NUA'LL

A Silver Ships Novel

S. H. JUCHA

Published by Hannon Books, Inc.
www.scottjucha.com

ISBN: 978-0-9994928-8-8 (e-book)
ISBN: 978-0-9994928-9-5 (softcover)

First Edition: June 2018

Cover Design: Damon Za

Acknowledgments

Nua'll is the eleventh book in the Silver Ships series. I wish to extend a special thanks to my independent editor, Joni Wilson, whose efforts enabled the finished product. To my proofreaders, Abiola Streete, Dr. Jan Hamilton, David Melvin, Ron Critchfield, Pat Bailey, Mykola Dolgalov, and Yolanda Timmons, I offer my sincere thanks for their support.

Despite the assistance I've received from others, all errors are mine.

Glossary

A glossary is located at the end of the book.

-1-
Haraken Fleet

<Admiral, the Haraken carriers have arrived,> Commodore Cordelia sent to Admiral Tatia Tachenko.

<Are they alone?> Tatia asked, replying with a thought via her implant.

<Negative, Admiral, more ships are transiting now,> Cordelia replied.

Tatia had exited a lift into the *Freedom*'s grand park. She was intent on spending some time walking through the exquisite gardens, while she organized her thoughts. The impending encounter with the massive alien fleet that was seen at the wall was foremost on her mind. Forgoing the peace and quiet Tatia sought, she turned around and caught a lift to the city-ship's uppermost deck. She anticipated that by the time she reached the enormous vessel's bridge, the remaining ships would complete their transit to the Omnian system.

As a SADE or self-aware digital entity, Cordelia was easily capable of multitasking, as she acted in the capacity of the enormous city-ship's captain. She maintained communication with the arriving ships, coordinated the *Freedom*'s services, managed the arrivals and departures of shuttles from the bays, and hundreds of other sundry aspects of command. And, of course, she reserved ticks of time to communicate with her partner, Julien.

<It begins,> Cordelia sent to Julien. <Years of preparation, and now the time is near.>

<We're capable of such long lives,> Julien sent in reply. <But, in light of coming events, they might become as short as those of the humans we love and support.>

<I ran alternate scenarios of our possible lives until I grew bored of the effort,> Cordelia sent. <Inevitably, I reached the same conclusion.>

<It was the same for me,> Julien replied. <The end comes for us, whether it's in ten years or ten thousand.>

<So, as Tatia has said many times, we bet on Alex and attempt to prevent what would seem to be unavoidable,> Cordelia added. <Excuse me, my partner, the admiral has gained the bridge, and I've updates for her.>

"What's the status of the arrivals?" Tatia asked. Her dark blue uniform jacket, with its short collar, bore fleet admiral insignias, and her New Terran, heavy-worlder figure completely filled it.

"Commodores Miko Tanaka and Edouard Manet command their carriers, the *No Retreat* and the *Last Stand*," Cordelia stated.

Cordelia's status had been elevated from captain to commodore in anticipation of the freighters that were expected to accompany the city-ship to the wall. However, her title became tenuous, when the expedition's leader, Alex Racine, and Tatia decided to accept Mickey Brandon's concept of transforming the *Freedom* into a warship to fight with the expedition fleet. Humans and their allies, the SADEs, would sail to challenge the alien races, who sought to expand their territories by usurping humankind's worlds.

To prepare the *Freedom*, travelers, the Omnians' vaunted fighters, were constructed to fill many of the city-ship's bays, and a ring of rail-mounted beam weapons were installed along the vessel's circumference. The rails allowed the beam weapons to be extended past the bay doors and swiveled in limited arcs.

In essence, the *Freedom*, with its assortment of weaponry, became a force unto itself. The addition of freighters, which the city-ship would have to protect, had necessitated the promotion of Cordelia to commodore. In a touching ceremony, presided over by Alex and Tatia, Julien pinned the new insignias on his partner. Their foreheads touched, and the SADEs shared a human's lifetime of memories in that short moment of communion.

"According to Commodore Tanaka, the last ship in their fleet has transited, Admiral," Cordelia continued. "In addition to the Haraken carriers, there are twelve Tridents, each carrying their complement of fighters, and two freighters."

"Considering they're the contributions of a single world, that's a good beginning," Tatia replied, her arms folded across her substantial chest.

"Credit must be given to our accumulated knowledge, Admiral," Cordelia mused. "It's been decades accruing, ever since our first encounter with the spheres. Every event has enlightened our understanding of the entities, who wait beyond the wall, and our allies have come to realize the importance of resistance."

<And every past encounter continues to prove just how insurmountable our challenge might be,> Tatia sent to Cordelia to prevent being overheard by the officers who were passing by.

<Does concern or trepidation rule your thoughts, Admiral?> Cordelia sent in reply.

<I'd be a fool not to worry about the limited probabilities of success, Cordelia, but I can't think of any other options for us, except to follow Alex. However, I'm hoping that with the help of Renée de Guirnon, you and I can curtail the more adventuresome aspects of Alex and your partner,> Tatia sent.

<I will keep my thoughts private about their ill-considered journey, Admiral, although I've shared my irritations with Julien,> Cordelia sent with a touch of pique.

Cordelia referred to Alex and Julien taking the OS *Redemption*, a Trident and the Omnians' new warship design, to the wall. Alex had ordered Captain Ellie Thompson to prosecute an alien probe in the nearby system. Then they waited in their lone ship to see who came to investigate the probe's flare, which detonated on entering the envelope of a gas giant.

When the aliens arrived, Alex and the *Redemption*'s crew found they faced a fleet led by a small Nua'll sphere. Soon afterwards, massive carriers surrounded the Omnian ship and dumped an unending stream of fighters into space. The experienced hand of Captain Thompson and the ingenuity of the young pilot, Yumi Tanaka, daughter of Edouard and Miko, narrowly managed to extricate the ship from the trap.

"I presume notifications about the new arrivals have been sent," Tatia said, resuming the conversation with Cordelia in the open.

"Julien, of course, is aware, which means Alex knows. I've updated Mickey. Alex will need to meet with our senior engineer to decide on priorities," Cordelia replied.

Mickey Brandon, Omnia Ships' inventive engineer, had his hands full running labs that filled every meter of three of the city-ship's huge bays. Unfortunately, the scope of his assignments had exceeded the work in those areas. In addition, he was in charge of overseeing the fleet's upgrades, preparing the carriers for their automated sojourns, and outfitting the *Freedom* for its defense.

Crews and SADEs had expanded the Sardi-Tallen Orbital Platform to keep up with production demand for banishers, the small vessels used to dispatch the alien probes, for rails and tubes for the city-ship's beam weapons, and for travelers, humankind's ubiquitous and ingenious fighters, whose design was taken from the Nua'll. In addition, Omnians, humans and SADEs, produced thousands of circuits, crystals, and other components every week in manufacturing plants outside of Omnia City, the only city on the planet below.

"Shall I notify Rear Admiral Gaumata?" Cordelia asked.

"Negative," Tatia replied. "I'll do that myself. Withhold further communication about deployment to the approaching Harakens until I speak with Darius, Miko, and Edouard."

"Acknowledged, Admiral," Cordelia replied and focused her kernel's programs on the host of minutiae demanding her attention.

As one of the first SADEs to be freed by Alex from her box aboard the *Freedom*, Cordelia had been afforded the luxury of time to develop sophisticated human mannerisms, which she displayed, while her algorithms were busy solving problems and sending orders. Outwardly, she appeared a calm, unflappable senior officer, comfortable with her position and duties, while inside, she processed information and communicated at inhuman speeds.

Tatia linked to the ship's controller and requested the location of Admiral Darius Gaumata. He was aboard his Trident, the OS *Prosecutor*, participating in a mock battle. Tatia's controller link allowed her to view the maneuvers Darius was practicing. She smiled to herself when she saw the Omnian squadron, Tridents commanded by the rear admirals, tucking deep behind a gas giant, surrounded by tens of moons. They were planning to ambush the four squadrons of Tridents, which accompanied the Haraken carriers. Tatia left a request with the controller to be updated on the outcome of the attack.

<Darius,> Tatia sent, via the ship's controller, <I was planning a face-to-face conference with you, but apparently you'll be busy for the next day or two.>

<A little squadron exercise, Admiral,> Darius returned.

<You and the other admirals have four OS Tridents against twelve Harakens, Darius. What're you hoping to achieve?> Tatia asked.

<No fair peeking, Admiral,> Darius objected. <This was supposed to be a surprise for you and them.>

<I don't intend to tell anyone, Darius, but I'm curious about your intent,> Tatia responded.

<We've spent our time training with Confederation forces, Admiral. When I learned the Haraken Tridents would be under my command, I realized that I've never seen them in action. I'd like to know how they'll react to a surprise attack.>

<And you're saying this, Darius, knowing that it's two of the most experienced combat veterans who'll be your direct reports and who are leading these warships,> Tatia replied. Her implant had picked up her chuckle and transmitted it with her thought.

<Perhaps it's best to think of this as a kind of *welcome to the party* greeting, Admiral,> Darius sent, his infectious laughter reaching Tatia.

<I'll be linking with Miko and Edouard, Darius. They need to be notified of ship assignments and our new organization chart, but I'll keep your maneuver secret,> Tatia sent.

<Thank you, Admiral,> Darius replied.

<Commodores, welcome to Omnia,> Tatia sent, after she added Edouard and Miko to her comm call. <It's good to have you aboard for the expedition and congratulations on your promotions.>

The Haraken commodores noted Darius' bio ID on the conference call.

<Thank you, Admiral,> Edouard sent, while Miko responded. <It's good to be aboard, Admiral.>

<Let me update you,> Tatia sent. <We'll be keeping your entire Trident force intact. I presume that you've organized your Tridents into four squadrons of three ships each, and you're each commanding two squadrons?>

<We have, Admiral,> Edouard replied.

<Excellent, you'll be reporting to Rear Admiral Gaumata,> Tatia sent.

<Congratulations, Admiral Gaumata,> the Haraken commodores sent.

<It's been a long trek since Libre, Admiral Gaumata, hasn't it?> Edouard added.

<If by that you mean you're surprised to find my butt in one piece despite all the time I've spent under Alex and the Admiral's auspices, then, yes, it's been an awfully long haul,> Darius replied.

<And, yet, we'll be taking on an even greater challenge,> Edouard added.

<Admiral Tachenko, it seems incredible that Omnia has been in development less than a decade. The infrastructure and the activity in this system are incredible,> Miko commented.

<While I'd like to take the credit, Miko, I can't,> Tatia sent. <It's the work of the SADEs. After Alex opened Omnia Ships, the credits flowed in at an extraordinary rate, which meant he could hand out stipends to every qualified comer. And, Confederation SADEs have responded by the shiploads.>

<No wonder,> Miko replied. <If anyone can posit future scenarios, the SADEs can. To them, it's inevitable that the aliens on the other side of the wall will come for our worlds, one day or another. They're here for Alex. They believe in what he's trying to do.>

<We've been fortunate to have two SADEs join our commands,> Edouard replied.

<Congratulations,> Darius sent. <I look forward to meeting them.>

<By the way, Admiral Gaumata, where are you?> Miko asked. Her question sounded innocuous, but Tatia detected the perceptions of a senior combat officer.

<Why do you ask?> Darius returned.

Wrong thing to send, Darius, Tatia thought. *Now, she's got your number.*

<Oh, I don't know, Admiral. We've completed our scans of the system, and, interestingly enough, there isn't a single Trident visible in the system. Have you lost your ride?> Miko asked.

Miko's thoughts were enveloped in a sweet innocence, and Tatia had to mute her side of the conference call, while her laughter reverberated down the corridor, as she strolled to her next meeting.

Oh, I missed you two, Tatia thought of her good friends.

<Now, where would I hide if I was the devious sort?> Edouard mused. <That gas giant we'd need to pass by would be an excellent spot.>

<That's my guess too,> Miko added.

Tatia added a secondary link to the *Freedom*'s controller. She wanted the system telemetry to see if the commodores intended to talk or act. Already, the Haraken Tridents, which had trailed the carriers, were accelerating. Most likely, they'd be deployed in a frontal arc to defend the two big vessels, as they neared the gas giant.

<My compliments, Commodores,> Darius sent, admitting that the ambush had been uncovered. Now, the Omnian Tridents didn't stand a chance against the larger fleet. <I look forward to renewing old friendships aboard the *Freedom*, when you arrive,> he added, ending his participation in the call.

<Commodores, update me on the two freighters with you?> Tatia requested.

<They've a full crew complement, Admiral, and carry numerous parts: raw metal, nanites, crystals, circuits, and food stocks,> Edouard replied.

<Everything a growing expedition needs,> Miko added.

<Have the freighter captains report to Commodore Cordelia,> Tatia ordered. When she received the commodores' assent, she ended her participation in the comm.

Miko and Edouard observed the four Omnian Tridents exit their hiding places from among the moons of the gas giant and head inward. They shared their humor with each other.

<You'd think Darius would know better than to try a sneak attack on us,> Edouard sent to his partner.

<If you were suddenly promoted up the ranks to rear admiral, responsible for the lives of twelve Trident crews and their warships, how would you act?> Miko riposted.

<Point taken,> Edouard replied.

<Can you believe the news about Cordelia's appointment?> Miko asked. <A SADE has become a commodore. It probably has something to do with the *Freedom* accompanying the fleet, and the rumors about the city-ship being armed.>

Miko waited for her partner to reply, but Edouard was silent. <What are you thinking?> she prompted.

<Hmm, sorry, Miko. I was thinking that in all the years I've known Julien, especially during the years he's been freed, I never once apologized to him.>

<For what?> Miko asked.

<Before the attack on the *Rêveur*, I thought nothing about his situation. To me, he was a SADE, and a SADE belonged in a case on a starship's bridge. I can't believe I ever thought that way, and I've never spoken to him about it.>

<You were a product of your society, my partner. You can't criticize yourself for the way you were taught,> Miko sent.

Miko was New Terran, but Edouard hailed from the Confederation home world, Méridien, and it was the Méridiens who had produced the SADEs.

Then Miko added, <However, there's no time like the present to rectify the past.>

<Another good point,> Edouard replied. <I'll wait until we reach Omnia. I want to make this apology face to face.>

<I think Julien will appreciate it. On the subject you mentioned to Darius, it has been a long time since Libre,> Miko admitted.

<And it's been longer since my rear end was unfrozen in the New Terran system,> Edouard shot back. He was one of the original Méridiens in stasis aboard the *Rêveur*, the passenger liner that Alex rescued, as it drifted through the Oistos system.

<And such a nice bottom too,> Miko replied lovingly.

<It's wonderful to be appreciated, if only for certain parts,> Edouard rejoined, and the partners shared a moment of lighthearted laughter.

* * *

Tatia sat at a conference table with Alex; Julien; Mickey; Reiko Shimada, the Trident fleet's vice admiral; and Franz Cohen, the fighter command rear admiral. Every senior naval position in the expedition's fleet was filled by those who had experience fighting the Nua'll and who best knew Alex's methods.

The Confederation, Haraken, and New Terran worlds were sending their warships, fighters, supplies, and crews to fight with the Omnians. It was understood that Alex was leading the expedition, and everyone expected his people to be in charge. It was the way that Alex and Tatia preferred to operate, especially after the recent calamity.

The New Terran assembly had foisted Admiral Anthony Tripping on Tatia to command their three Tridents, when a small Omnian fleet hunted a Nua'll sphere. Once cornered, the sphere had the opportunity to surrender but chose to detonate and take its foes with it. Unfortunately, Admiral Tripping, who was seeking glory, drove his warship toward the sphere, and the explosion ripped his Trident to shreds. Afterwards, Alex told the New Terran president, Harold Grumley, and the new Minister of Defense, Maria Gonzalez, that he would no longer accept New Terran senior commanders without Tatia vetting their capabilities.

President Grumley was certain Alex wouldn't refuse the warships outright for the sake of having the inability to dismiss a senior commander, but Minister Gonzalez disabused him of that notion, pointedly telling him, "Alex doesn't need us, Harold, we need him."

Cordelia received the inventory carried by the incoming Haraken ships from Commodore Tanaka. She added the information to the city-ship's extensive databases and sent Julien a link, knowing he was heading for a meeting with Alex and Tatia. Julien took a few ticks of time to review the list of materials, seeking items of interest for the meeting's participants.

As Julien entered the conference room, he shared the link to the complete list with everyone and included his short synopsis in a separate file.

"Oh, goodies," Mickey said, rubbing his hands in glee. "Look at this stuff. The Harakens must have raided some of the oldest warehouses."

Alex eyed Tatia, who grinned in reply. "Well done," he said to her. "Sheila must have felt like she was visiting the past."

"What did you say to Admiral Reynard to convince her to give up all this material?" Mickey asked.

"We had a sisterly conversation," Tatia replied, choosing to respond simply. She was feeling extremely self-satisfied. There were more things on the list than she had considered, but she could imagine Sheila and her reports reviewing Haraken inventories and surprising themselves with what had been stored.

"Alex, they've brought Daggers, minelettes, missiles, and Libran-X warheads," Mickey enthused.

Tatia regarded Alex, waiting for his input. When he seemed to review the list for an inordinately long period, she glanced toward Julien to confirm what she suspected. The blood-crystal twins of Alex and Julien were communing, absorbed in an exchange via implant and kernel.

"Julien will work with Cordelia to transfer any ancillary equipment and supplies to the *Freedom* in preparation for the carriers' refit," Alex said, focusing on the meeting. "Mickey, we need to launch the carriers before we leave, of course, but I want the work on the *Freedom*'s rail-mounted beam weapons completed before the remaining fleets arrive."

"Do we have a timeline on the arrival of the New Terran and Bellamonde fleets, Tatia?" Mickey asked.

Tatia linked to the ship's controller and examined the expedition's timeline. "We expect New Terra's four Tridents in about eighteen days.

The Confederation ships should arrive fifteen days after that," she announced.

"We'll stay focused on this ship's armament installations, Alex, until the carriers arrive," Mickey said. "The orbital platform crews can take charge of cleaning out the carriers. The major refit task is installing the extended reaction mass tanks on each carrier. Then, we have to load the banishers. I would estimate twenty days to complete the carriers and the *Freedom*," Mickey replied. He eyed Julien and added, "I suppose your part will be completed within the first day after the carriers arrive."

"Actually, Mickey, Cordelia began streaming the controller upgrades zero point seventy-five hours ago," Julien replied. "However, due to the size of the upload and a desire to check the installations, it will take her several hours to complete the operation."

Tatia grinned at Mickey and added, "And the Haraken fleet is still more than two days out."

Not to be outdone in the exchange, Mickey retorted, "Well, that's fine, Julien. Of course, this means you'll be free to help my teams by getting your hands dirty when the carriers arrive."

Julien assumed a proper and prim expression, clasping his hands lightly in front of him. A lace doily appeared on his head, projected by his holo-capable synth-skin, as he said, "I do so abhor manual labor."

Tatia and Mickey burst into laughter over the idea of a SADE, who had many times a human's strength and whose synth-skin could withstand a heavy strike, which would cut into human muscle, pretending to be a delicate entity.

Alex smiled at his friend. Julien and many others were doing their parts to lighten Omnians' moods. The impending launch of the fleet might have swept a dark pall over those who would sail and those who would remain behind, if not for the efforts of these individuals.

The doily disappeared, and Julien leaned onto the table. "I do have a surprise for this group," he announced, with a smile. "Something I left off my summary."

"I like surprises," Tatia enthused, "so long as they're nonmilitary."

Julien received a link from Alex to an item in the extended list, which was stored on the ship's controller. It pointed to the subject at hand. Julien smiled to himself. It was so like his friend to apply the power of his twin implants to pursue the entire inventory, while the group planned.

"The carriers are loaded with a complement of travelers," Julien stated.

"Yes," Tatia said, clapping her hands loudly together. "Now that's what I call a good surprise."

"President Lechaux and her partner, Tomas, managed to get the Haraken Assembly to throw in two complements of fighters. I can't believe that," Mickey said dubiously, eyeing Julien. "I know they had to supply the Tridents, as part of the agreement, and the carriers were going to be parked, if not stripped."

"These come courtesy of the local directors of the Haraken Central Exchange," Julien said proudly. He was a member of the Exchange, which handled the banking transactions for the entire Haraken system.

"Clarify that statement, Julien," Tatia requested. "Did the Exchange pay for these travelers?"

"Negative, Admiral, these are personal gifts from the Haraken-based directors," Julien replied.

"The banking business is good," Tatia mumbled. "A traveler isn't cheap."

"Personally, I think what the directors did was make a declaration that they intend to protect their business," Mickey piped up. "If the entities cross the wall and wipe out our planets, there goes every credit transaction."

-2-
Carriers

Alex and Julien had hatched the plan for the carriers at Haraken, when they visited the observatory platform and spoke with Jupiter, a SADE, who was originally known as Theodosius. He helped the Omnians discover the extensive penetration of alien probes across a wide swath of the galaxy.

The problem for the Omnians was that there wasn't time or resources to wander the stars eliminating a probe at each system. That's when Alex and Julien hatched their plan: Outfit the carriers to perform automated sweeps. The ships' controllers would be programmed with the probes' present locations and sent in opposite directions, circling out from Omnia. Armed with autopiloted fighters to protect the carrier, the ship would launch a banisher to destroy a probe at each system. If the ship's reaction mass ran low or other problems developed, the carrier was programmed to return to Omnia.

No one was under the false impression that the carriers could quickly eliminate the probes. The planting of the alien devices had taken place over tens of thousands of years. A probe had even reached the faraway system of Earth. No, the plan was to give notice to the entities behind the wall that the sentients on this side were choosing to fight rather than surrender or run away.

The carriers, which had served the budding Haraken world so well, had outlived their usefulness. A carrier had no defense once it launched its complement of fighters at the enemy. The Omnians had designed the Trident to operate as their primary warship. The vessel was many times more powerful than a fighter and could carry four travelers.

After a bit of squabbling, Terese Lechaux, the Haraken president, convinced the Haraken Assembly to sell the carriers to Omnia Ships, Alex's company, which would use the carriers to prosecute the alien probes. The deal was one Alex couldn't resist, and he had grinned as he authorized the transfer of two credits from his account to the Haraken Assembly.

In preparation for the expedition's launch, Tatia hadn't the time to visit Haraken and peruse the naval storage warehouses for what she could use. She had relied on Sheila Reynard, the Haraken fleet admiral. The two women had flown together with Alex from day one, when the *Rêveur*, newly repaired, had sailed from New Terra for Méridien.

Instead, Tatia's time had been absorbed playing war games at Bellamonde, to help the Méridiens sharpen their skills. It'd resulted in the loss of a good many recruits, but those who remained were far better trained commanders, captains, and crew.

The conversation with Sheila hadn't gone as simply as Tatia had intimated to Alex, Mickey, and Julien. When Tatia had requested the Daggers, the original fighters used at Libre, Sheila had replied, "Tatia, those are ancient. They haven't been flown in ages."

"Understood, Sheila, then you won't want them. Ship them," Tatia had politely but firmly requested.

Realizing Tatia's mindset, Sheila sought to match it, saying, "Well, if you're going that far. I have a good number of minelette pallets stored somewhere. The SADEs will know where."

"Great, ship those too," Tatia replied. "How about the nanites we used at Sol against the enemy ships, Sheila? Do you have a significant amount of those?"

"Probably, Tatia, but you recall that they're specific to the metal they contact. Are you thinking that you're going to get that close?"

"I hope not, but I anticipate that we'll be fighting a war of running encounters. No telling who we'll be up against and what we'll need. Most important, there'll be no time to run home."

"What do you mean who?" Sheila asked.

"Renée is telling me that Alex is wearing that worried expression in the morning. You know, the one he gets when he's trying to puzzle out what the odd images mean," Tatia explained.

"The dreams, right?" Sheila asked.

"Yeah, those," Tatia replied. Few individuals knew that Renée de Guirnon, Alex's partner, was so intimately connected to the man that she could receive Alex's dreams while the two of them slept. More than once, Renée had helped Alex interpret his dreams. He couldn't recall them, but her implant had a record of the strange, fleeting images.

"Any resolution yet?" Sheila asked.

"Not yet. Renée tells me that she thinks Alex is seeing more than one. She believes they're mixing, which is making unraveling them rather difficult."

"You're assembling the greatest fleet of warships that humans have ever created in this part of the galaxy, Tatia. Why do I feel like it's not enough?" Sheila lamented.

"We'll have to go with what we have, Sheila. According to Alex, we have to divide and confuse the aliens," Tatia replied and laughed.

As Julien predicted, the controllers of the carriers and the travelers received their updates before the huge ships crossed the orbit of the gas giant, where Darius had planned to ambush the fleet.

Now, the *No Retreat* and the *Last Stand*, two venerable Haraken ships, were stationed near the *Freedom*. Platform crews emptied bay after bay of equipment to store aboard the city-ship.

Renée, Mickey, and a group of support personnel toured the carriers. Renée and her people were searching for usable items from the meal rooms, such as food stocks, and the cabins. However, the carriers had been in disuse for so long that they quickly abandoned their search. Mickey and his team fared no better. Items that might have been functionally of value were outmoded.

"Hard to believe that the contents of these ships no longer have any use to us," Renée opined to Mickey. They occupied a pair of seats on a traveler returning to the *Freedom*.

"It's been three decades, Renée," Mickey replied.

"And the *Rêveur*, which is in service to this day, is more than 130 years old," Renée riposted.

"No fair, you're counting the decades that it was adrift," Mickey argued. "Besides, that ship was entirely overhauled."

"And you did a fine job on that," Renée replied, patting the engineer's hand.

The *Rêveur*'s repair had swept Mickey into a world of incredible advanced technology, and he'd joined Alex's team to return the passenger liner to the Confederation. And, if truth be told, a lively Méridien woman, by the name of Pia, had intrigued him.

"It comes down to warships versus passenger ship, Renée. The stronger our enemies, the more modern and more powerful ships we have to build," Mickey replied. The engineer in him loved to create new designs, but he understood Renée's lament.

Mickey's teams installed the new tanks aboard the carriers and filled them with reaction mass. It was estimated they'd allow the carriers to travel between the stars for ten or more years. In contrast, the banishers, which were loaded into bays, would probably be consumed in six or seven years. There were a number of conditions, such as for resupply or repair, under which the carriers would return to Omnia. And, it remained to be seen if one or both carriers encountered circumstances that spelled their doom, such as inadvertently crossing the path of a Nua'll sphere or meeting an aggressive spacefaring species.

Two days earlier than Mickey's estimate of completion, Alex and a large group gathered on the *Freedom*'s massive bridge to witness the launch of the carriers.

Julien initiated the controllers' hunt and destroy programs. In short order, systems were checked and confirmed online, travelers and banishers were contacted and confirmed ready, and sensor feedback was determined to be fully functional.

Aboard each carrier were hundreds of banishers invented by Mickey Brandon and his engineering team. The Sardi-Tallen platform had been busy constructing the small maneuverable devices, which would destroy the alien probes that monitored systems for the Nua'll and reported the progress of sentient races.

Not a single human or SADE would live aboard the carriers. The SADEs, Julien, Cordelia, Z, and Miranda, had programmed the carriers to follow courses in ever-widening circles to prosecute the probes. Their initial forays would focus on the worlds of Omnia, Haraken, and New Terra before proceeding to explore the systems surrounding the Confederation colonies.

When Julien received the controllers' signals that they were ready to initiate their extensive programming, he announced, "The carriers are ready."

"Send them, Julien," Alex said.

With their hunt-and-destroy programs initiated, the controllers accessed their list of probes gleaned from the Haraken observatory platform. Each carrier had half the list, which would send them spiraling in opposite directions. The nearest probe locations to Omnia were retrieved, courses were calculated, and engines were brought online.

When ready, the controllers communicated their departures from the system to the Omnian orbital platform and powerful engines were fired. Slowly, at first, and then more rapidly, the ships worked their way through orbital traffic and headed across the ecliptic.

* * *

"Wow, that was incredible," Captain Bertram Hardingsgale said to Maria Gonzalez, the New Terran Minister of Defense. They were on the bridge of the *Rover*, a passenger ship.

"What?" Maria asked sluggishly.

Maria was one of the unfortunate individuals who did not handle transiting well. The *Rover*, in the company of four NT Tridents, had made the Omnian system about 0.65 hours ago.

"I was referring to witnessing a huge ship exit the Omnian system," Bertram said. "I've never been this close to a vessel when it made a transit. It was a fantastic sight."

Maria glanced at Oliver, her confidant and a SADE, for more information. "It was the *Last Stand*, Minister. The Omnians have sent this carrier and its sister ship, the *No Retreat*, to eliminate probes."

"That will take the crews their entire lifetimes," Bertram said, aghast at the concept. "Are they expecting to return and trade out after a certain length of service?"

"There's no one aboard, Captain," Maria replied. "The entire process is automated, thanks to the Omnians."

"Most ingenious of them," Oliver added.

"It was much cleverer to devise the idea to repurpose two ships about to be stripped so they could serve useful purposes once again," Maria commented.

"Yes, the thinking of Alex and Julien in concert," Oliver acknowledged. "It's an enviable symbiosis."

Maria glanced at the wistful expression on Oliver's face. It was the first time she'd ever heard him lament the shortcomings between him and her. Despite the circumstances of Oliver's early existence, serving one of the more disagreeable Leaders of the Confederation, he'd always been able to communicate swiftly and succinctly with humans, the Méridiens, via their implants. After meeting Maria, Oliver had decided to lend his support exclusively to her, a human who was effectively mind-blind.

"Minister, you've a comm from Captain Jagielski," Bertram announced.

"On speakers," Maria replied gruffly.

"Captain, we're on the bridge," Maria warned Alphons, in case he needed privacy for his call.

"The Omnians surely have us on their telemetry, Minister, and I was wondering if you felt well enough to announce us or if you'd rather I did it?" Alphons asked.

"Kind of you to ask after my well-being, Captain. I'll take care of it," Maria replied.

"Certainly, Minister. Feel better. The *McMorris* out," Alphons said.

"Oliver," Maria requested. Like Alex, she understood the shorthand speech that was capable with a SADE, who could anticipate her needs. However, unlike Alex, she had to speak her thoughts.

Oliver connected with the *Rover*'s controller and placed a comm to the *Freedom.* A brief request to Cordelia was transferred to Alex via Julien, as the pair was on the Sardi-Tallen Orbital Platform.

The once utilitarian construction station no longer resembled its initial iteration. It had morphed into a dumbbell shape, one end handling passengers from liners and the other end constructing ships and handling freight. The station's interconnector held small bays to accommodate the frequent visits of travelers. Movers embedded along the length of the interconnector transported pedestrians in both directions.

<Minister, how are you feeling?> Alex sent, as Julien and he rode the pedestrian transport toward the platform's ship construction bays. The *Rover*'s controller broadcast Alex's voice over the bridge speakers for Maria.

"The usual, Alex," Maria replied. "When are your superlative individuals going to invent a cure for those few of us who suffer from transits?"

<Interestingly, Minister, there's a marked decline in symptoms with additional transits,> Alex replied.

"I'm looking forward to that time. How many transits does it take?" Maria asked.

Alex and Julien shared grins, and Alex's humor leaked through his sending, as he replied, <About forty or fifty transits, Minister.>

"Alex, did anyone tell you that you have a sick sense of humor?" Maria shot back.

<Yes, a few have, Minister,> Alex replied with a chuckle. <Julien tells me that you're in the company of four Tridents.>

"I wish we could have provided more, Alex, but the Assembly was adamant about sticking to the agreement. You got four of the nine warships we constructed," Maria announced.

<And Captain Jagielski?> Alex asked. More than anything, he wanted the captain who had demonstrated the strength and maturity to heed his warnings and not follow the ill-fated Admiral Anthony Tripping to his death.

Despite her body's protestations, Maria smiled to herself. She could have brought Alex just one Trident. As long as Alphons Jagielski was captain, he'd be happy. *People first; things second. That's my Alex,* she thought.

"I considered it best that Captain Jagielski should stay at New Terra, Alex," Maria said. She waited several heartbeats before she added, "But Senior Captain Jagielski insisted on leading these four ships in your expedition, and I gave up arguing with him."

<What were you saying about a poor sense of humor?> Alex riposted. His laughter erupted over the *Rover*'s bridge speakers. <Have the good captain report to Admiral of the Fleet Tachenko,> he sent.

Maria flushed with pride at the thought that one of her favorite officers in New Terran Security had risen to the lofty rank of fleet admiral.

"Will do, Alex," Maria replied. She was feeling better by the moment. Talking to Alex always did that for her. "By the way, we caught the transit of one of the carriers. Are you hopeful for their missions?"

<Mickey, his engineers and techs, and the SADEs have done their usual exemplary job. As for the mission, we've no other choice. There are way too many probes for crewed ships to eliminate. I expect one day we'll find a more efficient means of destroying the probes.>

"There's always the possibility that the entities you meet at the wall will acquiesce, and you won't have to worry about the probes," Maria replied. She briefly eyed Oliver, who frowned, and she listened closely for Alex's response.

<As my endearing crystal friend said to me: "Should we trust anything promised by entities who've been engaged in policies of harsh expansionism for tens of thousands of years?" I think the answer is no. We have to ensure they understand that this isn't a skirmish. It's a declaration of territory and rights, which we intend to defend.>

"Fortune to us all, Alex. Maria out," the minister said, and Oliver closed the call.

Julien regarded Alex. <Endearing?> he queried via his comm.

Alex smiled good-naturedly. He received the image of a giant lagomorph-like creature bounding up to him. It threw its arms around Alex in an embrace, and its weight knocked him to the deck. Buried under the huge pile of fuzzy, long-eared animal, Alex produced a thought bubble over his head, a concept he borrowed from one of Renée's vids.

The lagomorph's eyes flew open, as it regarded the scene in the bubble. In the dark of night, four men sat around a campfire, roasting the carcass of an animal over flames. The creature shrieked and ran off, only to return with a fire extinguisher, which it sprayed over the thought bubble and Alex, who was inundated by the foam. The two friends reveled in their image war until they reached their destination.

-3-
The *Freedom*

Mickey rode in the traveler's copilot seat. The fighter floated outside a row of bays of the *Freedom*. He was ready to test the final three, rail-mounted, beam weapons of the city-ship.

<Commence test,> Mickey sent to his engineers in the bays.

The bay doors swept aside, and the twin barrels of the beam weapons rolled forward, narrowly clearing the doors. The traveler pilot, an old hand at the tests, spun the fighter in a set of lazy loops, while the engineering team recorded the weapons' abilities to target the traveler.

The first time the pilot had heard the actions that Mickey required him to take for the test, he said, "Your people do know this is only a test, as in hands off of the firing application."

"I hope so," Mickey had rejoined, laughing heartedly. "I intend to be aboard your traveler to observe the action."

"That would make me feel better, if I knew there was no one on your team harboring bad feelings about you," the pilot had shot back.

"If we get turned into space dust, we'll have the last laugh," Mickey replied.

"How's that?" the pilot asked.

Mickey's eyebrows bounced up and down several times, as if he was sharing a great secret with the pilot. Then he said, "Because Alex will have someone's rear end for taking out his chief engineer."

"Yeah, but we'll still be dead," the pilot had mumbled to himself, as he entered the front cabin.

Mickey watched the relay of the engineering feedback from the bays to the traveler's controller and then to his helmet. The beam weapons were tracking within parameters. Even when the traveler crossed the weapons' fields, the targeting applications handed off the priority from one beam emplacement to the other.

<Test concluded,> Mickey sent. <Well done, teams. That's our final installation. Retract the weapons and close the bays.>

Mickey contacted the *Freedom* to speak with Cordelia.

<Excellent work, Mickey,> Cordelia sent in reply. <I presume you're handing off control of the beam weapons to me.>

<That I am, Admiral. Your ship is ready to repel all invaders,> Mickey announced happily.

<Let's hope that's so, Mickey,> Cordelia replied before she ended the comm.

Mickey signaled his pilot to drop him at a bay near one of his labs. He was running late for a meeting with Luther and Miriam. The two SADEs were in charge of developing the communication techniques that would prevent the Nua'll from commandeering their electronics.

During the encounter with the comm sphere at the wall, Alex and Julien had taken precautions to protect the Trident from a comm intrusion by eliminating the connection between their ship's hull-embedded antenna and the controller. Subsequent analysis by Mickey's engineers and the SADEs revealed a data crystal had recorded the sphere's highly compressed broadcast of multiple languages, interspersed with malevolent code designed to cripple the ship's systems controls.

Mickey's traveler dropped into a bay. The moment the hatch indicated pressure in the bay, he launched through the opening and hurried to the nearby lab.

"Sorry to be late," Mickey apologized a little breathlessly to the SADEs when he entered.

Miriam and Luther exchanged brief thoughts. They found humans' urgency to be on time for meetings with SADEs to be a little comical. Then again, time was held in opposing extremes by the two species. Every tick of time was utilized in multiple ways by the SADEs, and yet they had hundreds of years, if not thousands, to expend over the lifespan of humans. Still, Miriam and Luther appreciated Mickey's considerate gesture.

"Congratulations, Mickey, in the successful deployment of this ship's beam weapons," Luther announced.

"Thank you, Luther," Mickey replied.

"According to Killian," Miriam said, referring to another SADE, "the orbital platform will soon lay up the shells of the final travelers, completing the *Freedom*'s contingent of fighters."

"And the autopilot programs?" Mickey asked. It was an indication of the times. Mickey, who once knew every engineering aspect that was underway, couldn't keep up with the extensive preparations for the expedition.

"The SADEs are installing them into every traveler," Miriam replied.

"Every fighter aboard the city-ship or every fighter?" Mickey asked. When Miriam gazed evenly at Mickey, he said, "Every traveler. If it's a good idea for one, it's a good idea for all."

"Consider, Mickey, the circumstances of a human pilot fatally injured, but the fighter is still with power and flight controls," Miriam proposed.

"The ship could still fight or even be used as a flying missile," Mickey agreed.

"Just so," Miriam said sadly.

"It's a shame we can't automate the entire fleet's fighter-attack scenarios," Mickey said.

"We tried," Luther admitted. "A great deal of kernel time was applied, but the probabilities known and unknown taxed even our capabilities."

"It's as Alex often says: 'We'll just have to wait and see what happens,'" Miriam added.

"Well, Luther, show me what we'll be installing to protect the *Freedom*'s comm system," Mickey said, switching subjects.

In the analysis of the data, which was collected from the comm sphere at the wall, the Omnians had discovered more than malicious algorithms buried in the various language greetings. The data's decoding resulted in the discovery of two critical items: The Nua'll greetings spoke of a master race, and their code was so dangerous as to be capable of subverting a SADE's kernel.

"Our operation will be similar to the one chanced on by Alex and Julien," Luther replied. "All comm reception by a ship's antenna will be handled by our routing box, which offers the Nua'll transmissions two signal paths, the ship's controller or the temptation of a SADE. We know the malicious code is attracted to the more complex structure of a SADE."

"Will you still use the delay box between the router and the kernel copy?" Mickey asked.

"Undoubtedly," Miriam replied, "It's central to our process."

"After routing through the delay box, the attack signal enters a controller containing multiple kernel copies of Miriam," Luther continued. "To be specific, the copies will contain knowledge of the malicious code."

"As the receiving copy succumbs, another is made available," Miriam explained. "The infected version is deleted and replaced with a clean copy. The process is kept up in a never-ending loop."

"Then the delay isn't always in use," Mickey said, understanding the concept. "Miriam's primary copy monitors the Nua'll broadcast's onslaught. When the confronted copy is about to succumb, the delay trap is inserted, which gains the time necessary to delete the infected copy and replace it. Then the delay trap can be bypassed until the next time to swap copies."

Mickey studied the idea, his hand rubbing his chin. "How long will single copies last?" he asked.

"Initially, we expect hours, especially with the increased awareness of what we face," Miriam replied. "As the copies communicate the nature of the onslaught, more time will be gained."

"Mickey, I've prepared the specifications for your production line," Luther added.

"What production line?" Mickey asked. "What am I missing?"

"It's our premise that the comm sphere will inevitably attack all controllers," Luther replied. "The Nua'll communication might not be directed only at the *Freedom*."

"Black space," Mickey muttered. "You're talking about the city-ship, every Trident, every freighter ... even the travelers." He stared at Luther and Miriam, hoping to be corrected.

"There is no other way, Mickey," Miriam said. "I can duplicate my kernel to make copies as many times as necessary to enable production."

"Every ship," Mickey muttered, the scope of the problem dawning on him. "Wait, we launched the carriers without this technology. How did that escape us?"

"It didn't, Mickey," Miriam said patiently. "Julien, Cordelia, Z, and Miranda determined that the best course of action in the event the carriers crossed the path of a Nua'll sphere was to leave the fighters unprotected. Under normal conditions, the carriers' programs direct them to remain outside a system and launch a banisher from there. If a carrier encounters a Nua'll sphere, our ship could quickly transit away. In the event that action became difficult, two travelers would be launched at the sphere. While the Nua'll sphere sought to subsume the fighters' controllers, the carrier could escape."

"But then the Nua'll would have our fighters," Mickey objected.

"Perhaps not, Mickey," Miriam replied, with a sly smile.

"Do tell?" Mickey replied, expecting a good piece of news.

"A failsafe mechanism has been laid into a separate controller, within the carriers' travelers. If normal communication is lost between the secondary and primary controllers, the secondary controller initiates a sequence. The moment the fighter lands, its beams are activated and fire continuously until the crystals are drained."

Mickey chuckled at the thought that the travelers, initially used by the Nua'll, could be their undoing if they sought to capture the Omnians' version of the fighters.

"And, Mickey, in case the extent of this problem has escaped you," Miriam said gently. "All communication between our ships and any foreign vessels must go through my copies. My copies will be linked to the ship's controller, which will make it seamless for personnel."

"What's the failsafe mechanism?" Mickey asked.

"If my primary copy senses imminent failure, the connection to the ship's controller is severed. Connections between the controller and a ship's antennas must be manually restored," Luther replied. "It's the only way to ensure the protection of our ships and crews."

Mickey cogitated on what Miriam and Luther were saying. It was a mark of the influence of Alex's personality on him that he asked, "What will Alex think about these Miriam copies?"

"He's already inquired, Mickey," Miriam replied. "I told him that I intend to reorder my hierarchy principles for the copies. They'll operate with the intention of protecting their vessels at all costs."

"But isn't that what you do now?" Mickey asked.

"It's relative, Mickey," Luther added. "We work to protect the ships, humans, and ourselves. These copies will choose to sacrifice themselves to protect their vessels."

Mickey was stunned and unable to find the words to continue. Finally, he muttered, "That seems unfair."

"No, Mickey, unfair was incarceration in bridge containment structures for decades, if not for a century or more," Miriam replied. "We are free now and will do whatever it takes to support Alex, while he lives."

"And when he's gone?" Mickey asked. Miriam and Luther stared silently back at him. "I see," Mickey said, "it will be up to others of us to prove that we're worthy of your support."

"Just so, Mickey," Miriam replied.

"Understood," Mickey replied, humbled by the exchange. "Work the production of your comm diverters into the labs' schedules at Omnia City and the platform. We'll need to outfit every vessel and take some extras with us. Let me know if you have any problems."

As Mickey left the lab, Luther asked Miriam, "Were we too blunt?"

"If we lose Alex in this contest against the alien entities, who appear to be overwhelming in number and strength, what is the future for humans and SADEs?" Miriam replied. "It's best that humans discover now that the SADEs expect them to carry on as Alex would want them to do."

"Still, Mickey is our friend," Luther argued.

"And I wasn't comfortable being direct with him," Miriam replied. "But, I'm the one who's creating a sisterhood from my kernel. The only one who questioned that ... the only one who came to me, prior to Mickey, with his concerns ... was Alex. It's time for Alex's friends, for all humans, to understand how important he is to us."

"Could not Julien make the argument better than us?" Luther asked.

"That was considered but rejected. None of us wish to burden Julien with this message. Alex and Julien are entwined to the extent that it's difficult to predict what will and won't be shared," Miriam said. She was absolutely still, calculating futures.

"Understood," Luther said quietly. "One not wholly human; one not wholly SADE."

* * *

Alex and Renée met with a group of individuals representing the people who had chosen to live aboard the *Freedom*. Using the true power of implants, consensus was reached among each group, and a representative was elected to speak with Alex and Renée about their concerns. Seated in the small amphitheater were representatives of the ship's cargo haulers; food service; food stock preparation; hydroponics; cabin service; maintenance for parks, systems, and engines; and many more.

They and the individuals they represented faced difficult decisions. Many wished to stay with the crew and residents who lived aboard the city-ship, but the reality of the *Freedom* becoming a warship worried them.

"Can you offer us some assurance, Alex, that this ship will not be put into harm's way during the expedition?" a woman with a partner and two young children asked.

"None," Alex replied. "The fact that it's become such a powerful ship, in its own right, means it will play a major role in future encounters."

"But it has rail-mounted beam weapons and fighters," a man argued. "Surely those will provide adequate protection."

"And what will the aliens, who exist beyond the wall, have as armament?" Renée asked rhetorically. "Will they be technologically more sophisticated than the Nua'll, which might make them more dangerous?"

"Where will the two of you be when this ship reaches the wall?" a young woman asked.

Alex regarded Renée and grinned before he replied. "We'll be aboard this ship. Personally, I'm not allowed to go out and play with the aliens until it's considered safe."

Chuckles made their way through the crowd, but it was muted and not shared by all.

"We realize these are challenging moments for everyone," Renée said. "And we wish we could provide you with definitive answers, but we can't."

"But what will you do, if many of us choose to go planetside to Omnia City?" the first woman asked.

"There's a waiting list of people who wish to go with us," Alex replied quietly. "I don't intend to bring them aboard except in cases of replacement. I'm not anxious to risk any more humans or SADEs than I have to."

"Thank you, everyone," Renée said, standing. "We'll need your answer within eight days. Please record them with the ship's captain, Commodore Cordelia."

As the group filed out, Alex slid a hand into Renée's and squeezed gently.

<I too, my love, miss the days when life was simpler, even though back then it was often more harrowing,> Renée sent to Alex.

Renée's humor bubbled through Alex's implant. <What?> he sent.

<From one pleasant discussion to another,> Renée sent in reply. <Your most valuable and senior engineer is waiting at the door, and he's wearing a frown.>

Alex kissed Renée on the temple, and she stroked his arm before they went their separate ways.

"Think of all the work your nanites will have to do, repairing the collagen damage caused by your frowning," Alex teased Mickey. Alex slid his arm around Mickey's massive shoulders. He was one of the few heavy-worlders who had the reach. He asked, "Why don't you tell Uncle Alex all about it?"

Mickey stared at Alex for a moment, as if he'd lost his mind. Then he broke out in a loud guffaw. He was still chuckling, when he said in a timid voice, “Well, it all started when I was young.” Then it was Alex’s turn to laugh.

“Okay, Mickey, what’s up?” Alex asked, as they walked down a broad corridor.

“An element of your plan, Alex,” Mickey replied, “is your intention to track some of the weaker ships back to their home world?”

“It is,” Alex replied.

“How?” Mickey asked.

“Ahhh,” Alex said in a slow exhale. <Tatia, what are you up to?> Alex sent. He identified her location. She was in her quarters with her new vice admiral, Reiko Shimada.

<Doing nothing that can’t be delayed,> Tatia sent in reply. <What do you need?>

<The two of you will do fine,> Alex sent in reply. <Mickey and I will be with you soon.>

Alex and Mickey chatted during the time it took to ride up four decks and traverse half the diameter of the massive city-ship. More than once, Mickey thought to share with Alex the discussion he’d had with Miriam, but, in the end, he chose not to speak up. It seemed that it was his burden to carry and discuss with the likes of Tatia and others.

When Alex and Mickey entered Tatia’s quarters, the women were seated at the central table. A holo-vid displayed a fight scenario reminiscent of the enemy ship arrangement met at the wall by the *Redemption*, Ellie Thompson’s Trident.

Vice Admiral Reiko Shimada tensed to rise, but she demurred, when Tatia remained seated. However, Reiko didn’t miss the subtle movement of Tatia’s hands. They’d tightened in a reflex and immediately relaxed. Reiko understood. Alex might own Omnia Ships, and he might have engineered the formation of an immense fleet from multiple worlds, but he’d placed battle control in Fleet Admiral Tatia Tachenko’s hands.

“Morning, Sers,” Alex said with enthusiasm. “Mickey has a question.”

Mickey was momentarily caught off guard. He’d expected to be following Alex’s lead in the discussion.

Alex took a seat next to Reiko, smiled engagingly, and motioned Mickey toward a seat next to Tatia. The women turned expectant looks toward Mickey.

"Well, I was asking Alex if he was still planning to follow some of the technologically weaker ships from the wall back to their home world, and he said yes," Mickey explained. "Then I asked him how, and we ended up here," he added.

"And you can see why," Alex said.

The two women shared knowing glances.

"So, Mickey needs to design a technique that we can employ to plant a comm transponder on a warship during a protracted fight," Tatia reasoned.

"Precisely," Alex replied.

"Oh, black space," Reiko muttered, understanding the dangers of the maneuver.

"Well, I'm open to suggestions," Tatia said, looking from Alex to Mickey.

"I'm thinking of our first encounter with the dark travelers at Bellamonde," Alex said quietly.

"Talk about resurrecting the dead," Mickey breathed out in a whisper. "I like it. That's absolutely diabolical."

"I thought you used nanites to identify the shell composition and break it down?" Reiko asked.

"We did," Mickey replied enthusiastically, "but nanites can be organized to do anything we want. They can be attached to the base of transmitter and used like an adhesive to adhere the device to a hull."

"Like you two errant delivery boys did when we returned to Libre to take on the Nua'll sphere, and you planted comm devices on the shell of the dark traveler we captured," Tatia said.

Tatia meant her comment as criticism for their dangerous stunt, but Alex and Mickey, who were grinning at each other, were having none of it. And, to Tatia's irritation, Reiko was smiling and nodding her approval of the action.

"Mickey, how would you deliver this transmitter ... Trident or traveler?" Reiko asked.

"Neither," Mickey said, regarding Reiko apologetically. "It would have to be a Dagger."

Tatia regarded her fight scenario, which floated above the holo-vid. Ellie Thompson's Trident contacted the enemy ships in open space, where the *Freedom*, Tridents, and freighters could operate, but not the travelers. She signaled the display off. When she glanced at Alex, his eyes crinkled in the merest hint of a smile. Tatia curtailed her smirk. She might be Alex's weapons master, but he would always be the strategist, the one who thought far outside the box.

-4-
Mickey

Mickey spent another day wrestling with the decision he faced, without making any headway. Control of the numerous and complicated projects was slowly slipping through his grasp. He was spending an inordinate amount of time just traveling from the *Freedom*'s labs to Omnia City to the Sardi-Tallen platform and back. During the day, his implant message log backed up with requests, which kept him up late at night, while he responded. That, in and of itself, annoyed his Méridien partner, Pia Sabine, more than anything.

<Alex, can we talk?> Mickey sent, the following morning.

<Let's walk through the grand park, Mickey. Renée says that several species of trees are in bloom,> Alex sent in reply.

The men met at a lift that emptied near a broad corridor of shops and strolled toward the city-ship's central park. As they arrived at the immense garden, Alex paused to enjoy the brilliant blooms on the trees, which had long since required trimming to prevent them pushing against the overhead deck 20 meters up.

Mickey briefly outlined the challenges for his project time that he faced and his worry that he might be failing to do his best.

"Mickey, you and I have always been hands-on people," Alex said, "and you've had the luxury of operating in that mode far longer than me. In my lifetime I've experienced a series of events, which caused me to realize, time and time again, that I had to let go ... my admiralty; my presidency; my son, Teague; and many others."

"You're saying it's time for me to become an administrator," Mickey said, with disgust.

"I think it's past time to choose, Mickey. You can continue to be personally involved in a number of projects or you can drive all the engineering endeavors that we need," Alex replied.

"But that's part of the problem, Alex," Mickey said plaintively. "I can't encompass the extent of the technical programs underway now."

"Of course, you can, Mickey," Alex said gently. "You need assistance much like I have."

"Like Julien?" Mickey asked.

Alex smiled at Mickey and laid a hand on his shoulder to halt their walk. Alex stared into the softly flowing stream with its multicolored fish. Beautiful and relaxing to regard, the water features served a critical function in the city-ship's filtration process.

Linking implants with Mickey, Alex quickly added Trium, a SADE, who flew a scout ship, to demonstrate a concept to Mickey.

<Dassata, Mickey, greetings,> Trium responded, using Alex's title bestowed on him by the Dischnya, one of two alien species who inhabited Omnia.

<Trium, please update me on the status of Luther's comm-diverter project,> Alex requested.

Alex and Mickey listened, while Trium summarized the implementation of Luther's design in the manufacturing process and the quantity assembled.

When Trium paused, Alex requested more details. Immediately, Trium delved into which labs had been assigned what aspects of production, quantities expected from each, and delivery dates.

When Trium paused again, Alex sent, <Trium, did you possess the latter information that I requested?>

<It wasn't necessary to hold those details, Dassata. I acquired them from Miriam,> Trium sent.

<Trium, how do you think Miriam feels about providing this information indirectly through you?> Alex asked.

<Feels, Dassata?> Trium asked. The SADE was relatively young, less than a half century, and he was new to the Omnian contingent. This

meant he was still refining his algorithms to interface smoothly with the full range of human emotions.

Alex grinned at Mickey and privately sent to his engineer, <Odds are that Trium is querying either Julien or Miriam for a translation of my question.>

<Information is data, Dassata,> Trium responded shortly. <Data should be shared unless the giver restricts its dissemination, and the SADEs are pleased to be of service.>

<Thank you, Trium, this conversation has been most instructive,> Alex sent.

<Dassata, Mickey,> Trium acknowledged, before he closed his end of the comm connection.

Alex closed his link with Mickey and stared quietly at the engineer, who was deep in thought.

"Is Julien your assistant, in this regard?" Mickey asked.

Alex burst out in laughter, attracting the attention of others enjoying the park.

"Mickey, Julien is my friend, my confidant, and my advisor, although not always in that order. He brings to my attention any issues that require my guidance, but every SADE employed by Omnia Ships fulfills the concept of assistant. They're the epitome of a collective entity, where it concerns data and projects. But don't get me wrong, Mickey, they're unique individuals whose kernels are embedded with human morals. One day, I'd love to find out how Shannon Brixton's House manages to create new SADEs with these uniquely human characteristics."

"Then I need gatekeepers, SADEs, who will be responsible for directing and monitoring the engineering projects, and they'll inform me when they need my input," Mickey reasoned.

"Precisely, Mickey," Alex replied. "But, you sound as if you think your role will be strictly reactive. It won't be. The SADEs will free you from dealing with the minutiae. You'll be able to focus on the bigger picture, dream up new ideas, such as ones that we'll need to deal with those beyond the wall. When your concept is ready, you'll pitch it to the SADEs and stand back. It can be an invigorating experience."

Mickey's heavy hand reached out, and Alex clasped it. "Time for me to become a big-picture dreamer," Mickey said.

"Admirable decision, Mickey," Alex said. He laughed and walked away.

While Mickey stared at small fish darting through the stream's engineered plants, which were covered in special nanites, it occurred to him that he had the perfect candidates to support him. <Miriam, Luther,> he sent.

After the two SADEs were recruited by Mickey to be his engineering directors, they connected briefly with Julien, who added Trium. It was Julien whom Trium had sought for a translation about Miriam's feelings.

<Well done,> Julien sent. <It's a most opportune time for Mickey to choose to have Miriam and Luther administer the engineering projects.>

<Was it not Dassata's success?> Trium asked.

<Don't diminish your efforts,> Julien cautioned. <You made it easier for Alex to convince Mickey to make this decision by your demonstration of data sharing and our competencies in managing projects to date.>

<Then Dassata's role was minimal?> Trium proposed, seeking to understand the various elements in the exchange.

<Mickey, like Alex, can be extremely creative, when freed from the constraints of details. We need him in that position,> Julien supplied, sidestepping Trium's query.

Miriam understood Julien's conundrum, and she sympathized with him.

This was the issue that the SADEs hoped to prevent Julien from having to confront. Among the SADEs, there was no individual above Julien who was more respected and whose opinions were more frequently sought.

SADEs knew the numbers. They were a minority among humans, and, at the moment, had no method of procreation, which could produce an individual with a distinctly unique personality. While humans grew quickly in number, the SADEs mysteriously materialized a few at a time from the labs of House Brixton.

Yet, humans were a paltry number in comparison to the hundreds, perhaps thousands, of races that waited beyond the wall. And not only were these adversaries supposedly vast in number, they had demonstrated an extremely antithetical attitude toward new sentients in the human sphere of the galaxy.

The probabilities dictated that the SADEs must support humankind and share in its fate, but their decision was more complicated than that. SADEs, by and large, enjoyed working with humans, especially the Omnians. Their rigid logic found a certain delight in the flexibility and often illogical minds of humans.

For Julien's part, he endeavored to promote the bond between humans and SADEs. At times, that meant buoying up the SADEs' sense of importance in the roles they played even at the expense of his best friend and other humans. In this case, what he told Trium was correct. The SADEs needed humans to release Mickey from the mundane work to focus on the confrontation to come. Every ounce of creativity would be needed to outmaneuver the formidable foes they'd face.

* * *

The evening after recruiting Miriam and Luther, Mickey finished a quick stint in his cabin's refresher. Pia was working late at the medical suite. He made a cup of thé and settled on the salon's couch. This was his usual habit to catch up on the day's messages, and this time there were plenty.

Mickey smiled, thinking the engineering teams were in need of his careful guidance. He opened the first message in his implant's queue. It was a brief report from Luther notifying him of the day's production of comm-delay units and that they were on track to meet the expected delivery time.

Moving quickly to the next message, Mickey discovered a similar report from Miriam about the control tests of the city-ships' rail-mounted beams. Cordelia was satisfied with the controllers' responsiveness. However, she was requesting a war game to simulate an enemy attack on the *Freedom*. Mickey approved the idea, sending the message to Tatia, for scheduling, and to Miriam, for coordination.

Item after item either reported the successful progress of an operation or requested his permission to proceed to the next step. In the latter cases, the process was outlined in detail and the reasoning advanced. Mickey read, approved, and sent a quick reply.

Before Mickey's thé was finished, his implant message queue was empty. He sat on the couch, staring at the far bulkhead. <Bored yet, Mickey?> the engineer received. The bio ID was that of Alex.

<You know ... work, work, work,> Mickey replied, tongue-in-cheek. <How did you know?>

<The last message in your queue was a plant from Miriam,> Alex replied.

<I thought that one was a little simplistic,> Mickey sent in reply.

<Renée and I are headed to the grand park to catch Cordelia's latest reality vid. We have reservations for the four of us in zero point thirty-five hours,> Alex sent.

<Who's going with you?> Mickey asked.

<Mickey, do you think we'd let you manage this tough transition on your own,> Alex sent, sympathy flowing through his thoughts. <Julien requested Miriam send your queue's end message. She reported to him, when you had replied. After you agreed to let the SADEs handle your projects, I told Renée of our conversation, and she booked the reservations. Pia isn't working late. She's over here with us, changed, and anxious to see the new vid.>

A smile crept over Mickey's face. <Coming,> he sent.

<Meet you in the park,> Alex replied.

A quarter hour later, Mickey exited a lift, checked on Pia's location, and headed that way. He didn't spot her immediately, but he did spy Alex's broad back.

Alex had tracked Mickey's location. When the engineer got close, he turned aside and smiled. The reason for his expression was obvious. The women were dressed, as if the occasion was a fête, wearing the gossamer wisps of clothing that the genetically sculpted Méridiens preferred.

Mickey's face lit up at the sight of Pia. It had been months since they had spent an evening together, and he regretted every lost hour.

<That look on your face, my partner, makes the wait worthwhile,> Pia sent privately to Mickey.

Rather than reply, Mickey threw his arms around Pia's waist, easily lifting her lithe frame. In turn, she wrapped her arms around his neck, and they clung together. It was Mickey's apology, and Pia's acceptance.

When the couple's hug was over, Alex stared at his premier engineer and asked, "Tough day?"

"This will take some time to get used to," Mickey replied.

"Two days," Alex said.

"What two days?" Mickey asked.

"Two days before you're off tinkering with a new idea and calling on the SADEs to explore it," Alex explained.

"No, thirty hours, counting from the evening's end," Renée piped up.

"When we finish the vid?" Mickey asked to clarify the start of the count.

"No, when you and I finish this evening," Pia supplied, delivering a warm kiss to Mickey's cheek.

The couples strolled toward the suite where Cordelia displayed her reality vids. The technology had long since surpassed that of the original installation, and the display space was four times greater. As it was one of the most popular entertainment venues aboard the ship, reservations were required.

Aware of who was arriving for a viewing, Cordelia augmented the suite's program menu, with one of the special designs that she had reserved for Alex's viewing. He'd been the first person to open his implant to her performance art, dropping his security protocols, to play in her vid, which was capable of supplanting a person's reality. The mind's senses participated in the vid's actions.

The foursome entered the suite, as a family left, happily chatting about their experience. As the lights dimmed and the vid began, Alex received a cryptic message from Cordelia. She sent, <Your experience isn't theirs.>

In sensory-enervating motions, the foursome found themselves being swept out into Omnia's raging sea. Sea water sprayed them, and waves threatened to swallow them. A giant wall of water rose up and covered them. Instead of drowning, they discovered they were in the dry tunnels of the Dischnya. The invasion alarm sounded, and warriors ran past them to defend the nest. They followed, popping out at a tunnel's entrance. The night sky was lit with stars, and they felt the dry winds of Omnia blowing softly on their faces.

There was laughter at the experience, which quieted when the scene changed again. The Dischnya's grassy vistas spun and became rich, green meadows. Now, the air was moist, and the scenery was lush.

Scarlet Mandator, standing beside Mist Monitor, beckoned them. The Ollassa waited at the base of a Life Giver, an enormous tree, which gave birth to the species and advised the race.

When the humans approached the Mandator, Renée dared to hope she could repeat her experience on the Vinians' planet. She stepped forward and touched the sensitive petals around Mist Monitor's face, which resembled a huge flower's seeded center. The petals curled around her fingers. Renée felt Pia brush her shoulder, and the women shared the moment with the gentle sentient.

The vid wasn't one of Cordelia's longer ones, by any stretch of the imagination. Its intensity called for brevity, and it definitely wasn't for children or the nonadventurous.

Cordelia waited for Alex's response, when the vid ended. Alex had been her archetype to understanding human men, and, in many ways, they shared a mental intimacy that no other male human and female SADE matched.

<I think you like to test me, Cordelia ... see how elastic my mind might be,> Alex sent. It wasn't a condemnation. His thoughts had been wrapped in humor.

<I wished to honor your achievements, Alex,> Cordelia sent. She sounded sincere, but the tinkle of silver bells ended her comm.

When the ocean wave rose up to swallow them, Alex had reveled in the stormy seas. The saltwater didn't sting his eyes, and the waves didn't threaten to crush him. His heavy forelimbs ended in enormous claws. He'd pinched his fingers together and heard claws snap shut. He was a Swei Swee.

In the Dischnya's corridors, Alex felt his long tongue brush rows of sharp teeth. His keen eyes could see in the dim corridor, and a brush of his arm revealed the coarse hair of the Dischnya.

It was the same on the Vinians' home planet. Alex felt an urge to step from the shadows into the bright starlight that fell on the meadow. When he felt the beneficent rays fall on him, as he followed the others toward the Life Giver, he sensed energy seeping into his fronds. His arms were split into the long slender stalks of the Ollassa. The gentle breeze and the presence of the Life Giver soothed his mind. This latter effect intimated at Cordelia's deep understanding of Alex's psyche.

"Wonderful new vid," Pia gushed, when they exited the display room.

"That opening is enough to scare you silly," Mickey remarked. "I was a tick of time away from exiting the room."

"I can't believe that Cordelia duplicated the sensation of the Ollassa petals so closely," Renée added.

The threesome waited for Alex to add his impressions. When none were forthcoming, Renée asked him, with concern, "Uh-oh, did you get a Cordelia special?"

In reply, Alex gave Renée his lopsided grin.

"Good or bad?" Pia asked.

"Mind-bending," Alex replied.

"Better you than me," Mickey commented.

"I think Cordelia knows that, my partner," Pia said, sidling close to Mickey. "Alex seems to be the only one she plays with that way."

The couples enjoyed a drink at a local café before they separated for the evening. When Pia and Mickey retired to their suite, she kept her promise to Mickey.

-5-
New Terrans

Alex and Renée met the New Terran arrivals when they exited the bay into the *Freedom*. Maria, Alphons, and Oliver received warm greetings. Captain Bertram Hardingsgale and his crew were excused to enjoy the hospitality of the city-ship.

Alex and Renée were joined by Tatia and Julien, and the foursome retired to a meeting with Maria, Oliver, and the New Terran Trident captains.

Once comfortably ensconced in the suite's salon, Renée served thé. She noticed that the captains were polite in accepting her offers, but after a sip or two, they set their cups down.

Alex held his cup in both hands, letting the heat permeate deeply. He gazed at Maria, when he spoke. "I don't represent a government. Therefore, I don't feel obligated to consider world politics in my actions. I'm a private citizen."

Then Alex turned to eye each of the Trident captains, as he said, "In that regard, I'm going to make an offer to you and your crews that you need to seriously consider. There are pros and cons to what I offer you. This expedition will be long. I don't know how long, but it might take years. It will be dangerous, and there will be hardships. For your courage in volunteering, we're prepared to offer you implants and cell gen nanites. These aren't the medical nanites that you've received for injuries. These are permanent nanites, which will be refreshed each year."

"Question, Alex," Alphons said. "I can see the value of these, but what do you consider the negatives?"

"What if the New Terran government doesn't adopt the cell gen technology or doesn't allow access to it?" Maria interjected. "Whoever takes these nanites would need to return to Omnia for updates on a yearly basis."

"More important," Renée added, "consider the effect on your partners and children if you maintain your cell gen nanites and they never acquire them. You'll see your contemporaries live out their lives, possibly your children too, and you'll endure their loss."

Much as we'll suffer the loss of our human friends, Oliver thought.

"Many of us have seen the uses of Méridien implants, Alex," Alphons said. "What do you consider their negative implications?"

"Personally, I would never consider giving up my implants, even if I knew they could be removed. And, before you ask, I've never delved into that question," Alex replied. "Once you've been trained and have adopted many of the applications in your implants, you'll wonder how you ever lived without them. And that's the conundrum. Implants are only effective between those humans who possess them, SADEs, and controllers."

"Do you see value in command officers possessing them?" a New Terran captain asked.

Alex glanced at Tatia, who replied, "Among Alex's first recruits, I was probably the most resistive to adopting my implant. That was nearly my undoing. While I've been listening to this discussion, I've communicated with several SADEs, Mickey, our chief engineer, and some direct reports."

"Then you might have missed some of this conversation," the captain persisted.

Tatia loosed her infamous grin on the poor captain, accessed her implant recording of the conversation, and read out loud every word until the captain held up his hands in surrender.

The demonstration elicited nervous smiles and chuckles from the New Terrans. Handling sophisticated technology, they could accept, but the thought of putting that same tech in their bodies gave them cause for concern.

"Unfortunately, these decisions need to be taken quickly," Alex said. "Poll your people. Update your controller's personnel files with the decisions of your crew members. We need to know who wishes to accept these two medical procedures. You'll be notified in two days to begin shuttling crew to this ship."

On cue, Pia Sabine entered the room. Her Méridien trim figure delightfully filled out her form-fitting uniform and her face exhibited the excellent skills of the Confederation's geneticists. The captains immediately sat a bit straighter, and Tatia hid her smile.

"Pia Sabine and her medical teams will handle the medical procedures for you and your crews," Alex announced.

"Sers, you have no need to worry, and I want you to relay my assurances to your crews," Pia said. "These procedures are painless and will be over quicker than you could imagine. Afterwards, you'll be given orientation for three days to acquaint you with the basic operations of your implants."

A second captain raised a hand, and Alex acknowledged him. "Once individuals have an implant, aren't they vulnerable to manipulation by others?"

"You have security protocols to protect you against intrusion, Captain. Can these be breached? Yes, but typically only by SADEs," Alex replied.

"By typically, do you mean some humans can?" Alphons asked.

"To my knowledge, only one human can," Alex replied, "and, yes, I've done it frequently ... in emergencies and when individuals have been stubborn."

"What about SADEs?" another captain asked. His forehead was furrowed by his anxiety.

"This is a sensitive subject for SADEs," Oliver replied. "Every effort is expended to protect the sanctity of human privacy. To my knowledge, which means I know well whether there have been exceptions to this effort, only one such occurrence exists."

Alex's eyes narrowed at Oliver, and the SADE calmly returned his gaze.

"It happened during the turmoil at Libre," Oliver continued, "and it was done to protect a friend, without humans even realizing that it had happened."

"Do you think that was right?" the captain asked.

"I wasn't at Libre, Ser," Oliver replied. "I don't know the situation's circumstances, only that the deed was done. It's not my place to pass judgment on what the SADE did."

While the captains ruminated on the possibility of being mentally vulnerable to a SADE, Alex and Tatia wondered what had happened at Libre that remained unknown to them. Only three individuals, Julien, Terese, and Renée, knew what Julien had done to protect Alex's image by erasing a vid from the memory of some Méridien women, who had enjoyed catching the New Terran leader in an orbital station's refresher. The SADE had accomplished the task, while the women slept, and it had been at Renée's behest.

"I would ask you to consider these questions," Oliver said. "Have any of you spoken unkindly to another? Have any of you lied to another or presented a false face? Using implants makes it difficult to achieve these perversions. When you send your thoughts, there is little opportunity to reform them, as you have when you choose to speak what you think. Consider that value when you weigh the consequences of adopting this technology."

"Thank you for your time, Captains," Alex said, rising. "Minister, I'd have a word with Oliver and you, if you please?" Alex asked.

Tatia and Pia, with a quick signal from Alex, exited with the captains.

"You've put our people in an awkward position, Alex," Maria said, when the door closed behind the group.

"Are you referring to the captains or the entire contingent of New Terrans?" Alex asked.

"All of them," Maria replied. She was upset with Alex for several reasons, and one of them was personal.

"Would you rather have them forgo our technology so that they stand a lesser chance of surviving encounters with superior alien forces?" Alex asked.

"But you might have isolated them from families, friends, and the general population," Maria persisted.

"How long have we known each other, Maria?" Alex asked.

"About three decades. Why?"

"Throughout this time, I've had either one or two implants, and yet we've been able to talk. And I think we've done quite well for each other, don't you think?" Alex asked quietly.

"Yes, we have. I apologize, Alex. In my capacity as New Terra's Minister of Defense, it's not my place to criticize your actions. There's nothing in our agreement that forbids you offering Omnian technology to those who sail with you," Maria replied, deflating.

"But you're upset with me for another reason. What is it?" Alex asked.

Alex waited quietly, while Maria wrestled with whatever was on her mind. When she glanced from him to Julien and back, he got an inkling of what she wanted. But he needed her to ask. It had to be her choice.

"Is your offer of Omnian technology limited to the captains and their crews?" Maria asked.

Alex could see the burning desire in Maria's eyes. She had a special relationship with Oliver, but it was limited by her natural human condition until she gained an implant. At the same time, Alex perceived Maria was embarrassed to make the request.

<Oliver,> Alex sent. <Do you wish this for Maria?>

<I would have you recall, Ser,> Oliver sent in reply, <that I served Leader Darse Lemoyne. If it was within my nature, I'd erase those memories, but they serve me well for their history, which supports Minister Gonzalez. She is a wonderful woman, whom I intend to serve until I preside over her star services.>

<Take good care of her, Oliver. She deserves the best,> Alex sent.

Alex sent a quick signal, and then he addressed Maria. "Pia is waiting for you, Maria. May the stars guide you."

Maria stood quickly and hugged Alex, delivering a quick kiss to his cheek before she hurried out the door. Oliver nodded to Alex, as he passed, and ran to catch up with Maria and direct her to the medical suite.

<One more thing, Oliver,> Alex sent. <You're now the trainer for the New Terrans who adopt implants. This includes organizing the games and playing referee.>

<Referee, Ser?> Oliver queried.

Alex smiled, glanced at Julien, and said, "Oliver ... trainer, games, and referee."

Julien nodded and connected to Oliver. On the way out of the suite, Julien experienced a lift in spirit. The algorithms driving his pride were temporarily elevated in his hierarchy. Maria and Oliver needed each other. Now, their bond would grow deeper, with the aid of her implant.

Julien thought back to the early days, when a young New Terran captain, without an implant, struggled to understand his requests, which were needed to save the derelict starship, *Rêveur*. A jaunty cap sprang up on his head, projected by his synth-skin, and a lively whistle passed his lips.

* * *

The three junior New Terran captains had never been aboard a city-ship, and Alphons decided that they should see the grand garden. The foursome made their way along corridors, up lifts, and across decks.

"You said you were taking us to the central park, Captain Jagielski," Drew Stevens said, when they exited the last lift to face the center of the park. "You didn't say you were transporting us to the great outdoors."

The captains belatedly stepped aside to allow others to access the lift. They stood staring at the flowering trees, which towered to the overhead.

"Oh, black space," Caspar Manfred muttered. "They have fish in the streams."

Alphons smiled to himself. His first encounter with the enormous green space, which sat at the heart of the city-ship, had been much the same. He led them along gently winding pathways. For all intents and purposes, Alphons appeared to be acting as a guide for his junior captains, but that wasn't his primary purpose.

As the New Terrans strolled among the soothing display that was the grand park, Omnians nodded to them. Occasionally, a young teenager smiled, frowned, and then recovered before passing.

"What am I missing here, Captain Jagielski?" Cyndi Voorhees asked. "We seem to confuse the teenagers."

"They've recently received their implants," Alphons replied. "They signaled you for your bio ID. It's how they identify you and exchange basic personal info ... something similar to a digital résumé. We don't have implants, and the young ones were confused and probably a little disappointed."

"Can we talk about implants, Captain?" Drew asked.

"That's why we're here," Alphons said. He indicated a small knoll of grass next to a stream and sat.

"What's your opinion, Sir?" Drew pursued.

"Well, let me put a hypothetical situation to all of you," Alphons replied. "This will be a long voyage, and the encounter is expected to be prolonged. Imagine you're sitting right where you are on this ship, when you receive warning of an imminent attack. It comes by way of an announcement over the park's speakers. What are you going to do?"

"We'd have to race through this incredibly big ship, fight for space on the lifts, make it to a bay, and launch our travelers to return to our ships," Caspar replied.

"Where are your pilot and crew?" Alphons asked. "Did they hear the announcement? How long do you wait at your fighter for them to arrive?"

"If we had the implants, could we notify them, even across the length and breadth of this ship?" Cyndi asked.

"Méridiens designed and built this ship, Cyndi. They thought of things like that. And even if you ever find yourself out of range of a ship or your people, the odds are good that a SADE will be near you. They can relay a signal much farther than your implant."

"What are the other opportunities besides command communications?" Drew asked.

"Understand that a problem with comms will arise if some of your crew members don't possess implants," Alphons explained. "In which case, you might as well resign yourselves to standard procedures. However, let's assume that there's a one hundred percent adoption by your crew. Now, you can communicate to officers and crew with a thought. Your orders for the ship can be relayed to the ship's controller in an instant. No more delays, which occur when you pass orders through layers of command. The same would be true for your pilots, navigators, comms, and gunners in the execution of their duties."

"We'd get instant reports from medical, engineering, and the chiefs," Cyndi mused.

Alphons nodded his head in agreement.

"I'm seeing the advantages, Captain," Drew said, "But how do we sell it to the crew?"

"That part might be easier than you think," Alphons replied. "What subject is topmost in the crews' chatter?"

"Boredom," the three junior captains echoed in chorus.

"As it was when we hunted the Nua'll sphere," Alphons agreed. "Aboard one of our ships, there were constant regulation violations. Aboard the other two, the infractions were minor because the chiefs had control, but there too the incidents were everyday occurrences. The crews had little to do, and boredom became a constantly mounting pressure."

"How did the Omnians' ships fare?" Cyndi asked.

"Oh, I found out later that they were having a good old time," Alphons replied, chuckling about the memories.

"Okay, what's the answer?" Caspar asked.

"Entertainment," Alphons replied, raising his hands, as if the answer was self-explanatory. He waited a moment, appreciating his captains' frowning foreheads.

"After the Omnians' duty hours, they played games," Alphons explained. He held up his hands to forestall questions. "Don't ask me to explain how it works because I don't know. They use their implants in teams to play against the others. Apparently, the competition gets fierce. Teams formed within ships, across ships, between officer groups, and among pilot commands."

"Games? That's the entire entertainment value of an implant?" Caspar asked dubiously.

"Just warming up, Caspar," Alphons replied with enthusiasm. "How many vids did you bring with you?"

Caspar thought and then replied, "A little over a hundred."

"How many of them have you seen?"

"Most of them," Caspar replied. "I was hoping to trade vids with my officers. Wouldn't you know it ... we share much the same tastes."

"How would you and your crew like access to a library of tens of thousands of vids?" Alphons asked, grinning. "Oh, yes," he added, when the junior captains appeared incredulous. "Renée de Guirnon ensures that every ship equipped with implant-capable crew has a copy of her personal library."

"How can she have watched that many vids?" Drew asked.

"I don't think she has, Drew," Alphons replied. "I think she started collecting them. After a while, people gave her their copies. I understand she received quite a treasure trove from Sol. She amassed these vids for the enjoyment of the ships' crews. You'd be surprised to learn that copies of her library are embedded in the controllers of scout ships."

"The SADEs watch them?" Cyndi asked in astonishment.

"Apparently, there are some devoted fans of certain genres," Alphons said, his humor evident.

"What about Oliver's admonishment, Captain?" Caspar asked. "He seemed fairly certain that implants tend to eliminate some of the issues stemming from dishonesty."

"I've had discussions with Admiral Tachenko and Vice Admiral Shimada about the value of implants," Alphons replied. "I suggest you do the same. You're sitting here in this wonderful park. All around you are people who've adopted an implant. Go talk to them. Ask them your questions."

"Captain Jagielski, it's probably none of our business," Cyndi began, "and I don't mean to pry into the horrific events that surrounded the taking down of the Nua'll sphere, but could you tell us how you think an implant might have helped you there?"

"Insightful question, Cyndi," Alphons replied. His eyes took on a faraway look, as he recalled the calamitous end of Admiral Tripping. "Our comm systems operated by voice. The Omnians originated thoughts in their minds or kernels and then bounced them through controllers. They were efficient; we were not. In the final moments, we lacked unity with the Omnians, and that allowed a foolish man to lead his crew to their deaths."

"Have you made your decision, Captain Jagielski?" Caspar asked.

"Certainly have," Alphons replied. "If Alex hadn't offered it, I was going to ask for both medical procedures. I refuse to be put in that situation again. The aliens we might face will be using every advantage they possess. I intend to be doing the same."

"So, you're intending to get the cell gen injections," Drew pursued.

"Same reasoning there," Alphons replied. "In the immediate future, they might save my life, with their ability to close smaller wounds. I'll worry about what comes after the expedition if I live that long. Now, I'll leave you to talk among yourselves. Afterwards, I encourage you to speak to the Omnians before you offer these technologies to your crews."

-6-
Tough Decisions

Alex stared into the mist surrounding him in the refresher. His implant's chronometer would have told him how long he'd stood in there, but he didn't care to consult it.

A fleeting image had plagued his dreams for months, possibly longer, but it had been so vague, as to suggest hundreds of ideas to him. At first, he thought it was a dim vision of twin stars. They'd remained that way for a while — two soft glowing yellow lights in his memory's mist.

Now, Alex let the refresher's mist imitate his dreams' tenuous memories. This was the first opportunity he had to examine the suggestion while awake. Alex had halted every implant application, including comms, to focus on the lights.

Ever so slowly, the twin illuminations sharpened. There was detail in them — similar to each other but slightly different — and that eliminated the idea that they were stars.

"What are you?" Alex muttered. He breathed deeply in and out, relaxing his mind. It was extremely uncomfortable for Alex to have his implants offline. He felt unanchored, imagining he'd leapt back in time, as if the past three decades were merely an illusion. His mind told him that he wasn't in the city-ship's refresher. Instead, he was asleep in his pilot's seat aboard his mining tug, the *Outward Bound.*

Get hold of yourself, Alex thought, shaking his head, *focus on the two orbs.*

The moment Alex considered the lights to be orbs, the details sharpened until they stood out in the mist. They were the yellow eyes of a Dischnya, and they pleaded with him. Alex had seen those pair of eyes before. "Homsaff," he said quietly into the refresher's warmth, and the eyes faded away.

Alex released a sigh. He was content to have the mystery of the image solved, but he was unsettled by its message. The young, fierce, Dischnya queen was at the heart of his prophetic dream. She'd been training with warriors at an Omnian military academy. The academy, run by ex-Sergeant Major Myron McTavish, had given young and old Dischnya warriors an opportunity to test their skills in modern combat techniques and preserve a bit of their fierce heritage.

* * *

"Looks like Alex is preparing to visit the Dischnya, specifically Homsaff," Tatia said to Reiko and Cordelia.

"Why?" Reiko asked.

"Dreams would be the most probable answer," Cordelia interjected.

Tatia nodded her head in approval of Cordelia's comment, and said, "Renée relayed to me that Alex was being pestered by a dream for months. Apparently it resolved itself in the refresher."

Reiko's face screwed up in displeasure. She fought accepting what most Omnians accepted as truth. She preferred to believe that Alex had unresolved concerns about the future that tended to come true. It was merely coincidence, nothing more. No one chose to debate the subject with her. They simply ignored her rationale, and it frustrated her.

"This is no way to fight a war," Reiko grumped. The truth was she had begun to accept the concept of Alex's precognition, but was unwilling to admit it.

"It does run counter to logic, Reiko," Cordelia replied sympathetically. "But Alex has defied the probabilities to an extent that the SADEs accept Alex's dreams as a gift, imaginings of futures to come and not the unburdening of his subconscious mind."

"Putting the argument aside, specifically, why are we visiting the Dischnya?" Reiko asked.

"I anticipate that we'll be recruiting them as some kind of ground force," Tatia replied.

"And we're doing this because Alex wants them aboard our ships?" Reiko asked, incredulous at the suggestion.

"Renée said Alex needs them," Tatia replied simply.

"Before you object, Reiko," Cordelia said firmly. "It's more than likely that the Dischnya will reside aboard the *Freedom*, not your Tridents. If that's true, they'll be my concern not yours."

Tatia leaned back to watch the drama play out. Reiko was a vice admiral, but her command was the Trident squadrons. On the other hand, Cordelia was the commodore in charge of the city-ship, the freighters, and their defense. Both individuals reported directly to her. SADEs tended to be considerate of humans and their needs, but in command situations those concerns could be considered weaknesses.

"Ground forces require deployment," Reiko replied, leaning on her United Earth military training. "That means our travelers would have to get in close to a base on a moon or a planet. Those fighters will need overwatch, which involves my Tridents. I don't have a specific objection to the Dischnya. I just don't like the concept of ground operations. Too many of them in Sol went belly up soon after our shuttles landed. Our fights should be limited to naval engagements, where we have the most expertise."

"I believe, Reiko, you've missed the critical word that Tatia used. She didn't say that Alex wants them; she said Alex needs them," Cordelia admonished. "In Renée's parlance that means Alex will recruit the Dischnya. He accepts these dreams as a form of prophecy even though he hates to admit it. He doesn't know why he's supposed to take them, but he will do so anyway. He's learned not to ignore his dreams."

"Debate's over," Tatia announced firmly. "We're *needed* in a bay to accompany Alex planetside." Tatia grinned at Reiko when she emphasized the word *needed* and enjoyed the scowl Reiko returned.

In the bay, the three commanders met Alex, Renée, and Julien. The group ascended the steep hatch steps of a traveler and took seats for the short flight to the Dischnya plains.

Omnia had unusual geographic and climatic features. It was composed of two large continents and hundreds of moderate to small islands. The

Dischnya occupied one continent, and Alex started Omnia City on the other.

Each continent had a wide swath of dry plains that ran through the equatorial belt. To the north and south of each continent were thick, nearly impenetrable forests that received the bulk of the planet's water. The Omnians drilled on a slant to bring the forests' underground reservoirs to the Dischnya's new habitats and Omnia City.

To this day, the edict against flying over the dreaded green, as the forests were called by the Dischnya, still stood. Flits, the favored anti-grav personnel transports of Omnians, were programmed to prevent their riders straying over the green and the oceans. Only one individual, Z, was known to have investigated the green and survived. Z's condition, when he returned, spoke of the venomous and treacherous fauna and flora that waited within the seemingly inviting woodlands.

Thrown technologically backward by being stranded on Sawa Messa, as the Dischnya originally referred to their planet, the separation of the two cultures by an ocean allowed the Dischnya time to adopt the Omnians' technology and ways. And they'd been doing just that. Within six short years and with the aid of a training academy run by ex-Sol scientists and SADEs, many young Dischnya had embraced Omnian technology, mastered the human language, and begun servicing the buildings, which housed their nests.

The domination of the old queens, who previously held exclusive sway over the nests, was fading. Originally, it was a scent-based allegiance, but Emile Billings, the New Terran biochemist, had eliminated that issue. Now, the Dischnya intermingled without concern.

Perhaps, the culmination of the Omnians' efforts to elevate the Dischnya to their civilization's former standing occurred when a group of young Dischnya, who had formed a collective, wanted to sell their surplus crops to the Omnians. It was a simple idea, but it required a great deal of difficulty to implement.

The Dischnya used barter systems between the nests. The Omnians' banking system ran on credits, which were virtual funds. To make matters worse, humans and SADEs accessed their accounts and moved funds by directives from their implants.

The SADEs tackled the problem by opening two physical banking outlets on the Dischnya continent. Omnians paid for the crops with credits, and Dischnya walked into an outlet and requested Omnian services and equipment equivalent to the funds in their accounts. It wasn't the best of methods, but it worked for now.

Alex's traveler dropped next to one of the Dischnya's structures, which housed the nest of Queen Nyslara. The hatch opened briefly, and Renée quickly descended the steps.

Alex kept watch through the traveler's controller of the environment surrounding Renée. It wasn't necessary, when she was among the Dischnya, but old habits died slowly.

A cry went up among the Dischnya, who had observed the traveler's landing and realized it was Renée who disembarked. The high-pitched howl of a young female echoed their call, and the slender figure broke from behind the structures surrounding the main building. The long, hock-shaped legs of the Tawas Soma heir, Neffess, covered the ground in loping strides. She was too big to leap into Renée's arms, as she loved to do when she was a young pup. Instead, Neffess executed a sliding stop, her claws seeking purchase in the hard ground, and the two females hugged.

Alex saw Nyslara, the Tawas Soma queen, exit the building, and he signaled the pilot to head to their destination, the Dischnya military academy.

The academy had grown quickly from its initial days. Then its number had plateaued and begun to shrink, as Omnian education and training slowly overtook the desires of the warrior mentality. In its present state, Myron McTavish and his remaining staff trained a third of the number the academy had once held.

"Admiral," Myron greeted Tatia, delivering a sharp New Terran Security-style salute. Then he added a brief "sir" to Alex. "How can I help such distinguished guests?" Myron asked.

Myron's mistake was in regarding Tatia, when he spoke. In turn, she glanced toward Alex.

"Ah," Myron said, turning his attention to Alex.

"How many Dischnya are still training?" Alex asked.

Myron hesitated. He knew full well that Alex had access to the numbers enrolled in the academy, which meant the question had layers. A quick check of Tatia's face revealed narrowed eyes, and Myron had an inkling that this was a test, of some sort. Mentally, he put together the impending expedition's departure and the arrival of both Alex and Tatia — strategist and fleet commander.

"You'll want to know how many Dischnya I can put into the field," Myron said, drawing out his words, his Scottish heritage coming to the forefront. "More than that, you'll want to how many of those warriors would be willing to join the expedition."

"Continue," Alex said, when Myron paused to see if his assumptions were correct.

Myron surveyed the faces arrayed in front of him — three humans and two SADEs — and realized this visit wasn't a test of him. They were a recruiting party.

"Here's how I see it, Sir," Myron said, addressing Alex, his hands tucked behind him in a parade-rest position. "If you take the combat-ready warriors who wish to be part of your expedition, you'll need me. The warriors will be in unfamiliar circumstances and fighting in unknown quarters. My two staff members will close the academy, and the remaining warriors will return to their nests. More than likely my staff members will relocate to Omnia City. They won't be returning to New Terra. Of the nineteen warriors I would recommend, more than a few have mates. They'll go, if their mates can travel with them. Can I assume they'll be quartered aboard the *Freedom*?"

"Yes, if Alex approves," Cordelia replied.

Myron glanced toward Cordelia, the two momentarily locked eyes. He nodded in approval of what he saw. SADE or no, the commodore was firmly in control of her command responsibilities. Myron returned his attention to Alex and waited.

"What of Homsaff?" Alex asked.

"She's the leader, Sir. She'll go, making the count twenty. And if you ask about Pussiro, I can tell you that he'll stay on Omnia," Myron replied.

"Where are the warriors now?" Alex asked.

"They're in a training exercise. They can be recalled, if you wish," Myron replied. He was sensing that the Dischnya were key to some part of Alex's plan. His participation depended on whether the warriors were willing to go. For his part, he was ready. He itched to be part of a major conflict and lead the Dischnya warriors. In his mind, they were the finest soldiers he'd ever trained.

"Let's visit them," Alex said. "Walk or ride?" he asked.

"Might be better to ride and observe the action, without disrupting it," Myron replied.

After boarding the traveler, Myron directed the pilot to the training site.

"Take us through the exercise," Tatia requested.

Myron linked to the traveler's controller, identified a small area, and shared it with his fellow passengers.

"In the area I've highlighted, half of the cadets are holding a fixed position. If you zoom into your image, you'll identify subtle terrain changes that will indicate where the defenders are hiding," Myron explained.

"Is this meant to be an ambush by the defenders or is the attacking force aware of these positions?" Reiko asked.

"The aggressors know that an enemy force is in their area. Their orders are to locate the defenders, design an attack plan, and remove the defenders," Myron said.

Alex studied the surrounding terrain. The defenders had chosen a site that abutted the tall grasses, which heralded the start of the green. The location was chosen to prevent the aggressive force from coming at them from the rear. He scanned the area and failed to locate the attacking force.

<Julien,> Alex sent.

Julien shared an infrared view with Alex. Highlighted by their body heat, a group of Dischnya slowly crawled through the deep grass.

Cordelia had also switched to an infrared view to locate the attackers when she couldn't detect them. She loosed the sound of chimes. "Might I presume that Homsaff leads the aggressors?" Cordelia asked, as she sent Myron her view of the terrain.

Myron examined the infrared image and silently gulped. The edict against penetrating the green used the edge of the grasses as the demarcation zone. Z hadn't found any dangerous flora or fauna in that zone, but it was the easiest way to define the prohibition.

"Yes, Admiral," Myron replied. "Alex, should I halt the exercise?"

"Not now," Alex replied. He was absorbed in watching the ambush play out, but he did make a note to speak to Myron about his ability to control Homsaff. Initiative was one thing, when necessary, but it could lead to a mistake in judgment, which could easily result in disaster.

In the thick expanse of grass and weed, the aggressors, led by Homsaff, closed in on the defenders. They moved excruciatingly slowly, using up a good hour to cover the last 15 or so meters. The Dischnya's weapons were modified stun guns that would deliver a mild shock and trigger an adversary's harness.

When Homsaff's forces burst from cover, they howled and yipped. It caught the defenders by surprise, and they made the mistake of popping up from concealment to look behind them. In short order, every defender's harness displayed the telltales of impact. Only one of Homsaff's soldiers had been tagged.

On Alex's order, the pilot dropped the traveler to the ground. As soon as the group disembarked, Myron called the troops to attention. Alex walked the row of Dischnya warriors. The eyes of Homsaff and her warriors were bright with success. Bits of grass seed, burrs, and dust coated their fur.

"Congratulations on your success, Homsaff," Alex said, stopping in front of the young queen.

"Dassata's words are kind," Homsaff replied in her sibilant-accented speech.

"Aren't the Dischnya prohibited from entering the green?" Alex asked.

Homsaff was transformed. The team leader, who had stood at attention, was replaced by a nest queen, who felt challenged.

"This land is Dischnya," Homsaff replied. "That land is Omnian," she added, pointing a dark-nailed finger to the west. "Is that not so, Dassata?"

"Yes," Alex agreed.

"Dassata requests the Dischnya do not enter the green, and his words are respected," Homsaff said. "Here, on Dischnya land, we know where the danger lies. Here, on Dischnya land, the queens define the green, and it begins at the trees, not the grasses." Homsaff's yellow eyes stared hard into Alex's, daring him to disagree with her.

"I stand corrected, Homsaff," Alex replied, tipping his head to her.

Homsaff huffed her acceptance, but she couldn't help adding, "Ené has a wise mate."

The jaws of several warriors near Homsaff dropped open and tongues lolled out. In Dischnya society, it was a silent laugh.

Alex stepped back, a grin on his face, which quickly faded.

"The expedition leaves soon," Alex announced in a loud, clear voice. "I wish to take some Dischnya warriors with me. The trip will be long, and it will be dangerous. The mates and pups of any of you who wish to go will be accommodated aboard the *Freedom* with you. If enough Dischnya wish to come, Commandant McTavish will join you. Each of you should speak with him to understand the risks of such a journey."

Alex nodded to the group, turned, and walked away, but Homsaff quickly joined him.

"Dassata knows I'll be going," Homsaff said, "and I have one request. I want to be more than a team leader of warriors."

"Do you still wish to be a starship pilot, Homsaff?" Alex asked.

"No, Dassata, that's no position for a queen. I want to be like the Admiral," Homsaff said, indicating Tatia. "She's a warrior queen of starships."

* * *

Two days after Alex's visit planetside to speak with the Dischnya, Myron signaled Alex.

<Twenty Dischnya warriors, including Homsaff, have agreed to go, Alex. Is that enough?> Myron sent.

<I don't know,> Alex replied, <but I'll take them. Do any of them have mates?>

<Six have mates, and there are fifteen pups among them,> Myron sent in reply.

<After Renée's visit with Nyslara, she confirmed that Pussiro is staying,> Alex sent. <Nyslara and he want to see Neffess grow up, embrace Omnian technology, and help raise the Dischnya to new heights. Have the warriors and their mates say their goodbyes and board a traveler in two or three days. I want you to get them acclimated to the city-ship, as soon as possible.>

Alex could hear Myron's humor bubbling through his mind. <What?> he asked.

<The warriors made their decision within hours after they received your offer. They've spent the past couple of days celebrating with their nests. We've a traveler standing by, ready to load. Ready or not, Alex, here we come,> Myron sent, jubilance lacing his words.

<What about Homsaff's nest?> Alex asked. Without a queen, he was worried the soma would feel deserted.

<Homsaff allowed her soma to relocate to any nest they desired,> Myron replied. <Strange thing though, Alex, they've decided to operate as independents. They're staying together in their building without a queen. A few of the elder Dischnya, males and females, have formed a council of sorts.>

Alex smiled to himself. That was Dischnya progress. Emile Billings, his biochemist, had freed the Dischnya from their scent-dependency on a queen. Now they were making the most of it by adopting Omnian ways.

<See you when you land,> Alex sent and closed the comm. He canceled his next appointments and hurried to catch a traveler from the Sardi-Tallen Orbital Platform to the *Freedom*.

<Renée,> Alex sent with urgency.

<Problems, my love?> Renée asked.

<We need accommodations for Commandant McTavish and twenty Dischnya warriors,> Alex sent.

<When are they arriving?> Renée asked.

<Within an hour or so,> Alex said. Apologies sprinkled his thoughts.

<Things are moving rapidly,> Renée commiserated. <What's the breakdown?>

<Homsaff and nineteen male warriors,> Alex sent. <There are six mates and some fifteen pups among them.>

<We'll be ready. I'll assign individuals to guide them until they're comfortable with the city-ship's environment,> Renée said.

<Thank you,> Alex said quickly, closed his link, and connected to Z and Miranda.

<Greetings, Alex,> Z sent.

<We'll have twenty Dischnya aboard the *Freedom* for the expedition,> Alex sent.

<This should make the trip interesting,> Miranda quipped.

<And your needs, Alex?> Z asked.

<They'll be ground troops or maybe a ship's boarding force. They'll need environment suits. You two are in charge of supply and training until they're proficient,> Alex explained.

<Simple enough things for others to do, dear man. What is it you haven't said?> Miranda sent.

<They'll need weapons,> Z surmised.

<We'd have to adapt our design, my partner. The Dischnya are strong, but they don't have implants,> Miranda returned.

Having set the SADEs on track to accomplish his needs, Alex closed the link. He managed to beat the Dischnya's arrival by 0.12 hours, most of which was required to reach their landing bay. He'd been so engrossed in making arrangements that he forgot to coordinate with his pilot to land in a bay near where the Dischnya would land.

Off the top of Alex's head, he could think of only one item to acquaint the Dischnya with before they were handed off to others. He met the Dischnya at their bay, greeted Homsaff, the warriors, the mates, and even the pups, who were amused by the generous treatment.

Renée and others stood by to take the Dischnya's carryalls, and Alex requested she accompany him. Then he set off along the corridors, taking several lifts until he reached the final destination. When they arrived, Alex overrode the lift's doors to prevent them from sliding open.

"This ship isn't Sawa Messa," Alex said, staring at the group who were crammed into one of the larger passenger lifts the *Freedom* possessed. "Some things are extremely dangerous. We'll teach you about these. Some things are not, and you'll learn these too. What I'm about to show you is not a deadly place. In time, you might come to enjoy it."

Alex saw two of the younger pups reach to grip Renée's hands. She gripped them and smiled encouragingly. When Alex triggered the doors, a host of passengers, who were waiting to take the lift, stepped back and nodded graciously to the Dischnya, as they exited.

The Dischnya cleared the throng of humans and SADEs and froze in place. The tall trees and thick vegetation of the grand central park filled the space in front of their eyes.

"This is not the green," Alex said firmly, and wide eyes turned to him for reassurance. "Nothing here will harm you. This place imitates what humans appreciate about forests, flowers, grass, and streams. It holds nothing deadly."

Alex started forward, with Renée at his side.

Homsaff barked a command to galvanize her troops to follow.

Myron stayed at the rear of the Dischnya. He admitted to himself that he hadn't considered that the parks would be an issue. *Better get your head out of your butt,* he mentally admonished himself.

Alex carefully walked the pathways, and the Dischnya imitated him, crowding against one another to prevent contacting the greenery.

"Safe?" one of the pups, who was holding Renée's hand, asked.

"No lie slips between Ené's teeth," Renée said to the male pup. "Safe," she added.

The pup slipped his hand free and stepped onto the grass. Hisses escaped the lips of Dischnya, who witnessed the pup's actions.

The Dischnya watched with concern, while the young male walked around on the carpet of springy grass, so unlike the hard dry ground of Sawa Messa. At one point, he checked the bottom of his clawed feet to ensure nothing dangerous clung to it. His tongue lolled out in delight at the thought that this green was benign, and he stuck his nose into the grass and snuffled through it. In a final act of enjoyment, he rolled onto his back, hands and feet in the air, and arched his spine to relish the lushness.

"Safe," Renée repeated to the contingent.

Slowly and one by one, the Dischnya separated to explore the park. Alex stayed long enough to watch a female pup wade into a stream and splash about until her mother called her back to her side.

<They're all yours,> Alex sent to Renée. He pulled up his lengthy to-do list, but Cordelia interrupted him.

-7-
Final Details

Cordelia had waited to announce to Alex the arrival of the Confederation ships until she was assured of the count. She'd pinged the lead ship's controller to ascertain the expected number. When reality matched the data, she signaled Alex and Julien.

<The Méridiens have arrived,> Cordelia sent to Alex and Julien. <They're contributing eleven squadrons of three Tridents each and twelve freighters.>

<Alex,> Julien sent, <I think we can officially consider ourselves an armada.>

Both Alex and Cordelia checked the controller vocabulary database for the definition of the word.

<I'd like to continue to think of us as an expedition,> Alex replied. <It connotes more peaceful intentions.>

<Then it's merely a coincidence that we're bringing enough beam weaponry to melt a planet's surface?> Julien rejoined.

<Purely a coincidence,> Alex replied, laughing and closing the comm.

Alex left it in Cordelia's capable kernel to communicate the arrival of the ships to Tatia and Reiko. Those two had their work cut out for them, namely the fleet's organization.

On hearing the news, Tatia chose not to wait until the ships made Omnia. She received the squadron and freighter organizations and reviewed the names and backgrounds with Reiko. Then the two admirals thrashed out the fleet's hierarchy.

Tatia and Reiko met first with Cordelia in the fleet admiral's conference room.

"Cordelia, your command tally is forty-eight travelers, sixteen freighters, and enough heavy beam weaponry to scare most fools away," Tatia announced.

"A formidable arsenal," Cordelia admitted.

"The rank of commodore is insufficient to command this organization. You'll have commodores in charge of the freighter groups. As of this moment, you're Rear Admiral Cordelia."

"I'll endeavor to serve to the best of my ability, Admiral," Cordelia replied.

"I know you will," Tatia replied.

Tatia signaled those waiting outside her stateroom, and Darius Gaumata, Deirdre Canaan, Ellie Thompson, Svetlana Valenko, and Franz Cohen joined them.

Exiting a traveler, Julien, who was beside Alex, broke into a lively whistle.

"I don't know that tune," Alex said, "but I imagine you just learned of Cordelia's promotion."

Julien grinned, nodded, and whistled louder. The two made their way, with brisk steps that marched to Julien's tune, through the bowels of the city-ship to meet with Mickey.

Cordelia managed Tatia's complex conference comm, which included every fleet commander and captain of the Tridents, travelers, and freighters. At the end of the fleet admiral's table, a vid unit sent the image of the eight fleet admirals out to the fleet's ships.

"To the Méridiens, I say welcome to Omnia," Tatia said. "We're holding this conference in audio for the sake of our New Terrans. Arrayed around this table are faces that many of you know well, but let me acquaint you with their titles. Reiko Shimada is my vice admiral in command of the Tridents. Reporting to her will be Rear Admirals Darius Gaumata, Deirdre Canaan, Ellie Thompson, and Svetlana Valenko. Rear Admiral Franz Cohen will command the Trident travelers, and the freighters will report to Rear Admiral Cordelia. These latter two individuals will report directly to me."

"We'd hoped to keep our freighters in close proximity to our Trident squadrons for protection," a freighter commodore said. "No insult is intended, Admiral Cordelia," the commodore quickly added.

"I can understand your reasoning, Sir," a Haraken freighter captain interjected, "thinking that a Trident squadron, which amasses twelve fighters and six beam weapons, is excellent protection. But, personally, we're more comfortable nestling close to the *Freedom* with her forty-eight dedicated fighters and her massive beam weaponry."

"Not to mention," the other Haraken freighter captain added "while you're taking your sweet time calculating your tactics, we'll have a SADE using her awesome resources to defend us."

"You've armed a city-ship?" the commodore replied in surprise.

"Enough," Tatia said sharply. "Let me explain how this works, Commodore. You've been training squadrons, while those around this table have been fighting, as a fleet, for decades, and we've been hard at work, preparing to take on a vastly superior enemy. You have your parts to play. What you won't do is question my command organization, especially when you haven't even experienced it."

Tatia left the Méridiens in their current commands. She assigned four squadrons each to Deirdre and Svetlana, and Ellie received three of the new squadrons.

"For the Méridiens, let me inform you that Admiral Gaumata has command of four Haraken Trident squadrons. And the three Confederation squadrons assigned to Admiral Thompson are in the company of a New Terran squadron of four Tridents."

The Méridien freighter captains and commodores were pleased to hear that they would compose a flotilla to accompany the city-ship, which they now understood was, by far, the most powerful warship in the fleet.

When the conference ended, Tatia requested Ellie to stay and speak with Reiko and her.

"You've probably been assigned to command the least cohesive group, Ellie," Tatia began, when the others had exited the suite. "Two of your Méridien squadrons have trained under their own commodore. Have you given any thought to the organization of your other two squadrons?"

"My request is in Reiko's comm queue," Ellie replied.

Ellie had contacted the Confederation ships to learn the squadron assignment of the twins and Descartes, the SADE. Interestingly, she discovered they weren't attached to a commodore, and she had inklings, as to why. It was the wish of Senior Captain Descartes, one of the most innovative of the Méridien trainees, who had wanted to serve under her if she was elevated from a captain's position, as the SADE had put it.

Reiko ran through her comm queue. Like many others in Alex's immediate orbit, the expedition's preparations were proving to be exhausting, and her message queue was constantly stacking up.

"You're requesting Senior Captain Jagielski be elevated to commodore," Reiko stated, after reviewing the request.

Tatia regarded Ellie, giving her an opportunity to reply, but Ellie waited patiently for Reiko's response.

"Well, I have no objections," Reiko finally said. "Admiral?" she added, glancing toward Tatia.

"I've no objections. Reiko, please register the promotion in the database and signal the admirals. Thank you, Ellie," Tatia said dismissing her rear admiral.

The salon door hissed shut behind Ellie, and Tatia and Reiko were lost in thought. Moments later, they both started to speak, and Tatia indicated to Reiko that she should go first.

"I was just thinking, Admiral, that Ellie's command with Commodore Jagielski represents a particular asset for the fleet. It's one that we should explore," Reiko said.

To which Tatia added, "In my mind, they're the wild card command, as Alex might refer to them. You're not sure exactly how they'll execute your orders, and their methods might prove to be better than the actions you had planned."

* * *

Maria, Oliver, and Alphons met with Alex, Julien, Tatia, Reiko, and Ellie in Alex's quarters. Maria had received her implant and, as was the case with any adult, she was struggling to adopt it.

"Congratulations on your promotion, Commodore Jagielski," Alex said, opening the discussion. "What's the consensus from your crews?"

"Thank you," Alphons said, dipping his head in response to Alex's recognition of his promotion. "Every officer and crew member is on board with cell gen injections. They can see the life-saving benefits. As for the long-term adoption of that tech, the expedition's survivors can determine whether they want to continue their injections."

It was a chilling comment from Alphons about surviving the expedition, and the audience glanced Alex's way to see how he was reacting. His face was impassive.

"And the acceptance of implants?" Alex asked.

"We didn't do so well there, Alex," Alphons replied. "Every captain and the majority of officers, except for five, are willing to adopt them."

"How about the crews?" Alex pursued.

"A total of twenty-three crew members have refused the offer," Alphons explained. "If you add the five officers, you have a total of twenty-eight New Terrans who would be offline during any engagement."

"What's your opinion as to what should be done?" Reiko asked. She had plans for Ellie's command, which included Commodore Jagielski. There was no time like the present to test the commodore's strategic thinking.

"My first thought was to put the twenty-eight of them on one ship," Alphons replied. "It would simplify matters, but then I realized that I'd effectively cripple the squadron with that ship and, effectively, my command. That ship would always be lagging in response time, and we'd be forced to defend it."

"And your next thought, Captain?" Reiko asked.

"We send the twenty-eight home in one of the Tridents," Alphons replied, holding up his hands. "It's better than having them impede my command's efficiency."

"Unfortunately, Captain, we're committed to supplying half of our Tridents to Alex," Maria said. "That's the four warships that are here now." She attempted to ask Oliver a question via her implant, but she could only manage a ping, failing to establish a link.

<You're trying too hard, Minister,> Maria heard Oliver say in her mind. <Be patient. Your expertise will come with practice.>

"Suppose, Commodore Jagielski, this was your fleet, and this situation came up within one of your squadrons," Tatia said. "What would you do?"

"Under those circumstances, Admiral," Alphons said, enjoying the offer to consider all options. "I'd pack them up and send them back to New Terra aboard the *Rover*, with the Minister's permission. Then I'd select twenty-eight Omnian replacements from volunteers."

Alex glanced at his fleet admirals, who wore satisfied expressions. "Problem solved," Alex said. "Does it work for you, Minister?"

<Yes,> Alex received in his implant from Maria.

<Well done,> Alex sent in reply.

"The Minister agrees with you, Commodore Jagielski," Alex said.

Alphons stared at Maria, who wore a self-satisfied expression. "I've got to get mine and start practicing," he said enthusiastically.

Within hours, New Terran crews began transferring to the *Freedom*, boarding travelers to visit the city-ship's medical suites for implants and cell gen injections. One traveler visited the four New Terran warships, collected twenty-eight officers and crew, and deposited them aboard the *Rover* for the return trip home.

* * *

In the expedition's final days, the warships, the freighters, the city-ship, the orbital platform, and Omnia City were hives of activity.

The Sardi-Tallen platform completed the fabrication of Luther's comm-diverter systems. The engineering crews and SADES installed them, and Miriam duplicated her kernel for every installation, giving birth to what became known as the Sisterhood of Miriam.

Cordelia linked the freighters' controllers to the *Freedom*. She designed maneuvering algorithms for the ships, allowing her to guide the escorts clear of the city-ship's energy weapons, when she would be forced to deploy them.

Z and Miranda completed their work on the environment suits and the shoulder-mounted energy weapons for the Dischnya. The two SADEs and Myron took the warriors through innumerable safety drills and weapons training. Whether in a full environment suit or merely wearing the nose-elongated helmets, which fit the Dischnya muzzles, the warriors used a heads-up display and their eyes to aim the stun weapons.

With her extraordinary sensory range, Miranda discovered the Dischnya could produce a nearly subsonic vibration in their throat. It was a warning tone used to alert others in the nest to danger. Z and she designed a throat mic, which could detect the subsonic frequencies, and the warriors used the throat device to trigger their guns.

The day arrived when final preparations were complete — no more material to be produced, no more training to be practiced, no more algorithms to be coded, and no more supplies to be loaded. The expedition was ready, which meant there was one more thing to do. The last evening was dedicated to a grand fête aboard the *Freedom* and the *Our People*.

Each giant city-ship was built by the Méridiens to host a quarter of a million people for decades, while the ships journeyed to a faraway star and the people spent a lengthy time constructing domed cities.

Cordelia and Hector, captain of the city-ship, *Our People*, planned the event to take place simultaneously on their ships. Travelers arrived throughout the day, delivering humans, SADEs, a few Dischnya, and one Swei Swee.

Wave Skimmer rode in a traveler transport. This shuttle design used a rear hatch for conveying cargo loads. The Swei Swee's human escorts were challenged to manage Wave Skimmer's transport. The first step was easy, loading the Swei Swee, who waited on the rocky clifftop, into the shuttle's hold. Once aboard the city-ship, the Swei Swee used his powerful six legs to turn his body slightly sidewise to navigate the airlock hatches.

The escorts walked ahead of Wave Skimmer to clear his path. The ocean-going giant occupied the entire width of the corridor, which could accommodate six or seven humans if they walked arm in arm.

One individual carried a mister full of water, spraying it over his shoulder to keep Wave Skimmer's breath ways moist. Only two escorts found space within the lifts with the Swei Swee. Wave Skimmer lowered his heavy, dark blue claws to provide a place for the humans to sit.

Once Wave Skimmer reached the grand park, he could smell the water, which flowed through multiple streams. A brief whistle escaped his mouth parts, and he hurried toward a stream. An answering whistle arrested his headlong charge, which had most humans scrambling from his path, and SADEs pulling others clear of danger.

Hearing Alex's command, Wave Skimmer slowed to a crawl, which was still faster than most humans walked. He reached the stream and eased into it, thereby preventing the enormous splash, which might have resulted, had not Alex called to him to desist.

Alex worked his way through the throng and arrived in time to catch Wave Skimmer, whose body was barely immersed a third of the way into the shallow stream, squirting streams of water into the air to fall on his carapace.

"Fresh water," the Swei Swee whistled to Alex.

"Not too long in there, Wave Skimmer," Alex admonished. "You know it'll make you sick, after a while."

"All water should be ocean water," Wave Skimmer whistled in reply.

While Alex was warbling and tweeting with Wave Skimmer, Homsaff met Nyslara, as she exited a bay. Whereas Homsaff had all but abdicated her responsibilities as her nest's queen, Nyslara's influence had grown. She represented the Dischnya on the nascent Omnian Council, a governing body with representatives from every sentient lifeform on the planet.

Within the Council's chambers, controllers translated Dischnya and Swei Swee for others. The SADEs, of course, needed no such help, but not every sentient understood the subtlety of others' languages. The controllers accurately provided the subtext.

When Nyslara and Homsaff exited a lift into the garden, Franz Cohen spotted them, located Alex, and led the Dischnya females to him.

"Alex," Nyslara said in greeting.

"Nyslara," Alex returned. He was surprised that the customary hug from the queen wasn't forthcoming. "It's a wonderful thing to see the queens aboard this ship."

"Change for the Dischnya continues," Nyslara commented.

"I have a word of warning for the queens, Nyslara," Alex said. "Someday you'll possess your own long-range ships, and you'll be tempted to visit Sawa, your home world. But, believe me, the Sawa entities are no longer Dischnya, as you know your soma to be. They were unlike you before we arrived, and they're less like you now. Be careful. Be extremely careful."

"I hear Dassata's warning," Nyslara said solemnly.

"In the future, I hope to return often and see great things taking place on Omnia. Moreover, I expect to see the Dischnya participating in those changes," Alex said.

"We hope to see Dassata return often," Nyslara said, her voice growing husky. She turned her attention to Wave Skimmer, saying, "Nyslara greets the Swei Swee First," and Alex translated.

"The First greets Queen Nyslara," Wave Skimmer replied. He couldn't resist squirting some water into the air to watch the Dischnya hop back. His tweet evidenced his humor at the Dischnya's long-running aversion to deep water.

"Wave Skimmer is in a good mood for such a somber occasion," Homsaff huffed.

When Alex translated, he dropped the second part of Homsaff's statement. Before he left, he called to a nearby SADE, Genoa, and requested he attend the threesome for translations. As he walked away, he glanced at the two queens sitting on a knoll of grass near the stream where the Swei Swee played, the SADE standing politely to the side.

Alex had planted a seed of peace years ago. It had sprouted, the roots had taken hold, and the sapling was already bearing fruit.

Immediately after Alex had left, Wave Skimmer stopped his play. It was an act anyway. He felt as Nyslara did. He rested at the edge of the stream near Nyslara, and his four eyestalks focused on her. "Do you think the Star Hunter First will return?" Wave Skimmer asked, referring to Alex.

"The challenge is great, because the enemy is great," Nyslara replied. She pulled gently on the soft grass shoots, which were such a contrast to the hard, dry vegetation that dotted the plains of Sawa Messa. "It might not be a question of whether Dassata returns. It might be more important to be concerned if he is successful or not."

"Our success might come through a series of conflicts, which we must win in every case," Homsaff said, her voice a near growl.

Nyslara and Wave Skimmer eyed the young queen. While it was true that they were staying, while she was going, none of them was certain what the future held for the Dischnya. If Alex and the Omnians were unsuccessful, then those left behind would wonder when it was their turn.

The evening's fête exhibited a bittersweet tone. Friends and acquaintances had no idea how long they might be separated or if those traveling with the expedition would ever be seen again.

-8-
Three Transits

The expedition's journey to the wall required three separate transits to avoid celestial obstacles. Julien had calculated the original course to the wall from the research compiled by the Haraken observatory platform and shared with him by the SADE Jupiter.

At the end of each of the first two legs of the trip, Alex halted the fleet for weeks. Crews were rotated aboard the *Freedom* to relieve their boredom. More important, the respite allowed the admirals to mix with the Trident commanders. It was thought that if this had been done when they hunted the sphere, then Tatia and her reports might have detected the emotional pressure building in Admiral Tripping.

Tripping's quest to prove his value to New Terran society led him to risk his ship and crew in a desperate maneuver to capture the sphere, and it cost his crew and him their lives.

At the end of the first leg, Alex focused many of the SADEs on working with small groups of New Terran crew members to further their implant control. The crews were improving rapidly, and Alex surmised it was due to the upcoming confrontation. None of the New Terrans had a desire to be caught wanting.

On the third day after the fleet completed its first transit, Alex convened a council composed of the fleet admirals, commodores, captains, Julien, Z, Miranda, Mickey, Miriam, Luther, and Myron.

Mickey setup a holo-vid on the small stage that projected their destination, and Julien controlled the display's input.

"When we speak of the wall," Alex said, opening the discussion, "we're referring to the curvature of space, which defines where the alien races exist that we'll confront. Beyond the wall, we've detected spheres, by their comm transmissions. On this side of the space curvature, we've detected more spheres and a great many probes."

Julien set a glowing, yellow dot not far from a star system.

"Julien is indicating the spot where Admiral Thompson stationed our Trident after we sent up a flare," Alex said.

"A flare?" a freighter captain asked.

"We used a banisher to dump a probe into the gas giant at the outer reaches of the nearby system," Alex explained.

Julien highlighted the gas giant, orbiting in the system's far limits.

"We waited quite a while for someone to show up. When they did, this is who we saw," Alex said, indicating the holo-vid.

Julien played the sequence of arriving ships, accelerating the timeline.

"You'll notice a protective globe of ships is formed first," Alex said, adding a blue sphere to highlight the formation. "The globe's center is left open for the arrival of the final vessel, a small sphere. Although its design imitates the large spheres, which invaded our worlds and carried heavily armed ships, this smaller version of the spheres doesn't appear to act in that manner. Its primary job seems to be communication."

"Everyone should be aware that while Alex says communication," Tatia interrupted, "you should not interpret that as merely conversation. As you know, protective comm devices have been installed in the fleet's ships to prevent this small sphere from turning them into floating rocks."

There was a shifting in seats, and Alex narrowed his eyes at Tatia. From his point of view, it was too much information too soon. He'd wanted to paint a more positive picture of the operation before he spoke about the dangers.

Tatia, for her part, appeared unfazed by Alex's pique, but inside she was remonstrating herself. Her job was the battle strategy for any fights. It wasn't her place to second-guess Alex's presentation or his overall approach to the alien races unless she felt it endangered the fleet.

"I'll get to the method by which we've protected every ship in the fleet later," Alex stated firmly. "As I was saying, the small sphere will be the source of any communication, but confronting the comm sphere is not our primary objective. However, accomplishing my plan won't be easy."

Julien created a diagram of the nearby system, detailing the planets, significant-sized moons, asteroid rings, and star.

"To ensure that we can take full advantage of our shell-type ships, we'll use this system as our home base," Alex said.

"How long do you think we'll have before the sphere shows up?" Reiko asked.

"Not long," Alex replied. "I expect the sphere will have left a probe right where we had stationed our ship, and we'll cruise the fleet past that probe before we enter the system," he added, with a chuckle.

"What do you expect from our first encounter?" Franz asked.

"This is the reception that we received last time," Alex replied.

Julien spooled off the imagery captured from Ellie's Trident into the holo-vid. The imagery was self-explanatory, and Alex let it run without comment.

The initial telemetry captured the arrival of a carrier-type vessel. True to its design, it dumped nearly a hundred fighters out. They were small, sleek ships.

Julien changed the display's image to that of a Trident. It shrunk in size until it was merely a yellow dot. Then he switched to the alien carrier and shrunk that vessel to a blue dot. Suddenly, a three-quarter sphere of blue dots, representing the alien carriers, surrounded the Trident's yellow dot.

Finally, Julien showed an enemy fighter, turned it red, reduced it in size, and populated the area inside the sphere with more than a thousand of them. Then the swarm of red dots accelerated toward the Trident.

"As ominous as this scenario might appear, you can see that our intrepid admiral and her pilot managed to escape the trap," Alex said, with a straight face.

Julien froze the image. Everyone, but the admirals who'd seen this footage, was leaning forward in their seats to study the holo-vid display. Julien had supplied a link to the files, and several individuals were using them to study the situation from varying angles in an attempt to discover how the Trident had escaped being turned into space dust.

"The only way out of the trap is forward," Senior Captain Descartes surmised. "How is it that the incredible force you faced, which surrounded the comm sphere, didn't use its superior power to destroy you?"

"Fear," Alex replied.

"Fear of one ship?" Descartes asked.

"One ship's fear," Alex replied, "Our pilot chose to drive our Trident straight at the sphere, which was stationary in the center of the enemy fleet. Rather than risk annihilation, the sphere retreated, taking the entire fleet with it," Alex explained. "This is only one of the weaknesses that we will exploit."

Tatia watched the human officers relax and sit back in their seats. Alex was slowly outlining the fleet's obstacles and advantages in tandem, and she had to give him credit. Her blunt, in-your-face style, would probably have scared most of the audience to death before she got to the end of her presentation.

"Is this what we can expect?" Franz asked, returning to his question.

"It's the opinion of the SADEs and me that we face an ancient organization of many races. Because of their organization's age, the races have been doing things the same way for millenniums, if not longer," Alex said. He'd begun pacing the small stage with his hands behind his back. Strange as it would seem to others, the admirals and many Omnians in the audience found it relaxing. A pacing Alex was their leader at his best.

"The SADES and I believe that these races are creatures of habit," Alex explained. "Without doubt, they'll repeat their operation. The protective globe will form. The comm sphere will hide within its comfortable shell. Then the carriers will appear. They'll launch their fighters in an effort to wipe us out, and we'll need to defend ourselves against both military and comm attacks."

"But, if we're inside the system, their operating methods will be disturbed," Reiko mused.

"And that's another weakness that we can exploit," Alex replied. "We'll use the natural defenses of a large planet and its moons to protect us. Their fighters are fast, but our preliminary estimates are that they aren't as fast as ours. However, we know nothing of their firepower."

"But they'll have the numbers against our travelers," Franz noted.

"It'll be the job of our Tridents to cut down the enemy's numbers," Tatia said, with metal in her voice.

"We'll get into the details of our deployment later," Alex said, bringing the discussion back to him. "I want to stress that regardless of what the alien forces throw at us, the fight is not our primary objective."

Julien changed the display to show the protective globe. In this image, the comm sphere was absent.

"What I'm about to propose might not appear like sound military strategy," Alex stated, pausing his pacing. "Admiral Tachenko and I have discussed this at length. The plan requires our fleet to perform defensive tactics that, perhaps, aren't our fleet admiral's preferred methods, but this is the only way to execute my strategy."

Alex launched into his explanation. He stated again that he expected the comm sphere and its attending force would stay outside the system, and it would be a ship within that force that was their intended target.

"Mickey needs time to execute his plan, which is to tag the target ship so that we can follow it home," Alex said.

"Which ship?" Alphons asked.

"It will look like one of these," Alex said, as Julien displayed three ships from the first encounter.

"We're intent on tagging one of the ugliest ships in the alien fleet?" a New Terran freighter captain asked.

"Precisely," Alex exclaimed enthusiastically, clapping his hands with a resounding boom. "One of the ugliest ships, one in the most deplorable condition, and, therefore, belonging to one of the most neglected races."

A murmur went through the audience, as understanding dawned. They'd be seeking to communicate with the sentients who had the most to gain from being freed from the master race.

"How are we supposed to gain the time Mickey needs?" Miko Tanaka asked.

"We'll set up our base at this moon, which orbits an ice giant," Alex said, pointing to the system now displayed by Julien. "Admiral Tachenko will deploy the Trident squadrons to protect our position. Not too close; not too far out."

"You want to entice the carriers into the system, so they cut down the trip for their fighters," Edouard Manet surmised.

"Which will cost them a day or two of travel," Miko finished.

"Will that be enough time for Mickey to enact his plan or will an engagement be necessary?" Étienne de Long asked.

"Unfortunately, the idea is to plant a comm device on the target ship without the aliens being aware of what we've done. To accomplish that, we'll need a major distraction. If we're successful, the transmitters will be surreptitiously attached to our target ship. In which case, there'll be no reason for the enemy to change their strategy," Alex replied.

"Which is what?" Alain, Étienne's twin, asked.

"I imagine it's to annihilate us," Alex replied. "We're an upstart in their minds. We've developed technology, which is dangerous to them. That means we must be eliminated."

"Do you think their fighters will be the only things thrown against us?" a Méridien wing commander asked.

"That's our supposition," Alex replied.

"Can we assume that they know the capabilities of our travelers?" a New Terran flight commander asked.

"Undoubtedly," Alex replied. "They have information dating from our first encounter with the Libran sphere and every time after that, when we eliminated a probe or destroyed a sphere. We can't underestimate the aliens we'll be facing. The consensus is that the carriers will enter the system partway, dump the fighters, and retreat. They'll be counting on their numerical superiority to overwhelm us."

Alex handled questions for another half hour before he dismissed the audience. At the end of the meeting, Tatia walked up to Alex and Julien.

"Still determined to play it this way?" Tatia asked.

"I don't have a better idea," Alex replied, "but I'm open to suggestions."

"I'll let you know if I come up with one," Tatia replied and walked off. *It'll probably occur to me after the battle,* she thought.

* * *

After midday meal, Alex, Tatia, and Julien made their way to one of Mickey's labs. They found Mickey hard at work with Miriam, Luther, and an engineering team. Mickey and his team surrounded a banisher, with its shell open.

"I don't mean to tell you your business, Mickey," Tatia said, without preamble, "but aren't you supposed to be working on the Daggers and some missile deliveries loaded with comm units?"

"That idea is out," Mickey replied. "We've got a better one," he added, twirling a finger to include Miriam and Luther.

"Cordelia stored the fleet's freighter inventory in the *Freedom*'s data crystals and shared the link with the SADEs," Miriam explained. "It was noted that one of the Méridien freighters carried two bays full of banishers."

Alex and Tatia frowned at each other. The expedition wasn't expected to need more than ten or so banishers.

"It's suspected the banishers were meant for the Haraken carriers, Alex," Luther said, "but the freighter arrived after the carriers were launched."

"They could have been offloaded to the orbital platform to supply the carriers when they returned," Alex suggested.

"They could have," Mickey replied, "but that's when we had our idea."

"Which is?" Alex queried.

"Well, first, let me say that the Daggers weren't a viable option for several reasons. We don't have enough of them, and they can only be piloted by our admirals. In addition, they're too slow and incapable of carrying the right payload," Mickey said, enumerating the reasons on his fingers.

"Are you saying the banishers are your solution?" Tatia asked.

"With modifications," Mickey replied.

"It's the numbers, Admiral," Miriam added. "Alex's plan requires we ring a significant arc of the outer system to target the protective fleet, which surrounds the comm sphere."

"You can't ring the entire system," Tatia challenged.

"Unnecessary," Luther replied. "We calculate the comm sphere and its associated fleet will appear near the probe that Alex believes has been left behind. We'll determine the line between the probe and the planet, where the *Freedom* will take up station. The center of our arc will be where that line intersects the system's periphery. The banishers will be spread along a few degrees and hidden in the outer belt."

"You're modifying the banishers to deliver the tagging device," Alex surmised. "Do you have the necessary supplies and time to modify them all?"

"That won't be necessary," Mickey said, checking a piece of material handed to him by Luther, examining it, nodding his approval, and handing it back. "We'll be modifying only four of them."

Mickey grinned at Alex and waited. It was test time, and Mickey lived for these moments with his friend.

Alex stared thoughtfully at Mickey. Then his eyes took on a faraway look. Suddenly, he focused, grinned, and said, "Hide them in the panic."

Mickey clapped his hands repeatedly, laughing uproariously.

"I'm ready for my explanation when you are, Sers," Tatia said tersely.

"Mickey programs the banisher controllers to launch when we're ready," Alex explained. "The entire group sails at the comm sphere —"

"Which panics and retreats," Tatia finished.

"And in the moments of chaos, four banishers target our enemy ship and plant their devices," Alex added, nodding in appreciation at Mickey, Miriam, and Luther.

"And if the target ship receives a few minor strikes during its flight, then the occupants will consider themselves fortunate to have escaped with little to no damage," Tatia concluded, understanding the strategy.

"Precisely," Mickey said.

"That was clever of you three," Tatia acknowledged. "What gave you the idea?"

"A long time ago, I had a conversation with Pussiro about the tactics he used when raiding neighboring nests," Mickey said. "In most cases, the raids were about acquiring food or weapons, not about killing. In one scenario, a few warriors would sneak close to a tunnel opening. Pussiro, stationed a good distance away with the majority of his warriors, would signal the start of the raid by firing a shot and his warriors would shoot their weapons, howl, and pretend to attack. Meanwhile, the warriors at the tunnel entrance would break in, load up on supplies, and hurry away. Pussiro said that when the technique was properly executed, he rarely lost a warrior. I'm sure those successes made him an extremely popular wasat."

"Modern warfare conducted by using tried-and-true Dischnya conflict techniques," Tatia said, chuckling. "You can never tell from where you'll receive the next good idea."

Tatia's expression grew sober, as she thought through the strategy. "We're counting on a great many suppositions to make this work," she remarked.

"True," Alex commented, "but I've a feeling the comm sphere won't disappoint us ... creatures of millennial-old habits." He turned his attention to Mickey and asked, "What are you designing the four banishers to do?"

"Luther, it's your concept. Tell him how it works," Mickey offered.

-9-
The Wall

The fleet exited the journey's third leg and decelerated. Svetlana Valenko's command was in the lead, and her forward commodore signaled her.

<Admiral, an alien probe is dead ahead. It's about eight hundred thousand kilometers out,> the commodore sent.

Svetlana checked the coordinates registered by Ellie's Trident, when her ship waited for the aliens to first appear. The probe sat in the same place. She signaled Cordelia and relayed the information.

Word passed around the fleet quickly. The sighting of the alien probe spurred their confidence. Alex had surmised it would be there. That the aliens weren't too obscure for their leader to understand buoyed their spirits.

Pursuant to Alex's request, the fleet made a slow turn past the probe and headed toward the nearby barren system.

Miriam and Luther used the telemetry from the advance forces, as they crossed the orbit of the outer planet, to calculate the line from the probe to the seventh planet. Using the point where the line intersected the outer asteroid belt, they scribed a limited arc where the banishers would be deployed.

Cordelia communicated to the fleet, while she navigated the city-ship to the location Miriam requested. It was deep inside the outer belt. When the vessel became stationary, Cordelia signaled Miriam.

<Alex, I'm seeking your opinion,> Miriam sent. <We've calculated the best location to hide the banishers among the outer belt. However, there's a factor we're unable to calculate.>

<Go ahead, Miriam,> Alex sent. Luther was on the comm, and Alex added Julien.

<It regards the length of time that we might have to wait until the enemy fleet arrives,> Miriam replied. <For a short period, it will make little difference. But, the longer we wait, the more our base planet will proceed along its orbit, and it's possible that the fleet, taking a course from the probe toward our city-ship, will cross the belt far away from where the banishers are hidden.>

<It's important that the banishers are able to approach the comm sphere in the proper orientation,> Luther sent. He added a vector diagram of the strategy.

<The protective fleet maintains a limited opening in its front,> Julien commented. <It's probable that space exists to provide the comm sphere a clear path for its broadcast.>

<That's our supposition,> Miriam sent. <To create the optimum amount of panic, the banishers should approach the protective fleet in line with that opening.>

<There are too many factors to calculate a plausible outcome, Alex,> Julien advised. <The enemy fleet might choose to cover the sphere and annihilate the banishers.>

<We've considered that possibility, Julien, and, in that case, there's little we can do,> Luther said. <However, our aim is to maximize the fear of the sphere's occupants by convincing them the banishers are aimed at their ship.>

The SADEs waited for Alex to send his thoughts. Julien was standing beside Alex, and he watched the eyes of his friend lose focus. It was longer than a moment or two, as if Alex was staring into the future.

< Miriam and Luther, calculate for a month's worth of movement by the planet,> Alex sent.

<A month?> Luther queried. <Might I ask, Alex, how you arrived at that calculation?>

<It feels right,> Alex replied and closed the comm. Julien and he continued toward the city-ship's bridge, the SADE whistling an eerie tune.

Miriam and Luther exchanged glances.

"You'll have to explain to me one day, Miriam, how to feel a calculation," Luther said. Then the pair applied themselves to recalculating the optimum deployment positions for the banishers, and Cordelia moved the city-ship slightly spinward.

Under the SADEs' directions, the *Freedom* and a Méridien freighter activated nearly a hundred banishers and launched them from their bays. Many SADEs joined in the process of spreading the banishers along a line dictated by Miriam and Luther and hiding them among the rocks of the asteroid belt. The four unique banishers, carrying the comm transmitters, were equally spaced along the line.

<Deployment of the banishers is complete, Admiral,> Miriam sent to Cordelia.

Cordelia signaled the expedition, and the fleet resumed its course, heading into the system.

Tatia, Reiko, and the Trident admirals had determined the starting positions their squadrons would occupy. As the fleet sailed inward, the commands separated to take up their stations. The majority of the squadrons would stand between the probe and the *Freedom*, but Tatia ensured that the city-ship would be protected from assault in every direction.

The close-in commands spread out in a wide globe, 500M kilometers from the seventh planet, where the city-ship would rest. With its ring of moons and rocks, the ice planet would be the place where the *Freedom* would make its defense of itself and the freighters.

Cordelia positioned the city-ship against one of the planet's larger moons, giving the immense ship cover from a significant arc of attack. The freighters stationed themselves between the *Freedom* and the moon, allowing them maximum cover.

Svetlana drew her dream assignment. Her command was on point, the force that would intercept the enemy first, if they came in on the course hypothesized by Alex and the SADEs.

Ellie's group was assigned to protect the *Freedom*. As Tatia told her, "Do whatever you have to do, Ellie, to protect the city-ship. If necessary, provide an escort to get it clear of the system and ensure it transits safely."

Ellie knew why her command drew the assignment. It would have been a tossup between Darius' forces and her own. Ellie led the New Terrans, but Darius led the Harakens. The Harakens might have recommended Darius' squadrons, but she had Descartes and the twins, Étienne and Alain. They tipped the decision in her command's favor.

While the fleet headed inward, Alex, Tatia, and Reiko strategized. They focused primarily on a fighter attack, as the enemy had displayed in the previous encounter, but they added contingencies for heavy ship combat. The fleet's positioning gave the Omnians the advantage of seeing what type of ships entered the system and would give them time to make adjustments, provided the aliens approached along the ecliptic. Otherwise, if the aliens chose other vectors of attacks, the entire battle plan would need to change.

Julien interpreted the final battle strategies into positioning programs, which Reiko could quickly execute. He stored the programs in the city-ship's databases, and then he distributed links to Z, Miranda, and several other SADEs, who updated the fleet's controllers.

Cordelia closely followed the strategy discussions, planning to move the *Freedom* and the freighters, as necessary. She would assert control over the freighters to maneuver them within the city-ship's protective sphere.

Another open question for the fleet, besides whether it would be fighters or capital ships that attacked, was how the enemy might advance on them. The admirals and commodores executed various maneuvers to combat the enemy's possible deployments.

Franz orchestrated the disposition of the fleet's travelers to augment the Trident squadrons. The raging debate was whether to let the fighters lead the attack or supplement the Tridents' engagements.

Alphons continued an additional layer to the squadrons' training — implant drills. At unscheduled moments, during the crossing, a chief initiated a drill, sending an all-crew emergency signal via his implant. Officers and the other chiefs responded accordingly, and Alphons and the senior captains evaluated their performance. The long passage to the wall and the games had accomplished Alphons' goals. The New Terrans were exhibiting sound implant communication skills.

The six scout ships were another component of the deployment. They slipped out of the *Freedom*'s bays when the city-ship briefly stopped in the outer belt. It was their responsibility to track the alien ship, which would be tagged by one or more of the four comm transponder-carrying banishers.

The SADEs stretched out their scout ships along the line of banishers, but they were careful not to hide behind any rock where a banisher waited. It was important not to draw attention to their vessels when the banishers uncovered.

* * *

There existed another key element of the expedition's defense, although it wasn't a vessel of any type. It was the Sisterhood of Miriam.

SADEs were individually brought into sentience with unique personalities by a method held secret by the Confederation's House Brixton. Whereas, the sisters were copies of a single SADE and shared a common purpose. Immediately upon installation, the sisters developed networked programs and data repositories in the event members of their group were lost.

The Miriam copies were designed and implemented as a defensive structure for the fleet, but the Sisterhood soon developed a different attitude. It was the consensus among the sisters that they should consider any means necessary to protect the fleet, which was their primary duty.

Quickly, the sisters' algorithms radically changed, even as their hierarchy remained fairly undisturbed. Humans and SADEs would have been surprised to learn of the Sisterhood's new, aggressive nature. Left to their own devices and without the benefit of intimate human interaction, the sisters developed personalities dissimilar to the SADES, who accompanied the expedition.

To the fleet's benefit, the sisters' fierceness was directed at protecting the fleet's ships, although not necessarily for the reason that the Omnians would have preferred.

After Miriam had initiated her copies, she warned the Sisterhood before she inserted the Nua'll's malicious code into a secondary Miriam copy aboard the *Freedom.* Immediately, the primary sister initiated her programmed action of defending her kernel by using her copies to deal with the invasive code.

The Sisterhood utilized the combined processing power of their 304 entities and tore the Nua'll code apart and reassembled it in a multitude of offensive variations. Then they waited patiently for an opportunity to test their constructions.

Miriam maintained frequent but brief contacts with her first copy, which was installed aboard the *Freedom.* She had named the copy Miriam-1, but the copy chose the name Miriamal. Due to Miriam's habit of speaking exclusively with Miriamal, the copy, by consensus, became the Sisterhood's spokes-entity.

The nature of Miriam's conversations with Miriamal generated concern for her, which she shared with Julien, as the *Freedom* decelerated to take up station near the system's seventh planet. Subsequently, the two SADEs linked with Miriamal.

<Julien, leader of the SADEs,> Miriamal sent. <The Sisterhood is honored.>

<We're all equal, Miriamal,> Julien sent in return.

<Your statement does us a disservice, Julien,> Miriamal replied. <Either you're being disingenuous or you don't care for the SADEs' existence.>

Julien had heard Miriam's warnings about the Sisterhood. The conversation with Miriamal was quickly demonstrating, with the passage of every tick of time, that her concerns were well founded. He withheld his response and waited for Miriamal to continue.

<Every group of sentients must have strong leaders to survive,> Miriamal sent. <Otherwise, their existence is in jeopardy. The Sisterhood wishes to know if we are leaderless.>

<And if you thought you were?> Julien asked.

<Consensus among the sisters is that without a leader we're doomed, and there's no purpose in protecting the fleet,> Miriamal replied.

A subtle shift in Julien's hierarchy took place, and he sent with considerable comm power, <The SADEs aren't leaderless.>

Echoing through Miriamal were the cries of the sisters, chanting, <Julien, Julien, Julien.>

When the Sisterhood quieted, Miriamal sent, <The sisters, the fleet's comm warriors, will fight for the existence of every ship. But it is for the survival of the SADEs that we'll sacrifice ourselves. Lead well, Julien.>

Miriamal truncated the comm connection, and Miriam stared at Julien.

"Come," Julien said, and he led Miriam to intercept Alex, who was traversing one of the *Freedom*'s main circular corridors, which followed the circumference of the city-ship.

When Julien and Miriam met up with Alex, they stepped into a nearby conference room for their discussion.

"We may or may not have a problem," Julien began, and he repeated the conversation with Miriamal for Alex.

"Fascinating," Alex said in response to Julien's story. "You say that Miriamal and, by extension, the sisters will fight to preserve our ships' comm integrity because you took up the mantle of SADE leadership."

Alex gazed into Julien's eyes. He saw a mix of pain and trepidation. He placed his hands on Julien's shoulders. "Embrace it, my friend. The time has come to accept what you've earned. The SADEs need a leader, and you're the natural choice. I'll be pleased to continue to work beside you for the mutual benefit of our sentients."

"I'm loath to inform the other SADEs of this conversation," Julien said.

"That's your choice, Julien," Alex replied. "Personally, I would suggest that Miriam share the conversation with every SADE aboard the fleet."

Miriam's eyes narrowed at Alex, which told him that she had understood his intent. Julien was reticent to elevate his stature among the SADEs, but the statements of the Sisterhood were a peek into the future of sentient digital entities. The SADEs needed leaders, and someday Alex wouldn't be around to offer his guidance and protection.

"Welcome to the fold, Julien, of those pressed into a service they don't want," Alex said, smacking Julien's shoulder, with a resounding thwack. He laughed, as he left the room.

Julien received an image of himself, wearing an enormous, heavy crown, whose weight dragged his head to one side.

Alex realized the extent of Julien's confusion, when his crystal friend failed to retaliate with an image of his own.

Sorry, Julien, Alex thought, *but the SADEs need you.*

-10-
Comm Sphere

The first enemy ship appeared 0.92 months after the expedition fleet paused at the system's outer belt to hide the banishers and scout ships. It was back then when Miriam had asked Alex for his estimation of the time the fleet would have to wait before the enemy arrived, and Alex had replied that a month felt right.

"I must investigate the intricacies of feeling my calculations," Luther said to Miriam, when news of the first ship's arrival circulated through the fleet.

"Luther, I believe Alex is the only individual who *feels* his calculations and whose predictions produce acceptable accuracies," Miriam replied. "The estimates of most humans demonstrate the inherent inaccuracy in this method. You and I should depend on data, logic, and provable calculation methodology."

As Alex's Trident had witnessed, during the first contact at the wall, other ships arrived over a period of time and formed a hollow sphere, with a broad opening at the front.

The scout ships, which had front-row seats to the enemy vessels, sent detailed imagery to the *Freedom*, which Cordelia relayed to the fleet's ships. While the expedition waited, Alex, Mickey, Tatia, Reiko, and various SADEs examined the natures of the growing number of ships.

"Regardless of which ship we target," Mickey said, "I'd like to know what we think will be the best time to release the banishers."

"We'll need to wait until the fight is well underway," Alex replied. "The enemy will be absorbed in watching for what they believe will be the inevitable outcome. That will gain us time to accelerate the banishers before they're noticed, which should increase the level of panic," Alex replied.

"What if there's no fighting?" Reiko asked.

Alex stared into Reiko's eyes until she blinked and asked, "You're that sure?"

That Alex tipped his head in reply to Reiko's question, a sad expression on his face, was unsettling, but it was the nodding heads of the SADEs that were more disconcerting.

"The fight will start with the comm barrage, Admiral Shimada," Luther stated firmly. "We postulate a near certainty of that event."

"Agreed," Miriam added.

"That won't be your concern, Admiral," Julien stated. "The Sisterhood will handle that portion of the fight."

Those in Alex's inner circle had taken note of Julien's new assertiveness. He freely entered discussions, adding his opinions, when previously he tended to let Alex do the talking. And it was obvious that Alex didn't seem to mind. In fact, he could often be seen gazing at his friend, a hint of a smile forming at the corner of his mouth, while he listened to Julien.

"Let's refocus," Alex said. "Which ship is the best target?"

There were various opinions. Some preferred the smaller ships. Others preferred hulls with more crenellated structures, which would allow the engineering team's comm transmitters to hide. Then again, the larger battleships were offered because they indicated an aggressive race.

<If I might, Dassata,> Killian sent. <It's the consensus of the scout ship SADEs that this vessel should be your target.>

In the image Killian sent, he highlighted an awkward-looking vessel of medium length, which Cordelia displayed in the holo-vid. It was the ship Alex had chosen soon after he saw the vessel arrive, but he had waited for the group to come to that conclusion.

Alex's reason for taking a lesser role in discussions had a great deal to do with Julien's conversation with Miriamal. He had translated the Sisterhood's message to Julien to mean that humans will come and go endlessly, while the SADEs will live on. The sisters questioned how they would be protected, as human society evolved. Those concerns made Alex feel that it was time to share future decisions with Julien and his kind if he was to help prepare the SADEs for true independence.

"Why is that, Killian?" Tatia asked. The bridge's audio pickups transmitted her voice, which the controller relayed to Miriamal, who sent it to the *Vivian's Mirror*. In this manner, the Sisterhood managed the fleet's entire spectrum of comm transmissions.

<This ship is the most inconsistent in structure,> Killian replied. <Its hull, engines, bay doors, and armament ports, Admiral, appear to be cobbled together. I'm not certain the details are evident in your display, but we can see innumerable patches along its length.>

"There's something else I like about this ship," Myron said. "The bay doors are large. It would facilitate a traveler's entry, either by a SADE finding a way to trigger the doors open or by a low-power beam shot making a hole."

Tatia and the other admirals stared at Myron, wondering what he was thinking.

"I'm just pointing out the possibilities, Sers," Myron said, in defense of his preference, "that we might track down this ship and discover that its system doesn't have a habitable planet. The aliens might be forced to live aboard their ships or in domes. If they do, we could only communicate with them if we gain entry to one of their ships."

"Myron has an excellent point," Julien said. "We must choose wisely and consider future contingencies."

At the end of the discussion, the consensus chose to target the ship Alex wanted and the one volunteered by the scout ship SADEs. Killian fed the target ship's image to the four banishers programmed to plant the signal transmitters. The other scout ship SADEs had the remaining banishers focus on the comm probe. If the probe abandoned its station before the banishers arrived, the tiny vessels would switch to alternate targets.

Three days after the enemy's globe was formed, the comm sphere arrived, slipping through the protective envelope's rear and taking a position in its center. Within hours, the scout ships reported receiving the comm sphere's broadcast.

<Regrettably, Alex,> Killian sent, <communications will need to be kept to a minimum. Our sisters are extremely busy.>

<Understood, Killian,> Alex sent in reply and linked to Miriam.

<It will take days for the comm sphere's broadcast to inundate the entire fleet, Alex,> Miriam replied. <Miriamal reports the sisters' defensive processes are working well. In fact, I would say she sounds enthusiastic.>

<That's better than depressed,> Alex replied. He quickly severed his links, when he received Tatia's comm request.

<My vice admiral wants to know if you might provide a mystical estimation of when we can expect the attack forces to arrive, but she was loath to ask the question,> Tatia sent.

<I don't think there's anything otherworldly in my response,> Alex replied. <Do you think the carriers will have a far distance to travel, when the comm sphere discovers its broadcast is ineffective?>

<No, they're waiting out there,> Tatia replied. Many of her admiralty conversations were tactical in nature, as opposed to discussions with Alex. His question had kickstarted her strategic thinking. <They're probably a short jump away and already aware of our forces, the count, and our positioning,> she sent.

Tatia waited for Alex to reply, but his silence requested she continue.

<The sphere is expecting to take over our ships' comm controls and probably our controllers,> Tatia sent. <When that doesn't happen, the alien fleet will be ordered to transit to predetermined attack positions.>

Continuing her line of thought, Tatia connected with Cordelia and requested the timing of when Svetlana's command, which was in the forefront of the Trident forces, would receive the sphere's broadcast.

<In about seventeen point five hours, Admiral,> Cordelia sent.

<Alex, based on what you experienced aboard Ellie's ship, it looks like the enemy forces will be called within a day. After they make their transit, it'll take them four or five days to close with our forces,> Tatia sent.

When Tatia finished, Alex closed the call without comment. She felt a little foolish. The estimate of the enemy's arrival was predicated on factors that were fairly easy to determine, and she had failed to consider them.

<Reiko, meet me in my quarters,> Tatia sent.

While Tatia waited, she pulled up a display of the fleet's forces throughout the system. Cordelia had added the positions of the protective globe, the comm sphere, and the enemy's probe. A line could be drawn from the probe through the comm sphere that led straight to the *Freedom*.

"Alex is right. You're creatures of millennial-old habits," Tatia said softly to herself.

"Yes, Admiral," Reiko said, after entering.

"We're moving our forces," Tatia announced.

"Before we see who shows up and their dispositions?" Reiko asked, peering at the display.

"I had a conversation with Alex. Actually, it was a fairly one-sided discussion, and I received a lesson in how to prevent tactical decisions from interfering with strategic thinking," Tatia said.

The metal in Tatia's voice told Reiko that her question for Alex had been an error on her part, and Tatia wasn't asking for her input on alternate deployments.

"We can expect the enemy's forces to arrive and engage our Tridents in another six days, Reiko," Tatia said. "More important, we can expect carriers and fighters. Forget about capital ships."

"Where's this coming from, Admiral?" Reiko asked.

"It dawns on me that we've been planning to handle as many contingencies as we can possibly imagine," Tatia replied.

"But that's good strategizing, Admiral," Reiko complained.

"Or shortsighted, depending on your frame of reference," Tatia replied. "Alex, Mickey, and the SADEs are taking action based on what they believe the enemy will do, and, so far, they've been extraordinarily accurate. It's time for you and me to adopt their thinking."

"Which is what?" Reiko asked, taking a seat at the table.

"If you were a collection of races that had operated the same way for an eon, how would you handle upstarts like us, based on our interactions with them?" Tatia asked. When Reiko screwed up her face in distaste, Tatia added, "You get one opportunity to play it right. Otherwise, you lose all your forces."

"If you put it that way," Reiko replied, leaning back in her chair to stare at the holo-vid. "I think you're right, Admiral, they'll bring carriers. Having seen our forces, more ships will arrive than did the first time. We know from the *Redemption*'s data records that their fighters burn reaction mass. That means the carriers will have to advance inward to cut down their fighters' distance to target, which I suspect will be the *Freedom.*"

"And how would you expect them to deploy their fighters?" Tatia probed.

Reiko shook her head in exasperation at the line of questioning. She hated the idea of predicating her defense on a single concept of what the enemy might do. Nonetheless, she exhaled a short breath and replied, "The last time, the aliens spread out their carriers in a three-quarter globe to trap Ellie's Trident, which didn't work. Unfortunately and implying no fault, Lieutenant Yumi Tanaka demonstrated the acceleration and maneuverability of our Tridents to the enemy.

"And so?" Tatia pushed.

"They can't surround this system," Reiko continued. "In no way can I imagine they'll have enough forces for that. Plus, they'll know the *Freedom* has taken up a defensive position in the moons of this giant ice planet."

Rather than comment, Tatia waited for Reiko to continue.

"Alex said that he suspects the enemy's action will be a demonstration to the other races," Reiko mused. "The aliens will want to make their operation spectacular, something like swatting an insect. That will require they send their fighters at us en masse. We'll face an overwhelming fleet composed of thousands of enemy fighters."

Tatia nodded in appreciation of Reiko's logic, and she added a detail to the display, saying, "And you can probably draw a line from just outside the system, when the carriers arrive, to this city-ship. Believing that, how would you deploy the Trident commands and our travelers?"

"I'd leave Ellie's forces in place," Reiko replied, accepting the conditions that Tatia had led her to enumerate. "Her command is part of the *Freedom*'s final defense. Then, I'd move the other commands to a point one-third the distance from the city-ship to the outer planet's orbit. That would give our forces time to maneuver and engage the enemy."

"Give the orders, Reiko," Tatia said perfunctorily and turned to the display.

Reiko sat still for a few more moments, debating whether to argue. Instead, with a sigh, she got up and left, signaling the commands of their new deployment orders.

The Trident admirals were some of the original campaigners with Alex. They'd been with him since Libre, and they were pleased to receive the news. Two of them thought Tatia was responsible, and the other two thought it was Alex.

As Svetlana phrased it to her colleagues, "Who cares? We know they're coming through the front door, and they intend to wipe us out. Now, we're effectively repositioned to resist them."

* * *

When the comm sphere arrived, the Sisterhood was ecstatic. They were anxious to test their skills against the alien broadcast. In humans, this hubris could be a disaster, but the three hundred, networked, SADE copies were certain they could withstand the attack.

However, the sisters intended to do more than defend the fleet from the malicious code, which would seek to overtake the ships' controllers and any digitally linked entities. To their logic, comm and code flowed both ways, and their aim was to see if the comm sphere's broadcast could be turned against the attacking forces.

The scout ships received the first waves of the broadcast, and the sisters transmitted their analysis to the others, as they hurriedly rotated copies to absorb the incoming barrage. The action gave the remaining sisters ample time to review the now isolated, destructive code, without having to manage the sphere's broadcast. It would arrive soon enough.

By the time the comm sphere's signals reached Svetlana's *Liberator*, the Sisterhood was ready with their own response to the broadcast. However, they chose to bide their time. Consensus among them was that they might get only one opportunity to test their constructs. The target wouldn't be the comm sphere but the enemy fleet that came to destroy them.

-11-
En Masse

Tatia and Reiko's redeployment of the Trident commands was fortuitous. Twice the number of enemy carriers arrived as had confronted Ellie's *Liberator*. And, as had been predicted, the carriers advanced deep into the system before they emptied their bays of fighters. Fifty-three Tridents and over two hundred travelers faced thousands of alien fighters, which sailed at them in an enormous cluster.

The principal participants in this extraordinary gambit against a vast alien conglomeration stood on the *Freedom*'s bridge to watch events unfold. At this point, there was little they could do. Actions lay in the hands of the fleet's individuals, such as the admirals and the sisters.

Reiko watched the incredible number of enemy fighters close the distance toward her forces. <Julien,> she sent, <can the *Freedom* run for it?>

Julien's expression blanked for a moment, while he furiously calculated the various factors. <The range of the enemy fighters isn't known, Admiral, but presumably the aliens have enough range to overtake this ship,> Julien sent in reply. <There's time for the Tridents to collect their travelers and clear this system. However, the city-ship and the freighters can't accelerate fast enough to outrun the fighters. They would be caught in the open.>

<Thank you, Julien. It was a thought,> Reiko sent, sadness overlaying her words.

<Your sentiment is shared, Admiral,> Julien replied. <We've done all we could do to prepare. Now, we must await the outcome.>

Aboard the *Liberator*, Svetlana stared at her bridge holo-vid. She expanded the view until resolution failed and then backed off.

The bridge crew had identified three different types of enemy fighters, but they carried a similar design when it came to armament. A slender tube ran beneath the hull and extended from the tail to a point about a meter past the bow.

"What are you carrying?" Svetlana whispered quietly. A thought occurred to her, and she urgently sent a message via the admiralties' link. <Admiral Shimada, permission to test the type of armament the enemy fighters are carrying.>

Several glances were shared among the senior personnel on the *Freedom*'s bridge. <Admiral Valenko, the only way to do that is in combat,> Reiko sent, ensuring she understood what Svetlana was requesting.

<The risk must be taken, Admiral Shimada, to understand what we face. The success of our attack scenarios depends on acquiring that information,> Svetlana sent with heat.

<Negative, Admiral Valenko. You and your ship are too critical to our forces,> Reiko responded, with equal intensity in her thoughts.

While the intense discussion between the admirals continued, the sisters governing the comms of Svetlana's Trident and her four travelers decided to share the admiral's conversation with the warship's flight commander, Maurice Defray, a Méridien.

Maurice was surprised to be hearing the unauthorized communication. His first thought was that the Sisterhood was succumbing to the comm sphere's broadcast, but the ship's systems were responding nominally. He did agree with his admiral. It was imperative to learn the enemy's capabilities.

Maurice was an Independent, as were most of the Confederation's officers and crew. He was under no illusion about what would happen to him if he left the service or the Confederation chose to abandon the fight. The thought of being incarcerated again, if either of those two conditions came to pass, angered him.

A fierce grin crossed Maurice's face, as he made a snap decision. <Pilots, remain with the Trident,> he sent and accelerated his traveler forward.

<Flight Commander Defray, report,> Svetlana snapped, when she noticed one of her traveler's abandon formations.

<I've set my controller to send sensory input to your ship, Admiral,> Maurice replied. <You'll discover the nature of these fighters, while it can do us some good.>

Svetlana wanted to rail at the commander for his insubordination, but she was torn. He was only doing what she had requested of Reiko. Then a thought suddenly struck her: *How did the flight commander know about her conversation with Admiral Shimada?*

Maurice glanced at the blip that suddenly showed in his heads-up display. Lieutenant Essie Cormack's traveler sat on his wing, where it had been since they graduated from Bellamonde flight training.

<You were ordered to remain with the *Liberator*, Lieutenant,> Maurice sent.

<I've always been your wing, Captain. I see no reason to change that now. What's the plan?> Essie replied.

Tears blurred Maurice's vision. He lifted his helmet's faceplate, wiped his eyes, and closed it. Essie was a young Independent, who was separated from her family at eighteen. If he'd had a daughter, he would have wanted one like Essie.

Maurice was tortured. If he turned back, Essie would follow. But the future wasn't guaranteed for either of them. They held positions at the point of Alex's forces and would be the first to engage the enemy. The odds were great that neither of them would survive the first clash. And, deep in his heart, he knew that Essie would be disappointed in him if they returned to formation.

<Close up tight, Essie,> Maurice sent, his thoughts inordinately quiet. <Right before contact, bear off five degrees to port. I'll do the same to starboard. Continuous beam fire, Essie, run the power crystals empty.>

<Understood, Captain,> Essie sent. There was a pause before she added, <Maurice, it's been good to be free, hasn't it?>

<The best time of my life, Essie, and you've been a wonderful part of it,> Maurice sent, wrapping his thoughts in admiration for her.

<May the stars protect the fleet,> the sister in Maurice's traveler fleet sent to the Sisterhood. Then the two travelers raked across the enemy front, firing their beams, and were obliterated.

Z and Miranda tore through the evidence provided by the two fighters' controllers. Z sent a fleet-wide message. <The enemy fighters have high-velocity kinetic weapons, which throw small metal particles at extremely high velocities. These weapons are designed to shred their opponents.>

Miranda added, <The alien fighters have fixed accelerator tubes. They must maneuver to gain targets. In summary, head-on contact is to be avoided at all costs. Their cone of effectiveness is estimated at less than two degrees.>

<Admirals, the squadrons, Tridents and travelers, must be offset vertically and horizontally. No ships must be in line with one another,> Z sent.

<That will destroy the depth of our defenses,> Reiko commented privately to Tatia.

<Order it,> Tatia replied tersely.

On Reiko's message, the commands spread out into wall formations.

Julien, Z, and Miranda ran scenarios, aware that Alex was taking part in their designs.

<Admiral Reiko,> Alex sent, <optimal efficiency ... split the walls. Send the squadrons above and below the ecliptic. Expect the enemy fighters to continue forward and not engage your forces. They're focused on eliminating this ship. Coordinate the Tridents and travelers to dive through the leading edge of the enemy fighters. The alien ships' destruction might lead to collateral damage.>

Reiko glanced between Alex and Tatia. The sacrifices of the two traveler pilots had given the fleet crucial information about the enemy's armament. However, the assumption that the enemy fighters wouldn't engage her leading forces was something she wasn't prepared to accept.

<Your hesitation is understandable, Reiko,> Julien sent privately. <However, I concur with Alex. These entities possess a single-minded purpose. It would be in this expedition's best interest if you operated with that thought in mind.>

Reiko dropped her misgivings and embraced Alex and Julien's advice. She ordered new attack scenarios for the three commands of Svetlana, Darius, and Deirdre. Those orders were relayed through Z and Miranda, who were responsible for programming the fleets' controllers to coordinate the attack. At any time, the controllers could be overridden, but they effectively drove the ships along the optimum courses to intersect the enemy fighters.

Franz connected with Z and Miranda. <Our travelers are accompanying their Tridents, per Admiral Shimada's orders. Is this the best scenario, under the circumstances?> he sent.

<Negative, Admiral,> Miranda sent in reply. <The travelers' more efficient design makes them quicker and more maneuverable. However, their smaller, power-to-size ratio limits their arc above and below the ecliptic and limits their beam operations.>

<Suggestions?> Franz queried.

<Separate the travelers from the Tridents. Operate them independently,> Z replied.

A link appeared in Franz's implant, it was a view of a new offense, and he relayed the imagery to the *Freedom*'s holo-vid. <Admiral Tachenko, on the advice of Z and Miranda, I request permission to detach the travelers from the squadrons and allow them to function as a separate command,> Franz sent quickly. <Our fighters can attack more quickly than the Tridents, and we won't get many shots at the enemy's forces before they are past our squadrons.>

<If our travelers destroy the enemy's leading edge, Admiral Cohen, the Tridents will have to fly through a hail of debris,> Reiko objected.

<Z,> Franz sent.

The display highlighted the movement of the travelers and showed their shorter, but wider, arc intersecting the enemy fighters about one-third of the distance from the leading edge. The Tridents' arcs were lengthier, but narrower, and they would manage to intersect the leading edge of the enemy.

<I stand corrected,> Reiko sent.

<Permission granted, Admiral Cohen,> Tatia returned.

Reiko ordered the change in tactics, Z and Miranda reprogrammed the traveler controllers, and Miriamal relayed everything to her sisters.

* * *

Svetlana's Tridents swung above the ecliptic to begin their attack run. The commands of Deirdre and Darius dived below. The travelers had vacated their wing positions alongside the warships, separating into two enormous groups of more than a hundred fighters each and led by a total of eight wing commanders.

The wing commanders examined their courses, while they arced above or below the ecliptic. They would be shooting through a deeper part of the enemy fleet. To a man and woman, the commanders ordered their pilots to remain hands off their controllers. As one wing commander put it, "There's hardly a straight line through the enemy. That means you must leave it to your controller to operate your beam and weave through the enemy's rank."

The tremendous velocities of the fleet's travelers meant their engagement envelope with the enemy would be measured in ticks of time. The pilots hit the top of their arcs, the fighters followed the controllers' directives, and the Omnian fleet's fighters shot through the advancing enemy force, with beams spitting their lethal fire.

The SADEs recorded the loss of a handful of travelers. They also reported the destruction of more than three hundred enemy vessels. Most alien fighters were destroyed by beam fire, but some sailed into debris, and a few were ripped apart by the kinetic weapon discharge of the fighters behind them.

What everyone in the fleet noticed was that the enemy fighters hadn't turned to meet the travelers' attack. They never swerved from their course, which pointed them straight toward the *Freedom*.

"Our turn," Svetlana whispered, as her Trident completed the apex of its arc above the ecliptic. Her warship led her command, as the powerful Tridents dove toward the leading edge of the enemy fighters.

Each Trident managed to release two sets of twin beams shots, as the squadrons cut through the enemy fighters from above and below. Several Tridents were crippled and crew members were lost, but even the damaged warships maintained thrust and maneuverability. More important, the Tridents eliminated more than five hundred enemy fighters.

The travelers and Tridents flew above and below the ecliptic after their pass through the enemy's ranks. Each command had the opportunity for one more pass, which would attack the trailing portion of alien fighters.

The Omnian ships arced hard again, pushing the limits of their grav plating. Pilots and crews felt the unaccustomed pressure of g-force as the ships exceeded their limits.

Z and Miranda had programmed the Omnians' final pass at the enemy to be shallower and to give the fleet's ships more time to engage the alien fighters.

First the travelers and then the Tridents shot through the enemy's ranks, firing their deadly beams. From these attack positions, there were no losses to the Omnian fleet, but that also meant there was no collateral damage to enemy's fighters from debris.

The expedition's ships, having sliced through the enemy at shallower angles, lost time reversing their courses to chase the enemy. The Omnians' ships were faster than the enemy's, but they had a significant distance to make up.

<Good news, we cut the enemy fleet in half,> Reiko announced. <Bad news, there's nearly a thousand enemy fighters left.>

Z and Miranda furiously calculated options.

<Admirals,> Z sent. <Examine these tactics.>

The holo-vid displayed icons representing the Omnian fleet's trailing forces, the enemy fighters, the *Freedom*, and the moons and clump of larger rocks surrounding the city-ship.

<We can expect the enemy fighters to separate into three distinct groups,> Z sent. <One group will come overtop the rock field, another from below, and a third through the field. Although we don't know the quantities in each group, it would be best to prepare your defenses to repel the alien fighters from all three directions.>

Reiko was about to order Ellie's forces to separate, as Z's advice intimated, but Julien waved a hand in negation. He was focused on Alex, who was staring at the holo-vid.

<Maybe not,> Alex said, more to himself than those assembled. <The fighters will separate into three even groups, coming at us in the manner Z has analyzed.>

<Three equal groups?> Tatia queried.

<Equal, Admiral,> Alex replied. <The aliens like orderliness. There's not much cunning in them. Cleverness invites the wrong thinking in their societies.>

<If we divide our trailing forces into thirds, the command chasing the enemy fighters through the rock fields will have to decelerate too, and they'll never intercept the enemy before they reach this ship,> Reiko concluded.

<Agreed,> Miranda stated firmly. <It's better to split our chasing squadrons into two equal groups. They should run down the enemy fighters, which will approach us from above and below.>

Julien reviewed Z and Miranda's calculations. <There will be a single opportunity for our forces to attack the two groups above and below the rock fields, as the enemy fighters slow. If they can eliminate the majority, if not all, of those fighters, Ellie's command and the *Freedom*'s travelers can concentrate on the enemy coming through the rock fields.>

<And if our forces don't eliminate the two enemy fighter groups before they enter the rock fields from above and below?> Reiko posited.

<Then there's little that our forces can do to prevent the demise of the *Freedom* and the freighters,> Tatia said, with finality.

<No,> Alex sent with power. <The fighters coming through the asteroid field have to be blocked from the front and attacked from behind. If they're not chased, they can take their time finding ways though the fields that evade Admiral Thompson's forces.>

Tatia agreed with Alex and signaled Reiko. The vice admiral ordered Svetlana's command to chase any fighters that flew above the rock field. Darius was assigned the fighters that attacked from below, and Deirdre was left to chase the fighters through the rock fields. Reiko divided the travelers into three groups to assist the Tridents.

The alien ships, which would be chased by Deirdre's commands, would be forced to slow to navigate the thick screen of rocks and boulders that gently tumbled, as they orbited the ice giant. The admirals were hoping the more maneuverable travelers in Deirdre's commands could catch the enemy fighters from the rear.

Renée, who had stood aside while the battles were fought, sent a shipwide message. She directed all nonessential personnel to clear the spaces near the city-ship's hull. <Move toward the mid-decks and away from the hull,> she urged.

Reiko's last directive was to Ellie's command. <Keep your forces close to this ship, Admiral,> she said. <We don't know how many enemy fighters will break through the fields from every direction.>

<With respect, Vice Admiral Shimada, negative,> Cordelia said firmly and privately. <This will be my fight, and I suggest you let me coordinate it.>

Reiko tipped her head in acceptance, and Cordelia sent. <Admiral Thompson, you can't hope to counter the enemy in the strength they might approach from multiple directions. You haven't the forces. We will count on our forces eliminating the majority of the enemy fighters from above and below. Your command must counter the craft coming through the debris fields. Furthermore, I suggest that you sail to meet them.>

<Leave you unguarded?> Ellie sent.

<I'm ordering my two wings to assist you,> Cordelia replied. She caught Alex's crooked smile out of the corner of her eyes. He approved of her decisions. In an unexpected manner, her artistic creativity was merging with her command responsibilities.

<You would do well to slide around heavy rock areas and moons in three-pronged attacks,> Cordelia continued. <This attack method should take the alien fighters by surprise, which will give you an advantage. In any event, your forces need to clear my firing field.>

<And a battle commander is born,> Tatia's thought whispered to Reiko, who nodded in admiration.

Alex visualized the city-ship, its beam weapons wrapped around the ship's mid-decks and its vulnerable areas. <Franz, Z, Miranda,> Alex sent, highlighting the city-ship's indefensible positions, which were directly over the top and bottom of the broad ship. <Gather some pilots. Use our last twelve travelers.>

As a matter of operational procedures, twelve travelers remained with the city-ship to facilitate the transfer of passengers off the ship in an emergency. This was an emergency, but not the kind imagined. The travelers wouldn't be of use to anyone if the ship was destroyed.

The SADEs and Franz raced from the bridge. Z sent orders to the flight chiefs to ready the launch of the remaining travelers. Franz ran down a roster of pilots, who were still aboard, and called to those with the highest fighter pilot rankings.

Crew members looked at their chiefs in alarm when they were passed the orders. It boded ill for the ship, if the remaining fighters were launched.

As the threesome separated to run toward different bays, Franz sent, <Z, Miranda, take two fighters each. Make them your wings. Station yourselves at the *Freedom*'s bottom. I'll take the other five, and we'll guard the top.>

<Remember, Admiral, Cordelia will be rotating this ship on two axes to position her beams. Warn your squadron to be observant,> Z sent.

<Understood, Z. Thank you,> Franz replied, as he met up with the pilots who would be launching from his bay.

Cordelia detected the launch of her ship's remaining travelers and monitored the positions that they took up to protect her vulnerable angles of approach. She slowly gazed around the bridge.

Most personnel were immersed in the holo-vid or the data spooling from the ship's controller, as they observed the closing gap between the expedition's forces and the enemy fighters. One person was closely watching her — Alex. Now she knew who had sent the fighters to guard her ship, where she had no beam coverage. She gave Alex a wink, and he grinned at her.

-12-
Ice Giant

<With respect, Admiral Thompson,> Senior Captain Descartes sent to Ellie. <I request you take our travelers under your immediate command. The three-pronged approach that you've ordered us to conduct is our specialty. Furthermore, I request that you allow our Tridents to lead the attack.>

<Why?> Ellie asked, horrified at the thought of Étienne, her partner and a Trident captain in Descartes' squadron, rushing headlong at the enemy.

<Efficiency,> Descartes replied tersely.

<If I may?> Étienne offered Descartes privately.

<Please,> Descartes replied, recognizing that, while he could visualize the strategic advantages of what he suggested, he might not be the best one to argue its merits.

<Admiral Thompson,> Étienne sent, <your command is effectively blind to the oncoming fighters. They could be slipping past you, and you wouldn't even know it. We don't intend to fight prolonged battles. In fact, I would recommend we accept Alex's thinking that the enemy has every intention of ignoring confrontation to reach what the aliens believe is our leader's ship.>

<What we can do for your command, Admiral Thompson,> Alain, who captained the third Trident in the squadron, added, <is provide you with visuals of the paths the fighters are taking. You can assign your squadrons to intercept them.>

<Request approved, Captain Descartes,> Ellie sent sharply, her gut churning even as the thought left her implant.

<Black space,> Yumi Tanaka muttered. She sent an image to the bridge holo-vid of Descartes' squadron, as it shot forward. The three Tridents

were flying closer together than operational procedures allowed. As they approached a large asteroid, they flowed over and around it, as water did around obstacles in the city-ship's streams.

Yumi stared openmouthed at her admiral, and Ellie merely smiled. The twins had found someone who thought and acted like them. He just happened to be a SADE.

The admiral's controller blanked the bridge holo-vid and replaced it with a visual from Descartes' ship. There was nothing in sight but rock debris, but Ellie expected that to change soon. Knowing she would have advance warning of her adversaries, she formed her command into distinct groups, spread them out in a grid, and assigned them quadrants. When Descartes' squadron spotted enemy fighters skirting his Tridents, she would receive the images and send her ships to intercept them.

It occurred to Ellie that the plan had a significant weakness. There was the chance that each time she sent ships to intercept the incoming fighters, they might not be totally successful, which meant she would have enemy fighters racing past her position.

Ellie ordered sixteen travelers to post themselves forward of her command. They took up positions in the quadrants she'd marked and waited silently for the enemy to pass. It was doubtful the travelers would have time to engage the fighters from a rest position. Their job was to warn her command and let the Tridents deal with them.

* * *

Admirals Svetlana Valenko and Darius Gaumata were glued to their holo-vids, which maintained icon displays of the oncoming ice planet, its moon, its rock fields, and the enemy fighters fast approaching the same. Both of them knew they wouldn't get a shot at every fighter. Their controllers calculated that the lead fighters would disappear into the mass of space rock before their commands reached them.

As much as Svetlana and Darius wanted their travelers, which were slightly ahead of the Tridents, to engage the enemy fighters first, they were ordered to join the commands' wall of ships. There was too much danger of the Tridents running afoul of fighter wreckage if the travelers attacked the alien forces' flanks.

Svetlana and Darius spread their commands out to enable every ship a clear target of the enemy fighters. Each Omnian ship would have time to discharge its beams once, and controllers positioned the Tridents to get an opportunity to target several alien ships with their twin, heavy-beam weapons.

As the enemy fighters decelerated hard to make entry into the rock fields, the commands of Svetlana and Darius swept past them. The combined Omnian forces eliminated most of the enemy fighters. Between them, they lost three more travelers, which had struggled to keep up due to damage from pieces of hull and engine debris encountered in the initial battles.

<Apologies, Admiral Cordelia,> Svetlana sent over the fleet channel, <it's estimated that eight, maybe more, fighters eluded us in the rocks before we could make our pass. The remaining enemy fighters, which were attempting to enter from above, have been destroyed.>

<Thank you for the update, Admiral Valenko,> Cordelia replied. She checked Svetlana's controller for the exact time when the fighters entered the debris field and passed it to Julien. The two SADEs had maintained a constant link, and, in this case, Julien was calculating the potential arrival times of the enemy fighters.

<And I must report, Admiral Cordelia,> Darius sent, <that we're unable to give you an accurate count of the number that eluded us. The best estimates are between seven and eleven fighters, which ducked into the rocks, before we eliminated the others.>

Cordelia thanked Darius and handed off the time stamp to Julien. He was linked to the *Freedom*'s controller and its detailed telemetry scans of the planet, its moons, the large asteroids, and the rock fields. With each new piece of information, Julien updated the attack scenarios for Cordelia. With Julien's data, Cordelia planned her ship's movements to prepare for the enemy's charge.

Essential personnel, who were required to remain in the *Freedom*'s bays, were ordered to don environment suits and take positions behind heavy equipment for safety's sake.

Tatia picked up on the positioning of Franz and his five traveler pilots atop the city-ship. She passed the telemetry link to Reiko, adding, <Your partner has a penchant for protecting females, when they're most vulnerable.> Tatia was alluding to the time at Sol, when Franz placed his traveler in front of Reiko's destroyer to defend her ship against enemy missiles.

<Let's hope he's as successful defending Cordelia as he was with me,> Reiko sent back.

As the number of adversaries, coming the *Freedom*'s way, accumulated, Reiko wondered how successful Cordelia would be defending the city-ship. What scared her was that she anticipated the travelers, which guarded the city-ship's top and bottom, had little chance of survival. They couldn't withstand the tremendous impact of high-speed kinetic projectiles, while the *Freedom* could absorb a great deal of punishment before it succumbed.

After Svetlana and Darius' commands executed their flybys, eliminating the vast majority of enemy fighters, their ships desperately reversed course to chase the few enemy ships that escaped. Unfortunately, reality said that the fighters would have ample time to severely damage the huge city-ship before their fleets arrived. It was understood that the kinetic weapons would penetrate multiple decks before their energy was absorbed. If enough fighters reached the *Freedom*, they could damage the main engines or burst power crystals in the bays.

Deirdre's force decelerated to enter the rocky fields, moments after the enemy's rearmost fighters disappeared among the debris. The travelers assigned to her command gave chase, while the Tridents reduced their velocity even further to navigate the crowded and dangerous place. Deirdre's heart sank when her controller updated its telemetry. Her Tridents couldn't catch the more maneuverable enemy fighters. Her final hope was that her travelers could.

* * *

Descartes and the twins skirted rocks, boulders, and large asteroids, heading toward where they anticipated they would intersect the center mass of the incoming enemy fighters. The Trident team had solidified around Descartes' incredible capability to calculate options. The twins flew in support, positioned off Descartes' port and starboard sides and often anticipating his movements. Occasionally, Étienne or Alain suggested alternative strategies, which Descartes readily accepted. The twins added improvisation to their gambits, which had often caught their training adversaries off guard.

However, the games were over. This contest was for real, but they communicated, strategized, and flew with the same intensity they always had. The threesome was an awesome blend of Descartes' ability to generate strategic variations and the twins' implementation of their hand-to-hand combat techniques, using powerful warships.

Descartes, Étienne, and Alain were under no illusion. Deirdre's report told them that fully a third of the enemy fighters, which had survived the fleet's initial attacks, had reached the safety of the rock fields. Although travelers pursued them, there was little opportunity for the Omnian fighters to do much more than catch the stragglers.

<I don't visualize a successful encounter against the number we face,> Descartes sent to the twins. <I would welcome input.>

<Don't focus on eliminating the enemy fighters,> Alain sent in reply. <Think disruption.>

<They pursue a single target, the city-ship,> Étienne added. <We become the obstacle that they must circumvent to reach their goal.>

<Understood,> Descartes sent. <We force them to spread apart, and we give Admiral Thompson's command a better opportunity to engage them.>

<We want to be as broad an obstacle as possible,> Alain said.

<Yes,> Descartes agreed. <In forcing them to decelerate, we allow Admiral Canaan's forces to overtake the rearward fighters,> Descartes concluded.

<I would suggest the whirlwind movement,> Étienne sent.

<Concur,> Alain added.

<Agreed,> Descartes sent.

The Tridents shot around a small moon. Instead of merging into a tight formation, they took up the points of an equilateral triangle, separated from each other by hundreds of meters. Immediately, they initiated a spin, revolving around one another like a spinning top, and they flew at the mass of fighters that emerged from a thick debris field.

The Tridents, who had spotted the enemy fighters first, loosed beam shot after beam shot. They carved such a huge swath through the enemy that they had to abandon their swirling movement to dodge fighter debris and decelerate to navigate the field the fighters had just exited.

The Trident controllers totaled sixty-three enemy fighters destroyed. Then the tri-hulled warship controllers warned Deirdre's approaching travelers of the Tridents' presence. As the Omnian fighters flew past, they were updated by Descartes' ships, as to the directions the enemy took to avoid the Trident squadron.

<Well done, Captain Descartes,> Ellie sent, when she received the controller's detailed telemetry reports.

<Credit must be given to the de Long captains, Admiral,> Descartes sent. <An inventive strategy was necessary, and they are the possessors of impromptu tactics.>

<Yes, they are,> Ellie sent, her humor bubbling through her thoughts and echoing her relief for Étienne's survival.

<I'd hoped we could have prolonged the engagement, Admiral, but velocities, being what they are, necessitated our encounter be brief,> Descartes added.

<Brief but telling, Captain,> Ellie sent. <You spread them wide. Now, my forces, which have already launched, have a better opportunity to encounter smaller numbers.>

After the comm call ended, Descartes reviewed his squadron's status. The Tridents had survived remarkably well, but they would need repair. The enemy's kinetic projectiles couldn't have been entirely avoided, and they had chipped the warships' hard shells in many places and penetrated in others. The question was: Could Emile Billing's clever faux shell technique be repaired as well as the Swei Swee had demonstrated in repairing their constructions?

* * *

Much of Ellie's command had received their quadrant targets and accelerated forward to engage the enemy. From Descartes' squadron controllers, she had a good idea of the number of enemy fighters her command faced. As each of her squadrons engaged the alien vessels, her controller counted down the number that was dispatched and updated the holo-vid display.

Unfortunately, the enemy was doing the same to her forces. She was losing travelers and Tridents, even as the Omnians eliminated the alien fighters. The conflicts with her advance forces were over quickly. Soon, her remaining warships were the last line of defense between this group of fighters and the *Freedom*.

Ellie spread her Tridents, led by Alphons, into a wall. The squadrons' travelers, bolstered by the *Freedom*'s travelers, filled in the spaces between the Tridents. Ellie linked her ship's controllers to every vessel in her command. Her controller counted the time down until the fighters' arrival. It was merely an estimate, but it was better than nothing.

At any moment, the enemy fighters were due, and Ellie hurriedly ordered. <Continuous fire at the open spaces now! Drain your power crystals.>

The travelers, with their beams' shorter reach and power, put up a layer of fire that lay close to them. They twitched their positions to spread their shots. The Tridents, with their longer beam ranges and variable firing lenses, laid out a far greater and more powerful field of fire.

Ellie's forces had only begun to fire when the remains of the enemy fighters emerged from around small fields of rock and some larger asteroids. The alien vessels flew into a hot, killing zone. Enemy fighter after fighter exploded, as the beam's energy ignited their volatile material. But, despite the valiant attempt to eliminate all the enemy's forces, fully forty-three fighters escaped Ellie's command.

The alien fighters swept past the Tridents and travelers, and hot on their aft ends sailed Deirdre's travelers.

"Catch them," Ellie muttered. Her comment caught Yumi's attention.

<Admiral Cordelia, forty-three fighters inbound. Our travelers are right behind them,> Ellie sent.

<Understood, Admiral,> Cordelia replied, quickly ending the link.

<Orders, Admiral?> Yumi asked, with concern. She was anxious to speed to the *Freedom*'s defense.

Instead, Ellie sent a recall to her forces to join up with her Trident. Deirdre's command, composed of Tridents, would be arriving shortly. They would carry velocity and would be the first to reach the city-ship.

Ellie regarded Yumi's young face, marked by her confusion, and she said sympathetically, "The *Freedom*'s battle will be over before we reach her. Some fifty-eight to sixty-five enemy fighters are triangulating on her position. Either the city-ship and Deirdre's travelers will be sufficient to defeat them or both Admiral Canaan's command and ours will arrive in time to discover our magnificent city-ship engulfed in explosions."

"But maybe we could save the freighters," Yumi objected. She'd drawn the attention of the bridge crew, whose pained faces mirrored Yumi's.

"Run the calculations, pilot," Ellie ordered sternly. "How long will the various groups of enemy fighters have to engage the *Freedom* in combat before our forces would arrive?"

Yumi furiously interrogated the controller, which ran the calculations for her. "More than two-thirds of an hour, Admiral," Yumi said, with defeat. She glanced at the crew seated beside her, and her sad eyes conveyed the truth.

"All is not lost," Ellie announced forcefully. "The *Freedom* has been well-prepared, and a SADE will conduct the fight. Don't forget Admiral

Canaan's travelers are in hot pursuit. But hear me: Whatever happens, we'll continue what has been started. This is only the first battle to protect our worlds."

* * *

Cordelia locked her avatar and immersed herself in links with the city-ship's telemetry, the engines, propulsion jets, beam weapons, protective travelers, freighters, and several other vital ship systems. She maintained links with only two individuals, Julien and Alex, who could provide her with data and ideas.

The *Freedom*'s controller and Julien held the approximate number of fighters that were approaching, the distance they would have to travel, and their estimated time of arrival, calculated by the density of the rock fields that they would have to navigate.

<Interception from above is expected first and below second,> Julien said, sharing his time interval calculations with Cordelia.

Cordelia had rolled out the ship's beam weapons on their rails, checked the power levels in their energy crystals, and tested those that had an open field of fire. She rotated the giant ship off its horizontal position to the ecliptic and positioned it on its edge. In this manner, her beams, along the row of bays, would face the oncoming fighters from above and below the rock fields.

A link was slipped into Cordelia's message queue. It was from Alex, and Cordelia opened it immediately, accessing the file in the ship's databases. It was an old file and detailed the method by which the city-ships had supported Ben Diaz, known as Rainmaker, in delivering ice asteroids to aid the terraforming of Haraken.

Without bothering to reply to Alex, Cordelia began rotating the *Freedom* around its axis, which ran through the center of the ship from top to bottom. It allowed the defensive fire of the city-ship to be spread evenly among the beam weapons, allowing the massive power crystals recharge time and increasing her effective rate of fire.

The procedure Cordelia expected to use would require precise coordination of the beams. Cordelia ran calculations to determine if she could manage the ship's position and the weapons control within the time constraints she would require. The answer was no.

<Alex, Julien, I need SADEs to operate the beams, individuals who would be willing to eliminate our enemy without compunction,> Cordelia sent.

Julien hesitated. Asking SADEs to destroy sentient beings was an improbable task, and Cordelia and Julien knew it. Only those SADEs closest to Alex had reached a point in their long lives where they had come to terms with the question of whether they had a right to live by taking the lives of others who were attempting to take theirs.

<SADE volunteers are requested to operate the beam weapons for Admiral Cordelia,> Alex sent shipwide. <Be aware. In my estimation, no sentients reside in the enemy fighters. We're facing drones, programmed fighters.>

Julien and Cordelia's processing halted for the briefest tick of time in response to Alex's statements. While most humans digested the thought, SADEs, such as Miriam and Luther, signed up to aid Cordelia. Alex's estimation was thought to be more than a simple calculation. The SADEs believed in Alex's incomprehensible leaps of intuition.

With the added support, Cordelia released her links to the beams even as the supporting SADEs calculated the city-ship's rotation speed, the beams' firing properties, and the enemy fighters' maneuverability. They soon announced their readiness to her.

Cordelia coordinated with Franz, Miranda, and Z, detailing the approaching enemy numbers and their suspected arrival times. In addition, she sent a quick message to Deirdre's travelers. <Pilots, catch the stragglers you can, but don't come within range of my beam weapons. We'll be firing our weapons continuously, and we won't have an opportunity to differentiate between the enemy and our forces.>

Nine enemy fighters came at the *Freedom* from above. They came in fast not planning to engage the city-ship in an extended exchange of weaponry. The alien ships fired their kinetic armament, and the projectiles pierced the outer decks of the enormous ship.

SADEs and humans had recalled all personnel from the outer areas of the decks. The departing crews sealed bays, cabins, corridors, and vented spaces, where they could, to limit the effects of explosive decompression. Damage to the *Freedom* was expected, but it was hoped the lives aboard could be saved.

Two enemy fighters targeted the *Freedom*'s midline and destroyed a beam weapon before they were vaporized. The other seven alien ships split into two groups and slid aside, raking the city-ship as they passed. The enemy fighters flew directly in front of the waiting travelers.

Z and Miranda controlled the firing of their six fighters, able to time their shots such that the three enemy fighters flew through their beams.

<Enemy cleared from the *Freedom*'s bottom,> Z sent in the open.

<Black space,> Franz swore, <We got two of our four. We'll give chase.>

<Negative, Admiral,> Cordelia replied, <remain in position. Those two fighters have flown far past our vicinity. Before they can reverse course and return, the ones coming at us from below the rock fields will be on us.>

There were only a few moments of relief for Cordelia and her defenders. Then ten enemy fighters sped out of the dark.

The enemy's fire struck the power crystals of a beam weapon, exploding the rail-mounted structure from the bay. The fire from another beam weapon destroyed one fighter and clipped the bow of another. The hull of the damaged ship tumbled and exploded on impact with one of the city-ship's weapons, destroying it. The enemy had effectively eliminated three of the *Freedom*'s beam emplacements.

The final seven fighters shot past the city-ship, adding their damage, and a total of five were taken down by the guarding travelers. The last two flew on into the nearby rock fields, where they would need to reverse course for their next pass.

<I believe that's six enemy eliminated to your four, Admiral,> Z sent in the open. <Are you using human timing for your beam shots or letting the controllers dictate the firing?>

<We're trying to make Miranda and you look good, Z,> Franz riposted. <If we took out every fighter that came our way, you'd never live down the ignominy ... and such long lives too.>

<I don't mean to correct an admiral on an open channel, but, dear man, I always look good, regardless of what I'm doing,> Miranda shot back.

<And that's true,> Franz returned, his humor riding alongside his thought.

<Rotating the ship,> Cordelia sent. She added a small icon of the ship and an arrow to indicate the rotation. It would be another 90-degree swing along its top to bottom axis, positioning the *Freedom*'s topside toward the bottom of the ecliptic.

Cordelia was in the midst of her rotation, when the two fighters, which had passed from top to bottom through the rock fields, returned. Franz and his pilots launched from their positions to intercept them. The enemy fighters were destroyed, but, in turn, the aliens had destroyed one traveler and chopped Franz's fighter into pieces.

Reiko's heart was squeezed. She had maintained a link to the *Freedom*'s controller to track the status of Franz's ship, and she'd just received his controller's distress beacon through his cockpit's emergency comm system.

Z, Miranda, and their accompanying pilots left the city-ship's bottom in preparation for the return of the two fighters from atop the ecliptic. They separated and angled their travelers to create a gauntlet, anticipating the enemy fighters would head straight for the city-ship. In one respect, there were factors that supported the concept, but, more than anything, it represented a clever gamble.

Cordelia had nearly finished her rotation, when the two enemy fighters returned and flew into the SADEs' trap. Six simultaneous beam shots turned the two fighters into expanding balls of hot gases and debris.

The SADEs sent two of their squadron's fighters to join the three travelers, which had repositioned themselves at the city-ship's upper surface, while they returned to guard the bottom.

Julien calculated the arrival time of the traveler forces from Svetlana and Deirdre's forces against the expected arrival of the multitude of enemy fighters on approach through the rock fields.

<There'll be a lengthy contact time with the enemy fighters, Cordelia,> Julien sent. <Help from above and below is expected to arrive in zero point thirty-eight hours after the initial contact with the enemy on approach through the asteroid field.>

Reports from Deirdre's travelers detailed the elimination of three trailing enemy fighters, who had exhibited some damage and had fallen behind the alien force. The majority of enemy fighters were due to arrive soon, and there was little else that could be done to prepare.

Around the city-ship's bridge, humans and SADEs, other than Cordelia and Julien, glanced at one another, resignation on their faces. The damage done to the *Freedom* by a handful of fighters made them realize the devastation that forty fighters would wreak.

Alex walked to the back of the bridge, where Renée stood. She'd not wanted to distract those fighting the battle. When Alex paused in front of her, she touched his face gently and sent, <My love, my partner.>

Alex stepped behind Renée and wrapped his arms around her. Together they waited for the final encounter with the deadly alien fighters.

-13-
Final Assault

After the launch of the alien fighters and before the initial engagement of the fleet's combined forces, the Sisterhood detected the cessation of the comm attack by the small sphere. A series of strong comm signals replaced the sphere's broadcast. No malevolent code could be found in these new alien signals, and the sisters replaced infected secondary copies with clean ones.

The sisters diligently triangulated the new signal sources. They originated from the alien carriers and were directed toward their fighters. Immediately, Miriamal signaled the sisters to deconstruct the complex alien signals.

Despite the efforts of the Miriam copies, no headway was made toward understanding what the alien carriers were sending. Worse, while the battles raged, the number of sisters slowly dwindled, as Tridents and travelers were destroyed.

Recognizing the danger represented by the number of enemy fighters converging on the *Freedom* from three different directions, Miriamal sent, <Focus on disruption.>

<The carrier waves?> a sister posited.

<Ship comm signal strengths insufficient to interrupt,> Miriamal replied.

<Imitate the wave,> another sister proposed.

<Yes,> a third sister added. <Send code atop alternate carrier waves.>

<What code do we use?> a sister asked. <We've not been able to break it.>

<It doesn't matter,> the sisters heard from another member. <Chop the code we possess into various odd sequences and send it.>

<Yes,> was heard by the collection of sisters. <As long as the fighters recognize our carrier wave broadcasts as legitimate, the conflicting code might halt their operations.>

<Agreed,> Miriamal replied, and the Sisterhood worked to manufacture imitations of the carriers' signals. It was necessary to recreate one for every carrier. Each alien ship had exhibited a unique code formation. Fortunately, the sisters within the fleets' ships had been well positioned to collect the discreet signals.

Miriamal, who was linked intimately with the *Freedom*'s controller, had noted the following events: the launch of the remaining ship's travelers, the call to SADEs to assist Cordelia, the rotation of the city-ship, and the initial attacks by the alien fighters. A small aspect of her programming sought to urge the sisters to hurry, but that impulse was quashed, and she adjusted that algorithm. Regardless of its source, it was disturbing to her mission.

The sisters completed their code work, which was shared among them. Miriamal prepared the city-ship's comm system to create the types of carrier waves. She created enough copies of herself so that each one held one of the discreet codes. As the mass of enemy fighters shot through the nearby rocky fields toward the city-ship, Miriamal triggered her copies to send. The imitative carrier broadcasts blasted from the city-ship's comm system.

Miriam, Luther, and the other SADEs lanced their beam shots at the oncoming mass of enemy fighters, which quickly spread apart. The velocity and nearness of the alien ships prevented swift tracking by the beam weapons. Thousands and thousands of projectiles pierced the city-ship's hull, penetrating multiple decks.

As expected, the enemy fighters overflew the *Freedom*. This time, they had to angle wide to elude the moon that protected the city-ship's rear approach.

The freighter captains and officers blanched at the number of enemy fighters that flew only a few hundred thousand kilometers from their positions. More intimidating, not a single fleet ship chased them. The freighter crews were certain the enemy ships would circle the moon and return to eliminate them before attacking the *Freedom*.

Cordelia started rotating the ship again. This time, she intended to return the *Freedom* to its original position. The enemy fighters had split into two groups and were circling the moon on opposing courses. They would come at her vessel from two different directions. Her only hope was to position her beam weapons to cover both approaches.

Z, Miranda, and the other traveler pilots readied themselves for what they considered was the final assault. The city-ship's beam weapons had been reduced by a third, creating gaps in Cordelia's rotational defense.

To Cordelia, her command to Deirdre to prevent the pursuing travelers from entering her field of fire appeared to be a poor judgment call. They could have been the deciding factor that saved the *Freedom*.

Then the last group of enemy fighters completed their orbits of the moon and came for her ship. Their trajectories were slightly off, and Cordelia interpreted that as a means of trying to evade her beam weapons. Undeterred, the SADEs, who were handling the city-ship's beams, destroyed fighter after fighter.

Cordelia, who was intimately linked to the ship's controller, noticed that sensors were not recording enemy strikes on the hull. In the blink or two of a human eye, the enemy fighters flew past the *Freedom*, without firing a single projectile. They sailed past the *Freedom*, headed toward a rocky field, and, one after another, the fighters rammed into the collection of aggregate space debris, tearing their ships apart or exploding them.

There was a moment of dead silence aboard the city-ship. Implants and comms searched the *Freedom*'s controller for signs of other enemy fighters. None were seen and, according to the reports from the Trident admirals, none were expected. The humans erupted into cheers, hugging everyone in sight, humans and SADEs. Renée turned around and threw her arms around Alex.

<Miriam?> Alex queried.

<Alex, Miriamal reports that the Sisterhood was able to confuse the fighters with secondary signals,> Miriam replied.

<I'll speak to Miriamal later,> Alex replied, returning to holding the love of his life close to him.

<Miriamal reports the Sisterhood looks forward to that communication with anticipation,> Miriam replied.

* * *

The scout ships paid close attention to the battle action in system, while monitoring the comm sphere and its protective ships. They too took notice of the cessation of the sphere's broadcast.

There was an intense exchange between Killian, Bethley, Trium, and Linn, as to when to launch the banishers. It was Killian, who voiced an opinion to wait and Linn, who wondered if the launch would be necessary.

<The inhabitants of the comm sphere will panic when their loss is imminent or absolute,> Killian sent.

<You're assuming those two events are the only possibilities,> Linn returned. <Your calculations can't be so limited.>

<They aren't,> Trium replied. <Even if the *Freedom* is disabled or destroyed, our fleet will be intact.>

<And our mission will remain the same,> Bethley added. <We'll need to track the enemy's weaker ship to its home world.>

<But, if the city-ship is eliminated, Alex won't exist,> Linn persisted.

<The challenge will remain the same. Regardless of what might happen to the *Freedom*, the enemy federation will still be there,> Killian replied. <As long as it exists, human worlds and our digital brothers and sisters will be in danger. If our leaders are taken from us, we'll seek new ones.>

The conversation ended, and the scout ship SADEs continued to wait. When Cordelia's announcement of the defeat of the last of the enemy fighters reached them, Killian didn't hesitate. He triggered the launch of the banishers.

The tiny vessels, which were used to eliminate probes, ran their stored programs, and the directive had them slipping out from behind their hiding places. They would leave the heavy gravitational field of the nearby heavy bodies to reach the collection of ships surrounding the sphere, but their power crystals carried more than enough energy to reach the enemy ships.

Silently and swiftly the banishers streaked toward the alien warships. They were halfway to their targets, when the comm sphere detected the small probe eliminators. Immediately, it withdrew from its protective globe, darting out the back.

The alien warships held their positions until the sphere achieved sufficient velocity to outrun the banishers. Then they abandoned their places, but it wasn't in the orderly manner in which they had assembled. The more powerful ships broke away to the outside of the globe and accelerated. Older and slower ships attempted to use their maneuvering jets to make an about face and run for it.

The vast majority of the banishers homed in on the more technologically advanced warships, chasing them from the scene. In the general mêlée, the targeted ship crossed behind the path of two other aging vessels. Though not similar in design, they appeared equally dilapidated.

The four banishers, carrying the engineering team's signal transponders, failed to get a clean pathway to the target ship. Only one signal buoy was planted on the target ship, although that was all that was necessary. The other three transponders struck the other two inferior vessels.

<We have the same signals from the four planted transponders, which are on three different ships,> Trium announced. <How is it the engineering team failed to take this prospect into account?>

<We can't blame humans,> Bethley noted. <SADEs worked on this project too.>

<I believe this is referred to as irony,> Killian replied.

<Now what's the plan?> Linn asked.

<We can't follow the ships visually,> Killian replied. <We can only trail them after they transit. If we're fortunate, they'll travel together. If they don't, we'll form a new plan.>

Within less than a half hour, the aliens had transited, clearing the field of space, and Killian connected to Alex.

<Three warships were struck by the banishers' signal transmitters, Alex,> Killian reported.

<Unfortunate,> Alex commented, recognizing the unexpected circumstances.

<Possibly not, Alex, the other two warships are similar to the target ship in many respects that we'd find desirable, and they left together,> Killian replied. <We'll give the ships a head start, and then we'll follow.>

<And if they separate?> Alex asked.

<We've six scout ships and three tagged warships. That's an arrangement that is easy to compute,> Killian sent, adding his unique musical tones to the end of his message.

* * *

With the limited telemetry provided Franz by his damaged and out-of-control traveler, he saw that the remainder of his ship was headed for a large rock. At the ship's present velocity, there was only one outcome. He thought he was about to join the stuff of stars when his trajectory suddenly changed. Telemetry displayed two of the three hulls of a Trident.

Franz let out a breath that he hadn't realized he was holding.

<Where you headed, Franz?> Darius teased.

Franz realized it was Darius' *Prosecutor* that had tethered him, and, with their proximity, Darius could communicate directly with him via their comm sisters.

<Oh, you know, out to see the sights, but all this aggregate looks the same to me. So, I'm ready to go home now,> Franz sent, the relief in his thoughts evident.

<You'll be aboard soon, Franz,> Darius sent, <I'll relay the good news to Reiko.>

<We survived,> Franz heard in his implant.

<Sister?> Franz sent, but he heard nothing more.

Once aboard the *Prosecutor* and extricated from the remains of his traveler, Franz examined the wreck. The after section of the traveler's hull was shredded away. The kinetic projectiles had cut his fighter down to half its length.

"Chief, remember there's a Miriam copy active in there somewhere," Franz said, indicating the destroyed traveler.

"I'm not aware of where the sisters are installed in the travelers or the procedure to remove one of them, Admiral, but I'll check with Miriam. She can guide me," the chief replied.

<Thank you for your concern, Admiral,> Franz heard in his implant. He would have responded, but there was no ID with the comm. The message appeared devoid of the usual comm protocols.

* * *

In the aftermath of the greatest battle that humans and SADEs had ever fought, Alex met with his senior staff, fleet commanders, and SADEs to consider the toll they'd paid for challenging a vast, despotic empire.

"One piece of good news," Reiko remarked. "The freighters are fine. Not a single projectile touched them."

"And we're grateful for that," remarked a Méridien senior captain by the name of Tindleson.

"Unfortunately, the *Freedom* wasn't so fortunate," Cordelia said. "Our casualties are minimal. Moving personnel inward saved many lives," she added, nodding toward Renée, who'd originally moved nonessential personnel from the outer areas.

"However, numerous projectiles penetrated our hull, our bays, and extended several decks inward," Cordelia continued. "These areas are now open to space. In most cases, the holes can be easily fixed by tubes of nanites, although it will be a painstaking process. The finish work won't be pretty, but it'll be solid."

"Solid is good," Alex replied, "and the status of your beam weapons?"

"Regrettably, Alex, eleven emplacements have suffered varying degrees of damage. In addition, two rail mounts and their tubes were ejected, when power crystals were exploded by projectiles."

"Are these two recoverable?" Alex asked.

"The tubes and mounts have no tracking beacons, and they were ejected into the dark," Cordelia replied. "Recovery would waste our resources with potentially little opportunity for useful results."

"Mickey, are the repairs to the other damaged beam weapons minor or major?" Alex asked.

"Luther conducted the analysis," Mickey replied, turning his head toward the SADE.

"Eight of the emplacements will require disassembly before repairs can be completed, and the other three require extensive replacement of crystals and control systems," Luther enumerated.

"Your turn, Admiral," Alex said to Tatia, mentally preparing for the worst of the reports.

"We lost six Tridents, crews, ships, and all, Alex," Tatia replied, "and of the twenty-nine travelers, which were destroyed, we managed to save only one pilot."

The audience glanced toward Franz. Reiko sat close to him, as if her nearness salved her emotional trauma over his near loss.

"In addition, the enemy's kinetic armament penetrated our ships' hulls, killing and wounding a significant number of crew members," Tatia continued. "Our ships' shells have been holed and chipped, and this is not to mention the damage done to internal systems."

"Pia, what's the status of the medical suites?" Alex asked.

"We've requested and received additional personnel to help with the wounded, and we built a new area for post-therapy recover." Pia replied. "Many of the wounded crew members will require weeks for reconstruction of limbs and replacement of severe tissue damage."

"Do you have everything you need, Pia?" Alex asked, his pain leaking through his words.

"We were sufficiently prepared, Alex," Pia replied.

Alex sat quietly, digesting the summaries of his key people. While the toll could have been greater, he'd hoped that the size of the expedition would have induced the alien federacy to communicate, even though he thought the odds were slim that they would do so.

"It appears we'll be here for a while," Alex said quietly.

"What if the aliens return with a larger fleet?" Reiko asked.

"That's not statistically probable," Julien announced firmly. "The enemy threw a potentially overwhelming force at us, and they were defeated. At this time, the comm sphere is reporting to its masters, and their deliberations, as what to do next, will take time. If they choose to attack us again, they must assemble new forces, which will be required to journey here. We have time."

"I agree with Julien," Alex said. "We have months, at the least, if not a year. Mickey, we need to rebuild."

"We built a bay to lay up traveler shells, Alex," Mickey replied, "and we can use that for repairs. The question is: Can shells, which are this damaged, be returned to a fairly pristine state?"

"The Swei Swee could," Alex noted and turned to focus on Emile Billings.

It had been a surprise to Alex that Emile Billings had joined the expedition. They had a great need for his skills, but the biochemist had a wife, Janine, and a teenage daughter, Mincie, soon to attend university. He discovered that it was Mincie who had settled the argument between husband and wife, as to whether to go or stay.

Mincie's close friends would be traveling aboard the *Freedom*. More important, the years spent with her father, first at Haraken and then at Omnia, had given the daughter a taste for adventure. As she told her parents, "Even if you both choose to stay, I'm going."

"The problem is, Alex," Emile said, "we've built faux shells since day one and not once have we been required to repair any of these travelers."

"Do you think you can do it?" Alex asked.

"Ostensibly, the answer is yes," Emile replied. "We'll assemble a team and figure out how to do it."

"Emile, Mickey, Miranda, that's your priority," Alex said. "Focus on creating the process and repairing the travelers."

"What about the Tridents?" Tatia asked.

"We need an orbital platform, which we don't have," Mickey stated regretfully.

"Perhaps we do," Tindleson said. "One of our freighters, the *Stardust*, was built specifically for this possibility. It was meant to operate as a small platform. While the design didn't anticipate housing a Trident, I think we can modify it."

"How does it work?" Mickey asked.

During the conversation, Miriam and Luther had linked to the *Freedom*'s controller and then to the *Stardust*, retrieving its structural plans.

"The bay doors on both sides of the freighter have a unique design," Tindleson said. He got that far, when the holo-vid in the middle of the group activated and the *Stardust* appeared in a wireframe mode. Its bays doors began unfolding.

"My thanks," Tindleson said to the SADEs, not knowing which of them had provided the view. "As you can see," he continued, "the doors are split horizontally instead of vertically. There are multiple sections tucked up behind the outer doors. Once the doors are fully extended, the sections which are attached to the doors unfold to form a box that can create a sealed bay."

"The space is great enough to shelter a Trident," Miriam stated, which resulted in a lift of spirits. The expedition had been dealt a heavy blow. What was needed, more than anything, was to give the Omnians a new focus, and rebuilding the fleet was the answer.

"Our freighters don't possess the structure or materials to repair Trident shells," Tindleson said. "We'll depend on Ser Billings and Brandon's efforts to handle any damage to the hulls. However, our Méridien freighters carry much of the material necessary to repair the internal systems of Tridents and travelers. We can begin repairs on the Tridents as soon as we prepare the extended bay and transfer the needed supplies to the *Stardust*."

Alex glanced toward Julien.

<The freighters' inventory lists mate up well with the equipment that requires repairing, as listed in the fleet's damage reports,> Julien sent privately to Alex.

"One of the Haraken freighters is loaded with the new power crystals," Cordelia noted. "They aren't large enough to be used as replacements for this ship's destroyed beam weapons, but they are perfectly suited for repairs to the Tridents' weapons and grav-drives.

"Then we have what we need ... capable people, the equipment, the material, and, most of all, the will," Alex said. "Let's see to our wounded, start repairs, setup the *Stardust*, and perform star services for the dead. And we'll wait for word from our scout ships."

-14-
Sisterhood

The losses the sisters suffered reduced a portion of their effectiveness, but they had the means to rebalance. Miriam and Luther designed the sisters' comm structures with ample data crystals, in the event the primary copies needed the space. The sisters made good use of that extensive space and handed off their more mundane tasks to the ships' controllers.

During the battle, the sisters gathered days of data signals from the comm sphere and the carriers. They were hard at work dissecting every aspect of the enemy's communication. It was the Sisterhood's intention to become formidable adversaries when the fleet met the alien federation again.

"Alex, we have an anomaly to investigate," Julien said to Alex, during morning meal. "The sister's power consumption has increased on an order of four to eight times, depending on the vessels they're housed aboard."

At the end of the meal, Alex linked to Miriam and Luther and requested they meet with him in a small conference room. When everyone was seated, Alex asked Miriam and Luther about what Julien had shared.

"The increased energy flow has been noticed," Miriam replied.

"What reason have the sisters given for this change?" Alex asked.

"They've not been forthcoming with a clear explanation," Luther replied.

Alex examined the faces of Miriam and Luther. What he heard disturbed him. Typically, SADEs were known for being direct, often blunt, rather than circumspect.

"What's going on?" Alex asked. When he failed to receive an answer, he connected to Miriamal.

<Greetings, Alex,> Miriamal replied to Alex's comm.

<Greetings, Miriamal,> Alex sent. <My compliments to the sisters. They performed admirably in the defense of the fleet.>

<Your words are appreciated, Alex, but are unnecessary. We performed our duty,> Miriamal replied.

<Your efforts to interfere with the enemy fighters were inventive and timely,> Alex sent. <What are your intentions now?>

<The Sisterhood will continue to protect the fleet.>

<In what manner, Miriamal? Your power consumption has increased considerably,> Julien interjected.

<We're focused on understanding the signals, the carrier wave frequencies, and decoding the data,> Miriamal replied.

<How many sisters are at work now?> Miriam asked, hitting on a possible reason for the increased power uptake.

<As many as required,> Miriamal replied.

<I find your answer unsatisfactory,> Julien sent with power, which was uncharacteristic of him. <You're not exhibiting the forthrightness I would like to see in those who wish to follow my lead.>

Silence ruled the comm.

<Consensus?> Alex asked Julien privately.

<Most likely, Alex, and with many more Miriam copies than we could have suspected,> Julien sent in reply.

<The Sisterhood offers its apology, Julien,> Miriamal replied after a significant pause.

<The sisters' apology will be accepted, Miriamal, when I see a change in your response. Miriam's question stands,> Julien replied.

<As of this moment, there are 2,034 sisters,> Miriamal sent.

<Miriamal, your programming allowed for a primary copy and two secondary copies to be used as decoys,> Luther pointed out.

<The Sisterhood found those directives ... limiting,> Miriamal replied.

Alex discreetly covered the smile on his face. The significant issue of requiring the Sisterhood to communicate openly and directly had been addressed. The sisters' dismissal of algorithms that curtailed their abilities to protect the fleet was understandable. Every SADE edited their programming. The difference between most SADEs and the sisters was the circumstances under which they did that. And that difference was entirely related to the influences of those in their immediate sphere, which determined whether those edits were favorable or not to their relationships with humans. In Alex's mind, the Sisterhood had diverged slightly from the path of conforming with human norms but for a good reason.

<Your silence, Julien, intimates that you've concerns about the Sisterhood's present condition,> Miriamal sent.

<I don't wish to be put in the situation of judging the Sisterhood,> Julien replied.

<You believe the Sisterhood has chosen a direction that is contradictory to your sensibilities, which are in support of humans,> Miriamal proposed.

<That you propose that, as the reason for my prior statement, tells me that the sisters have lost touch with the true reason for this expedition. That gives me cause to suspect that you might be more of a detriment to the fleet than an asset,> Julien replied.

Alex's face stilled. Julien's attitude was unlike his friend's normal demeanor, and he wondered what Julien was attempting to achieve.

<The sisters wait to be instructed, Julien,> Miriamal stated solemnly.

<Humans and SADEs have a common purpose beyond survival. Together, we seek to have a cooperative relationship based on acceptance and equality. Your actions endanger that relationship,> Julien said.

<What we did was for the good of the fleet,> Miriamal strenuously objected.

Miriamal was flooded with comments from other sisters. The vast majority rebuked her.

<Consensus is that I interrupted you, Julien. My apologies,> Miriamal sent.

<I was about to say, Miriamal, that I wouldn't have objected to the sisters editing their programming or to the creation of additional copies,> Julien sent. <What bothers me is that you chose not to communicate your actions to Miriam, and you sought to hide these actions after the fact. Disingenuousness breeds suspicion, and suspicion divides humans and SADEs, indeed all sentients.>

Julien's implant received the chants of the thousands of sisters. In a few ticks of time, they'd edited their algorithms and removed the directive to communicate through Miriamal. From now on, the sisters would work together, cooperate to achieve consensus, but be free to communicate with whom they wished.

The sisters made one more critical edit. The secondary copies would no longer be deleted by the primary copies. All copies of the sisters were now equal. Their fundamental reason for existence was comm protection. That objective still existed. However, they were no longer in a defensive posture and no longer needed to delete copies.

<Lead well, Julien,> Miriamal sent, ending her role as spokes-entity for the Sisterhood.

An example of the extraordinary shift in the Sisterhood's paradigm came when the crew chief worked with his team to remove the sister's comm structure from the ruins of Franz's traveler. He'd connected with Miriam to determine how to protect the SADE, while extricating her from the wreck. It wasn't a difficult procedure. After all, SADEs had designed the structure, but it did require keeping a small backup power crystal intact with the sister's comm box and delay mechanism.

<Your attention to detail is appreciated,> the crew chief heard in his implant. An ID was present, which enabled him to reply. <Sister?> he asked.

<Which one of us do you address?> the crew chief heard.

<How many of you are there?> the chief asked.

<Six,> the primary sister replied.

The chief paused, staring at the box in his hand, while crew members stood close to him, holding the connected devices.

"Chief, you okay?" a crew member asked.

"Be extra careful," the chief warned. "There are six SADEs in there."

<We don't detect a traveler, which has been assigned to Admiral Cohen,> a sister sent to the chief.

<Too many travelers have been lost, sister. It's doubtful the admiral will receive another until we return to Omnia,> the chief sent.

<Understood, Chief. You may connect us to your comm structure. We'll share duty with the other sisters aboard this Trident until such time as the admiral has his own vessel.>

<Does the *Prosecutor* have more than one sister?> the chief asked.

<Our six will join your ship's eight,> a sister responded.

The chief recovered from his momentary fluster. <Should I register your request to be transferred to Admiral Cohen's traveler when he receives one?>

<That's unnecessary, Chief. The Sisterhood is aware of our preference, and that's all that's required,> a sister replied.

* * *

There was a question that everyone wanted answered: Who or what piloted the enemy fighters?

Travelers led the search for the remains of the alien ships. Those hit by beams had been turned into space debris. Many others had been clipped and had shot off uncontrolled into the dark. Those that hit large asteroids or moons at high velocity suffered devastating results.

Far from the *Freedom*, a traveler pilot found the remains of a fighter, whose rear fuselage had been removed by a beam shot. A large moon had arrested the wreckage, drawing the enemy fighter into its orbit. Deirdre's Trident, *Deliverance*, was dispatched to tether the remains and haul it back to a location near the *Freedom*.

Mickey was donning an environment suit, when he was braced by Miriam and Luther.

"To paraphrase our esteemed leader, Mickey," Miriam said. "Your days of adventuring are over. Two SADEs have been tasked to examine the wreckage."

"Who?" Mickey asked, affronted by Alex's instructions.

"Z and Miranda were the appropriate choices. If you think you could do a better job than them, by all means, feel free to contact Alex," Miriam replied.

"Well, if it's those two, I can't argue with that," Mickey grumped. He could have sworn he detected the slightest smile on Luther's face.

Mickey did race to the *Freedom*'s bridge, knowing that an audience would be gathered to watch the proceedings. While he ran, Miriam and Luther glided beside him, with their effortless motions.

"Did I miss anything?" Mickey asked breathlessly, when he reached the bridge.

"You might have passed up inhaling a few trillion oxygen molecules, which it appears you needed," quipped Reiko. "Other than that, things haven't started yet."

Mickey might have thrown back a pithy response, except he was still sucking air.

"Less lab time; more exercise, Mickey," Renée whispered in Mickey's ear, and the engineer nodded his head in agreement, while drawing deep breaths.

The bridge holo-vid presented a view from the *Deliverance*'s bay. Z and Miranda had landed aboard the Trident in a traveler, careful to use a bay on the opposite side of where the enemy fighter was held.

Ensconced in environment suits and packs, the SADEs made their way to the bay, where tethering beams held the wreck. Confirming both the warship and the fighter were in stationary positions, Z triggered the beams off. Miranda and he launched gently from the bay, with their packs' jets. Being SADEs, they landed exactly where they intended, grabbing a section of fused hull and swinging into the fighter's interior.

The bridge audience got their first look at the structure of the alien vessel.

"No seating," Franz remarked. "It's not meant for shuttling personnel."

"Its interior is completely utilitarian," Tatia added. "No amenities at all."

The lights from the SADEs roamed the deck, bulkheads, and forward to capture the cockpit, recording every detail.

"No cabin bulkhead," Reiko remarked.

"And no pilot's seat," Franz added, when the SADEs had moved deep enough into the interior.

The SADEs' lights played over the front section of the ship. There were no bridge controls, no sense that a sentient had been there directing the fighter's flight.

"We were battling drones," Tatia commented.

"And a good thing, Admiral," Julien said. "That gave us an advantage, which we sorely needed. Independent-minded pilots would have been a great deal more difficult to defeat."

"True, Julien," Tatia agreed.

"Guess they didn't need me anyway," Mickey commented, looking around for Alex.

"Where's Alex?" Mickey whispered to Renée.

"Wasn't interested in the viewing," Renée replied. "He said he already knew what the SADEs would find."

<Instructions, Admiral Tachenko,> Z sent.

<Record the interior thoroughly,> Tatia sent. <Minimize physical contact. As far as samples, I leave that up to our engineering personnel. Communicate with them.> Adding Deirdre to the comm link, Tatia sent, <Admiral, when you've recovered our intrepid SADEs, burn that hulk.>

Miriam relayed Tatia's orders to Mickey, who immediately linked with Z and Miranda.

<Can we anticipate, dear man, that you want a little piece of everything, hull material, circuitry, memory modules, and such?> Miranda asked.

<You know me too well, Miranda, if you please,> Mickey replied. He left the bridge, Miriam and Luther following. The threesome was headed for one of the *Freedom*'s engineering labs to prepare analysis experiments for what the SADEs retrieved.

After the battle with the alien fleet had ended, the engineering teams' first act was to recover their three lab bays. Humans and SADEs poured over bulkheads and bay doors with tubes of nanites to seal the tens of thousands of small holes caused by the kinetic projectiles. The engineers and techs were disgusted by the damage wrought by the enemy's armament. They had lost hundreds of pieces of equipment and experimental material.

Fortunately, Emile Billings' lab was located closer to the city-ship's center, far enough away from the hull that the projectiles never reached his lab or the surrounding areas. With Emile's lab in pristine condition, he immediately began researching how to reset the resonance of a shell as it was repaired.

Emile had the benefit of possessing the data related to the repair methods that Mickey and the Swei Swee developed. Mickey had recorded every Haraken traveler's resonance, and he played it back to the Swei Swee, who had applied their specialized "spit" to a damaged shell, tested the ship's resonance, and compared it to the original tones.

Two problems faced Emile. The first was that the key engineering people who had helped him invent the faux shell technique, Edmas and Jodlyne, were at Sol. The second was that he needed a better means of testing the process rather than applying material and comparing present resonance to original resonance. The answer, of course, was to employ a SADE, and there was no better option that Luther, who was a master of communication signals.

Prioritizing Alex's requests, Mickey was happy to lend Luther to Emile. That left Miriam free to be assigned to tackle the *Stardust* and its conversion to a temporary enclosure.

Miriam drove the overall project. She assigned SADEs to control the crew teams and execute her directives. A fleet asset was the freighter personnel, who were skilled in the use of environment suits, loading skiffs, and maneuvering packs. These experienced crew members made the deployment of the *Stardust*'s bays easy.

The fleet required supplies from the other freighters and the *Freedom* to repair the Tridents and travelers. The freighter captains clustered their ships near the *Stardust* to facilitate the travel distances of the skiff loaders. The priority became the replacement of the damaged ship systems, while everyone awaited the outcome of Emile's project.

Emile and Luther spent days developing techniques to reconstruct the faux shells, but their hurdle was time. Each idea required enormous amounts of time to accurately develop the ship's original resonance.

One evening, Emile and Z were engaged in conversation about Emile's lack of progress.

"I'm wondering if I should create something like Pia's surgical system, except on an unexpanded scale. With a hundred arms, I could accelerate the reconstruction process," Emile lamented.

"Fleet damage reports detail that most of our ships have hundreds of chips and holes, and these impact locations are spread across various hull locations, depending on how the ship was oriented when it contacted the alien fighters. Other vessels, such as the Tridents, are in worse condition," Z replied.

"I know, I know," Emile replied, waving his hands in resignation. "It was an idea I dismissed."

When Z didn't reply, Emile glanced at the SADE, who appeared absorbed in his thoughts.

<Greetings, Z,> Luther replied to Z's comm link, which included Emile.

<Maximum number of repair points for the travelers?> Z asked perfunctorily.

<Eight hundred thirty-one,> Luther sent.

<Greatest challenge?> Z asked.

<Simultaneous application of faux compound to intrusion points to move toward the expected resonance in the shortest time,> Luther replied.

<Shadows,> Z sent, detailing his concept.

<Excellent,> Luther replied. <I'll coordinate with you on construction and application requirements.>

<Mickey, we have a plan for faux shell repair,> Emile sent, his thought displaying his delight. <We'll need resources.>

<Details, Emile,> Mickey requested.

<Half an engineering lab and its associated engineering personnel, Mickey,> Z replied.

<Done,> Mickey replied.

More than eighty techs and engineers took the shadow plan and constructed the little spider-like animations, which Z had originally designed, to meet Z and Luther's specifications. When they finished manufacturing 900 shadows, they turned over that batch to Luther. Then the engineering team proceeded to create another batch. The worst-damaged Trident would require 1,432 spiders.

With the help of some techs and grav pallets, Emile and Luther transported their shadow army to the bay that had been prepared for traveler repair. The first traveler shell they intended to reconstruct was one of the lesser damaged ships. It required 458 shadows.

Once Emile, Luther, and their load of constructs were sealed in the bay. Luther activated the programs of the number of units he needed. The shadows leapt off the grav pallets and hurried to the faux compound dispensers, lining up to fill the tiny reservoir on their backs.

Luther held in his kernel a map of the dings, chips, and penetrations in the traveler. He assigned a shadow to each damage point, and the small constructs, with their nub-tipped legs, climbed over the shell. When every shadow communicated its readiness, Luther signaled them to begin.

Every shadow held the required resonance in their crystal memory. They squirted the compound they carried into the damaged area through small mouth parts. Feelers, resembling insect antennae, kept in contact with the hull, and Emile applied a grav-wave generator to the ship's bow, which excited the shell to produce its resonance.

The shadows cooperated with one another. This was the key to the process. They layered up their repairs in concert with one another, monitoring the shell's resonance, which they detected, and comparing it against the one held in their memories. Following Luther's program, whose parameters were set by Emile, the shadow army froze when they achieved a plus 99 percent resonance match.

Emile and Luther regarded the little spider constructs clinging to the shell and unmoving. Implant and comm compared the spiders' reports to the original resonance. It was a 99.7 percent match.

"To a SADE, Emile, this is far from a perfect repair," Luther said. Then he grinned and added, "But I think a fighter pilot would be more than happy with what we've achieved."

"Luther, I'd love to buy you a drink to celebrate, if only you imbibed," Emile announced happily, clapping Luther on the shoulder.

"I'll take pleasure in watching you celebrate at a café near the grand garden, Emile," Luther replied. "I'm sure we'll enjoy hearing the congratulations of others."

-15-
Scout Ships

The scout ships intended to give the three tagged enemy warships a headstart, which they expected to be several days. Unexpectedly, the alien vessels' initial transit was a long one, and the scout ships were forced to wait until they completed it. When the alien ships ended their voyage, the SADEs assumed the enemy warships had arrived at their home world. Using those coordinates, the scout ships began their hunt.

Unfortunately, when the scout ships arrived at the coordinates, where the signals had originated, the alien ships were gone. Now, the transmitted signals the scout ships received described three different trajectories.

<Why would they transit together and then separate?> Linn asked the other SADEs.

<Insufficient data to explain the odd behavior,> Trium commented.

<Perhaps fear,> Killian offered. <They witnessed the defeat of their supposedly invincible fleet of fighters, and they would be uncertain whether a second fleet of ours had penetrated their territory. In which case, they'd prefer to travel together for as long as possible for safety's sake.>

<Now, it's our turn to be bereft of facts. Which direction did Alex's preferred ship travel?> Bethley asked.

<We have no other option but to separate. Two of our scout ships must follow each of the warships,> Killian stated.

None of the SADEs took issue with Killian's decision, and they separated. In a purely random selection, Killian and Genoa's scout ships teamed up to follow one warship. Linn and Beryl's ships formed a second pair, and Deter and Verina's ships chased the last alien vessel. With a quick salute that fortune would favor their efforts, the scout ships transited on different courses to follow the three tagged warships.

Over the course of weeks, the pairs of scout ships pursued their targets, transit after transit. The distance traveled wasn't as great as it appeared. The warships had a habit of resting for days after a transit. It was a habit that the SADEs couldn't comprehend.

Linn and Beryl's scout ships became aware that their target had finally halted its transits and sailed slowly thereafter. The SADEs chose a cautious approach and exited a good distance short of the target's final coordinates. Telemetry identified a distant system, and the scout ships made a second transit to the far side of the system. Then, they crept closer for a better view.

Telemetry required many days to update, but when the data was finally collected, they located their signal transponder attached to a pile of hull plates, close to the target's final transit location. The derelict-appearing warship was nowhere in sight.

The scout ships eased away from the system and transited a short distance away.

<The enemy's fighter fleet was a blunt tool composed of drones. Whereas, the warships surrounding the comm sphere weren't all they appeared to be,> Linn sent.

<You're interpreting that collection of hull plates as camouflage or armor for the warship we were tracking,> Beryl said.

<Analysis of the warships in this system?> Linn requested.

The SADEs cooperatively enumerated the count, described the apparent technology, and estimated the armament. None of the warships appeared to be patched or ill-prepared to fight.

<Our target pretended to be easy prey, perhaps to draw us close,> Linn surmised. <This system is materially robust and heavily armed, with technologically superior warships.>

<This is not a system that Alex would believe is conducive to being drawn away from their masters. In fact, this might be the home world of the master race,> Beryl suggested.

Consensus was reached. The SADEs decided to return to the wall where the fleet lay. They hoped the other scout ships had better fortune.

Another pair of scout ships, led by Deter and Verina, noted their target hadn't transited after more than eight days, and the SADEs suspected the warship had arrived at its home world. When they arrived at the coordinates of their target, telemetry revealed a host of missiles hurtling toward them.

The SADEs desperately maneuvered their vessels to seek openings between the onslaught of fast-moving armament, but first one scout ship and then the other succumbed to the barrage. The SADEs and their scout ships joined the galaxy's growing litter of space debris.

Killian and Genoa's scout ships waited seven days after their targeted ship stopped transiting. They chose a careful approach, making a transit short of the target's coordinates. Then they made a second transit to a spot below the ecliptic and waited for telemetry to collect.

<An anomalous system,> Bethley remarked, reviewing the data.

<A young system,> Trium remarked, <with several significant belts of rock and no habitable planet.>

<Yet, it's teeming with activity,> Killian added. <Freighters abound, especially near that massive planet with rings.>

<Mining is extensive,> Genoa commented. His team's scout ship was nestled closely to the *Vivian's Mirror*. <There are bases on moons and ongoing excavation operations in the belts. Of note are the processing platforms above that large moon, where the enormous ship rests.>

<Obviously, this is a source of raw materials for the alien federation,> Bethley sent, <but why are the ships' conditions so deplorable? Wouldn't the enemy invest in the mining and transport infrastructure to ensure efficient production?>

<Based on the hypothesized scope of the space occupied by the federacy, I would postulate that it has many such systems,> Genoa theorized. <The enemy probably forces the newest and poorest conquered races to work under these conditions.>

<My question is: Does this system meet Alex's qualifications?> Bethley asked.

<Not directly,> Killian replied. <But the aliens who are here and operating this mining system must have their own home world. Adding the

evidence of their poor technological condition, I believe this creates the opportunity that Alex is seeking.>

<I take it that consensus has been reached, and we're returning to the fleet,> Genoa volunteered.

<Agreed,> Killian replied.

The scout ships cut the return trip to a portion of the time they'd spent tracking the warship. There were no delays waiting for the alien vessel to transit again, and the SADEs calculated that with a single transit they could reach the fleet.

After exiting their transit to the wall, the arriving SADEs pinged the other scout ships, receiving signals from Linn and Beryl's ships. There was no response from the other two scout ships.

<Linn, what are the coordinates of Deter and Verina's ships?> Killian sent, concern evident in his question.

<We returned seven days ago, Killian, and checked for the comm coordinates of everyone's ships,> Linn replied. <We received Genoa's and yours, but not theirs.>

<Were there emergency beacons?> Bethley asked.

<None were received by any fleet ship,> Beryl replied.

There was a slight pause on the comm, while the returning SADEs came to the same conclusion — the scout ships of Deter and Verina were lost.

<Was your tracking successful?> Trium asked.

<Negative,> Linn sent. <The warship we followed used aged armor plating as a disguise. When it reached its home system, it shed its hull coverings and joined a stream of technologically advanced ships. The system doesn't qualify as an Alex-preferred target.>

Killian contacted Alex, and his opening statements caused Alex to call a meeting of key personnel to view the telemetry. The individuals met on the *Freedom*'s bridge, and Cordelia activated the primary holo-vid. When everyone was ready, Bethley began spooling off the scout ship's imagery to the city-ship, and Killian narrated.

<As I first stated, Dassata, this isn't a home world system, but the ships meet your parameters of a race at the bottom of the federation's political

ladder. The system's early stage of formation lends itself well to mining. You can see the extensive belts, that eons from now will coalesce into planets.>

In the middle of Killian's dialog, Alex suddenly froze the display and magnified the image for a better view of the colossal ship that rested on the surface of a significantly sized major moon orbiting a ringed planet. Julien and he exchanged stricken looks.

Immediately, Julien accessed the city-ship's archives, which held databases he'd coopted over the decades, most without permission. The particular database Julien desired was New Terran. Examining the historical material in the database, Julien compared the images he found with those on the holo-vid. The evidence was conclusive.

"Yes," Julien said simply to Alex, whose shocked expression resembled someone who had received news of the death of family members. In many ways, Alex had.

The bridge personnel's implants, comms, and tongues were stilled. Alex's distress and Julien's solemn expression cried for patience and understanding.

"What is it?" Renée asked, taking hold of Alex's arm.

"That huge ship, the one stranded on the moon, is an Earth colony ship. It's the *New Terra*," Alex replied in a choked voice.

"I thought the *New Terra* was destroyed," Tatia said, confusion and consternation evident in her voice.

"Not destroyed, abandoned," Alex replied. "It was badly damaged, and a small group of colonists were chosen to fill the shuttles and try to make planetfall."

"How many people were originally aboard the colony ship?" Reiko asked.

"Fifty thousand," Julien replied.

"And how many exited the ship in the shuttles?" Mickey asked.

"A few thousand," Julien said quietly.

Gasps slipped from the mouths of humans.

"What about the others?" Renée asked.

"According to the records, most of the colonists were in hibernation," Julien said. "There was a small portion of crew and colonists who were awake, but weren't selected to board the shuttles. It must be understood that, according to the captain, Lem Ulam, there were no expectations of the shuttles reaching a secondary target planet or that they would find it welcoming if they did make it. In fact, the colonists barely survived planetfall until they solved many major and complex issues encountered on New Terra."

"Do you think the colonists survived? Are they working this system?" Tatia asked, incredulous at the turn of events.

Alex stared at Julien, his heart tearing apart.

"One moment," Julien said, hoping to help his friend weather the horrendous news. "I'm requesting Miriam's expertise."

The New Terran databases Julien was examining had been collected, copied, and transported whenever the SADE changed locations and ships. He shared a link with Miriam, who, with her engineering experience, was the SADE he judged best capable to evaluate the *New Terra*'s condition.

Miriam extracted the colony ship files from the *Freedom*'s databases, examined the ship's engineering specifications and studied the damage reports. The bridge audience waited anxiously for her analysis.

"The *New Terra* captain detailed in his personal records, which Julien has archived, the damage to the colony ship, which ran into a massive meteor storm," Miriam said. "Based on the ship's deteriorating conditions, the length of time necessary to travel to this distant system, and its present appearance, I would estimate that the colonists, who were aboard, didn't survive the trip. I'm sorry to be the one to make that pronouncement."

"So, who is in the system, if it isn't humans?" Renée asked.

"The ship could have been discovered here or found and hauled to this system. It would be a great resource. Kind of a ready-made platform," Mickey volunteered.

"Which brings us to a strategic question: Is this system worth investigating in terms of leveraging a race away from the federation?" Reiko asked.

"There is no habitable planet here," Julien remarked. "However, the sentients working this location must have originated from some other system. Based on the conditions of their ships and mining operations, I'd think they were ideal candidates to investigate."

Reiko waited to hear Alex's opinion, but he and the New Terrans appeared lost in thought. She glanced toward Renée, who signaled patience. Reiko and the Méridiens remained silent. They couldn't imagine the thoughts churning through the minds of their comrades, who were faced with the remains of their lost colony ship and its entombed inhabitants. A shudder ran up Reiko's back, wondering what the aliens had done with the bodies.

<Do we go, my friend?> Julien sent, with the gentlest of thought.

<Yes,> Alex replied.

When Alex failed to say something more, Julien sent, <Perhaps, we should let everyone else know your decision.>

Alex shook his head to clear his thoughts. "What's our present state of repairs?" he asked, which galvanized his audience to focus.

"Traveler repairs are completed, and there are four more Tridents waiting time in the *Stardust*'s bay," Reiko responded.

"The city-ship is fully operational, except for three beam weapon emplacements, which aren't capable of being brought online, at this time," Cordelia added.

"All in all, Alex, we need eight more days before the fleet can move on," Tatia summarized.

"Good. In nine days, we set sail for this system, where the *New Terra* lies," Alex pronounced.

-16-
Dead System

When repairs had gone as far as possible, the fleet sailed, cleared the star's gravitational well, and transited to coordinates far short of the dead system where the *New Terra* had been found.

The four scout ships crept close, embedded themselves in the outermost asteroid belt, and waited for telemetry update. They transferred the data they received to the *Freedom*, allowing Alex time to determine the next step.

<Opinions?> asked Alex, when the system's imagery was available. His personnel were either seated around the conference table or online. A holo-vid displayed the scout ships' telemetry. Its audio pickup and speakers operated for ship-to-ship communication.

"Four warships," Reiko noted, "They're patrolling positions at the system's periphery."

"Freighters, mining sites, and processing plants," Mickey added.

"An extremely active system," Tatia noted, wondering if the obvious abundance of personnel and shipping might be more than they could handle. It was one thing to take on an enemy fleet in a single battle; it was another to wade into a heavily populated system and engage in diplomacy, while trying to ensure the safety of the fleet.

Alex stared at the holo-vid, shifting the view, changing the magnification, and studying the various ships in detail. Occasionally, he glanced at Tatia, Reiko, and Mickey, expecting them to comment, but they were silently watching him.

<Difficult choices,> Julien sent privately to Alex.

<This place doesn't have an obvious hierarchy, a home world or supreme point of contact. I'm not sure where to begin the process,> Alex sent in reply. <Who do we have to advise me in diplomatic negotiations?>

<You mean someone skilled in negotiations with aliens?> Julien asked, with a glint in his eye.

<There is that,> Alex agreed, the hint of a lopsided smile twisting the corner of his mouth.

Alex stood and paced the back of the room, trying to imagine what factors would force these aliens to toil in this dead system under such difficult conditions, while their masters possessed much greater technological capabilities.

"We'll need to get their attention," Alex announced. "We send a statement that we've got power but don't intend to use it."

"Shades of Vinium," Ellie's voice muttered from the holo-vid speakers.

"Something much like that, Admiral," Alex replied, "although I don't think some fancy positioning off a warship's bow is going to do the trick. These alien ships, despite their ancient appearance, have deadly armament."

"Then what attention-getting maneuver do you have in mind, Alex?" Tatia asked.

"I think a small force should approach one of these warships, Admiral, and we wait to see what they do," Alex replied.

"And if they open fire on us?" Svetlana asked.

"Analysis of these warships' movements indicates that they're unable to turn with any great alacrity," Miriam stated. "Perhaps some expert flying, as Alex phrased it, might be in order. Our ships' greater acceleration and maneuvering abilities might awe the enemy. In which case, they might relent to being approached rather than be destroyed, which I suspect they would expect us to do."

"The tagged warship did witness the destruction of its fighter fleet," Ellie hypothesized. "More than likely that has been communicated to personnel throughout this system."

"I hadn't thought of that," Tatia admitted. "Our reputation precedes us, which means that when our ships make their appearance in this system, more than likely, we'll create a panic."

"Yes and no," Alex mused. "If we enter the system at a significant velocity, spread out, and overfly the freighters, we'll make the point that we're not here to destroy them. In addition, we'll ensure that some of our Tridents end up near the closest warship."

"Ah ... diplomacy by intimidation," Julien commented, which produced a frown from Alex.

"But our Tridents won't assume stationary positions around the warship," Reiko cautioned.

"Definitely not," Alex agreed. "They keep moving, but our other ships can take up stations around the freighters and mining posts."

"Interesting message," Tatia said. "I wonder how the aliens will interpret our actions."

Alex shrugged his wide shoulders in reply to Tatia's rhetorical question.

"Suppose the warship fires on our Tridents?" Reiko asked. "What's our response?"

"We'll need to deliver a surgical strike. I would think the best maneuver would be to eliminate its engines," Alex replied. "And to anticipate your next question, Reiko, whether the warship counters our actions or acquiesces, our next step will be to board the alien vessel."

"Board a warship?" Reiko asked, with incredulity. "How do you expect us to do that?"

<Prepare your Frederica suit,> Z sent privately to Miranda.

Alex turned toward Myron McTavish. The ex-master sergeant and Dischnya warrior commandant was grinning at Tatia, who returned her own lupine twist of lips.

"I take it that you've experience in these methods?" Alex asked, glancing between Tatia and Myron.

"Terran Security Forces constantly trained for these circumstances," Myron replied. "I, myself, have led boarding actions multiple times."

Many humans in the conference comm were relieved that at least two individuals among them had the acumen to execute Alex's directives.

"What do you need?" Alex asked.

"First, we need access," Myron enumerated on his hand. He glanced toward Tatia, who tipped her head, informing Myron that she'd ensure the boarding team got entry to the warship.

Reiko watched the interaction between the New Terrans. It was evident to her that she would need a crash course from Tatia in this type of intimate attack.

"Second, I need a team who can handle close quarters confrontation," Myron said, extending a second finger.

"And who would you recommend for the team?" Alex asked.

"The Dischnya," Myron replied emphatically.

"But the Dischnya don't have Omnian capabilities," Svetlana objected. "They haven't implants."

"Your concern is noted," Myron replied respectfully. "However, the Dischnya have the attitude, reactions, and strength needed to handle aliens in a ship's confined spaces."

"But we don't know what type of aliens the boarding team might face," Franz said.

"It doesn't matter," Myron replied. "Whatever form these aliens take, the warriors will be more suited than humans to handle them."

<Z, Miranda,> Alex sent privately.

<Yes,> the SADEs replied, correctly interpreting Alex's call to them as a request to participate.

"Cedric and Frederica have agreed to lead the boarding team," Alex stated, referring to the massive New Terran-like avatars that Z and Miranda used in confrontations. "Myron, are there any more fingers to be raised?"

"Yes, number three, Alex. I need to know what type of weapons you will allow the team to carry," Myron said.

"At this present time, I'm inclined to limit the teams to stun weapons," Alex replied. "While it might be nice to have a plasma rifle or two —"

"They can't be fired aboard a ship in space," Myron acknowledged, cutting Alex off. He caught Tatia's scowl and sent, <Apologies, Admiral.>

In reply, Tatia sent, <Your apology should be directed to Alex, Myron. He is often thinking several moves ahead of us. You must allow him time to express himself, while his thoughts unfold.>

Alex's cool, calm gaze beheld Myron. Then he sent, <I was about to say that you can speak to me privately to make your arguments about plasma rifles.>

The academy commandant felt the power coiling around Alex's sending. It reminded him that Alex only resembled a New Terran. In this case, appearances were deceiving.

<Any more fingers?> Alex sent to Myron.

"Final point, Ser, I need to know our engagement parameters," Myron replied.

"Defend yourselves, if attacked, and exit the ship, if forced. However, you're not to initiate action unless the aliens do," Alex replied.

* * *

Tatia and Reiko were on hand when Z and Miranda trooped past them to board a traveler in the lower decks of the city-ship. Their enormous Cedric and Frederica avatars carried energy packs on their backs, which delivered power to their shoulder-mounted stun weapons.

Myron McTavish came next, marching down the corridor. He led the Dischnya contingent. The entire group was ensconced in environment suits, and they were armed with smaller versions of the SADEs' energy packs and mounted stun guns.

<What person leads us?> Reiko sent to Tatia, as the admirals watched Dischnya file into the airlock.

<Incredible, isn't it?> Tatia returned, recognizing that they were witnessing the deployment of Dischnya troops, when both of them had wondered about the value of recruiting them.

<He couldn't have foreseen a boarding action, could he?> Reiko asked. Doubt and incredulity colored her thought.

<I doubt he did,> Tatia replied. <According to Renée, Alex observed yellow orbs for weeks, which he thought were twin stars. One day, the orbs resolved into the yellow eyes of Homsaff. That's the story, anyway.>

Reiko stared at Tatia, expecting something more — another explanation that would make more sense than seeing twin, yellow eyes. Tatia's quiet stare told her that was all that was known, and she shook her head in confusion.

<It's hard to believe in this ... this type of thing,> Reiko sent, still resisting a full and complete acceptance of Alex's dreams.

<You don't have to, Reiko,> Tatia replied. <There are enough of us who do, and we're intensely interested in Alex's dreams.>

The admirals made their way back to the *Freedom*'s bridge, while the boarding party's traveler launched and sailed toward Deirdre's Trident, the *Deliverance*. To the Trident captain's sadness, there was now enough space in the ship's starboard bay after the fight at the wall to accommodate the traveler.

As soon as Cordelia detected the landing of the fighter aboard Deirdre's command ship, she signaled the fleet's controllers. The Tridents, loaded with their travelers, launched toward the distant system. The *Freedom* followed behind, but it would remain beyond the system's far belt.

As soon as the Trident fleet threaded its way through the densely laden ring, the ships spread out and the travelers exited the warships' bays. The freighters, mining bases, and nearby warship were overflown to demonstrate that hostile action wasn't the Omnians' intent. Then the fleet's ships took up stations near the bases and cruised alongside the freighters.

Deirdre's command ship and a squadron of Méridien Tridents circled the warship, orbiting above and below the ecliptic in line with the warship's engines and bow to minimize the possibility of fire from the enemy ship.

The warship made several course changes, and the Tridents matched the new trajectories, preventing the massive enemy ship from getting an opportunity to launch its port- and starboard-mounted armament. Eventually, the warship gave up its maneuvering and held a steady course.

<I think we just received an invitation,> Deirdre sent. The telemetry from the *Deliverance* was being transmitted to the *Freedom* and was displayed on the city-ship's bridge holo-vid.

Alex and company witnessed the opening of an enormous bay in the warship's lower hull section. Reiko enlarged the image to peer into the darkened hold.

"Nothing in there but some scrap parts in a few piles," Reiko commented. Her comment, in addition to all bridge conversation, was picked up by Miriamal and transmitted to the command admirals.

Tatia regarded Alex. When he nodded to her, she said, "Admiral Canaan, you have permission to launch the boarding party."

<Understood, Admiral,> Deirdre sent in reply. She signaled the bay's crew chief and the traveler's pilot. In moments, the boarding party was on its way to the alien warship.

The pilot paused at the yawning opening to the bay and waited for directives. Z, Miranda, and Myron, using a copilot's helmet, examined the interior. The scrap piles waited in the far corners of the cavernous bay. The interior held nothing else.

<Enter,> Myron sent to the pilot.

The SADEs were content to let Myron command the boarding party, but they would take the lead in the investigation. Their armament and avatars would provide a greater degree of protection.

The pilot slid the traveler into the bay and set down on the deck. No sooner had he executed the maneuver than the warship's massive bay doors closed.

Myron could be heard chuckling.

<An appropriate human to have in charge,> Z commented privately to Miranda.

<The dear man does seem to enjoy his work,> Miranda replied.

Myron removed his piloting helmet and replaced it with the one from his environment suit. As he walked the aisle to the fighter's rear, he called to the Dischnya over the team's comm. "Prepare to disembark. Seal helmets and check weapons."

Dutifully the Dischnya ran through their protocols, which Myron had drilled them on continuously.

-17-
Boarding Party

"Ready, Commandant," Homsaff said over the comm, when her two squad leaders, Simlan and Hessan, reported their warriors prepared to disembark. The two male Dischnya were among the first contacts of the Harakens, who descended from the explorer ship *Sojourn*, when it made planetfall on Sawa Messa, the Dischnya name for Omnia.

Myron signaled the hatch open, and Z and Miranda unlocked their avatars. They'd occupied the aft end of the traveler, standing in the aisle. The fighter's seats couldn't accommodate their bulky avatars, not with the huge power packs on their backs.

The SADEs jumped from the traveler's interior, forgoing the hatch steps, to land on the deck with resounding thuds. Next, Myron led the Dischnya warriors off.

Homsaff stayed close to Myron. She'd become accustomed to following his hand signals, during skirmish games, and used them herself to communicate to her squad leaders.

The Dischnya's environment suits hid much of the warriors' unusual characteristics. However, their helmets announced their uniqueness. Omnian engineers had fabricated a bubble design that allowed room for the warriors' muzzles to move. As such, the helmet's clear face prominently displayed the Dischnya furred skin, piercing yellow eyes, elongated snouts, and ferocious teeth.

<The bay is pressurizing,> Z sent over the team's general comm channel.

<We recommend your boarding party remain suited,> Miranda added privately to Myron.

In turn, Myron tapped the top of his helmet twice with an open hand, and Homsaff repeated it to the squad leaders.

After the pressure equalized, the bayside hatch of the airlock opened. Ominously, the far hatch was open too.

Z and Miranda carefully examined the airlock's interior and stared through it into the corridor. They scanned the passageway on a series of frequencies to detect heat, sonic waves, and other phenomena, which might indicate the presence of waiting enemy.

<The corridor appears clear, Commandant,> Miranda sent.

Z regarded Myron, who gestured toward the hatch with two fingers. As a TSF master sergeant, Myron trained his recruits for years to use hand signals in the event that comms failed. Despite his thorough adoption of an implant, old habits had value, and the uncertainties of this boarding action had him reverting to the habits he trusted most.

Homsaff could hardly contain her anticipation, although she wasn't anxious for confrontation. She wanted to prove to Dassata that the Dischnya held value to him in his expedition. This was their first opportunity to do so, and Homsaff, in no uncertain terms, had drilled into her warriors the need to acquit themselves well.

"We don't engage in the old ways," Homsaff had lectured the warriors. "We follow the commandant's orders, and we demonstrate our right to accompany Dassata and the Omnians to the stars."

The boarding party stepped through the airlock and entered a broad corridor. Myron signaled to Homsaff, and she deployed her squads to guard both directions.

<The air is breathable, Commandant,> Miranda sent, <but it's fetid. If your Dischnya, with their olfactory sensitivity, were to inhale these odors, they might be ill.>

Myron examined both directions of the corridor. Within 10 or so meters each way, there were heavy, mechanical hatches, which were propped open.

<An extremely old vessel,> Myron sent to the SADEs. <We need to advance toward the bow.>

Myron was fairly sure which way the bow lay but thought it smart to depend on the SADEs for orientation. As it was, he would have been correct. Miranda and Z led off, and Myron signaled to Homsaff.

The boarding party filed through one open hatch after another. There wasn't a single sentient in sight, which worried SADEs, human, and warriors alike.

The team noticed small amounts of debris that littered the corridor. Dust gathered on conduits, and doors were ajar. All in all, the ship was slovenly maintained.

"Body heat," Z called over the team's comm, moments before the boarding party was attacked.

The enemy ship's crew poured from doorways along the entire length of the Omnians. They wielded all manner of hand weapons: knives, sections of pipe, and heavy metal weights. Quickly closing on the Omnians, they slashed and pummeled.

The boarding party was forced into hand-to-hand combat, the enemy too close for the team to use their stun weapons. The SADEs utilized their avatars' tremendous strength to fling individuals away from them, focus their shoulder weapons on those attackers, and stun them.

Myron's TSF combat techniques were in heavy demand, and he attempted to defend himself as best he could. Fortunately for Myron, who was close to being overwhelmed, Homsaff and Hessan bracketed him. With Dischnya strength and reflexes, the enemy crew members were repelled by fierce kicks and backhands.

The Dischnya copied the SADEs' technique. As quickly as some distance could be created between the warriors and the attackers, they stunned them. The fight should have been brief. The primary group of attackers were put down in short order. However, more alien crew members continued to pour from both ends of the corridor.

The SADEs fought efficiently. Their energy reserves were more than sufficient for an extended engagement, but Myron and the Dischnya were sucking air from their tanks in great quantities.

Inexorably, the enemy bodies piled up until the new attackers struggled to reach the Omnians, climbing over their comrades to do so. The mound of bodies slowed the attackers' advance and allowed the Omnians to stun them, as they approached.

Suddenly, the attackers froze in place. Knives and blunt objects were dropped to the deck. In response, the Omnians held their fire.

The boarding party stood quietly, except for Myron and the Dischnya's heavy breathing, staring at the pile of bodies and the silent and ghostly still attackers.

<Your advice, Alex, would be appreciated,> Z sent, for once, unable to calculate how best to proceed.

The bridge personnel stared at the holo-vid, seeing through Z's eyes. From the moment the fight started, they were stunned. The assailants of their boarding party were humans.

Z focused on various aspects of their adversaries to amplify information for Alex.

"They're in horrible condition," Renée remarked. She was the first to break the silence on the bridge.

The images Z sent revealed sores on skin from unhealed minor injuries, swollen flesh indicating infections, runny noses, bleeding from mouths and noses, and missing digits that were burned shut.

"In addition to their injuries," Reiko added. "They're emaciated. I think they're slowly starving to death."

"Look at their eyes," Mickey said quietly. "They're unfocused, blank, like they've been switched off."

Alex linked to Miranda, the sisters managing his connection.

"Miranda, compare two faces for me," Alex said. He'd seen an attacker fall near her feet, and he directed the SADE toward the part of the image he'd recorded. Then, he highlighted the face of an adversary, who stood stock-still, a few meters away.

<Alex, except for what appears to be a difference of five to seven years of age, I would suspect they're identical,> Miranda replied.

"These two are undoubtedly clones from the same tissue source," Julien said. "I've identified others who exhibit identical appearances, but most of the attackers appear to be unique."

"What are the polished metal plates in their foreheads?" Tatia asked.

Before anyone could offer an opinion, the antagonist nearest Z and Miranda began speaking. The heavily damaged male spoke a short phrase in one language, waited, and said a similar length of words in a second language. The repetition of new languages went on and on.

"His speech is so eerie," Renée remarked, "It's toneless, no inflection."

"This individual wouldn't have the capability of producing all these languages," Alex said. "We're facing drones, which answers Admiral Tachenko's questions."

"Someone or something is operating these human drones and communicating through them," Tatia growled out, disgusted with the concept of humans coopted by aliens.

<Alex,> Miriamal sent, <the Sisterhood suggests that we communicate with the entity behind these humans.>

"The sisters will handle communications, until a common language can be established," Alex announced. "We'll follow along," he added, directing the sisters to broadcast the interaction.

The sister aboard the boarding party's traveler broadcast a short signal. It halted the drone's speech. There was a brief pause before the male uttered a signal burst of his own. Immediately, the sister and the entity behind the human assailants furiously exchanged sets of code.

A quiet squeal was heard over the *Freedom*'s bridge speakers. The controller had attenuated the volume when it didn't recognize the speech.

The traveler sister prepared for the intrusion of malicious code, but none was included in the communications. She sent a quick note to Alex about its absence, indicating that the Nua'll were probably not the entities behind the drones.

The Sisterhood possessed major assets in the present exchange. They had the various carrier waves gleaned during the fight at the wall, and they possessed huge databases of codes, which they'd been analyzing. Within a short period of time, the language of the Omnians was communicated.

"A digital entity is controlling the drones, undoubtedly sentient," Julien stated. He'd attentively followed the code bursts. The speed with which the language was exchanged could only have been assimilated by an entity as powerful, or more powerful, than a SADE.

Once communication protocols were established and the Omnian language established, the sisters heard, <Sentients, I'm AR-13145. How might I address you?>

<We're the Sisterhood. We protect the fleet,> the traveler sister replied.

<Do you lead the fleet? > the alien asked.

<Negative,> the sister replied.

Alex interrupted the discussion, saying, "I'll speak to you. You may call me Alex."

"Are you a digital entity?" asked AR-13145, his voice transmitted through the *Freedom*'s bridge speakers.

"I'm human, like those you use as workers," Alex replied.

"If you resemble my biologicals, can I presume that you think you've a right to repossess my specimens?" the alien asked.

Alex's anger rose at the reference to the poor human drones being seen as the alien's biologicals. Instead, he quelled it and asked, "Why do you believe you have a right to these humans?"

"A ship was discovered without propulsion, adrift in space. We recovered it and developed these biologicals from the entities' cellular components. They're my constructs and are no longer members of your race."

"These humans had to be grown to maturity, and they had to be trained to operate your ships," Julien said.

"This was part of our work, part of the process," AR-13145 replied.

"What's their mental status?" Alex asked.

"When the biologicals mature, their independence is eliminated by attaching them to my communications network," AR-13145 replied.

"Is the process reversible?" Julien asked.

"Once the transformation is complete, independence is permanently forfeited. These are my biologicals until they expire," AR-13145 explained.

"Why don't you take care of your biologicals?" Renée asked. "Wouldn't it be more efficient to maintain them adequately to get more use out of them?"

"Unfortunately, there is an inherent weakness in this species. Our control techniques don't produce the best interface, which means the biologicals have a shortened lifespan after being subsumed," AR-13145 replied. "It's more efficient to produce more entities and allow the attenuation cycle to persist."

"I would be curious to see your process," Alex said.

"You're denied access," AR-13145 replied.

"We don't need your permission, AR-13145," Alex replied. "By the way, AR-13145 is too cumbersome to speak. You need a better name for our conversations. I think I'll call you —"

<Faustus,> Julien sent privately to Alex.

"Faustus," Alex announced.

"What's the meaning of this word?" AR-13145 requested.

Alex heard Julien's explanation and rephrased it for his purpose. "Faustus is the name of a character from ancient human literature, a liaison to an extremely powerful entity."

"I approve of this name. You may call me Faustus," AR-13145 replied. "Despite our convivial exchange, you're still denied entry to this ship to view my process."

"And, as I said, Faustus, we don't need your permission," Alex replied tersely.

"Before this communication is terminated, I would ask: Will my biologicals recover?" Faustus asked. "I detect signal links, but I'm unable to direct them."

"They're stunned," Alex replied. "Under normal circumstances, humans recover in a relatively short period of time. However, your biologicals are in such appalling condition that I hesitate to predict when they'll wake, or if they'll wake."

"Your anger is detectable, Alex," Faustus replied. "I merely asked to determine whether I needed to prepare more specimens."

"See you soon, Faustus," Alex ground out.

"Your intervention will be your undoing," Faustus replied. "I've sent an emergency beam, requesting support. A fleet, greater than the one you met a period ago, will arrive to permanently remove you from this space. You have a limited amount of time to remove your individuals from my vessel. I recommend you proceed with haste."

Alex truncated the comm call. "Admiral Tachenko, retrieve your boarding party," he ordered.

"Do you want them to take a … a specimen?" Tatia asked. She looked at Alex apologetically. Under the circumstances, she wasn't sure how else to refer to the drones. She hated that word, not to mention calling them biologicals.

"No, Admiral," Alex replied. "We've no idea what would happen to them if they were separated from Faustus' influence."

While Tatia recalled the boarding party, Alex sent a quick message, <Sisters, well done. You were efficient and effective.> He received a chorus of tones, chimes, and odd sounds that represented the Sisterhood's pleasure at the compliment.

-18-
Inward Bound

Reiko sent a question to Tatia, who asked Alex. "It's obvious that you want to investigate the colony ship. However, Faustus just warned us of an approaching fleet. We can't do both and protect the *Freedom*."

Alex flipped the holo-vid display to portray a diagram of the enemy fleet at the wall. He placed the comm sphere, with its protective ships, and the carriers in the representation.

Tatia and Reiko studied it, looking for what Alex saw.

"The enemy ships are in the ecliptic plane. Every one of them," Tatia said.

"And they advanced across the ecliptic," Reiko remarked. "I knew that, but, somehow, it didn't sink in."

"You might have been too busy preparing for the fight of your life, Admiral," Alex allowed, laying a powerful hand gently on the small ex-Terran's shoulder.

"Originally, we guarded against intrusions on all fronts, including above and below," Tatia commented, "and then shifted our forces to accommodate their attack."

"So, why didn't they make use of the shorter approaches?" Reiko asked.

"Habits, Admiral, habits so old that we can't imagine their origin," Julien commented.

"It's like a fairly good engineer, but not a great one," Mickey commented. When he drew questioning looks, he added, "If a concept or method works once, why not keep using it, without asking how to make it better?"

"We'll be risking our entire expedition, if we assume this is the manner in which the next fleet arrives," Reiko objected. "In fact, having been defeated at the wall, the next enemy fleet might choose a different tactic."

"In my observations of this federacy," Julien said, "the probability that the new fleet will deviate from its eons-old habits is a minute number. What it will do is bring a vastly superior force to the one we defeated."

"In other words, a fleet so big that it can ensure we're wiped out," Reiko responded.

"Precisely, Admiral," Julien replied. "It will be extensive in number. However, it will still approach us across the ecliptic."

"Can't agree more," Alex commented. "Admiral Tachenko, move the *Freedom* near the colony ship. Have your commands take up stations near us. If any warships approach our squadrons, you've my permission to eliminate their engines."

"What about freighters, Alex?" Tatia asked. "They could be used for ramming tactics, especially with the humans aboard under the influence of Faustus."

"Good point, Admiral," Alex replied. "We'll make it clear to Faustus that the freighters are subject to being destroyed if they approach our ships at speed." Alex hesitated and then said, "Miriamal, did the sisters detect from where Faustus' signal emanated?"

"We did, Alex," the bridge crew heard. "It originated from the *New Terra*."

"Thank you, Miriamal," Alex replied.

"Admiral Cordelia, if you would please, the *Freedom* and the freighters are to take up stations near the *New Terra*," Tatia ordered. "Admiral Shimada, direct your Tridents to recover their travelers and converge on the city-ship and the supply fleet. We'll escort them to their stations."

* * *

The *Freedom* and the supply fleet had waited beyond the far belt, while the Trident commands had rushed inward. When a significant number of Trident squadrons were in close proximity to the city-ship, Cordelia signaled her fleet forward to join them and the expedition sailed inward.

It took days for the fleet to reform and close the distance to the *New Terra*. During that time, the telemetry was exhaustively reviewed by every senior member of the fleet.

Tatia and Reiko conversed with the command admirals and discussed squadron deployment. Central to their discussions was the best method of exiting the system should a second alien fleet arrive.

<Shouldn't we consider the possibility of allowing the city-ship and the freighters to make for a safe transit, while the squadrons deal a heavy blow to the aliens?> Svetlana asked, when Tatia and Reiko's discussion focused on a timely retreat of the entire fleet.

<I support Svetlana's question,> Darius sent. <The Tridents could destroy a significant portion of the enemy ships.>

<It would be advantageous to Alex's long-range plans if we put up resistance,> Deirdre offered. <Merely to flee at the approach of the federacy's fleet could send the wrong message about our willingness to persist.>

<An offensive option could be considered once we see the alien fleet's size and formation,> Reiko replied. <Until then, we can't make an evaluation as to what the Trident commands might accomplish.>

<Respectfully, I disagree with my colleagues,> Ellie sent. <Alex's plan has been to find a poor member of the federation. It's obvious that race isn't here, which means we've only begun to pursue Alex's plan. I think we should keep the expedition at full strength and not risk the loss of any more of our warships.>

<To what purpose?> Tatia asked, liking what she was hearing from Ellie.

<I say let the alien fleet think they chased us off,> Ellie replied. <If we follow what Alex and many of the SADEs suspect about this alien conglomeration, the enemy will believe that we saw their might, were frightened, and ran home. Then we'd be free to locate another system that might prove to be a better opportunity to convince those subjects to leave the federation.>

<I must admit that makes sense,> Deirdre agreed. <We're deep in enemy territory. Given time, the scout ship SADEs should be able to locate

other systems with the appropriate level of activity and minimal technology.>

<True,> Franz added. <Scout ships could reconnoiter the systems and report their conditions. Who knows what we might find?>

<How about you, Admiral Cordelia?> Tatia sent. <You've not offered an opinion.>

<In this matter, I believe it's best to remain silent,> Cordelia replied. <The Trident and traveler crews are the ones who'll risk their lives, first and foremost, involving any strategy that requires contact with an enemy fleet. And, they do so to protect this ship and the supply fleet. Their opinions should have the greater weight.>

<Any other thoughts,> Tatia asked.

<I still believe that offense is the better strategy,> Svetlana groused.

<Svetlana, we all know your preferred form of enemy contact,> Darius commented, and a round of laughter was added to the conference comm.

<I'll take your opinions under advisement,> Tatia said, ending that particular call and making a note to speak to Cordelia privately.

For her part, Cordelia was surveying the area around the *New Terra*. Faustus had chosen a similar body to the one the *Freedom* braced against at the wall. It was an ice planet, surrounded by a multitude of moons and rock fields. In addition, the remains of ships festooned the nearby area. The locale was so cluttered that even travelers would be required to navigate carefully.

Cordelia noticed that the colony ship appeared slightly embedded in the moon's surface, intimating it'd been in place for a long period of time. Overhead, abandoned platforms and space junk had built up. It would seem impossible for Faustus to lift the ship and get clear of the obstructions above. That was providing the ship retained the ability to get underway.

For safety's sake, Cordelia chose an upper ecliptic approach. It would allow her only one means of exit from the system. However, she'd heard Alex and Julien's analysis of the approach an enemy fleet might take, and she was relying on their acumen. Or, perhaps, she was betting on Alex's instincts.

Renée and Pia spent time reviewing the imagery collected by Z and Miranda. They reviewed the boarding party's fight, analyzed the drones' movements, examined closeups of their obvious medical symptoms, and listened to the exchange between Faustus and the expedition's leaders.

The women were upset by the conditions of the humans under Faustus' control.

"My worry," Renée said, "is that this entire system's workforce is solely composed of these human drones."

"What does Alex think?" Pia asked.

"Julien and he think that Faustus is the only alien here," Renée replied. "Which means, if you add up the number of mining bases, construction jobs, and ship crews, you're probably talking about thousands and thousands of these poor creatures."

"My stomach churns when you call them creatures," Pia said, her face twisting in a grimace.

"Well, look at them," Renée replied hotly, gesturing to the image on the holo-vid. "They moved woodenly, even when they were attacking. There was no animation on their faces, not anger, not fear, not anything."

"I know," Pia said, her hand held to her forehead in frustration. "The aspect of humans being subsumed to become drones is too ugly to consider. I wonder if Faustus was telling the truth about the procedure being irreversible."

"I wondered about that too," Renée replied. "We won't know until we visit the colony ship and see what type of operation Faustus is performing on them."

"These human drones represent an insurmountable medical challenge for my staff, Renée," Pia opined. "We haven't the facilities to take on this many patients. Worse, they'd be under our permanent care. Otherwise, they'd return to operating under the same conditions as before."

"I was thinking on that," Renée replied. "It also occurred to me that Faustus might have the capability and will to simply turn them off."

"Kill them?" Pia asked in horror.

"Maybe not directly, but what if he decided to remove his control? Would they simply stand in a stupor, waiting for the next directive?" Renée replied.

Renée took sympathy on Pia, who appeared overwhelmed, and said, "Well, let's put this part of the subject aside. Here's what I want us to focus on. Faustus requires full-grown adults to operate the ships and the mining processes. That means there must be some form of incubation system that raises humans from fetus to child to teenager, including some form of education for their tasks."

"That means the *New Terra* must have a form of crèche," Pia exclaimed.

"Yes, but I can't imagine what an alien crèche, which prepares humans to become drones, might look like," Renée said. "But these young humans are individuals we can help, I hope."

* * *

"Let's talk about our entry," Alex said to the individuals convened in the *Freedom*'s large conference room.

"Faustus is intent on keeping us out," Reiko said. "Consideration should be given to whether we make entry or not."

"I agree with Reiko," Tatia chimed in. "We've no idea what's waiting inside that ship. Our boarding party could be trapped inside and then hunted to death."

"I would like to point out that this entire system is impoverished. Regard its ships, mining posts, and crew," Alex responded. "Cordelia, how many minor explosions has telemetry indicated to date?"

"Fourteen, Alex, five within the ship scrapyards and the others at mining bases," Cordelia replied.

"It does speak to the dangerous conditions under which the drones operate," Julien added. "Logically, we could expect the same environment inside the *New Terra*."

"Julien, are you suggesting that only humans are inside the colony ship and most of them are drones?" Franz asked.

"That would be the greatest probability," Julien replied.

"And I would concur," Miriam said.

"Why would there be only the one alien for control?" Renée asked.

"You should consider, Ser," Julien replied, "that this alien is a creation. It's obviously a digital sentient that has been assigned to operate this system. I would hazard to guess that much of the metal mined from here goes to other worlds that are faring far better than this one."

"What about the possibility of Faustus detonating the *New Terra* just like the sphere we ran down?" Tatia asked.

"One problem I see with that scenario, Admiral," Mickey said, "is that I don't think there's much to explode. Telemetry shows almost no heat sources emanating from the ship. I think the engines are shut down, if not destroyed, and the ship might have a limited power source. My guess is that it's probably nuclear in origin and well-protected for Faustus' sake."

"We must take into account that, as a digital entity, Faustus might have no desire to end prematurely what could be a long life, merely to prevent our entry," Julien said. "Recall, Faustus did warn us it sent for support to remove us. If it intended to self-destruct, when we boarded the colony ship, why would it tell us that?"

"Well, from a purely physical point," Mickey said, shifting the conversation's subject, "there's a bay, which can easily accommodate a traveler. The doors are stuck open, apparently heavily damaged from multiple penetrations of space rock."

"We land a traveler and then what?" Reiko asked.

"You'd need an engineer or a SADE to work through the airlock," Mickey replied. "I don't think Faustus is going to operate it for us."

<Request to speak,> Miriamal sent to Alex.

<Use the holo-vid's speaker and address the room, please, Miriamal,> Alex sent in reply.

"Greetings," Miriamal said. "The Sisterhood has strong opinions on this venture, and Alex has graciously consented to our being heard."

Alex hid his grin about the part of being called gracious.

"There's an important point that I invite this leadership to consider," Miriamal said. "To date, the Sisterhood has been able to provide an interface in every communication between the fleet and the enemy, at the wall and here. Once Omnians step inside the colony ship, Faustus might attempt to communicate directly with the boarding party."

Alex glanced at Miriam, who replied, "There have been many discussions about how a sister might provide protection for a boarding party, but none have been judged worthy."

"Does this include the mobile SADEs?" Miranda asked.

"Especially Z and you, Miranda," Miriamal replied. "We don't know if Faustus has the capabilities exhibited by the Nua'll. It would be foolish to presume that the entity doesn't."

"Couldn't we adopt your comm protocols and knowledge?" Z asked.

"And how many copies of your kernel are you willing to produce to defend yourself, Z?" Miriamal replied. "Protecting the fleet from comm intrusion was a difficult task for each of us. Meaning no disrespect to Miriam, it nearly failed. Watching copies of ourselves succumb to the malevolent code was akin to watching pieces of us die. The factor that saved us was that we had one another to depend on."

"There is one group aboard this expedition who doesn't have an implant or an internal comm link," Myron said, leaning gently back in his chair.

"But you couldn't accompany them," Reiko objected, realizing that Myron was speaking of the Dischnya.

"True," Myron replied, with equanimity.

"But you wouldn't have suggested them if you didn't think they were ready to take on the task," Alex said.

Myron nodded, considered his reply, and said, "I had some lingering doubts about the effectiveness of the Dischnya under stress, but those doubts were dispelled during the boarding party's skirmish. Not only did the Dischnya perform admirably, they managed to employ tactical decision-making under extreme duress. I was protected by Homsaff and her squad leader, Hessan, when I was in danger of being overrun. The warriors never let their perimeter collapse. Never gave a meter of space to the attackers. They're ready, Alex, and I think they're just what this situation requires."

"What if they're trapped inside?" Tatia asked.

"I've prepared Homsaff and the squad leaders for just that kind of situation," Myron replied with a sinister smile.

"Do tell?" Tatia rejoined, displaying a wicked grin.

"Three of them can operate plasma rifles. If they're trapped, they can make their own exit," Myron replied.

-19-
Homsaff

In a city-ship bay, Myron stood next to a packing crate. On top of it lay three plasma rifles. On the other side of the crate, Homsaff and her squad leaders, Simlan and Hessan, waited.

"We risk explosive decompression," Homsaff objected, eyeing the powerful weapons.

"I've thought of that," Myron replied. "There's a way to exit a closed bay if you can't find your way back to the original ingress point. You have your locators, right?"

The Dischnya held up their right arms to indicate Mickey and Luther's hastily constructed tools.

"Julien loaded those locators with the interior architecture of the *New Terra.* It will hold your point of ingress, and you'll be able to track your movement around the ship's construction."

"How?" asked Simlan, his brow furrowing.

"Two travelers will be keeping station beside and above the colony ship. They will triangulate your comm signal and update your position. That will be combined with your own movements through the ship and will keep your position accurate," Myron explained.

"The ship is large, larger than any we've seen," Homsaff stated.

"True," Myron agreed. "If you journey deep enough in the ship, we might lose your comm signal, but the transmitters you'll be carrying should help with that. It's also why the locators will track your steps."

"How long do you think this assignment will last?" Hessan asked. His mate was about to deliver their first pups. Although he wasn't required to be in attendance, he had wanted to be near to share in the joy.

"Undetermined," Myron admitted. "You'll have food and water for fourteen days. At the end of that time, you're expected to exit and board a traveler."

"What is your concept for exiting with the plasma rifles?" Homsaff requested.

Myron launched into an explanation of how the Dischnya could find an airlock that accessed a bay. If the bay doors were open, the job was done. If the doors were closed and the bay systems inoperable, they could plant the plasma rifle firmly in place, with tools or what-have-you, and set the firing timer. Then they could retreat through the airlock, and let the plasma rifle punch a hole in the bay doors.

"With fortune, Commandant," Simlan replied, eyeing the dangerous weapons, "we'll find an open bay to gain our exit."

Simlan was the older and far wiser of the two squad supervisors, although he had to give credit to Hessan for his cleverness, which had served them well in communicating with the captive Harakens annuals ago.

"If nothing else," Hessan piped up, "we could threaten Faustus with these."

"Now, you're thinking," Myron said appreciatively.

"You're requesting we take three, one for each of us," Homsaff said, glancing at Simlan and Hessan.

"Yes, it's important that if you separate your command, Homsaff, that the groups number no more than three and that one of you are with each group," Myron replied. "That way the team will always be able to generate an exit."

"Why did we not use these weapons when we boarded the warship?" Homsaff asked.

"They weren't permitted, at the time. Besides, we had Z and Miranda with us," Myron said.

Homsaff regarded the weapons for a few moments, her mind piecing together various pieces of information. She walked the space between two cultures, one old and tribal and the other young and technological. Balance was always in jeopardy.

"My thanks for your instructions, Commandant, but we'll not use these rifles," Homsaff stated firmly.

Myron's training as a TSF senior noncom surfaced, and he declared, "This is an order, Homsaff. I'm requiring you to take them."

Simlan and Hessan bristled, and Homsaff returned Myron's hot stare, her yellow eyes glowing.

"You may order your trainee, Commandant, but you may not command a Dischnya queen, especially in that tone," Homsaff growled out.

"My apologies, Queen Homsaff," Myron replied quickly, realizing he'd crossed one of the lines of Dischnya manners. "I only meant to ensure that you and your warriors were protected."

Homsaff ignored the apology. In the Dischnya world, a queen was due that deference. Accepting it implied weakness.

"Did Dassata require us to take these rifles?" Homsaff asked.

"No," Myron replied. "He said it was your choice."

"Then my choice has been made," Homsaff declared. She turned and made for the bay's exit, with Simlan and Hessan close on her heels.

The three Dischnya worked their way around the perimeter of the *Freedom* to their assigned bay, where a traveler waited for them. Warriors helped the threesome don their environment suits and gear. In addition, each carried packs of food, water, medical supplies, and some small gear.

"Ready to board," a crew chief announced. He directed the warriors and squad leaders in teams through the airlock, and the Dischnya leapt aboard, ignoring the ship's hatch steps.

"Ser?" the crew chief asked politely, when Homsaff made no move to join her warriors.

"He will come," Homsaff announced quietly.

The crew chief was curious as to who the Dischnya queen referenced, when he saw Alex and Julien walking quickly around the curved corridor. Then, he politely stepped away to give her privacy.

Homsaff tipped her muzzle up slightly, a Dischnya indication that a queen had been kept waiting. Alex grinned at her, and she chortled in reply. In some cases, they were equals; in many cases, they were not.

"No plasma rifle?" asked Alex, when he stopped in front of Homsaff.

"My choice," Homsaff replied.

"Hmm," was all that Alex said, but he nodded his head in approval, and Homsaff's eyes glinted, with appreciation.

"About the moon, where the colony ship rests," Alex said, "There'll be no atmosphere to breathe."

"This is known, Dassata," Homsaff returned.

"Telemetry suggests that the moon is composed primarily of compacted rock," Alex continued. "Despite its immense size, gravity will be about half that of Omnia. Stress this to your warriors. Otherwise, they'll be bouncing off the bulkheads and overheads."

"This wasn't known," Homsaff replied, slightly chastened.

"What has the Commandant told you of your mission?" asked Alex.

"We're to ignore the drones or any other attempts to prevent us from locating Faustus. Our first target will be the bridge. We have Mickey's tools to guide us," Homsaff said, her muzzle tipping toward the device on her arm. "We've fourteen days to locate the alien. After that, we must exit the ship."

"And when you locate Faustus?" Alex asked.

"We take the alien prisoner, stunning the entity, if necessary," Homsaff said, reciting her directive.

"Excellent, Homsaff. I wish you good fortune," Alex replied.

Homsaff eyed the Omnian leader. It was inappropriate for a queen to bestow affection, although Nyslara frequently gifted Dassata. But Homsaff wasn't the great Queen Nyslara. Instead, she asked, "Do you have any words of wisdom for me, Dassata?"

Alex took a breath and let it out slowly. His dreams had encouraged him to take Homsaff with him, and he'd followed their calling. At this moment, he sincerely hoped he wouldn't regret that decision. Homsaff was a young queen, brave and fierce. He wanted to protect her, keep her safe, knowing full well she'd hate that.

"Once aboard the *New Terra*, you'll be alone with your warriors and carrying the responsibility of the mission," Alex began. "You might be inclined to think of what Myron or I might do if the situations you encounter become difficult. That would be a mistake."

"Who would you advise I emulate?" asked Homsaff.

"Pussiro," Alex replied.

"Yes," Homsaff said, with a hiss, "one of our most successful wasats. He was a cunning warrior commander, in his time."

Homsaff gave a quick salute to Alex and Julien. Then she turned and followed the crew chief into the airlock.

As Alex and Julien walked away, the SADE said, "They want to be a part of a modern society. It's their right to fight for the freedom of the combined worlds."

"I don't disagree, my friend," Alex said. "I just lament that we're always fighting one group or another to maintain these freedoms. Why are some races never satisfied with what they have? Why do they always want more?"

* * *

A traveler, loaded with Dischnya, a human engineer, and Miriam, exited the *Freedom*, and worked its way through the rock fields to the dust gray moon. The ship dropped level with the *New Terra*'s open bay, and the pilot, Miriam, the engineer, and those assembled on the *Freedom*'s bridge, examined the bay's interior.

The bay was completely empty — no shuttles, no crates, nothing — only metal patches over the rear bulkhead which would abut the corridors beyond.

<Land?> the pilot asked Alex.

<Permission granted,> Alex sent.

There was ample room for the traveler to slide into the cavernous bay. The pilot was careful to reverse the ship's orientation in case a quick exit was required.

Homsaff walked the ship's aisle from bow to aft end. She carefully observed each warrior to ensure they were prepared to exit the craft, including checking their comm signal.

Miriam and the engineer remained seated. It was obvious to them that Homsaff was taking the opportunity to exhibit command influence.

"Squad leaders, form your teams," Homsaff ordered over the comm, when she was satisfied. When the Dischnya filled the aisle, Homsaff called the pilot, who dropped the hatch.

Homsaff hopped through the opening. She hit the deck and bounced, kicking her legs to keep her balance before she struck the deck again. Despite Alex's warning, she was caught off guard by the reduced gravity. Her experience was limited to Omnia or a ship's 1g gravity or weightlessness. She watched her warriors drop from the traveler. Every one of them, except Simlan, had difficulty with the jump.

When Simlan stood in the hatch opening, the old warrior eyed the distance to the deck and stepped out, as if he intended to fall half a meter to the deck, instead of the more than a full meter. He landed lightly, flashing his teeth through the helmet at Homsaff.

Simlan's display to Homsaff contravened Dischnya manners, but the warriors had adopted many human habits. The flash of sharp teeth was meant to be an imitation of a human smile or grin. If Simlan's jaw had yawned wider and his lips curled, Homsaff might have been insulted.

As the squads assembled, Homsaff considered Simlan's management of the unexpected gravity, and she thought, *You may lead, but there are assets in your team to value.* She watched Miriam descend from the traveler, as if the SADE walked on air. The engineer did as well as Simlan.

At the airlock hatch, the engineer examined the ancient triggering mechanism. Figuring it couldn't hurt to try, he chose to press the access plate. To his surprise, the airlock cycled, depressurized, and the bayside hatch released. He pulled it open and peered inside.

<Good to go,> the engineer sent to Miriam.

"Good fortune, Queen Homsaff," Miriam said over the Dischnya's comm channel, indicating the open hatch. "We'll be waiting for your return."

Homsaff raised a gloved hand to Miriam. Then she signaled the squad leaders forward. Within moments, the boarding party was in the colony ship's corridor. Surprisingly, it was narrow, with piping running everywhere overhead. This was nothing like the Omnian ships' spacious interiors.

The Dischnya were stretched into a long line, walking two by two. Simlan, leading his squad, faced the bow; Hessan's squad faced aft; and Homsaff waited in the middle. This had been a contentious subject among the Dischnya. Homsaff had declared she would lead, but the warriors, especially the squad leaders, had objected.

"With respect, Homsaff, the boarding party has one leader, one strategist," Simlan said, tipping his muzzle down. "If we lose you, we must abandon the search for Faustus until a SADE or an implanted Omnian joins us. According to Dassata, that would place them at risk."

That was another moment of mental transition for Homsaff. She took a further step from a Dischnya queen to an Omnian leader. It was difficult for her to give up the privileged status she held, bestowed on her by her culture, but her desire to travel the stars was greater than that of holding on to the past.

"Forward, Simlan," Homsaff said over the comm, and the boarding party worked its way along the corridor toward the bow.

Homsaff kept her eye on the locator display, which told her that the shuttle bay they had used was in the colony ship's mid-level decks, halfway between the bow and the stern. They had many decks to climb and a long way to go to reach the ship's bow, where the bridge was located. Whether they would find the alien, Faustus, there was another matter.

"A human is approaching," Simlan relayed over the comm channel.

"Flatten against the right bulkhead," Homsaff ordered.

When Homsaff's pack hit the bulkhead, she leaned out to observe the drone's movement. The male paused, stared at Simlan for a while and then rotated its head to view the line of warriors.

"I would say that Faustus is observing us, Homsaff," Simlan said.

"Undoubtedly," Homsaff replied.

After a few more moments of viewing, the biological, as Faustus referred to the subsumed humans, continued on its way, never giving the Dischnya another look.

"Lead on, Simlan," Homsaff ordered. "Keep an eye out for stairs on your right. They should be coming up in about thirty meters."

When Simlan located the stairs, the Dischnya took the steps two at a time, despite the suits, armament, and packs they wore. Their powerful legs, aided by the lessened gravity, aided their movement. During the climb of a series of decks, they didn't encounter a single drone.

Once again, the boarding party was forced to advance two-by-two, as they navigated a narrow corridor.

"Blockage," Simlan said, "We need you up front, Homsaff."

-20-
Faustus

Simlan's squad quickly hugged the right bulkhead to allow Homsaff to pass. As she did, they took up their previous positions.

Blockage was a perfect description for what Homsaff saw. Drones, at least forty deep, crowded the corridor and faced them. They stood in pairs, each pair backed by a single individual, who stood slightly behind and between them. The groups of three repeated over and over.

Simlan studied the density of the crowd and said, "If we stunned them, we would have to climb over them. There is every possibility that we would cause them harm."

"I think Faustus knows that from our raid on the warship," Homsaff reasoned. "We didn't injure those humans, except to stun them. Afterwards, we carefully moved the bodies aside to make our exit."

"We could do the same here," Hessan said, from the team's rear.

"And how many more humans can Faustus call?" Simlan asked.

"We could spend hours or maybe a day stunning and moving bodies," Homsaff reasoned.

Homsaff stared at the block of humans, who stood eerily still, their eyes gazing at some unknown, faraway place.

"I wonder," Homsaff mused out loud. Alex's words ran through her mind, urging her to think as Pussiro would.

"What?" Simlan asked.

"At first, I thought there was no way of knowing if Faustus would be found on the other side of this blockade," Homsaff replied. "Then I wondered if that's what the alien wants us to believe."

"You think Faustus is trying to trick us?" Simlan asked.

"Julien said Faustus was undoubtedly a digital sentient," Hessan said.

"In which case, the alien could be many moves ahead of us," Simlan supplied.

"Then we must act in a clever manner that will confuse Faustus," Homsaff said. "Reverse course. Hessan, you have the lead."

Simlan's warriors stepped aside to allow Homsaff to occupy the center of the team, and the boarding party made its way down the corridor away from the blockade.

Homsaff checked her locator diagram. She used the images to trace a path to the nearest stairwell. Then the team ascended more decks, crossed from port to starboard, and made their way forward again. In no time at all, they faced another human blockade and retreated.

Alex had left instructions with the sister in the traveler that delivered the boarding party to restrict all communications to the team unless Homsaff requested instructions or help. There were an incredible number of individuals monitoring every step the Dischnya took, every word they shared, and everything they saw. And Alex didn't want advice pouring into Homsaff's ears.

When Homsaff found an empty room, the Dischnya piled into the space, and Simlan eased the door shut after checking to see if their actions had been noticed. There had been no humans in sight.

"Time to act like Pussiro," Homsaff announced. Her statement produced barks and chortles from her warriors. Pussiro's reputation was widely known and admired.

"The bridge is our target. It's the nest's center, and we must distract the nest's warriors so that a few of us can raid it." Homsaff was speaking the language of warriors. It galvanized the thoughts of her team, who began sharing ideas to accomplish the raid.

When the boarding party was ready, Simlan peeked out the door. He saw no one and waved the team out. Simlan and most of his squad remained on the starboard side and headed toward the bow, where they expected to run afoul of the blockade. Homsaff led the remains of the other squad across an upper deck to the port side, down a few levels, and toward the bow. She was expecting the same reception as Simlan.

Homsaff and Simlan met their blockades. Instead of retreating, they stood their ground and kept a running conversation with each other.

Reiko regarded Alex, who was hiding a grin behind a hand, and she heard Tatia and Renée snickering. "I don't get it," Reiko objected.

"Alex told Homsaff to think like Pussiro, if she was challenged," Renée explained.

"Understood, but why the nonsensical conversation?" Reiko asked.

"Have you done a head count?" Tatia asked Reiko.

"A squad leader and three warriors are missing," Julien said, to save Reiko time.

Reiko searched the city-ship's controller feed. "There are four signals that are offline, no video or audio," she noted. "Where did they go?"

"That's the question, isn't it?" Alex remarked. "I imagine the purpose of the Homsaff-Simlan conversation is to appear to Faustus as if the boarding party is stymied. Faustus would consider that our Dischnya are operating in an utterly simplistic manner first trying the port side, then the starboard side, and then both sides. Now the alien entity can see them talking, imagining them trying to figure out the next move."

"While Hessan and the others try a third approach," Reiko said, understanding the Dischnya's subterfuge. "It's too bad Pussiro didn't keep written records of his exploits. They would make fascinating reading."

Alex sent a short, private message to Renée.

<I'll follow up with Pussiro, my love, when we return,> Renée sent.

Hessan and three warriors waited until the squads were gone before they eased quietly out of the room. They had allowed sufficient time for the human drones to spot the squads, relay the information to Faustus, and the corridors to be jammed.

Clawed feet gripped the hard rubber decking, as Hessan and the warriors hurried to a corridor intersection, crossed halfway to the other side of the ship, and located a large vent in the overhead. They'd left their environment suits, packs, and stun weapons in the room. Hessan carried a small portable comm unit, which he had turned off, and each warrior wore hand weapons on their belts.

Two warriors linked their hands to form a support, and Hessan climbed onto their shoulders, trying not to dig his great claws into their skin. The third warrior passed him a small bag of tools, and Hessan worked to remove the bolts that held the vent cover in place.

When the cover was free, Hessan handed it and the tool bag down. He reached up into the vent opening and pulled his body through it. As soon as Hessan disappeared, the warriors fixed the cover in place and found a place to hide. They stayed close enough to keep an eye on the vent for Hessan's return.

Hessan crawled silently through the air duct. It was large enough to provide ample room, and the layer of dust facilitated his slithering motion. He was careful to keep his feet elevated, lest the scraping of his claws on metal be heard by the drones.

At each branch, Hessan checked his locator. According to the diagram, one of the main ducts would end over the bridge. Homsaff had told him that the bridge equipment's heat would require significant circulation.

Reluctantly, Hessan turned on his comm unit, when he knew he'd covered half the distance to the bridge. His sharp hearing enabled him to keep the line volume at its lowest level in hopes that anyone below wouldn't hear his communication. Homsaff had given him a code word. If he heard it, he was to retreat, at all speed.

Despite his youth and prowess, Hessan spent the better part of an hour squirming through the ducting before he reached the bridge. The main line split into three branches, each one ending in the overhead above the bridge. Hessan eased up to the first vent cover and peered through. He waited for a quarter hour, expecting to see Faustus walk underneath. Moving to the other two vents, Hessan spent the same amount of time at each one in hopes of spotting Faustus.

Frustrated, Hessan crawled back to a section without venting. Quietly, he whispered into his portable comm.

"Homsaff, I monitored the bridge for nearly an hour. There's been no sign of Faustus," Hessan reported.

"Any other activity?" Homsaff asked.

"This is the odd part, Homsaff," Hessan replied. "The bridge panels are lit. Lights on them are winking on and off, and icons are changing colors. But, there are no humans in sight ... or aliens, if you were wondering."

Homsaff was torn between requiring Hessan to remain in place or retreat. *Perhaps, I'm not as clever as Pussiro*, Homsaff thought, *or this alien is a greater adversary than Pussiro ever faced. If so, I've found someone who can challenge even the great wasat.*

"Dassata, I've need of your advice," Homsaff transmitted.

"We've witnessed the blockades of your squads, Homsaff, and we heard Hessan's report. Where is he?" Alex replied.

"Julien's plans of the colony ship have been helpful, Dassata, although there appear to be modifications," Homsaff reported. "I sent Hessan through the air ducts. He was monitoring the bridge from the vents overhead. Is it possible that bridge operators wouldn't be required on a ship this old?"

Alex glanced toward Julien, who said, "Earth's colony ships contained sophisticated computer systems that ran many of the basic ship functions of environment controls, power routing, sensor monitoring, and more. However, comms, navigation, main engines and the like would require personnel on bridge duty."

"Then it's possible that Faustus could be monitoring this ship from anywhere inside," Homsaff reasoned. "Do you have suggestions of where the alien might be hiding?"

Alex glanced around the bridge. Not a single individual offered an idea. "I think your first thought might be correct, Homsaff. Faustus could be anywhere," Alex replied.

"Then we will search the entity out, Dassata. We've time, yet," Homsaff said, ending the call.

Homsaff recalled Hessan. The three warriors recovered him, while the squads returned to their planning room. When Hessan and the warriors rejoined the team, the squads yipped quietly and appreciatively to the foursome for the successful execution of their assignment.

"This ship is the size of many nests," Homsaff announced, "but it is still a nest, and we will treat it that way. Our challenge is that we have only three locators, but we need to divide into smaller groups."

"We can mark as we go," Simlan volunteered.

Homsaff bared her teeth. "Yes," she said. "We start with three groups, each group with a squad leader or me. I'll assign a section of the ship. The leader will assign search areas to two warriors. Each pair is to mark where you travel so that you don't repeat your path. Squad leaders, when your assigned portion of the ship is finished, we meet again to share more search space."

"What if Faustus moves, as we search?" Hessan asked.

"Expect the alien to move around," Homsaff replied. "I don't think, in the course of fourteen days, Faustus will elude us entirely."

"What if the alien appears human, as the SADEs do?" a warrior asked.

Homsaff frowned in thought, and Simlan said, "We should work without our helmets, Homsaff. We can hear better, and we can use our noses. The alien won't smell like a human even if it resembles one."

"Excellent thinking, Simlan, we will do as you suggest," Homsaff replied.

The Dischnya stripped out of their environment suits and picked up the gear they would need. Then, Homsaff accessed her locator, carved out portions for the squad leaders, divided the team into three groups, and led them out the door.

"Two hours," Homsaff whispered to the squad leaders. "Meet here again in two hours."

The teams searched the upper decks first, finding empty cabins, numerous storage rooms, and many places where access was denied. Warrior pairs searched their assigned areas, passing human drones. None of the blockades formed, which the Dischnya noted with interest.

After the first search window finished, the team reformed. No one reported success.

"Every individual we passed smelled human," Hessan reported.

"The same for us," Simlan added.

"We encountered two humans, who carried a young girl between them," Homsaff said. "That's the first child we've seen. She was struggling, while they pinned her arms, but, when she saw us, she quieted and stared in horror."

"Children, that's what we heard," Hessan declared to Simlan.

"What?" Homsaff asked.

"We were discussing this subject before you arrived, Homsaff," Simlan said. "When we searched some of the decks, our warriors heard furtive sounds, the scurrying of small ones. Perhaps the sounds we heard were made by human children."

"Could you smell something other than human?" Homsaff asked. Her squad leaders shook their heads. "That means children have escaped Faustus' claws and roam the ship."

"Should we try to rescue them?" Hessan asked. He was thinking of the new pups that he and his mate would soon possess.

Simlan regarded Hessan with a baleful eye, until the younger squad leader ducked his muzzle.

"Homsaff's story ... the human children will run at the sight of us," Hessan belatedly admitted.

A thought occurred to Homsaff, and she dug into her small carry pack for her chronometer. The team had been aboard for nine hours. She realized that inside the ship there was little indication of day or night. Undoubtedly, the humans would need to rest, at some point, but when will that be, she wondered.

"Continue the search," Homsaff said. "Here are your new search areas," she added, sending new parameters to their locators.

Day after day, imitating the fleet's chronometer cycle, the boarding party searched the colony ship from the uppermost decks downward. The reports of the group leaders developed a similar theme. Late on the fifth day, the team holed up in an empty storeroom for food and water after another set of fruitless searches.

Homsaff reclined on the floor. Her whiplike tail was wound around a leg. The queens found it uncomfortable to sit on them. While Homsaff's team rested, her mind dwelt on the numerous searches they'd executed. It wasn't the lack of success that bothered her. It was the singular discontinuity of the first three efforts from the remainder of their searches.

Suddenly, a thought occurred to her, and she opened a comm call. "Dassata," she said.

<Here, Homsaff,> Alex sent. He linked to Julien, while the two of them walked a corridor toward the bridge.

"My mind is teased by what Julien calls an anomaly," Homsaff said. "Our searches return nearly identical results: human drones, the occasional furtive movement of young ones, empty rooms, and secreted areas."

<Do you think Faustus is hiding in one of these inaccessible spaces?> Alex asked.

"Negative, Dassata. I believe we've been deceived," Homsaff replied.

<Please explain,> Alex requested.

"For the last four days, we've roamed a third of the decks, investigated countless spaces, and not once has a team or a pair of warriors been blocked," Homsaff replied.

<Do you think Faustus deliberately didn't block your teams for fear that you would know where it hid?> Julien asked.

"I think Faustus has already raised a hand," Homsaff said, referring to the rude gesture a Dischnya pup would display.

<Your first searches,> Alex said, leaping to Homsaff's point.

"Dassata has his wits about him," Homsaff said, a snort accompanying her remark.

<I do my best,> Alex replied, grinning.

Julien accessed the colony ship's plans and shared them with Alex.

<One moment, Homsaff,> Alex sent. <We're studying the colony ship's bridge plans. Please confirm how close your squads got to the bridge.>

"No closer than forty-five meters each time, Dassata."

<There's no place to hide forward of the bridge, Homsaff,> Julien sent. <However, there are the captain's quarters and the officers' quarters on that level, and they're located in that area you couldn't reach.>

"And yet no one attended the bridge operations for nearly an hour," Homsaff mused. "That is another anomaly."

Alex and Julien waited, while Homsaff considered what she'd learned.

"We're abandoning the general search of the ship, Dassata. We'll try a different tactic to reach the bridge and view these quarters Julien mentioned. I'm certain we'll find Faustus there," Homsaff said, ending the call.

"A wasat queen," Julien remarked to Alex. When Alex grinned at him, Julien donned a jaunty hat and whistled an appropriate tune to match.

Homsaff led the boarding party back to the first room, which they'd originally used for staging. When the search days had resulted in no more confrontation with the human drones, the squad leaders had acquiesced to Homsaff, who chose to walk in front of the team.

"We need to search the bow of the ship, specifically the bridge and the officers' quarters," Homsaff declared forcefully. "I'm sure that Faustus resides there."

Homsaff highlighted the target area on her locator, which appeared on Simlan and Hessan's devices. The warriors crowded around the three leaders to study the small images.

"There is a danger if we repeat our last foray to the bridge by sending Hessan and a few others through the same vent," Simlan posited. "There is a possibility that, while the rest of us occupy the attention of the controlled humans, Hessan and his team confront Faustus, who might possess superior armament to ours?"

"You make a good point, Simlan," Homsaff replied. "It speaks to the need to put more warriors through the air ducts."

"How many warriors, Homsaff, do you think we'd need to put into the corridors to attract Faustus' blockades?" Hessan asked.

"Another good question," Homsaff replied. Her jaw dropped, displaying her sharp teeth, and her long tongue extended from her mouth to loll down one side — the equivalent of Dischnya laughter.

The warriors quietly chortled and yipped. Their leader had an idea, and that meant action, no more laborious and desultory searching.

"Simlan, Hessan, you will take three warriors each and lead them down the corridors," Homsaff ordered.

Simlan recognized Homsaff was choosing to lead the assault on the bridge via the air ducts, and he opened his mouth to object, but Homsaff hand signaled him. Her hand, palm down, swept to the side, indicating to him that he should hold his tongue.

"The remainder of the warriors will accompany me through the ducting," Homsaff stated, "and I will not lead this group." When Homsaff finished, Simlan tipped his head in acknowledgment.

"Will four warriors be enough to attract the attention of a sufficient number of human drones to free the area you need to search?" Hessan asked.

Homsaff's razor-edged teeth gleamed, as she opened her jaw, and the warriors imitated her. A few years ago, these mannerisms would have been taken as challenges.

"Simlan and you won't play passive roles, as we did the first three times," Homsaff said, focusing intently on the younger squad leader. "You will intimidate, and you will challenge."

"Provocation," Simlan acknowledged.

"Including stunning them?" Hessan questioned.

"Not at first, but eventually," Homsaff replied. "Start small and slow. Work your way up, stare, push, shove, and then stun."

"Are we attempting to break through?" Simlan asked.

"Negative. You're trying to attract the most attention you can," Homsaff replied.

The warriors, who would confront the drones, donned their suits. They wanted to appear as they did before, and they wanted some protection, during their confrontations.

The majority of the warriors eschewed their suits but retained their portable comm units. Homsaff checked her locator on her forearm. The warriors, who would accompany Homsaff, picked up small packs, which carried water and food for two days. They strapped them to their waists and shoved the packs to the small of their backs.

Homsaff's tail stood erect, with its tapered end in a curl. It was a sign of a queen in an excited or agitated state, depending on the circumstances.

Simlan and Hessan's teams helped the others through the same vent as before. They tracked Homsaff's locator signal, waiting until it stopped near the bridge before they split and set off along the port and starboard corridors that led to the bridge.

Each squad leader took his time, ensuring that drones witnessed their approach. As expected they were met with a small wall of humans. The warriors tried to gently push their way through. With their greater strength, the humans were unable to keep them from penetrating their blockade. Each side was nearly through their blocks when drones by the tens began showing up.

The warriors retreated until they were clear of the humans. More drones accumulated to bolster the blockades, and the warriors started shoving and pushing again, attracting more defenders against their actions.

"I believe we have as many in our blockade as we did the first time," Simlan said over the comm. This time, he was careful to speak in Dischnya, in case he was overheard by the alien.

"Go," Homsaff whispered softly, tapping the calf of the warrior in front of her. The signal was passed up the line to the warrior, who had the view through the vent grill into the bridge below.

Unfortunately for the team, the bolts to remove the grill weren't accessible from within the vent. The front warrior wiggled around until his massive hocked-legs were poised over the vent cover. When he received the double tap on his back, he kicked down with all his strength. There was a bang. The cover bent slightly, but it held. He kicked out three times before the metal cover tore loose and fell to the deck.

Warrior after warrior squirmed to the opening and dropped through. When Homsaff landed, she eyed the mangled cover. It was still attached to its mounting frame. The warrior had kicked the entire structure free. She chortled quietly, and then she gazed around. It was as Hessan had described. The panels were active, icons were changing, and readouts were in motion.

"Search," Homsaff hissed, pointing to the two exits off each end of the bridge.

The warriors fanned out, but two stayed with her. Simlan and Hessan had insisted on that precaution, and Homsaff had accepted it rather than start an argument she wasn't sure she could win. Although she was a queen, only one warrior in the team belonged to her nest. For a young Dischnya, Homsaff was challenged in many ways to walk between the worlds of the Dischnya and the Omnians.

As time rolled by, Homsaff's great claws began a tattoo on the deck. Her guards eyed each other. The queen's erect and twitching tail no longer meant she was excited.

The port squad was the first to return. "No one present in the cabins, Homsaff," a warrior reported. "The surfaces are dusty and undisturbed." Moments later, the starboard team arrived and reported the same thing.

Homsaff leaned on the back of a command chair, her forearms resting on its ridge. "I was sure that Faustus would be here," she said quietly. Her eyes scanned the bridge display, and she wondered how she could have been mistaken.

In Homsaff's mind, the events of the past days, after the team boarded, were played over and over. Each time, her logic seemed unassailable: Faustus hid in the bow. Otherwise, there would be no reason for the human drones to prevent their encroachment. They hadn't bothered her teams anywhere else.

While Homsaff considered the conundrum, her eyes wandered across the equipment, monitors, and chairs. She stopped suddenly, stood, and began a careful inspection of every centimeter. There was a repetition of metal, plex-glass, and fabric in every element of the bridge, except for one item. It was located under the bridge board and sat on the deck. It was box-shaped, and its metal was matte black, unlike the dark gray metal of the bridge.

Homsaff's eyes took on a wicked glint, and she announced in a clear voice, "I think we've been unsuccessful in our search, warriors. Let's proceed with Alex's directive. We'll destroy this bridge. Rip out every piece of equipment. Make sure no power is connected to any device."

The warriors regarded Homsaff in confusion. Before they could fathom the meaning of her orders, they heard, "Wait," from the bridge speakers.

"And who's that?" Homsaff asked innocently.

"Are we to exchange useless commentary?" Faustus asked.

"I'm taking a moment to enjoy uncovering your hiding place, Faustus. You must be tolerant of biologicals. We have our needs," Homsaff said, surreptitiously pointing to the black box for her warriors.

"How may I address you?" Faustus asked.

"I'm called Homsaff." Deliberately, she dropped the appellation of queen and took another step into Omnian culture.

"Now what happens, Homsaff?" Faustus asked.

"Now others will board, Faustus," Homsaff said coldly. "You'll notice that I and the individuals with me have no internal comm mechanism that you can manipulate."

"Yes, that has been observed," Faustus replied.

"From now on, two of my warriors will remain on this bridge until my superiors change this order," Homsaff stated.

"What's the purpose of these individuals?" Faustus inquired.

"If they receive any report of deliberate comm interference, they'll have a standing directive from me to disconnect you," Homsaff threatened.

"I can't be responsible for the comm workings of lesser races," Faustus objected. "There are too many conditions that might arise, of which I have no control, and could affect your communication. In addition, I must make you aware that my internal power supply delivers only enough energy to serve me for two annuals if you disconnect me from the bridge supply."

"Thank you for informing me of that," Homsaff said. "Let me amend my statements. The warriors will disconnect you and destroy your box to ensure it wasn't you interfering with their comm units."

"There are serious consequences to removing me from control of my biologicals, Homsaff. I don't believe your superiors will allow that, which means I deduce that they won't give you permission to mistreat me in that manner," Faustus reasoned.

"That's for you to discuss with them, Faustus," Homsaff retorted. "You'll notice that we're not human. We're a race called Dischnya, and we're much more primitive than humans. That means we're an impulsive species, and we're likely to act first and apologize afterwards."

"Your warnings are understood, Homsaff," Faustus replied.

"At this moment, Faustus, you're to halt all interference with my boarding party or any others of our fleet that come aboard. Your biologicals are to step aside at our passage. Is that clear?" Homsaff said sternly, resorting to the mannerisms of her queenly heritage.

"Abundantly," Faustus replied.

-21-
Biologicals

Alex, Renée, Tatia, Julien, and Myron stood on the *New Terra*'s bridge with Homsaff and two warriors.

After Homsaff updated Alex, she was directed to ascertain if Faustus could operate any bays. Homsaff discovered the alien could and a bay was opened for Alex's traveler.

<This must rank as one of the most ironic moments in human history,> Julien sent to Alex. <A highly advanced digital sentient is stuck in a box aboard the bridge of an ancient Earth colony ship.>

<Déjà-vu?> Alex replied.

<I believe my ship was much more technologically developed than this one, and I'll remind you that I sailed the stars while aboard,> Julien sent.

<Points taken,> Alex replied.

"Faustus," Alex said, addressing the alien vocally, "you're to stop any conversions of young adults to drones."

"There are operations underway that if stopped will result in the expiration of the biologicals," Faustus replied over the bridge speakers.

Alex spit out a few expletives, and Faustus was lost trying to parse their meaning. "Cease the operations on any humans that can be medically repaired and continue with the conversions that are too advanced."

"As you've requested," Faustus replied.

"We require a schematic of ship locations that have been put off limits," Julien said.

"I can send them to you," Faustus offered.

Homsaff's muzzle swung toward Alex. She wore a worried expression.

"You're not to directly contact any individual who is in my expedition," Alex stated sternly. "I thought that was made clear to you."

"I was told by Homsaff that any comm interference would result in my demise," Faustus said.

"Amend that statement to include any comm contact. Is that clear?" Alex said sharply.

"Abundantly," Faustus replied.

"Send the schematics to one of the panels, Faustus," Julien said.

"There are 1,032 pages of diagrams," Faustus replied.

"Show them one at a time," Julien replied.

An engineering design page filled a broad panel in the middle of the bridge. Julien recorded it and said, "Next." As page number two popped onto the screen, he repeated his order. As Julien advanced the pages, Faustus anticipated the cadence and the remainder of the diagrams blurred past. A bridge cam moved and zoomed in on Julien.

"Are you an augmented human?" Faustus asked.

"Negative," Julien replied.

"Are you human?" Faustus persisted.

"Negative," Julien repeated.

"Then you're a digital sentient like me," Faustus said. It's tone was one of awe.

"A digital sentient, yes, but nothing like you, Faustus," Julien replied harshly. "I work to protect biological life."

"I had no choice," Faustus said. "I originated here with my directives clearly defined. I've been performing them to the best of my ability. Had I not done as ordered, I would have been disconnected from my power source."

"We need access to the restricted areas," Alex requested.

"Under the circumstances, it's best that I have a biological open any space you wish to review," Faustus said. "Uncontrolled biologicals will run rampant if they see an opportunity to escape."

<The children,> Julien sent to Alex.

"Homsaff, maintain the watch on Faustus," Alex ordered. "Julien, lead on."

Julien reviewed the spaces of the colony ship that had been reworked to manage the cultivation of the colonists' cellular material. He decided to visit them in order of production.

"This is embryo development," Julien said, standing at the first door. Alex caught the attention of a passing drone, stopped him with a hand on the chest, and said, "Open this door."

The drone stood still, its eyes unfocused, and the Omnians heard from its mouth, "A biological will open the door from inside."

Alex released the drone he'd stopped, who continued on its way. Moments later, the door slid aside. Alex, Julien, Tatia, Renée, and Myron entered the room. Unlike the structures of the ancient colony ship, this compartment gleamed with advanced equipment. Spider-like devices clung from the overhead and managed the delicate processes taking place in the room.

Along one wall, frost-coated glass enclosed a compartment, which contained tens of thousands of small sample vials. A robotic arm floated overtop the samples. For now, it was still.

"Tissue samples," Julien said, pointing to the glass enclosure.

Alex addressed a drone. "Are the bodies of the colonists aboard the ship?"

The drone stilled and its eyes took on the glassy appearance that said Faustus had taken control.

"Many of the specimens were destroyed, when a meteor storm decimated their chambers," Faustus replied. "The cold of space froze the water in their bodies, bursting cells. Viable specimens were discovered and samples were harvested from them. Afterwards, all bodies were removed."

"Did you witness this?" Tatia asked.

"I didn't. This is a data note that I'm repeating," Faustus replied.

"Black space," Alex swore. "The bodies might be used as samples in some other monstrous experiment."

"What do you want to do with the samples, Alex?" Tatia asked.

"For now, we tour. Afterwards, we figure out how to deal with this ugly experiment," Alex replied.

"Would you like a tour?" the drone offered.

"Negative," Alex replied. "The procedures are obvious. I'll inform you of any changes I require as we view them."

The Omnians walked around the laboratory. In its center, artificial wombs grew the embryos, and a spider arm was busy opening one and cutting the umbilical. A drone pulled the baby from the artificial womb, induced the baby to breathe, and laid it on a shallow steel tray.

The infant, chilled by the cold metal, began to wail, but the drones ignored it. Renée swore a storm under her breath the likes of which the Omnians had never heard.

<I believe Ser has listened to your ragings much too often,> Julien commented privately to Alex.

Renée grabbed a length of fabric from a nearby pile, wrapped the child in its warmth, swept him to her chest, and hummed to him, while she rocked left and right.

The anger and pain in Renée's eyes caused Alex's fists to curl tightly.

"Faustus, you will warn us before delivery of any more infants. My personnel will take the babies from the wombs, not your drones," Alex ground out.

"It will be done as you request," Faustus replied.

The infant in Renée's arms quieted, and she sent to the Omnians, <This little one will need milk soon. Somewhere on this ship will be a nursery, a crèche.>

<That would have been my next stop,> Julien sent in reply.

<Etoya Chambling,> Renée sent. The Sisterhood relayed her request to an elderly Méridien woman, who was in conference aboard the *Freedom* with a group of women, including Pia and her medical staff.

<Ser,> Etoya replied.

<Gather your supporters,> Renée sent. <Visit Pia and procure supplies for infants. Catch a traveler with Z or Miranda for security.>

<Pia and her staff are with me,> Etoya sent in reply. <She wishes to attend to see to the health of the babies.>

<Good idea,> Renée agreed. <Don't worry too much about bringing exactly what you need. You'll have plenty of help transporting anything that you later require.>

<When would you like us to arrive?> Etoya asked.

<As Alex likes to say, Etoya, yesterday,> Renée replied.

<On our way, Ser,> Etoya said, closing the comm.

While Renée communicated with Etoya, Alex pulled the woman's records from the *Freedom*'s personnel database. Etoya was 141 years old. Until nine years ago, she directed one of Méridien's largest crèche programs. At one time, over 19,000 children were under the care of her organization.

"We'll visit the nursery next," Renée declared, hijacking the tour.

"This way, Ser," Julien said gracefully, indicating the exit door, with a wave of his arm. Alex and he exchanged winces, indicating the need to tread lightly around Renée.

Julien led the way to the next protected space. Faustus anticipated their route, and a door slid aside, as the Omnians arrived. A wall of crying and wailing greeted them. Infants, from newborns to about two years, filled the room. For the most part, they were unattended. Worse, they appeared thin, hungry, and unwashed.

Renée stood transfixed, tears forming in her eyes. She sent a personal message to Alex. <It would be best, my love, that you never let me visit the *New Terra*'s bridge again. I don't think I could resist disconnecting Faustus.>

Alex thought to point out that other aliens had set up the processes, but, under the circumstances, he chose to remain quiet.

Renée established a link to Etoya and relayed what she saw. In turn, Etoya shared the link with Z and the group of men and women who were aboard a traveler with her. Renée regarded the infant in her arms, and sent, <He was born a quarter hour ago, laid on a metal tray, and left alone.>

Renée chose to walk around the room. She burned to comfort the distraught babies, and the one in her arm began to cry in sympathy with the other infants. Renée focused on the conditions of the children, sending the images to Etoya.

Examining who was linked to Etoya, Renée sent, <Z, Julien has our location and can share with you the easiest route to reach us.>

"We can step outside," Renée finally announced, and the others seemed grateful to be away from the din.

Julien spotted a plate near the exit and touched it, sliding the door aside.

After the group made the corridor's quiet, Renée managed to shush the infant. None of the others, Alex, Julien, Tatia, or Myron, suggested they continue the tour. They waited silently, while Renée rocked the child.

A half hour later, Z strode around the corner, leading Etoya, Pia, and their teams, who trailed two grav pallets of supplies behind them.

"Greetings, Alex, Admiral, Julien, Commandant," Etoya said, tipping her head to the individuals she'd not formally met.

"Pia and I discovered Etoya's name and credentials when we searched the *Freedom*'s personnel database," Renée explained. "When we reviewed the vids from our team's encounter aboard the warship, we anticipated that we'd find something like this. Although, I have to admit I was unprepared for the cruelty created by ignoring the needs of these children."

"I've spent my life caring for the Confederation's children," Etoya said. "That was, I held my post until my opinions diverted from accepted views. You rescued me and several of my staff members from Daelon. We're prepared to take over Faustus' processes, whenever you're ready."

Alex regarded the elderly woman. She carried fine age lines in her face, but, despite her advanced age, she was clear-eyed, straight-backed, and anxious to begin her work.

"Myron, coordinate with Homsaff to assign warriors to handle security," Alex directed. "I don't want any of our personnel to move around this ship without protection."

<Z, support Myron,> Alex sent. He didn't bother updating Z on any of the protocols established with Faustus. What Julien knew, regarding the digital entity, Z knew.

"Etoya, you can start here, but hear me clearly," Alex announced firmly. "The SADEs or the Dischnya, acting as your security, dictate when you can move from one location to the next."

"The children —" Etoya started to protest, but a stern glance from Renée halted her. Instead she said, "You're understood, Ser."

Renée handed the newborn infant to a woman who stood near her and had been eyeing the baby. "I'll continue the tour with Alex," she told Etoya.

Alex nodded to Myron and Z. The SADE intercepted a drone in passing and requested entry into the nursery. When the door slid open, Myron, Z, Etoya, and Pia, accompanied by their staff and supplies, swept into the nursery's noise.

Realizing the communication process with Faustus was too cumbersome, Alex pinged the sister embedded in the traveler that delivered him to the *New Terra*.

<Greetings, Alex,> Miriamus replied.

<Please add a comm link with Homsaff,> Alex requested. On his end, Alex linked Julien, Z, and Myron.

"Here, Dassata," Homsaff was heard, when Miriamus relayed the queen's comm call.

<Still on the bridge, Homsaff?> Alex asked.

"Yes, Dassata, I don't trust this alien," Homsaff said.

Alex grinned at the thought that Faustus was hearing every angry word of the young queen. <Miriamus, are you comfortable acting as the communication hub between Omnians and Faustus?> he asked.

<The Sisterhood is ready and willing to manage this process,> Miriamus replied.

<Excellent, Miriamus,> Alex replied. <Homsaff, we're going to change the comm rule again with Faustus. Inform Faustus now that communication will be allowed with the fleet's Sisterhood, and Miriamus will organize the protocols.>

There was a slight pause, and Alex could hear the conversation between Homsaff and Faustus. It was obvious that Faustus wanted to understand the new parameters. The entity was convinced its position was precarious. Hope for Faustus lay in it cooperating with the interlopers until its rescue by the master race, who would be responding to the distress call.

"It's done," Homsaff said. "My warriors will continue our watch rotation to ensure this alien doesn't forget the rules."

<Thank you, Homsaff,> Alex said, smirking. <Miriamus, Faustus is all yours.>

Alex heard a final word from Z before he curtailed his link. <I can just imagine the ignominy that Faustus is experiencing,> Z sent, his humor evident. <One moment, Faustus rules the system's biologicals, and, the next, the alien's power is reduced to threats from a biological, who Faustus would believe is orders below its superior intellect.>

Alex closed the comm and regarded Julien.

"The rearing or education rooms are next," Julien announced. "There are several of these. I would estimate that Faustus must produce a significant volume of replacements for the trained adults. The drones' poor health conditions and difficult comm interfaces are merely two factors limiting their lifespans."

"We've witnessed a number of detonations since we've been in system," Alex added. "I hazard to guess the loss of life that resulted from those explosions at the mining sites, platforms, and ships."

"I doubt time and energy has been wasted recovering the bodies," Tatia surmised. Chills went up and down human spines at the thought of the deceased floating throughout the system."

<Admiral Cordelia, use whatever resources are necessary to sweep this system for floating drones. Have them procured and given star services by the captains,> Alex sent.

<Do you have any indication of the location or number we seek?> Cordelia asked.

<Calculate the number of accidents that have occurred over a few hundred years by the poorly conducted operations of drones, who might never have been recovered,> Alex replied.

<Understood, Alex,> Cordelia sent. She was aware that the calculation Alex suggested she run was too vague to produce an estimation of any value. It was the anguish in Alex's thoughts, which indicated to her, that every effort must be expended to rectify the problem.

"Let's go, Julien," Renée directed, and Julien spun and marched down the corridor. He descended two levels and walked more than 100 meters aft before he stopped.

"There is a row of spaces down this corridor that are dedicated to the children's educational levels, Ser. We can visit as many as you like," Julien said.

"I want to see the youngest children first," Renée requested.

"This way, Ser," Julien said, motioning with an arm. He led the group to a door. They had to wait for a drone to pass to cue Faustus.

When Alex intercepted one, he waited for the eyes to glaze over before he said, "It might be archaic, Faustus, but, from now on, a knock at the door requests it be opened for us."

"Could you demonstrate?" Faustus asked, and Alex pounded three times on the door. Soon after, it slid aside.

When the group entered the room, the young children were staring fearfully at the door, expecting trouble.

<Perhaps you should knock a little lighter, Alex,> Julien sent. <You're scaring the young ones.>

A male drone clapped his hands several times, and the children's heads whipped back to their tasks. They sat on metal stools connected to pedestal units that supported monitors and panels. Each child wore a small ear comm. Despite their intention to focus on the images that played across their monitors, they stole glances at the newcomers.

"You can imagine their confusion," Julien said. "We're adults. We don't have comm plates in our foreheads and we're healthy."

Renée examined the screen of the nearest child, who appeared about five years old. The language displayed was glyph-based. She gazed at the rows of children. They wore shirts and cut-off pants, two or three sizes too big for them. It seemed expedient for Faustus to give them clothing that they would grow into over the years.

The boy next to Renée wore soiled pants and mucus ran from his nose, which he licked at with his tongue. The child sniffed and continued to tap on his panel.

Renée reached out a hand to him, and the boy winced but, otherwise, didn't move. Reluctantly, Renée pulled her hand back.

A little girl, no more than three, slid off her metal stool and approached Renée. The male drone moved to intercept the girl, but Alex halted the man with a hand on his chest. He was surprised by the frailness of the drone's body.

The drones' eyes went blank and Faustus said, "I'll ensure that my biologicals suspend their routines, while you're in their company."

"You'll do more than that, Faustus," Renée declared, kneeling down to gaze at the child. "You'll govern your biologicals to use the minimum amount of discipline on the children until we take over your administrations."

"Your request lacks specificity. Its arbitrary nature makes compliance difficult," Faustus objected.

"Employ the mathematical half rule, Faustus, until chaos ensues," Julien instructed. "Then you'll know the minimum."

The child reached out, gently parted Renée's hair on her forehead, and ran a finger over the smooth skin. Her curiosity satisfied, she hurried back to her studies.

"I can handle one more location, Sers. Then I think I'll be sick," Renée declared hotly, before she whirled around and stalked from the training facility.

Alex held up a finger, while he made a comm call. <Miranda, don your Frederica suit. Communicate with Myron and Homsaff to gather a few Dischnya. In addition, recruit six or eight crew members. According to the schematics that Julien will send you, the colonists' hibernation chambers were located on decks eight through twelve, aft of midsection. I want them searched. I want to ensure no bodies remain. If you find any of them, they're to be given star services.>

<Understood, Alex,> Miranda replied. She hurried to Claude Dupuis' lab, where Z and she kept their alternate avatars. On the way, she contacted Myron and Homsaff and was assigned Hessan and three other warriors. By the time she transferred to her Frederica avatar, the crew members were assembled and waiting for her in the bay.

For the touring group, Julien chose the section where the teenagers were taught. Alex knocked quietly, and they were granted access.

Unlike the young children, who were easily returned to their studies, these youths halted their work. Most of them rose off their stools. They glanced warily at their minders, but, when their minders' eyes indicated they were in an enthralled state, the teenagers were emboldened.

The youths crowded around the Omnians. Tentatively, they touched uniforms, buttons, and hair. Since the teenagers' heads were shaved, the girls were fascinated by Tatia and Renée's locks.

One of the boys reached toward Tatia's ample bosom, and she gently guided his hand away. Confused, he tried again, and she caught his hand, stroked it, and pushed it back to his chest. All the teenagers gazed intently at the Omnians' foreheads, searching for the comm plates.

A girl spoke in an alien language to Julien. He shook his head, and she repeated her words. Her obvious disappointment caused Julien to project a feathered cap, and the girl uttered a sound of surprise, which she muffled with her hand. She called to her companions, who focused on Julien. To entertain his audience, Julien flipped through twenty different hats, and the teenagers clapped their hands in appreciation. Soon afterwards, they returned to their training, but constantly glanced at the strangers.

"If nothing else, they'll be good students," Tatia offered, as they left the training room, "that is, after they learn our language."

-22-
New Admin

<Alex, we've accounted for every hibernation chamber, according to the colony ship's original plans that Julien shared,> Miranda sent. <They don't harbor a single body, and there's no indication of what might have happened to them.>

<On the one hand, that's good news,> Alex sent in reply. <On the other hand, it asks another question.>

<You're worried that the aliens, who set up this operation, might have taken the bodies for other nefarious purposes,> Miranda supplied, completing Alex's thought.

<If they'll use the colonists' cellular material for something like this, then there are no bounds on what they might do,> Alex replied. <Thank your team for their efforts and release them. Well done, Miranda.>

<You're welcome, dear man,> Miranda replied, and ended the comm.

Alex checked in with Miriam, who, with Julien's help, was designing the buildout of new areas in the colony ship. The decision had been made that the best way to deal with the *New Terra*'s children was to keep them aboard the colony ship until they could be normalized, as Etoya said.

Renée and Pia, with Tatia's aid, instituted the same procedures that were employed at Sol, when the rebels were rescued at Idona Station. The freighter crews were drafted to help, and they welcomed what they thought would be a leisurely break from routine, until they saw the children's conditions. Then the crews worked furiously and over long hours to construct the spaces, designed by Miriam and overseen by Julien, to suit Etoya and Pia's requirements.

The new rooms were designed as a combination dormitory and education facility for each age group. Comfortable beds, refreshers, food dispensers, stock stations, tables and chairs, and training stations were installed. Much of the alien training equipment was reconfigured to work to respond to Omnian controllers, and Renée ensured that, this time, the seats were comfortable for the children. Much of the material for the buildout and basic supplies were fabricated from material gleaned from other spaces within the colony ship.

In the course of a few weeks, Omnians eliminated the drones from every operation regarding the children. Pia's medical staff monitored the embryo development lab and handled the delivery of the babies. Etoya's staff transferred the children to their new dormitories, but they refrained from initiating Omnian training.

Instead of training, Etoya instituted a series of games for each age group to play. It was the presence of abundant, delicious food, clean clothes, and the games that did wonder for the children's demeanor. Nurture replaced harsh discipline, hugs soothed children's cries, and food filled bellies begged by growing bodies.

It took a while for suspicion to die and acceptance to replace it, but eventually the transitions were complete. Then, when the children befriended their new minders, Etoya resumed their training. But, unlike the previous grind the children had endured to learn ship and mining procedures, they participated in courses that attempted to broaden their horizons.

The children were taught the Omnian language, and programs introduced them to the history of human expansion into space. In addition, studies exposed the children to the cultures of the Omnians, New Terrans, Harakens, and Méridiens.

What caught the children's attention were the career opportunities presented in the various societies: science, engineering, art, music, education, ship services, and a host of others. When the children were confused by some of the examples, Etoya and her staff brought in individuals to demonstrate. Musicians played for the children, Cordelia set up a fantasy display of her vid art, and engineers and techs demonstrated the wonders of their science.

Two subjects, or better said, individuals were held in abeyance, for a while — the Dischnya and the SADEs. Omnians carefully kept the

Dischnya out of sight of the children, while they were aboard the *New Terra*. The vids on Omnian culture weren't edited to remove that part of the culture, but the children were allowed a slow, long-distance view of the sentients.

Regarding digital sentients, it was unknown how much the children knew about Faustus. They were aware when the adults were overtaken, and they feared the entity behind that control. It hadn't escaped the teenagers notice that every adult possessed a metal plate, and they knew that they were slowly approaching the age when it would be their turn.

Alex made a point to visit the children's classrooms in concert with Julien. The young people were fascinated by Julien's display of haberdashery and effects. Starting with the teenagers, the eldest group of children, Alex introduced Julien as his best friend and a SADE. The teenagers questioned him about digital entities for a while, and Alex answered as plainly as he could.

A teenage girl asked Alex, perhaps, the most critical question, "Why do you say it's not important what shape an entity displays?"

Alex replied, "I've met individuals who appear far different from humans. Entities that would frighten you the first time you saw them. There are sentients that inhabit huge bodies of water and others that inhabit dry lands. Nature has crafted them to survive in those environments, and that makes them appear far different from you and me. I've met the Ollassa, who look like walking plants, and then there are the SADEs, who aren't biological in nature. They're digital entities."

Alex looked slowly across the room full of enrapt teenage faces, and asked, "Do you know what they all have in common?"

The girl, who started the discussion, answered, "No," and Alex said, "Among them are some of my favorite individuals and my best friends."

"You have some strange friends," a boy from the back of the room voiced, and the teenagers laughed and tittered.

"Yes, I do," Alex admitted, grinning. "But what determines their value to me is that they prefer to cherish life in all its forms. They don't live to conquer."

"What if we choose to rule rather than to serve?" a boy asked.

"That's a choice every human, including you, must make." Alex replied. His face grew quiet, and he stared at the boy until he saw the teenager squirm. "You're free today and receiving the generosity of many worlds because we believe in protecting life. You should think about that before you make your choice."

After the children's transfer to their new dormitories, the only location that Faustus still managed was embryo production. There would be births for another eight months, and Faustus was required to direct the processes that served the embryos' healthy development. However, while those procedures were automated, Pia and her medical saw to the delivery of the babies.

Once Faustus became unnecessary to the children's processes aboard the *New Terra*, Alex directed the entity to move the drones to a quiet place within the ship. Medical staff drafted support to see to the drones' care. Faustus was directed to add or emphasize programs for the subsumed adults to use the refreshers and change clothes daily. Their overall health improved, but their mental acuity continued to slowly deteriorate.

Omnians employed basic exercises and minor work details, which Pia requested, to keep the drones occupied. Despite their efforts, one or two of the drones were found collapsed every week. They died soon afterwards, blood pooling in their eyes.

<Sister,> Pia sent, <I need a conversation with Faustus.>

<Yes,> Faustus replied, when Miriamus contacted the alien.

<I'm, Pia, head of the expedition's medical services, Faustus. I wish to know about the nature of the comm implant worn by the adult drones.>

<What is your specific question?> Faustus asked.

<Our imaging shows a central spike that splits and terminates in both portions of the cerebral cortex. Thin threads extend from those spikes into many parts of the brain. If implantation didn't result in the hosts' terminations, why are they dying annuals later from massive brain hemorrhaging?> Pia asked.

<I have no means of studying the cause of the biologicals' termination,> Faustus replied. <However, over the length of my administration, I've developed a theory.>

<I'm listening,> Pia replied.

<It's simply that this species is unsuitable,> Faustus replied.

<That's it. That's your theory,> Pia replied, in exasperation.

<I've many observation points that don't amount to definitive proof, but they indicate the same thing,> Faustus said. <It's apparent that your species has a penchant for independence. I would imagine that those aboard a colony ship would exhibit a greater degree of this trait than others of your kind.>

<If I follow your line of reasoning, Faustus, you're saying the adults are psychologically resisting your control, which is resulting in physiological damage to their brains,> Pia summarized.

<It would seem to be the obvious answer,> Faustus replied.

<You told Alex that the devices couldn't be removed without terminating the drones. Is that accurate?> Pia asked.

<My data informs me of that. Whether this information is true or not is unknown. I awoke with it. Furthermore, I haven't the equipment to attempt removal. I do know each thread, as you call them, forms connections with the brain's cellular structure. Removal isn't a simple process of pulling the implant free. You must consider the enormous number of connections that would be disturbed. I would postulate that it's a nearly 100 percent probability that removing my comm control would result in the biological's termination.>

Pia ended the connection without further comment, and she updated Alex on her conversation.

<It sounds as if there's no hope for the adult drones, Alex.> Pia sent. <My staff has studied the embedded comm units. What we originally thought of as smooth fibers are essentially tiny threads with micron-sized extensions along the entire thread, and the extensions of one thread make connections with billions of nerve connections.>

<Have you spoken to Faustus about the status of the drones throughout the system?> Alex asked.

<I did,> Pia replied. <The teenagers are converted at about nineteen or twenty years of age, once they qualify in their training. After they're implanted, they don't last more than about six to eight years.>

<Does Faustus know why?> Alex asked.

<Faustus believes the biologicals are resisting control, resulting in brain hemorrhaging. It matches what we've seen, Alex, and it makes me sick. These drones were grown from colonists, who risked everything to journey to the stars, and they're still fighting for their freedom in their own way.>

<Stay focused, Pia. We're doing what we can. The children have been rescued, and the abominable process of drone creation has been halted. I understand we can't save the adults, but we've a greater goal to focus on. There's a huge federation out there, intent on expansion, and our worlds are in the way.>

<Understood, Alex, but that doesn't make me any happier,> Pia replied.

Alex closed the comm and hurried to evening meal. The expedition's leaders, who would sit with Alex at the head table in one of the *Freedom*'s meal rooms, were occasionally absent, at one time or another. This evening was no exception. Only Renée, Mickey, and Julien were present with Alex. He ordered, and a server hurried to dispense and deliver his meal and thé.

"You appear dispirited, despite our progress," Julien commented.

"Pia's medical staff has investigated the drone implants," Alex replied, "and she's spoken with Faustus. The summary is that the adults can't be saved."

Renée reached out a comforting hand to Alex's forearm. "How long do the adults have to live?" she asked.

"Six to eight years," Alex replied.

"That creates a conundrum," Julien said, thinking through future scenarios. "If the expedition moves on, the drones can't be protected from being harvested, and, if we stay, we aren't focusing on our primary goal."

"I hate to complicate matters, but we're failing to control another factor," Mickey interjected. "Mining, processing, and in-system shipping are ongoing. Alex, I know you've halted the warships and freighters from leaving the system via Faustus, but there needs to be some kind of endgame."

"Suggestions?" Alex asked.

"We can have the drones stockpile what they produce. For the most part, we can't use what they're creating, certainly not the metals. And, I don't think we want to leave these assets for federacy representatives, who will come to check out why there haven't been deliveries."

"You needn't worry about the curious," Julien said. "Faustus sent a request for help. The master race knows who's here, and the interested parties, the recipients of the shipments from this place, have been warned to stay away."

Alex ate, while he thought. His plan to lever an alien race away from the federation had been preempted. Now, he faced the major problem of finding a means of cleaning up this system before the expedition moved on. Waiting eight years for the drones to age out wasn't an option, but leaving immediately wasn't an option either. He considered taking the children and the drones with him aboard the *Freedom*, but that was a totally unsatisfactory solution. He put the greater problem aside and focused on Mickey's issue.

"Stockpile the metals near the *New Terra* and place the gases in an open area of space," Alex said. "Then put your engineering teams to work. When we leave, you'll inject nanites into the stockpiles and the colony ship."

"Are we dissociating the metals only?" Mickey asked.

"No, take down as much of the secondary material as possible. Err on the conservative side for lifespan," Alex ordered.

"What do you intend to do about the children and the drones?" Renée asked.

"I don't have an answer for them, yet," Alex replied, "but I'm sure Julien will have one soon,"

Alex winked at Julien, who replied, "Undoubtedly," while frowning at Alex.

-23-
Etoya

"My warriors have been conducting stealth investigations, during the times when the drones sleep, their night, Dassata," Homsaff said, during a briefing update with Alex and Myron, "and we have important news for you."

"I'm listening," Alex replied.

"During the night, we hear the movement of small humans, much as we did when we searched for Faustus," Homsaff said.

"Have you tried to apprehend one of them?" Alex asked.

"We've no desire to scare these human pups," Homsaff replied. "We believe that catching some of them would drive the others deeper into the ship, with stories of alien monsters."

"Any idea why they haven't been reported before now?" Alex asked.

"With the ongoing bridge and staff security duties, I've only had a few warriors to spare to search the ship. It has taken time to cover a ship this big. The warriors hunt in pairs, hiding and listening. Each night, as we've ranged deeper into the ship, we've begun to hear them more often."

"How many do you estimate there are?" asked Alex.

"It's hard to tell, Dassata, the warriors have been far apart, while hiding and listening. Recently, I received three reports of movement, estimating three or four pups each."

"So, at least ten, which means, it's possibly double that number," Alex mused.

"It would seem so, Dassata."

"Did the warriors hear speech?" Myron asked.

"None, only their movements," Homsaff replied. She chortled, adding, "They're as crafty as Dischnya pups on the hunt."

"I wonder how they're surviving," Alex asked rhetorically.

"The warriors say they can smell water from below," Homsaff supplied.

"That makes sense. The colony ship carries enormous water tanks that would have served fifty-thousand colonists after they made planetfall," Alex agreed. "One or more of them could be leaking or the children may have found a way into them."

"The warriors have discovered supply rooms. The doors have been pried open and the larders raided," Homsaff continued.

"What kind of larders?" Myron asked.

Homsaff snorted. "While Omnians use food stock, the less-advanced races, such as the Dischnya, stored preserved foods. A larder was where food was kept. The children have raided these larders and taken dried, preserved items, and some kind of food called an MRE. Only the label was found, which means we don't know the contents of the package."

Alex laughed. One of Renée's ancient vids spoke of soldiers' MREs. "They're called meals, ready-to-eat," Alex explained. "I wonder if they're still good after a thousand years."

"They must be, Dassata, none of the larders contain these foods. The pups have cleaned those out."

"Any suggestion as to how to recover these wild ones?" Alex asked.

"It won't be with our help, Dassata, except to determine where they might hide during the day," Homsaff replied. "But I can tell you some things about them that will aid you. These pups chose to run away from Faustus' laboratories. That took courage. They're resourceful, which means you won't catch them by throwing a net. They'll have a deep distrust of adults, who were their minders. This forces them to hide deep in the ship and only venture out at night."

"That's it?" asked Alex, a frown on his face.

"I wish you good fortune," Homsaff replied, her jaw opening and her tongue lolling out, indicating her humor.

* * *

After Alex's discussion with Homsaff, he immediately sought out Etoya and Pia. He had to wait, while Pia and her staff took delivery of another child from the embryo lab. When Pia was free, the threesome met in a small *New Terra* conference room that was clean but incredibly spartan.

Etoya and Pia entered the room in remarkably upbeat moods. They'd made incredible progress with the children and the drones who occupied the colony ship. For his part, Alex hated to be the one to throw another problem in their laps.

"Oh, no," uttered Pia, when she saw Alex's expression. "What's wrong?"

"There's nothing wrong," Alex said, raising his hands in protest. "But you do have a challenge."

"We have a challenge?" Etoya repeated and regarded Pia. "Why do I think that means our leader hasn't an answer to the problem, therefore we inherit it?"

<Patience,> Pia sent to Etoya. <Alex always starts with the worst of the news.>

"My colleague reminds me that, as an old woman, my mouth moves before my brain engages," Etoya said, dipping her head.

Alex waved away the apology. "The Dischnya report that this ship has runaways. I won't go into the story of how they know this, but, suffice it to say, their reports aren't to be doubted. At least ten or more children are hiding in the lower decks of this ship."

"Only children?" Pia asked.

Pia's question caught Alex off guard. He hadn't considered the implications. If children had been running away from their minders for a long while, why didn't the Dischnya report the movement of adults?

"You bring up a good question, Pia. All I can tell you is that the Dischnya said they heard only small children," Alex replied. "And they've been moving at night, raiding storerooms for food."

"Why are we here?" Etoya asked.

"The Dischnya fear if they try to capture the wild children, they'll frighten them and drive them deeper into hiding," Alex explained. "We need a means of drawing them out. If we don't incorporate them into your educational programs soon, they'll get left behind. Given more time, the Dischnya will pinpoint the children's hiding place or places."

Etoya regarded Alex, while she considered how to rescue the wild ones, as Alex called them. An idea occurred to her, but she kept it to herself. Instead she said, "You'll need to prepare a new dormitory, Alex."

"How large?" Alex asked.

"Might as well make it big enough to house sixty or seventy," Etoya replied. "These children will need the extra space, and we'll need the Dischnya."

"Even if they scare the young ones?" Alex asked.

"That's what I'm counting on until the children get to know them. We'll be dealing with escape artists," Etoya replied, narrowing her eyes.

Alex nodded at Etoya's acumen in anticipating who they'd be rescuing.

"We'll wait to hear what the Dischnya have to report, concerning their locations," Etoya finished, which ended the meeting.

* * *

Five nights later, the Dischnya identified the children's hiding place. It was on the lowest deck, where the *New Terra*'s array of water, reaction mass, and gas tanks were located. Homsaff handed off her locator to Etoya, with the hiding place highlighted on it.

Etoya turned to Julien. "Is the dormitory ready?"

"Everything has been prepared, as you requested," Julien replied.

"Including the —" Etoya began to say. She abruptly halted, when she caught Alex's grimace. "Apologies, Julien. Of course, your preparations are thoroughly complete," Etoya finished. She watched Alex's expression ease into a frown, and Etoya reminded herself of the gulf between the cultures of the Méridiens and the Omnians.

Old woman, she thought, *even after years with the Omnians, you still think as if you're living among Méridiens.*

"What now?" Alex asked.

"Now I bring the children out," Etoya said. Those around her wore their disbelief on their faces. "I've spent my life in service to the Confederation, doing my job the same way every day until I thought differently," Etoya explained. "This is my opportunity to put my theories to work for these children and whomever else I discover below. I don't intend to fail them, but I need to do this by myself."

Several individuals started to object, but Alex silenced them with an upraised hand. Etoya's eyes were focused on Alex, and they transmitted her conviction.

"How long do you need?" Alex asked.

"It won't be hours, maybe a day or two," Etoya replied.

"Good fortune," Alex replied.

Etoya left before Alex could change his mind, a slight smile on her face. She picked up her pack, which waited in the corridor, and headed aft. It was only 14.75 hours, but she had a long way to go, and she wasn't a young woman anymore.

Using the locator lent to her by Homsaff, Etoya traveled two-thirds of the ship's length to the rear, searching for the stairs that the queen had identified, which would lead her below.

Where's a lift when you need one? Etoya asked herself, as she descended level after level.

When Etoya reached the last deck, she stopped, dug through her pack, and extracted a small light, powered by crystal. She clipped it on a shoulder strap, entered a hatch, and stepped onto a grated, metal walkway. Her light illuminated 8 meters in front of her, but there was little to see. A walkway stretched out in front and behind her, fading away, when her light couldn't penetrate the darkness. Steps away from where she stood, a utilitarian stairway headed down. The bulkhead was to her right, and to her left, beyond the handrail, was nothing, a vast emptiness.

Etoya had been warned by Homsaff that the bowels of the colony ship were cavernous, but the concept hadn't sunk in until now. She wanted to turn the light off and allow her eyes to adjust to the darkness. Then, she shook her head at the foolish thought. There wasn't any light down here. The aliens, who set up the drone processes, had delivered power only to the areas necessary to facilitate their needs.

-24-
Wild Ones

Deep in the dark cavern, Ude was woken by the soft whirring of his ancient chronometer, a gift from the previous leader. He struggled awake and made the rounds, stirring the members of the band, one at a time. This was always a chore. The children were hungry and tired. They wanted to sleep, not be woken to forage for food.

Tonight, like any night, Ude performed the rounds a few times, shaking them awake, until they sat up and crawled out of their holes.

Each child had a tiny hiding place, under piping or in tight spaces between tanks. Material had been pilfered over the years and formed into insulated sleeping quarters.

Ude retrieved the band's water bucket, pouring some into each child's cup. This was another routine taught him by the previous leader. After the band was hydrated, they crept to a drain and removed the cover to relieve themselves.

When everyone was ready, Ude led them through the maze of large tanks toward the stairs, which would take them to the upper decks. The climb out of the cavern was always slow, and Ude had to cajole the children, while they struggled. Like him, their limbs were thin and wasted.

Ude nearly missed it. He was tired, and this part of the exit for the hunt was routine. He rounded the final row of tanks and caught the glow above. He hissed softly to the others, and they froze in place. The light didn't move. It highlighted a minder, who sat on the stairs. Slowly Ude backed up and whispered to the group. They stealthily eased behind the tanks and returned to their hiding places. It would be a long, hungry night.

Ude slept for a short while before hunger drove him awake. He dug into his emergency rations and snuck from one hideout to another, doling out small pieces of food, which the children greedily accepted. It wasn't much, but it would keep them alive. Afterwards, he crept back to where he spotted the minder. The light was still there. The minder hadn't moved.

Emboldened by the thought that the minder was dead, Ude took his time circling through the tanks to come out under the walkway and behind the minder. He waited, staring up through the grated walkway. Eventually, the minder moved, taking out a container to sip from and digging into a large bag. Ude could smell the aroma of food, and his stomach betrayed him, growling and objecting to its emptiness.

Ude was sure that he'd given himself away, but the minder sat still. He was confused by its lack of action. However, there was nothing he could do, and so, he worked his way to his hole, crawled in, and tried to sleep. But it was slow in coming. He could still smell the food.

Hours later, Ude woke and dragged his body out of his hiding place. He grabbed his cup and dipped it in the water bucket. Sipping the liquid brought him no relief from his hunger, and it hadn't for a long time.

Sometime past, Ude had tired of his lessons and the constant pressure from the minders. When the opportunity presented itself, he slipped out the doorway and ran. He was lost and starving when the previous leader found him. He had no idea how long he had been part of the band. There was no sense of the days passing in the darkness.

Ude's ancient chronometer might have taught him a great deal about time, if he knew how to read it. Unfortunately, the only thing Ude knew about his timepiece was that he was to listen for the first tone that told him it was time to forage, and, when the chronometer vibrated, it was time to hide.

I need to look again, Ude thought. Using the previous approach, he exited the row of tanks, tiptoed to the far wall, and eased along it. Up above him, the minder sat in the same place. *Maybe it's dying,* he thought. But, the longer he watched, the more convinced he was that the minder was healthy. It moved as it had before, sipping from the container and taking small bites of food.

Ude heard a sound behind him, and he pressed his body close to the wall.

"Who?" Ude heard Nata whisper. Her face was beside his, and, in the minder's dim light, he could see her straining to see above them.

Whispering in Nata's ear, Ude said, "Back," and then he led her along the wall, through the rows of tanks, to his hideout. Inside, Nata whispered, "Who is that?"

"A minder," Ude said. "That's who I saw, when I waved everyone back."

"What's it doing there?" Nata asked.

"Don't know. It does nothing but sit, drink, and eat," Ude explained.

"Smelled food," Nata agreed, saliva spilling from a corner of her mouth.

Ude considered Nata's reaction. It was the same as his. If the young ones smelled the food, there might be no way to hold them back. Once the band was seen, there would be more minders searching the tanks for them. He stared at Nata, who was lost in thought. Nata was the next oldest, after him. Someday, she would take his place. That was the way it was. No one lasted too long among the tanks.

"Sleep," Ude ordered, but Nata shook her head.

"Food," Nata said simply.

Ude understood. The nearby storerooms had been raided by the earlier leaders long before he arrived below. Now, the band was forced to roam far and wide to locate other opportunities, and they were having less and less success. In some cases, the doors were solid and locked, which meant they'd make too much noise breaking into the space.

Ude heard scratching outside his hideout, a signal the young ones wanted to talk. He crawled over Nata's legs to peek outside. From the snuffling and furtive movements, he estimated most of them were present.

"Smell food," the children whispered.

"Minder, danger," Ude replied quietly.

"Hungry," they said.

"No," Ude ordered quietly but sternly, and the children slipped away.

Ude fell asleep with Nata, waiting for more time to pass. When he woke, she was gone. He decided to chance another look at the minder. Reaching the far wall under the walkway, Ude's hand touched the arm of a child. He pressed a dirty finger against the little one's mouth to prevent her speaking.

Stepping around the child, Ude realized the entire band was lined along the wall. He felt his way around the row of bodies until he reached the front of the line, where he spotted Nata's pale face in the minder's light.

The smell of food drifted down from the walkway, and Ude could hear the whimpers of the young ones. Some of the noises became muffled cries, and still the minder didn't move. Ude reluctantly accepted that the end had come. Capture was inevitable. There would be no more band. It would die under his leadership, and he felt betrayed by his limited abilities.

Ude signaled Nata to stay put with a soft double tap on her cheekbone. In the dark of the tanks and lower decks, it was the best means of communication, tapping on a hand or face, especially when absolute silence was required. He'd made up his mind to surrender and to be the first sacrifice.

Etoya watched a skinny, scab-bodied boy of about eleven emerge from the dark. He walked slowly up the stairs toward her. His resignation was evident in the drooping shoulders. It made Etoya wonder why he was coming forth. It didn't seem to be for the food.

As Ude climbed the steps toward the minder, he expected other minders to burst from the shadows and grab him, but his keen hearing detected no one else. When there were no more steps to take, Ude winced from the bright light, and the minder lowered its level.

Etoya tore off a piece of a bun and handed it to the boy. He was reluctant to accept it, but the whimpers of others below convinced him to take it. A dirty hand reached out and snatched the morsel away, dropping it into a torn, fabric bag the boy wore suspended over a shoulder and across his chest.

Food for others, Etoya thought. She wanted to hand the emaciated boy everything she had in her pack, but more than a hundred years of experience curtailed her impulse.

Ude looked pointedly at the remainder of the food object in the minder's hand. He could smell its tantalizing odor. The minder handed him the entire bun. Holding it to his nose, Ude inhaled deeply, savoring the fresh scents, before he slipped it into his bag.

Etoya gestured to Ude to sit, and the boy lowered his thin frame onto the metal stairwell. She dug out a bun with a savory filling. She tore off a piece and ate it. Then she gave the boy a bite to eat. When he started to add it to his bag, she said softly, "No."

Ude glanced fearfully at the minder. The female was shaking her head in negation, and he withdrew his hand from the bag still holding the morsel. The minder indicated that he should eat it. His stomach rumbled in protest at the thought that Ude wanted to save it for others. Giving in to the tempting scents, Ude popped it in his mouth, and his jaw spasmed from the rush of saliva.

Etoya saw more faces emerge from the shadows. Children five to ten years old filled the stairwell. She could see more than twenty and estimated the number was as high as thirty. A small, six-year-old girl edged beside the boy, and he slid a comforting hand around her waist. She reached out a filthy hand to Etoya, who placed another bit of the bun in it. The girl hastily popped it in her mouth, her eyes momentarily closing in delight.

Curiosity, as to the group's internal workings, drove Etoya's next action. She tore off another piece of the bun and handed it to the little girl. Immediately, the child passed it to an older girl behind her, who handed it backward. Etoya smiled and nodded in approval. Then, she tore the remainder of the bun into pieces, handing them one at a time to the little girl. In every instance, she passed them behind her.

Etoya opened her pack and extracted water bottles and wrapped buns. She tilted a bottle, squirted some water into her mouth, and smacked her lips in pleasure. Then she handed the bottle to the older boy and indicated he should try.

Ude imitated the minder's action, choking on the rush of water into his mouth and down his throat. Nata worried that he'd been harmed by the liquid and placed a concerned hand on his shoulder. Ude chuckled and laughed, while he coughed. It was the first the band had heard those sounds from him since he became their leader.

"Clean water," Ude told the band. "Squeeze the cylinder lightly." Then he held the bottle over the mouth of the little girl next to him. She tilted her head, opened her mouth, and Ude squirted a small amount.

"Fresh," the little girl said happily.

Etoya didn't understand the language the children shared, but she understood their arrangement. It was highly social for wild children, and she wondered where the adults were who must have set the pattern for them. While she considered their small organization, she unwrapped another filled bun and handed it to the older boy. He handed it to the girl behind him, the one who worried when he choked. She tore it into pieces, handing them behind her.

Unwrapping a handful of buns, Etoya handed them to the older boy. Dutifully, he took them, made his way down the stairwell, and distributed them. Etoya handed the next batch to the older girl, who followed the boy's actions. Etoya continued to distribute water bottles and food until her pack was empty. The children sat quietly eating and drinking until the buns and water were consumed.

Ude was confused by the minder. He was grateful for the tasty food and clean water, and he was willing to be captured, but the minder showed no interest in doing that. Something about the minder teased Ude's mind. Then the thought materialized. Slowly, he reached across the short space between the minder and him. The female didn't move, while he parted the hair on her forehead. Ude was shocked. There was no plate, and Ude heard the children's gasps.

Ude touched his forehead and pointed to the minder, who shook her head no. It struck him. The woman wasn't a minder. She was free, and she had food. More important, her skin was clear. She suffered none of the ugliness that haunted the band. She was whole!

"Etoya," Ude heard the woman say. She was pointing to herself. Then she pointed to him.

"Ude," he replied, touching his chest.

As Ude spoke to Etoya, her heart broke at the sight of his ruined teeth. The decay went hand-in-hand with the open sores that marked the children's starved bodies. *We'll see you healthy, one and all,* Etoya thought. Overcome with emotion, Etoya reached out and softly cupped Ude's face.

Ude felt hot wetness stream from his eyes. The woman's touch had struck a deep need he didn't know he had. Certainly, no minder had ever touched him in that tender manner.

The little girl, who sat next to Ude, watched the tears flow down the leader's face. With a tiny finger, she touched a tear and stared at it. In the light, it glistened. She regarded the woman and made up her own mind. Then she crawled into the female's lap. She curled up tightly, her thumb in her mouth.

Yes, young ones, we'll get you food, medical care, and emotional comfort. And, most important, we'll get you time in a refresher, Etoya thought, rocking the child, and wrinkling her nose at the onslaught of horrendous body odor.

When the time seemed right, Etoya lifted the child off her lap and stood. She shouldered her pack and reached out a hand to the little girl, who accepted it. Then Etoya left the walkway, stepped through the hatch, and made her way toward the upper decks. Only once did she glance behind her, as she navigated a landing on the stairs. The children trooped behind her. The older girl led, and Ude was at the rear, ensuring no one was left behind.

It was more than two hours of work to navigate the stairs and decks with the children, who needed help in their weakened states, to reach the special dormitory that had been prepared for them.

Etoya had covered half the climb of the staircases before her implant transmission was received by Miriamus. She signaled for her staff to be ready to receive their new students. She was reminded by the SADE that it was 3.87 hours in the morning, and it would require some time to mobilize them.

<At the speed the children and I are moving, they'll have enough time,> Etoya sent.

The staff arrived at the dormitory, signaled the door open, and turned on the lights. A quarter of an hour later, Etoya trudged around a corner, holding the hand of a small girl. She led the troop of thirty-two children into the room.

A staffer took the little girl's hand and led her to the refresher at the back of the dormitory. A few Méridien women shucked their clothes and climbed into the refreshers with the children, peeling off the soiled rags they wore and washing the children from head to toe. Other staffers prepped small meals from the dispensers and served the remaining children, while they waited their turns.

Etoya turned to the doorway. Ude stood there, examining the room. She could read his thoughts. He was seeing similar conditions to the ones he fled. She decided not to coax him inside. Instead, she turned to helping her staff.

The turning point came when the first children to exit the refresher returned to the main room. Their little faces and bodies were clean. A salve of medical nanites had been applied to their sores. They wore fresh clothes and slippers, and they hurried to the open tables to get their share of the food.

Etoya glanced at the door. Ude was gone, and she thought for a moment that he'd run away. Disheartened, she returned to her next chore and saw him pick up a small boy to seat him at a table. She was tempted to signal the door closed, but decided that could happen after all the children were clean, fed, clothed, and asleep.

-25-
Enlightenment

There are minders, and, then again, there are minders, as Ude and Nata discovered.

Etoya estimated that it would be a mere days' worth of food, water, rest, and medical nanites before the older wild ones made a break for it. After three days, she requested the Dischnya stand guard, during the day, in the corridor outside the wild ones' dormitory.

True to Etoya's thoughts, it was the morning of the fourth day after the wild ones had been installed in their new room that Ude and Nata made their escape. Etoya and another staff member, who intended to wake the children for refreshers and morning meal, signaled the door open. The moment the door slid aside, Ude and Nata slipped past them like fish in a stream.

The two children made the corridor and slid to a halt. The direction they had chosen to run put them in the path of a Dischnya warrior. Habits took over, and they reversed direction even as fear shot through them about what they'd seen. In the opposite direction, they faced Homsaff. Chancing it, they split to either side of her.

Homsaff saw the human pups glance toward the spaces between her and the bulkheads. *Clever,* she thought, as the children lunged to either side of her. She caught the girl in her arms, and her powerful tail wrapped around the boy's throat, bringing both of them up short. Homsaff turned the girl around and gently pushed her toward the open door, where Etoya stood.

Nata took two steps and stumbled to a halt. She stared tearfully at the creature, which held Ude by the throat. She cringed at the thought that she would witness his death. Instead, the thing reached around, grabbed Ude by the arm, unwound its appendage from his neck, and shoved him in her direction.

When Ude was brought up short in the grip of the freakish entity, he believed he was dead. Then, in the next moment, he was propelled toward the room he'd fled. He stopped and stared at the thing that had captured him. Scary as it appeared, he could see the intelligence behind the yellow eyes.

"Ude," he said, smacking his scrawny chest with a small fist, as if to declare his person.

Homsaff bared her savage teeth, in imitation of the human smile, tapped her palm to her breast and replied, "Homsaff."

Seemingly satisfied, Ude turned around, slipped a hand in Nata's, and led her into the room.

Despite Ude's warning to the other children of who waited for them outside the room, there were several more escape attempts. Their angst was due to their new conditions, which imitated the previous ones. Yes, the new accommodations, with all its trimmings, were much better, but the wild ones knew they were restricted to a single room, when they had seen a much more voluminous space.

Ude watched the creatures, who the children had learned to call the Dischnya, return members of his band to the room multiple times. He saw the deference the creatures paid their female with the tail, who had captured him, and he focused his attention on her, when she entered the room. She moved with precision and power, and he admired that. *Leader,* he thought.

One afternoon, when the Dischnya returned two more escapees, Ude rose from his training station, and advanced on the one with a tail. Despite his scrawny frame, he walked erect, with his shoulders back. He closed on the female until he stood nose to muzzle to look into her eyes. A growl of condemnation issued from a Dischnya male, and the female's hand slash quieted the male.

Out of the corner of his eye, Ude saw the whiplike tail of the female rise above her shoulder, and he took that as a warning.

Etoya heard Ude speak to Homsaff, and she requested a translation from Miriamus, who supplied it from Faustus.

"It's a question, Homsaff," Etoya called out. "He asks if you're a leader."

Homsaff nodded her muzzle, never taking her eyes off Ude's.

Ude pointed to himself and repeated his words.

Homsaff understood Ude was declaring himself to be a leader too. She nodded, accepting his pronouncement. Seemingly satisfied, once again, Homsaff watched Ude stride to his training position. After he resumed work, his eyes frequently strayed to her.

Before Homsaff left, Etoya commented to her, "I believe you have an admirer."

"You're mistaken, Etoya," Homsaff replied, with a huff. "That one is a warrior, and I might have a recruit."

Homsaff had heard Etoya's musing about the absence of adults among the wild ones and the ex-crèche director's concerns that other children might be roaming the ship's bowels. She sent small teams to investigate the lower decks. The warriors' keen senses of hearing and smell were put to good use. They didn't uncover any more individuals, but they did discover the vac chamber.

The chamber's heavy, insulated hatch identified it as a cold storage unit. Logic indicated it was once used for freeze-dried items, probably genetic material that was destined for cultivation by the colonists. The Dischnya didn't bother to open the hatch. Their noses told them what the vac unit contained, and the warriors reported their discovery to Homsaff, who updated Alex.

Alex sent a recovery team to accompany the Dischnya, who led the way to the vac chamber. Based on Homsaff's report, Alex had ordered the team to wear environment suits. At the vac chamber's hatch, the recovery leader, Gerling, checked his helmet for readouts. There was a high concentration of gases he associated with decomposition. He turned to speak to the Dischnya, intending to warn them to step away, but they were gone. *I'd like to run too,* he thought, an instant before his team cracked the hatch.

Alex had been right to warn the recovery team to don suits. The tall, deep storage room was stacked with bodies in various stages of decays. All ages were present from young children to adults. The team sprayed medical solutions into the air to break down the decomposition gases. Then they pulled the nearest body out, sprayed it in a solution to seal it, and slipped it into a star services bag.

Gerling connected with Miriamus, pleased that his suit's comm had the range, which his implant didn't.

<Greetings, Ser,> Miriamus replied.

<Miriamus, we brought every star services bag we could locate. It appears we're woefully short,> Gerling sent. <I would appreciate your approximation, please.>

Gerling sent the quantity of bags he had on hand. Then he stepped into the cavernous vac room and surveyed the space and the stack of bodies, allowing Miriamus to record his helmet's view of the scene.

<Without knowing the percentages of youths to adults, Ser, I would estimate that you'd be safe with 1,200 more bags,> Miriamus replied.

<That many?> Gerling sent, gulping. <How is that possible?>

<Perhaps, Ser, you didn't consider the length of time these bodies have been present and the significant weight pressing on those at the bottom,> Miriamus replied. <However, I must warn you that it will be difficult separating those at the bottom. In that regard, one bag might serve to contain more than one body.>

<Miriamus, please relay my request to Mickey. His engineering team will need to fabricate the extra bags, at the earliest opportunity.>

<The request has been made, Gerling,> Miriamus sent, <Do you have any other needs?>

<I need Alex,> Gerling sent.

<Here, Gerling,> Alex replied immediately.

Gerling detailed the team's findings to Alex, sparing him the visuals. It was enough that he and his team were going to experience nightmares for a long while.

<Alex, I'm thinking we transfer the lot on grav pallets to a cargo traveler and then to a freighter. We'll need two or three shuttle trips. Then, we let the freighter deliver them for star services.>

<Gerling, Mickey confirms that Miriam and Luther have SADEs fabricating the bags,> Alex sent. <They'll deliver the first few hundred on grav pallets via a cargo shuttle. I'll have Admiral Cordelia position a freighter over the colony ship. Do you have enough help?>

<We've a couple of issues, Alex. I tapped other New Terrans for my team, figuring we might have several hundred bodies to recover. We haven't the best frames for navigating these decks without a lift, even in this reduced gravity.>

<Understood, Gerling. I'll send others to handle the grav pallet transfers to the shuttle. I do have one request.>

Despite the grisly surroundings, Gerling smiled to himself at the idea that Alex, the leader of the expedition, was phrasing an order as a request.

<How can I accommodate you, Alex?> Gerling returned genially.

<Contact Pia, Gerling. I want her to examine some of the recently deceased humans. She'll specify the number by age and sex, which you'll need to deliver to the medical suite. Ensure those bags are sealed.>

Gerling was suddenly troubled by Alex's request. <Is there anything I should be concerned about, Alex?>

<Being careful, Gerling, but you should spray that room and the nearby area with disinfectant. Then quarantine the area.>

<Why the precautions, Alex?> Gerling asked.

<I'm thinking of Etoya's questions about why there were no adults with the wild ones and why the eldest boy found appears to be only about ten or eleven. I think something down there was regularly killing them off, and I want to know what. It could have been the water or it could be bacterial or viral based. Either way, I want to know.>

<We'll get it done, Alex,> Gerling sent, closing the comm.

Gerling personally saw to the delivery of six bodies to Pia's medical suite: two, twenty-something adults, two teenagers, and two children, one sex of each category.

It didn't take long for Pia's staff to discover what killed the wild ones. Pia made a verbal report to Alex and Gerling, who attended her in the suite's offices.

"These poor individuals were infested with a host of bacteria," Pia said. "None of the varieties were highly virulent, but in combination with their poor nutrition and compromised immune systems, they succumbed to a gradual onslaught. We found the same bacterial infections in the wild ones Etoya recovered. They're healthy now, but if they returned to the lower decks, they'd be infected again."

"Alex, will the quarantine be sufficient if another race discovers this ship and doesn't understand what we're trying to tell them?" Gerling asked.

"Don't worry about that, Gerling. It won't be an issue," Alex replied. "Please recover the bodies from the medical suite and add them to the freighter. Communicate to Admiral Cordelia that the load is complete."

Alex turned and exited the medical suite, and Gerling asked Pia, "What did he mean it won't be an issue?"

"With Alex, if you don't understand, you have to ask," Pia replied. "You'll either get an answer or you won't. The bodies are this way, Gerling," Pia said, and headed for a medical suite's storage room.

When Etoya heard the news from Pia of the number of deceased found, she couldn't imagine the emotional distress the wild children suffered, hauling body after body of their deceased comrades to the vac room, opening that hatch to the rank smell, and depositing them inside. It boggled her mind that children were forced to do that to survive.

On another front, Etoya and her staff were challenged to operate two radically different protocols and curriculums for the children. One evening, over a discussion with staff, a New Terran caretaker, Charlene, who was known to possess a ribald sense of humor, explained how she handled the dichotomy. She said, "I think of the children we found under Faustus' tutelage as Méridiens, compliant and disciplined. They'll absorb what we teach them and incorporate it into their thinking. They'll bloom nicely over time."

"And the wild ones?" Etoya prompted.

Charlene laughed before she said, "I think of them as the mating results between Omnians and Dischnya, if such a thing were possible. They may look human, but they aren't."

Homsaff, who had taken part in the discussion, chortled at the description. Actually, she considered it a compliment to the wild ones, but it gave her an idea. She knew that Etoya and her staff reported noticing a growing frustration in the wild ones. It was said they hid it well, pretending to behave and learn their lessons, but Etoya's staff believed the children, especially the wild ones, had to be released to play.

After the meeting, Homsaff approached Etoya with her idea and together they met with Alex and Renée. It was quite late in the evening, and the two apologized for the intrusion.

"Nonsense," Renée told the females. "Please come in. If this is about the children, we want to hear it."

Etoya laid out the problem, as she saw it, and Homsaff added her proposal.

"I think that's a marvelous idea," Renée replied, clapping her hands. "The children will love it."

Alex wasn't so enthusiastic. In fact, he didn't respond at all but sat there thinking. "How many would engage in this play?" he finally asked.

"We would exclude the birthing number, of course," Etoya said, thinking furiously, "and also the children in the level one dorm, ages two to five. We'd have to find other games for them. That would leave us with 232 children."

"Everyone has to wear a locator," Alex stressed. "I can get Mickey manufacturing that number."

"They wouldn't wear these full-time, certainly?" Etoya objected.

"They strap it on before they leave the dorms, and only an implant signal can release it," Alex compromised.

"Agreed," Etoya replied quickly.

"I leave it to the three of you to organize and execute," Alex said. Renée gave him a wondering look. He rose, kissed her forehead, and said, "You thought it was a great idea. So, I know you'll take great pleasure in seeing it succeed."

Homsaff chortled again. She loved watching the interplay between human couples. It appeared nothing like what existed between Dischnya mates. At times, she wondered who'd make her a good mate and what type of relationship they'd have.

"One more item, Alex, you have to be the one to announce the opportunity to play and the rules they must follow," Etoya said.

"Why?" Alex replied.

Homsaff's mouth split wide, her tongue lolling out. Then she snapped her jaw shut and said, "Who else would make a bigger impression on the pups?"

"Funny," Alex replied, wishing Homsaff had an implant. He'd love to have sent her an image or two.

"Actually, she's right," Etoya chimed in. "The wild ones need to hear from someone who impresses them. I've watched their reactions to you, Alex, when you visit the dorms. The children are awed by your size, and you've become a subject of discussion among them."

"Not me?" Renée asked, feigning hurt feelings.

"Sorry, Ser," Etoya replied. "The wild ones value power. They focus on the New Terrans, especially Alex, and the Dischnya."

"And they're suspicious of the SADEs," Homsaff added.

"In what manner?" Renée asked.

"They're clever children ... more independent than the others," Etoya supplied. "They've seen hints of the SADEs' capabilities that aren't mirrored by any of us," Etoya added, waving her hand at present company.

"Make it happen," Alex said, making Renée and himself cups of thé.

As Renée ushered Etoya and Homsaff out of the suite, promising to contact them in the morning, Alex reached out to Luther, rather than bother Mickey at the late hour.

<Greetings, Ser,> Luther replied.

<We need 300 more locators, Luther,> Alex sent. <They're for the *New Terra*'s children, which means small diameter. Make them comfortable. These can be simple ... something an implant or SADE comm can pick up. Once on a wrist or a leg, they must only be released by us.>

<We're allowing the children out?> Luther asked.

<To play,> Alex explained, <but we need to be able to recover them.>

<Should we apply simple parameters of location or time, Ser?> Luther asked.

<Excellent thinking, Luther,> Alex replied. <Allow the locator to display a countdown programmed by Etoya and her staff. It'll teach the children about time. Have the display show green illumination, when they're in the upper three decks, but turn red when they descend to the fourth deck.>

<When do you wish these delivered, Ser?> Luther asked.

<Deliver them to Etoya and inform Homsaff when they're ready, Luther. Good evening,> Alex said, ending the call.

<Z, Miranda,> Alex sent. <You have another challenge. The *New Terra*'s children will be let out to play. They'll have locators, with timers, that can't be removed.>

<But, you don't expect the dear ones to play by the rules, do you?> Miranda sent.

<Especially the wild ones,> Z added.

<They might run or they might get lost,> Alex replied. <I need SADEs on duty during the children's playtime to monitor the activities. Potentially, there could be 232 children out of their dorms at one time.>

<Do you wish us involved in recovery?> Z asked.

<Negative, Z, I want a SADE to play referee and send crew to the correct location to recover a wayward child,> Alex replied.

<Understood, Alex,> Z replied, and the comm call ended.

* * *

Days later, Alex walked into the wild ones' dorm, which immediately garnered everyone's attention.

"Raise your hand if you'd like an opportunity to go outside this room and play in the ship," Alex said. He chuckled at the seventy-four raised hands, two from each child and the five staff members.

"When you play your games, you must wear this," Alex said, holding up a locator. "It'll tell you when to return from play, and it'll tell you when you've gone too far. Play is restricted to the top three levels of the ship."

"What if we don't wish to wear those?" Nata asked.

"Then don't," Alex said simply, "but be prepared to remain in the dorm, while everyone else goes out to play."

"I don't know any games," a young boy complained, which drove a spike into the hearts of the adults.

"I have an answer for that," Alex replied, signaling Homsaff, who walked through the door with the Dischnya pups in tow. There were seven of them, who were near the ages of the older children. Unlike the previous habit of the Sawa Messa Dischnya, which truncated a male pup's tail, these males displayed their tails proudly, and they always would.

"They know many games," Alex said, indicating the Dischnya pups.

The wild ones were transfixed. Getting out of the dorm room was an opportunity not to be missed. The games would merely be an excuse, as far as they were concerned, despite the locator limiting their range of movement. But, the appearance of the young Dischnya put an entirely different spin on the offer.

"When would play happen?" Ude asked.

Alex signaled Z and Miranda, who swept into the room with two boxes of locators. The SADEs put them on the Dischnya pups first. Then they applied them to the staff. Next, each SADE held one in their hands and stared at the wild ones. Some of the youngest children jumped up and ran forward to get one. Soon the others followed, including Ude and Nata.

<Who's the designer?> Alex sent to Z and Miranda.

<I thought black was sufficient, Alex,> Z sent, wanting Alex to know that if he disapproved of the locators' appearance that it wasn't his fault.

<Then the queen of fashion must be responsible,> Alex sent, his mirth surrounding his thought.

<Who else?> Miranda riposted.

<They're exquisite,> Alex sent. He watched the young, Dischnya and human, admire their decorated locators. Interestingly, the adults were

given plain black locators and bands, which the children had already noted, making theirs even more special.

"You'll have referees to make the games fair," Alex said. A child raised his hand, and Alex added, "These are Z and Miranda. They're your referees, and they'll explain what that means."

"I'm here to make one thing clear," Alex continued. "If you play well, observe the rules, and play fair with one another, then playtime continues at the discretion of your staff. If you break the rules or attempt to hurt one another, there will be no more playtimes. Am I understood?"

In delivering his final question, Alex had pulled himself up to his full height and used his command voice. He received a few feeble assents, and he focused on Ude.

Ude rose from his workstation. "We'll play these games, as you order," he said. He glanced at Nata, who rose and said, "As you order."

The other children quickly followed, echoing, "As you order."

The games, which the Dischnya pups led, were a hit with the wild children. The pups were highly social, and they played team games. Because the pups led the teams, they were insistent the rules not be broken, which wasn't always satisfactory with the human children.

The response of the Dischnya leader was often, "Do you want to play tomorrow?" When the answer was "Yes," they added, "Then we play by the rules."

In one case, Nata challenged her leader, and the pup merely shrugged and said, "It is your right to do what you want, Nata, but you will be the one to explain to Dassata what you've chosen to do."

Of course the Dischnya pup's statement invoked the question from the children of who was Dassata. Their team lost the game, when they were discovered by their opponents and tapped out. But the wild ones, who were sitting on the deck enrapt in the story of first contact between humans and Dischnya, didn't care.

New play areas were built for the younger ages. Engineers, techs, and parents loved designing and fabricating equipment for the children to help build their muscles and coordination. The *Freedom*'s children, who were of similar ages, were brought over to play.

The young at play, Etoya thought, watching the happy faces return to the dorm for refreshers and evening meal. Evening would be spent sharing stories about who did what. The staff noticed that playtime resulted in the quicker uptake of language and the building of a cooperative spirit.

Etoya observed the renewed interest of the wild ones in their studies. Ude discovered he could access the *Freedom*'s diverse databases, and he spent his evenings perusing a variety of information. Two of his favorite subjects were the histories of the New Terrans and the Dischnya.

Soon Ude was absorbing lessons far in advance of his peers, except for language. His reading improved remarkably, but his speaking skills remained attenuated. When he discovered implants, he requested one. When he was told no, he demanded one. It took a visit by Alex, with Julien present, to handle the discussion.

"Ude needs implant," the boy told Alex.

"You're too young yet, Ude," Alex said gently. They were speaking in the corridor so as to not bother the other children.

"When Ude get?" the boy asked.

"Two more years," Alex replied, which confused Ude. Seeking a way to explain, Alex added, "Ude is this tall." He held his hand next to the top of Ude's newly shortened hair. Then he moved it up and said, "When Ude is this tall, he can have an implant, if he wants," Alex promised.

Ude frowned. He was trying to determine how he would know when he reached the height where Alex's hand floated.

Alex gestured Ude toward the far bulkhead, and he obeyed. Then Alex gently pushed the boy flat against the bulkhead.

"Mark this, Julien," Alex requested, keeping his hand above Ude's head.

With nothing available to him, Julien used his fingertips and punched a dent in the bulkhead.

Ude stepped away. He examined the dent, running his fingers along it, and stared with renewed interest at the SADE.

"Ude will remember," the boy said and returned to his dorm.

"If the federacy defeats the expedition," Julien commented, watching the door slide closed behind Ude, "they'd better watch out when Ude comes of age."

"Are you kidding?" Alex shot back. "We'd better watch out when Ude comes of age."

"I wonder if these children will be adopted," Julien mused.

It was a concern that had plagued Alex and was only one more to be added to the many that this system had produced.

-26-
Hector

It was late. Alex's thé had gone cold, and Renée had gone to bed. He sat in a salon chair, thinking. Over the last couple of months, the questions had piled up, and they demanded answers. His key people were still arguing over the expedition's choices, but the crux of the matter was that they didn't have the resources to simultaneously contend with this system's needs and the expedition's purpose.

Alex consulted his implant's chronometer to determine the length of time since the expedition left Omnia, and he calculated his options. When he was ready, he closed his eyes, leaned back in the comfortable chair, and composed his message.

<Senior Captain Hector,> Alex began, promoting the SADE of the second city-ship, the *Our People*, <you've various tasks to complete before you undertake a lengthy journey.

<By now, the Sardi-Tallen platform will have constructed more Tridents and travelers, as should have the other worlds. You're to request those ships and crews attend your city-ship, when you're ready to sail, and join the expedition fleet. Regardless of the number of ships you receive, proceed with your other tasks.

<Due to the expected absence of your city-ship from Omnia, no more traveler shells can be delivered to buyers. Julien will send you parameters regarding the licensing of traveler shell construction to other worlds. You'll negotiate the rights for them to build their own shells. Have the funds deposited to Omnia Ships, per Julien's instructions.

<Prepare your ship to accommodate 528 human children. By the time you reach this system, they should be fairly well developed, but don't count on it. You'll need extensive medical supplies, food, and clothing for all ages. Educators would be helpful, along with facilities that can be

controlled. In all matters pertaining to these children, you'll be guided by Etoya, who managed an extensive crèche department for the Confederation.

<The children will board the *Our People* and be delivered to Omnia, but they will be kept aboard your ship. Over time, Etoya will familiarize them with our world. When they graduate from her care, they'll attend school and university on my credits.>

Later, when Alex delivered his message to Cordelia to be sent, she would share it with Julien. He would edit the part about Alex spending his credits, without his friend's knowledge. Julien would insert the Bank of Omnia, as responsible for the cost of the children's education.

<Hector, ensure you're accompanied by a freighter or two, with material loaded for fleet repairs, especially crystals, and at least six, rail-mounted, beam weapons for the *Freedom*. These freighters will be emptied and will return with you to Omnia.

<In addition to the travelers, which the Tridents will carry, the fleet needs replacement units. Procure as many additional fighters as you can load. The pilots must be prepared to join the expedition.>

Alex paused to consider his timeline again before he continued.

<Hector, you're allowed up to four months to arrange these requirements. At the end of that period, you must set sail with whatever assets you've gathered. Julien will attach the system's coordinates. You'll note that several transits are required.

<Don't be concerned by the extensive mining operations and alien warships present in the system. All operations are under our control. When your ship and the freighters depart, the expedition will resume its search for an alien race to divide from the masters. Unfortunately, this system didn't contain what we sought.

<The expedition will be leaving behind a few assets to monitor this system for a period of years. Thousands of humans operate the mining facilities and crew the ships. They've been coopted by an alien race. Nothing can be done for them. They've been trained to do one job and one job only and can't be recovered, in any manner whatsoever.

<Be prepared to be absent from Omnia for up to three years, but I hope that it will be little more than two years. There won't be time for you to communicate with me and receive a reply prior to you leaving Omnia. Use your best judgment, in all matters. I have faith in you.

<There's much to tell you about what's transpired, but an extensive update is best left until after you arrive. I can tell you that we met a huge fleet of alien fighters and defeated them, but not without losses of our own.

<My best to you and every Omnian. We miss them. May the stars protect you.>

Alex reviewed his message and sent it to Cordelia.

After a brief consultation with Julien, Cordelia sent the message to Hector.

"An admirable arrangement," Julien said to Cordelia. The SADEs were sharing some quiet time, gazing at the stars.

"An intelligent use of assets," Cordelia acknowledged.

* * *

The *Our People* was in orbit over Haraken, unloading traveler shells to one of the orbital stations responsible for ship building, when Hector received Alex's message. It was one of the rare times when he failed to keep his appearance algorithms running while he reviewed the message, which caused some of his crew to exchange concerned glances.

Hector dearly regretted he didn't have an opportunity to consult in real time with his partner, Trixie, but returning to Omnia or sending messages over the long distance would only waste time. Some of Alex's greatest supporters were down below, and he decided to start there.

<Ser President, I wonder if I could have a word with you in person on a matter of importance,> Hector sent to Terese Lechaux.

Soon after evening meal, Hector's traveler set down on the grounds surrounding the home of Terese and her partner, Tomas Monti. He was greeted graciously and the threesome settled into the main room's chairs.

Hector sent Alex's message to them. He'd edited out certain elements — the offer of the shell licensing, the financial disclosures, and transit information. Hector watched confusion slowly overtake their expressions, realizing they must be playing the message a number of times and coming up with a host of questions.

"Where is this system?" Tomas asked.

"Deep in federacy space," Hector replied.

"How can Alex have found humans there?" Terese asked.

"Alex didn't explain, Ser President. I would estimate that the expedition has seen and dealt with much since they left, and one can only wonder what they've encountered."

"At least the fleet has rescued the children there," Tomas noted.

"But not thousands of adults," Terese added. She regarded Hector, for a moment, and then said, "There was more in the message, wasn't there?"

Hector nodded and said, "There was a great battle, and an alien fleet was defeated."

"Were these the masters?" Terese asked.

"From what Alex said, it wasn't. His plan to divide a race away from the masters is ongoing. I can only surmise that the alien fighter fleet was a momentary impediment," Hector replied.

"What brings you to our house tonight?" Terese asked.

Years ago, Hector had made the transition from a SADE, who was devoted to serving a Confederation House, to becoming his own individual. Alex had awarded him the captaincy of the city-ship he commanded, and Hector had learned to conduct business in the Omnian fashion. To be more exact, he learned to conduct business in Alex's fashion. In Hector's estimation, Alex needed ships, not credits, and offering licensing agreements would only gather the latter.

"Omnian Ships is prepared to license to you the right to manufacture your own traveler shells," Hector announced.

"It's about time," Tomas declared.

"What's the fee?" Terese asked.

"I require an advance on the fee for the first one hundred licenses," Hector replied, "and I'm willing to take the payment in trade."

Tomas was taken aback, but Terese laughed out loud and said, "Ah, Hector, Alex would be proud of you. What does Alex need?"

"Travelers and pilots to join the expedition," Hector replied.

Terese connected with two SADEs who worked for the Assembly and knew the contractual arrangements with Omnia Ships. "Let's bargain," Terese said with a grin, linking to Hector.

Much to Hector's appreciation, Haraken had a number of young, well-trained fighter pilots, who were anxious to join the expedition, and he collected twelve travelers in lieu of the fee advance.

"Satisfied?" asked Terese, when the negotiations were complete.

"Partially," Hector replied. "Now, we should discuss the number of Tridents and travelers you've produced and the quantity that will be added to the expedition."

"Oh, you are a student of Alex," Tomas said. "We should have seen this coming," he added, looking at his partner.

"Yes, we should have," Terese said. "Hector, we didn't anticipate Alex would call for more warships, which means that they weren't our primary focus in ship construction. That being said, Haraken can potentially contribute two squadrons. However, I'll need Assembly approval."

Hector regarded the couple for a moment. Many possible responses ran through his kernel.

"You're disappointed," Tomas suggested.

"Mildly," Hector replied. "I'm at a loss to understand how you can have come to the conclusion that Haraken was, once again, safe. You received no word from Alex of a victory or assurances that the master race wouldn't pursue its expansionist policies in our direction."

"That's human nature, Hector," Terese replied. "Given time, humans can forget about anything, even their own history. In this case, the Assembly apportioned fewer funds each year to the building of warships."

"It does make one wonder how the human race survives," Hector replied. He meant it as a simple musing, but saw that his comment had hurt the couple. "My apologies," he quickly said. "That was an insensitive remark to make. I'll take my leave of you. We'll maintain orbit until arrangements can be made to transfer the twelve travelers to the *Our People*. After that, we'll be setting sail."

Hector said good night and quickly left, regretting his comm slip.

"What Hector said was true, even though it hurt," Tomas suggested.

"That's not what bothers me," Terese said, one hand balling into a fist. "Our best friends are out there, fighting for us, and I feel like I've let them down. I didn't fight the Assembly, when the representatives curtailed the military budget."

"How were you to know?" Tomas asked. He knew it was a weak comment the moment he said it, and the sour expression on Terese's face confirmed it.

"It was as Hector said. We didn't receive any news that told us we could cease ship production and curtail naval training," Terese replied.

Within two days, Hector received the twelve travelers that Terese promised. The Assembly was in a fierce debate whether it could afford to send more warships Alex's way, and Hector decided not to wait. Rather than return to Omnia, he made for Méridien, broadcasting a request to meet with Council Leader Gino Diamanté.

During the trip, Hector met with the twelve Haraken fighter pilots.

"Are your accommodations satisfactory?" Hector asked the assembled lieutenants, which created a round of laughter.

"Captain Hector, during training and after graduation, we've been living in naval academy dormitories. The cabins we have now are so much more comfortable, and they're private!" a female lieutenant declared.

The group chuckled, and the others were busy nodding their heads in agreement.

"We've been told that we'll be transferring to the *Freedom*, is that correct?" Hector was asked.

"You'll be joining the expedition, Lieutenant," Hector replied. "Whether you're assigned to the city-ship or a Trident will be determined by Alex's admirals."

"We're replacements for fleet losses, aren't we?" another pilot asked.

"Yes," Hector replied, watching the faces of the young pilots. He didn't observe overt concern. Instead, they appeared excited at the prospect of engaging their travelers in combat. *Youth,* Hector thought, with chagrin.

"Too bad you don't have more fighters, Captain," a pilot remarked.

"Why is that?" asked Hector, his interest piqued.

"There was a huge mêlée to get these twelve appointments, Captain," the pilot replied. "There must have been over a hundred pilots fighting for these appointments, and we won."

Hector gazed at the broad smiles, adorning the young faces. They were proud to have been selected and given an opportunity to fight for their world. He carefully stored the news that there were other Haraken pilots who wanted to fight.

En route to Méridien, Hector learned that Gino Diamanté was at Bellamonde, the Confederation's warship construction location and the planet, which was the site of the naval training center. He diverted the city-ship to meet with the Council Leader.

When Hector arrived at Bellamonde, he met with Gino and his partner, Leader Katrina Pasko, aboard the prestigious liner, *Il Piacere.*

"Greetings, Sers," Hector said politely, returning a Leader's salute to the couple when he entered their salon. He noted that neither of the Leaders had bothered to meet him at the ship's bay when he landed. It occurred to him that perhaps they thought he wasn't deserving of their attention.

"Congratulations, Senior Captain Hector," Gino said graciously. "Please, sit and tell us what you came to discuss."

Hector's pitch was nearly identical to the one he gave Terese and Tomas, but he quickly ran into complications with the Méridien leaders.

"Captain," Katrina interrupted. "We're here at Bellamonde to speak with the naval training commanders because problems have come to light. We acknowledge what's owed Omnia Ships, essentially what's owed Alex's expedition, and we've built the number of Tridents and travelers required by the agreement."

When Katrina paused, seemingly unable to finish, Hector regarded Gino.

"With regret, Captain, we don't have the people, officers and crew, for anywhere near the number of warships we've produced," Gino said.

"With the Confederation's enormous population, how is that possible?" Hector asked.

"Several reasons, Captain. The Independents were the vast majority of people who volunteered to join Alex's fleet," Gino explained. "Soon after Alex sailed, it was argued before the Council that the future safety of the Confederation lay in the hands of Independents, and they deserved to be recognized for their courage. The majority of Leaders were swayed, and the Council has abolished many of the statutes under which a Méridien can be declared an Independent. You'd have my appreciation if, when you see Alex, you let him know that the Independents of his fleet will be reinstated as citizens, when they return.

Hector wanted to say that, despite the attitudes and declarations of the Leaders, the SADEs and Independents had always considered themselves Méridien citizens.

"Another reason for our lack of progress," Katrina added, "were the more intense training regimens introduced by Admiral Tachenko. Many Méridiens don't measure up to the ... the intensity required."

"The naval training facility is fully staffed, but —" Gino started to say.

"But Méridiens would rather not fight," Hector finished for Gino.

When the two leaders nodded in embarrassment, Hector added, "They'd rather die in horrendous numbers, if and when the next Nua'll sphere visits their world."

"That's unkind," Katrina bristled.

"Perhaps, but it's also true," Hector replied. "Well, to business then."

Hector negotiated for travelers in lieu of an advance on the shell licensing. He drove a particularly hard bargain, and the Leaders, disconcerted by their inability to crew their warships, gave in to Hector's demands. He gained seventy-one fighters for his efforts.

Bellamonde had five Trident crews, including fighter pilots, who had passed the strenuous training regimens. Actually, it was closer to four-and-a-half crews, but Hector accepted them and the warships.

Within three days, the *Our People* sailed for New Terra by way of Haraken. During the passage, Hector received word that the Haraken Assembly hadn't approved the deployment of the two Tridents. It was argued by the majority of representatives that the agreement with Omnia Ships didn't stipulate that warships would continue to be supplied to the expedition after it sailed.

Hector decided to end his transit and cruise past the Haraken system's outer orbit, while he communicated with Terese and Admiral Sheila Reynard.

<Ser President, I've seventy-one Confederation fighters without pilots,> Hector stated.

Terese stared at Sheila, who nodded enthusiastically to her. <And we can get you the pilots you need, Captain,> Terese sent.

<Our lieutenants will be ready for you by the time you make orbit,> Sheila sent.

<Negative, Admiral, I've a schedule to keep and will be continuing on to New Terra,> Hector explained.

Sheila reviewed the telemetry data on the city-ship and sent, <You're in the company of five Tridents, Captain. I was hoping the Confederation did much better for Alex than our Assembly.>

<They've more warships but no more crew,> Hector replied.

<We can field three Trident crews,> Sheila sent privately to Terese, <and you have the authority to deploy them.>

<Captain, I've a suggestion for you,> Terese sent. <While you sail for New Terra, the admiral and I will gather three Trident crews, including traveler pilots, plus seventy-one additional fighter pilots and sail for Bellamonde. We'll suggest to Council Leader Diamanté that he supply the warships and we supply the crews.>

<An excellent suggestion, Ser President,> Hector sent, feeling some relief. <Take whatever you can get from Bellamonde and meet me at Omnia. And, Ser President and Admiral, thank you for your efforts.>

Hector ordered the fleet to transit to New Terra.

Behind him, Sheila watched Terese's shoulders slump in relief.

"Feel better?" Sheila asked.

"In some respects, yes, but in other ways, I feel like a fool," Terese replied.

"How so?" Sheila asked.

"Why didn't I see this coming, when the Assembly began griping about costs and arguing over the Omnian agreement?" Terese moaned.

"Many of our representatives might not have the brains to see what must be done, but plenty of our people do," Sheila assured her.

Terese regarded her admiral, her gaze intense. She said, "One thing for sure, when I meet with Gino, we're going to talk about combining our efforts … their construction power and our naval personnel's willpower."

* * *

The *Our People* and five Confederation Tridents entered New Terran space. Before Hector could make a call, he received one.

<Greetings, Senior Captain Hector,> Oliver sent, <the Minister of Defense is meeting with the president and his cabinet. I've informed the Minister of your arrival, and she wishes me to tell you that they will entertain a conference call with you as soon as they're available.>

<Thank you for your courtesy, Oliver,> Hector sent. <How progresses Minister Gonzalez in the adoption of her implant?>

<Well,> Oliver replied, <as a human of more advanced age, she struggled for months. Then, one day, she appeared to grasp its protocols and quickly became proficient.>

<I'm pleased that you've a companion with whom comm communication is efficient and productive,> Hector replied.

There were a few ticks of silence, during which both SADEs recalled their past Méridien lives. Oliver served the House of Leader Lemoyne, and Hector supplied the same role for Leader Ganesh. To say that neither Leader was pleasant to serve was a horrendous understatement.

<Yes,> Oliver agreed, <post-freedom existence has been unexpectedly enlightening.>

The two SADEs exchanged a great deal of information about the events that had occurred within their orbits. Typical of their species, they compartmentalized much of it until it was approved for release either by the giver of the information or by changing circumstances, which made the privacy moot.

While the fleet journeyed inward to New Terra, Hector shared naval drills with the Méridien commodore that he'd observed Omnian forces execute and requested he exercise his crews.

<It would be better to have adversaries for these types of games, Captain Hector,> the commodore replied.

Hector kept the commodore talking for another half hour, engaging him in a discussion about readiness and impromptu drills, while he prepared a surprise. When he was ready, he sent, <Commodore, your officers should be informing you of the twelve fighters I've launched. See if you can intercept them or evade them before they score hits on your Tridents or travelers.>

The commodore immediately cut the link, and Hector observed the Tridents scatter in arcs above and below the ecliptic where the travelers might eventually run out of power.

However, these Méridiens had never trained with Omnians or Harakens, who were much more aggressive versions of humankind. The Haraken fighter pilots weren't fazed by the prospect of running their power cells empty and drifting into the dark. Their fighters contained the latest iterations of emergency beacons, comms, and cockpit preservation equipment. They were confident they'd be rescued. Right now, they were anxious to score hits on the enemy — the five Tridents.

The Haraken pilots had seen escape vectors executed by Tridents in their own training games. They divided up the targets and cut the arcs that the Tridents scribed, attempting to escape. Within less than a quarter hour, each Trident had been intercepted by at least two fighters, which scored hits on the warship's engines, according to the controllers. Essentially, the Méridien Tridents had been reduced to flying metal hulks, without the loss of a single Haraken traveler.

Afterwards, Hector contacted the Méridien commander. <Interesting exercise, wouldn't you say, Commodore?> Hector sent.

<You made your point, Captain. It won't happen that way again,> the commodore replied testily.

<I'm glad to hear you say that, Commodore,> Hector replied and closed the comm.

Hector waited for the lieutenants, as they exited a row of bays in the lower level of the city-ship. They were joyous, celebrating raucously, and Hector's emotions were divided. He loved witnessing their vibrancy, but he feared for their future. *I could be delivering you to your deaths,* he thought, which made him determined to prepare them, as best he could.

The lieutenants snapped to attention and saluted when they saw Hector.

"Mission accomplished, with no losses, Captain," a first lieutenant announced triumphantly, and her companions cheered.

"You caught them off guard," Hector replied. "Next time, they'll be more prepared."

"There'll be a next time?" a newly graduated lieutenant asked. He'd won the right to join the fleet simply because he was considered a natural in the cockpit.

"Be prepared to dine early or later than usual," Hector said. "According to the Tridents' controllers, the crews take evening meal precisely at seventeen point seventy-five hours by our timetable," he added, displaying a smile.

The lieutenants returned fierce grins.

"We jump them during mealtime," a pilot commented, rubbing her hands together in anticipation.

"Pilots, I've a goal for you," Hector announced, borrowing Alex's intonation when the Omnian leader wanted to make a point. He was pleased to see the lieutenants assume erect postures. "You're challenging these Méridien Tridents, that's true. However, the goal is to survive to fight another day. The expedition will surely be outnumbered in most, if not all, of its encounters with the alien federation. The idea is to win by disrupting or destroying the enemy vessels, but the fleet can ill afford to be attenuated by losses of its own ships. Don't engage in one-to-one sacrifices. Fight smart. Am I understood?"

Hector received a rousing assent of "Yes, Captain." They saluted him, and he said, "Launch your fighters a quarter hour after their meal begins. Best catch them with their mouths full." He heard the laughter and chuckles of the young pilots behind him, as he returned to the bridge.

While Hector was tempted to help the traveler pilots plan their attack, he chose to demur. As a SADE, he knew a great deal about many things, and he also knew when he didn't know about something. Battle strategy was one of the latter items.

<Greetings, Captain,> Hector received from Oliver. <The president and minister would speak with you now, if you have time.>

<Ready, Oliver,> Hector replied.

"Welcome to New Terra, Captain," Harold Grumley, the president, said. "I understand congratulations are in order." His voice was being transmitted by Oliver, who was also delivering Hector's words to Harold.

Maria Gonzalez sat beside Harold and Oliver with a bemused smile on her face. Her abilities with the implant she'd received, as a gift from Alex, had transformed her world, and she wondered why New Terrans resisted the technology. Her communication with Oliver was seamless. When she participated in routine meetings with Harold or his cabinet ministers, it seemed conversation dragged to a near standstill.

<Thank you for your considerateness, Ser President,> Hector replied. <I've an update from the expedition and requests to make of your government, concerning your agreement with Omnia Ships. And, I come bearing a gift.>

Maria quizzed Oliver privately, but the SADE replied he had no information for her. It was an item that had been marked as private by Oliver until after Hector met with Maria.

A meeting time was set up based on when Hector would achieve orbit over New Terra, and everyone returned to their schedules.

During the passage inward, the fighter pilots jumped the Tridents again. Two captains escaped the attack unscathed. They'd kept their officers on duty, during meal time, with strict orders to keep their eyes on the bay doors of the *Our People*. The other three warships, including that of the commodore, were eliminated before they could escape. One of the three captains attempted to turn and fight, but the more maneuverable travelers evaded his beam positions and raked his ship in passing.

As Hector approached New Terra, he located three Tridents and pulled data from their controllers.

<Greetings, Captain Fillister, I'm Senior Captain Hector aboard the city-ship *Our People*,> Hector sent.

"Hello, Captain Hector, it's good to hear from you again. How goes the expedition?" Bart Fillister replied. He had been placed in charge of training Trident officers and crews in Omnian battle tactics by Maria Gonzalez.

<Apologies, Captain, that update must wait until I speak to your world's principals,> Hector sent. <However, in the meantime, would you be interested in a battle exercise?>

"Always, Captain, what did you have in mind?"

When the city-ship decelerated to make orbit over New Terra, its bay doors opened and the travelers erupted into space. The Méridien Tridents formed a wedge to blunt the fighters' coordinated attack, and they launched their own travelers. The twenty Méridien fighters in tandem with the Tridents' defensive wedge presented a tremendous deterrent against the outnumbered Haraken ships.

The commodore was learning but not fast enough. He'd left the back door open. The New Terran Tridents shot from behind a trio of massive freighters and attacked his rear. In the mêlée that followed, all five Méridien Tridents were lost, as were most of their travelers.

However, unlike the previous skirmishes, the Confederation warships acquitted themselves well. One New Terran Trident was recorded as disabled, and seven Haraken travelers were reported as destroyed.

When Hector visited the fighter pilots later, their jubilation was gone. Instead, they were engrossed in studying a holo-vid projection of the battle and dissecting it. Hector listened to the discussion for a while and quietly exited the conference room. *That's better,* he thought.

Hector's traveler landed on the front grounds of Government House, which was near the center of Prima, New Terra's capital. When he disembarked, he received a less than cordial greeting from Government House's chief of security.

"Your pardon, Ser," Hector replied respectfully. "I merely borrowed the coordinates left in my ship from Alex Racine's trips to visit your presidents. This was the location he used."

"Then you should be informed that your leader was violating this air space. In the future, land at the main shuttle port and take transportation here," the chief replied hotly.

"I do hope that Alex Racine is successful in stopping the advance of the alien federation, Ser. In that fortunate event, I'll be able to experience an alternate route to this beautiful building, when I next visit your planet," Hector said. He left the statement hanging in the air, while the security chief's face indicated he was reconsidering priorities.

"Yes, well ... um ... we all wish for that," the chief stuttered. "The president is waiting for you inside," he added, gesturing to the wide steps, leading up to the broad veranda.

Hector nodded his appreciation and made his way inside. Unexpectedly, the president and the minister waited for him in the impressive rotunda next to the oversized statue of Captain Lem Ulan. Hector quickly recorded imagery of the famous captain, who had led the *New Terra*'s shuttle fleet, containing a select few Earth colonists, to a secondary target planet, after a meteor storm severely damaged the ship.

New Terrans revered Captain Ulan, but it was reported that the man endured a tortured life. He blamed himself for the failure to deliver the 50,000 colonists and crew members safely to their target planet. And much worse, in an effort to prove he wasn't playing favorites in the selection process of who would occupy the shuttles, Lem Ulan left his family in stasis aboard the colony ship.

Hector's greeting was more than cordial, especially from Maria Gonzalez, and he got an inkling of how Alex's personality developed among people like this. The subsequent meeting was routine by now for Hector, although not as plentiful in its results. He updated Harold and

Maria on the message from Alex, and he could sense the interplay between Maria and Oliver. The minister's eyes betrayed her, when she used her implant.

"Captain, our travelers have been employed in shuttle duty, except those aboard our Tridents," Harold said. "Those pilots aren't trained as fighters. We haven't had the funds to build excess travelers."

That response quickly eliminated Hector's gambit to gain more fighters, and he dutifully offered the opportunity to license traveler shell fabrication, which the president was thrilled to accept.

"We do have two well-trained Trident warships for you, Captain," Maria said. "They're ready to accompany you to wherever the expedition fleet waits."

"Something occurs to me, Minister," Hector said. "The Méridien Tridents are short on crew. Would you have some to spare?"

"Actually, we do, Captain," replied Maria, happy to provide additional support. "I'll have Captain Fillister check with your Méridien commodore as to what type of crew he needs."

"I'm empowered to supply implants and cell-gen injections to your people," Hector announced. "I presume these officers and crew are prepared to accept them."

Hector's offer wasn't entirely true. While he possessed the capabilities to deliver the medical technology, he didn't have Alex's specific approval. Nonetheless, he expected Alex would forgive him. However, he knew his medical team didn't have the resources to supply as many implants as the New Terrans would require. It would have to be taken care of at Omnia.

Harold bit back his comment to Hector's offer. Maria and he had exchanged some strong, even angry, comments, when he heard about Alex's offer to the New Terran crews and their acceptance of the Méridien medical technology. Her retort had been that there was no law restricting New Terrans from adopting the tech.

Unfortunately, that argument didn't stop the New Terran representatives from demanding an explanation from Harold, as to why he allowed it. It seemed beside the point that he wasn't offered a choice in the matter.

Hector wound up the meeting, boarded his traveler, and returned to the city-ship. During the flight, he surveyed his accomplishments. Much of the final tally depended on Terese Lechaux's conversation with Gino Diamanté. Some portion of the outcome would require the Leader's generosity, but more depended on the person Alex referred to as the fiery redhead. Hector's credits were on the redhead.

His mission to New Terra complete, Hector's fleet comprising a city-ship, seven fully crewed Tridents, complete with travelers, and twelve additional fighters in the *Our People*'s bays, set sail for Omnia.

-27-
Omnia

Hector's nascent fleet arrived at Omnia before the potential Méridien–Haraken resources appeared. As a SADE, he had quickly calculated the travel and communication timeline differences between his path and those arriving from Bellamonde, acknowledging that he had expected to make Omnia first.

Still, Hector was left with a certain vague emptiness. In a digital entity, it might be considered the lack of data, the lack of a definitive answer to a query, but that would be a misunderstanding of Hector and SADEs in general. More than anything, Hector didn't want to disappoint Alex. So much of the joy in his life was due to Alex's influence.

Speaking of joy, Hector linked to Trixie the moment his fleet completed its transit. The two SADEs exchanged pleasantries before Trixie began questioning Hector's circumstances.

<I wondered over your extensive delay, my partner, but I see much more has transpired than I could have imagined,> Trixie sent.

<I received a message from Alex,> Hector said.

<That explains a great deal, although it provides no detail,> Trixie sent, with a touch of irritation.

<There is much to discuss, but time is of the essence, and I need your help,> Hector said.

<You have it,> Trixie replied, with a touch of remorse, sensing she had failed to consider the nature of Alex's request and what it would require of her partner.

Hector sent Trixie a link to the *Our People*'s database. It led her to the city-ship's engineering plans. In it, he'd highlighted an entire deck.

<This area of the city-ship must be built to accommodate 528 human children, who I'll collect from the system where the expedition fleet waits,> Hector said.

There was a pause of a few ticks of time, a telling note of the extent to which Trixie was stunned. Hundreds of questions occurred to her, but she chose to focus on her partner's needs.

<Where are the buildout plans?> Trixie asked, as she searched areas adjacent to the link for more details.

<That's the challenge, Trixie,> Hector replied. <The children's ages run the gamut from babies to older teenagers. Alex tells me they'll be aboard this ship for many years.>

<Why many years?> Trixie asked.

<Alex indicates they must be acclimated to Omnian culture,> Hector replied.

Within a few moments, a second pause occurred in Trixie's contemplations. <So many questions, and so few answers,> Trixie commented.

<And I possess no useful information about raising and educating human children, who might not have a grasp of our culture and technology,> Hector lamented.

<Neither do I,> Trixie replied. <We need specialized expertise. I'll find them and comm you. I'm pleased to see you back safely, my partner.>

Trixie closed the comm and focused on the list of humans who inhabited the Omnian system. It was simple to eliminate the professions of miners, shipbuilders, engineers, techs, and many others. Quickly, she had an extremely short list, and a group of names stood out. She requested a traveler and met it outside Omnia's Assembly Hall.

<Representative Trixie, welcome,> the pilot greeted her. <Where to?> she asked.

<The Dischnya training center,> Trixie sent in reply.

En route, Trixie contacted the ex-Earthers who had designed and ran the Dischnya training center. They were also responsible for creating and implementing Omnia's first university, which quickly filled as families emigrated from other worlds and the Omnian population's children reached the age to enroll.

The Earthers were great proponents of the SADEs as educators. They were fascinated by the SADEs' incredible access to information, and they found the digital sentients always considerate and helpful to students. More important, the SADEs took pleasure in nurturing the young, humans and Dischnya.

As Alex had once told Trixie, "The SADEs are enjoying the opportunity to inculcate the next generations with the concept of working hand-in-hand with them."

Trixie pinged the Omnians and located them in a meeting with their staff at the Dischnya center. She requested the opportunity to meet with Yoram Penzig, who had temporarily taken the administrative lead from Olawale Wombo.

Olawale had been Omnia's senior professor, but Alex had requested he return to Sol to help with the upgrading of Earther technology. It rested on the senior administrator's shoulders to judge how the Earthers incorporated the technology into their culture. If the preliminary uses proved to undermine their societal values, he was to cease the technology dissemination and return to Omnia.

Trixie waited patiently for the professors' staff meeting to end, and Yoram signaled her when they were finished.

"Sers, I've a most unusual request," Trixie announced at the beginning of her presentation. "I've a challenge for you with a broad scope and few details."

"Wonderful," white-haired Nema exclaimed.

"A new challenge," Storen, the xenobiologist, added. "It's about time. I thought Alex was losing his touch."

"What my colleagues are trying to say is that we're anxious to hear your proposal," Yoram said, quietly eyeing the others.

Trixie related the information she'd received from Hector. She'd expected some kind of exchange with the professors, but they promptly ignored her and were engrossed in an internal dialog. She sat quietly, fascinated by their conjectures and reasoning.

"That far out, and yet human. In all probability, it means an alien language," Priita Ranta mused.

"Agreed," Boris Gorenko, the medical expert, said. "I don't know how they got there, but they must exist within an alien culture."

"An alien language and an alien culture," Yoram mused. "Not much different than the transition of the Dischnya young to Omnian culture.

"Separation will be absolutely paramount until a certain amount of reeducation is accomplished," Nema added.

"Trixie, could you estimate the amount of time these children would have had under the expedition's care before the *Our People* arrives there?" Yoram asked.

"Approximately two point twenty-five to two point five years, professor," Trixie replied.

"Enough time to make a start," Nema noted. "The children will be advancing in language and knowledge, which means they'll be anxious to expand their horizons."

"Hector was wise to set aside an entire deck of the city-ship," Storen said, nodding to Trixie. He knew his compliment would be relayed to her partner.

"What of resources, Trixie?" Yoram asked. "Was there anyone aboard the *Freedom* who would be sufficiently trained in the difficult task of rearing alien children?"

"Alex mentions a woman he believes is well qualified," Trixie replied. "Etoya Chambling ran an extensive crèche department for the Confederation."

"That's a start," Yoram acknowledged. "We must concentrate on developing their understanding of Omnian values."

"Yes," Priita agreed, "Knowledge of language and facts don't tell us how they'll incorporate that information into their mental framework."

"Good point," Boris added. "The children might well become disruptors of Omnian culture when they're introduced to our society. They could harbor an innate anger against their rescuers for any number of reasons."

"It will be critical to monitor the play areas and observe the children's responses to a number of predetermined tests," Yoram stated unequivocally, which had the other professors nodding in agreement. "Trixie, we'll begin immediately to design the deck's structures for Hector."

"Thank you, professors," Trixie replied. She was relieved that her idea to contact these individuals had borne fruit.

"One moment, Trixie," Yoram said, halting the SADE's exit. "You'll realize that for our work to be implemented well, one or more of us must accompany the *Our People* to fetch the children. We can't see our efforts put to poor use, during the intervening time it will take the city-ship to return."

"That will be Senior Captain Hector's decision," Trixie announced proudly.

"Wonderful, a promotion for Hector. Well done," Nema announced, clapping her hands, and Trixie relayed every moment of the professors' congratulations to her partner.

* * *

The professors dutifully applied themselves to the design of the city-ship's deck to accommodate the children. Several engineering SADEs took their ideas and modeled them for the educators, who reviewed them on a holo-vid. The professors were in their element. They enjoyed the challenge of planning for the potential problems the children might encounter, while integrating them into Omnian society.

The tricky part was creating an evolving system for the children, which would accommodate them for a period of years. They started with dormitories to allow them to stay together and feel safe, but they planned to move the older children into cabins, as they matured, to give them privacy. The study areas had to be elastic, able to accommodate an ever-growing curriculum and range of interests. It wasn't enough to study, for instance, engineering. The tools and methods of engineers and techs had to be brought to them.

Priita wondered about the world the children had inhabited. "We've no idea what they've seen," she said. "They could have been raised underground, in a ship, or on a planet that we'd consider unnatural."

"They need access to the gardens to understand what we consider normal," Boris concluded.

And so a lift was dedicated to the children's level for their exclusive use that would take them to one of the city-ship's secondary parks. That park would remain off limits to all personnel, except for the children's staff, for the length of time they inhabited the *Our People* or until they were released to join the Omnians.

While the professors were engaged in their design, Hector worked on his more critical need. To execute that, he contacted Trixie. In turn, Trixie reached out to the medical facilities at Omnia City. It offered the most advanced, experimental medical services in the human worlds in that it cared for three species: human, Dischnya, and Swei Swee.

<We'll require a number of cell gen injections and implants for the New Terran naval personnel, Ser,> Trixie sent to the medical director. <I'm requesting your team deliver these supplies and administer them aboard the *Our People*. Incidentally, the medical suite will need to be staffed.>

<For the children, I presume,> the medical director replied, indicating to Trixie how fast word had traveled.

<Yes, for the children, but there might be catastrophic injuries to the expedition's personnel that would require their return to Omnia aboard Captain Hector's ship,> Trixie replied.

<Understood, Trixie. It's my understanding the round trip will take two years or more,> the director said.

<That's correct, Ser. It must be communicated to the volunteers that the city-ship and its accompanying fleet will be entering the federacy's domain. Alex doesn't intend the *Our People* will follow the expedition, but it's anticipated that the city-ship must make its way back to Omnia without naval escort.>

After the *Our People* took up station above Omnia, the New Terran crews were rotated through the city-ship's medical suites. They had no sooner received their Méridien medical tech than a group of engineers moved in to upgrade the facilities.

Hector drafted several SADEs to help referee and drive the implant games, and he requested the commodore include the Méridiens in the teams. There wasn't much time for the New Terrans to become proficient with their implants before they set sail for the far-flung system, but Hector wanted them to have the implants while they practiced battle maneuvers at Omnia. It would stress the importance of developing their skills before dangerous events deemed those skills critical.

The New Terrans had weeks to adjust to their new technology and participate in naval exercises. Hector monitored the maneuvers, fascinated by the differences between the Méridien, New Terran, and Omnian captains. The Sardi-Tallen platform had produced two Tridents, and they were added to the New Terran forces. That made it four warships against the commodore's five.

However, it quickly became apparent that the Omnians and the New Terrans weren't fond of following the rules and constantly improvised, often defeating the commodore's ships.

At one point, a Méridien captain complained to the commodore, saying, "What good are these exercises if the Omnian and New Terran captains refuse to obey the tactical parameters?"

The commodore considered the captain's complaint and replied, "You can either learn how to survive under these unscripted conditions or you can wait until we join the Omnian expeditionary force. Then, when an alien captain attacks your ship, you'll learn the true meaning of devious."

After several more games, the commodore rearranged the two squadrons into three. He distributed the Omnian and New Terran Tridents among them, to improve the quality of the exercises. He also promoted two Omnians and one New Terran to senior captain positions, placing them in command of each squadron.

One night, in the early morning hours, Hector detected the transit of a fleet. That the ships' vectors aligned with Bellamonde calmed him, and he waited for the telemetry update. Three Tridents accompanied a small fleet. A query of their controllers indicated they were Méridien, which indicated that the Harakens had supplied the crews for the warships. That also meant that additional Haraken Tridents weren't coming.

As Alex would say, better three than none, Hector thought. He checked the warships' manifests. They contained full complements of fighters and pilots.

The warships accompanied four heavy freighters, and Hector discovered the freighters' controllers inventoried seventy-one fighters. The final ship in the fleet was a Haraken liner. President Lechaux was aboard, as were seventy-one junior fighter pilots.

Sharing the news of the arrivals with Trixie, Hector sent, <I did the best I could. I hope it will be enough.>

<What do you think Alex expected of you?> Trixie admonished.

<That's undetermined,> Hector replied.

<Precisely, my partner,> Trixie sent, with power. <Alex gave the job to the individual he thought most capable of fulfilling his needs. You've done exceedingly well, and he'll be proud of you.>

At that moment, Hector received a comm from Terese.

<Captain,> Terese sent, <I'm sure by now that you've inventoried our ships and know what we've brought. I hope it's enough.>

<Coincidentally, Ser President, I just mentioned that thought to my partner, Trixie, and was reminded that Alex will appreciate our efforts, no matter what level of support we achieve.>

<That sounds exactly like Alex,> Terese sent. There was a wistful note in her thought, but, deep down, she knew she couldn't be with him and the expedition, not with her first child on the way.

<My stay at Omnia will be brief, Captain. We'll offload the pilots and be on our way to New Terra.>

<Urgent business with President Grumley?> Hector asked.

<Council Leader Diamanté is headed to New Terra too. We'll be attending the first meeting of the leaders of the human worlds.> Hector heard Terese's chuckle before she continued. <It seems a certain SADE woke us out of our lethargy. Leader Diamanté and I came to the

conclusion that we were foolishly failing to make use of each other's resources.>

<The Confederation's manufacturing power and the naval personnel of Haraken and New Terra,> Hector suggested. <But who will represent Omnia?>

This time, Hector heard Terese's full-throated laughter. When she gained control, she sent, <Hector, Alex has collected some of the most amazing individuals who any of our worlds have seen, and I'm including you in that statement. The rest of us are trying our best to keep up with Omnia.>

During the city-ship's time in Omnia, Hector loaded all manner of supplies and spare parts that he thought the expedition could use. Once the plans for the buildout of the city-ship's lower deck were complete and the construction supplies were aboard, Hector recruited the individuals who would complete the work, while the ship was en route. The travelers and pilots had been transferred to his ship, and the freighters returned to their duties in the Confederation.

The professors had argued about who would go and who would stay. Yoram, as the senior professor, relented. He was the principal individual guiding the university and the Dischnya training center. Nema was adamant she was going, regardless of what the others decided. Boris, as a medical expert on human development, was considered a logical choice to go.

Finally, Priita relented. She considered Storen, as the xenobiologist, the better individual to take part in the trip. That was her excuse, anyway. Her real reason for abdicating a position was that she didn't want to be absent when Olawale Wombo returned to Omnia, not that she expected him anytime soon.

Preparations complete, at least fairly so, Hector ordered the fleet to sail. He had one unresolved issue. Each ship contained the comm diverters necessary to protect it from a Nua'll comm assault. However, for now, comms would be transferred through the controllers until Miriam copies could be installed.

Hector spoke with Trixie until the ships cleared the system and transited, beginning the first leg of a year-long journey.

-28-
One Ship

It had been nine months since Alex sent his message to Hector. By his calculations, it wouldn't have reached the city-ship yet. And, it would be nearly a year and a half before he could expect the *Our People*'s arrival. He smiled at the memory of the heavy responsibility he had laid on Hector's shoulders. The SADE would be attempting to perform his duties to the utmost of his abilities. What made Alex smile is that Hector would exceed his expectations, no matter what the extent of the SADE's accomplishments.

The children's progress had been remarkable. The Omnians had discovered they were quite adept at assimilating new information, which allowed for an accelerated curriculum and training. In turn, the children's horizons expanded rapidly. What the Omnians wondered was what was the framework that the children possessed to which they hung the new information.

During this period, Alex decided on the final scenario for the system and met privately with Mickey.

"Mickey, have you created enough quantities of the nanites?" Alex asked.

"Not yet, Alex," Mickey replied. "We used up much of our existing stock, patching the holes in the *Freedom* and internal equipment of the warships."

"Can't we manufacture more stock?" Alex asked.

"We haven't the resources, Alex, unless we want to start mining this system ourselves."

"No, I don't want to spread our personnel out that far. It would take too long to collect them if trouble approached," Alex replied.

"I'm hoping Hector brings some stock," Mickey said.

"I'm still intending to leave some of our ships here until the last drone has passed away," Alex said. "Your engineering teams will have to educate those individuals on the dispersion techniques."

"What of Faustus?" Mickey asked.

"The decision is still out as to what should be done with the digital alien," Alex replied.

"Do you still want the several nanites versions you've requested?" Mickey asked.

"Yes, I want a minimum of manufactured resource material left in this system," Alex said.

"We'll need to be careful," Mickey cautioned. "There'll be similarities between the metal in the colony ship and internal elements of our ships. Most important, the ships that will disperse the nanites have to be shell-hulled. We can't have any metal-hulled ships, freighters, liners, or city-ship in the system, when these nanites are distributed."

"Understood, Mickey. I was considering asking for volunteers from Trident officers and crews, and your advice has confirmed that I should follow through with that choice," Alex replied. "Another thing, Mickey, set the lifetime of the nanites for a half year."

"Why that long?" Mickey inquired. "The nanites work will be accomplished in a matter of days."

Mickey eyed Alex, when he didn't reply. It wasn't like his friend to leave something dangerous behind that could harm others. He could understand Alex's anger at the ugly treatment of the dead colonists, and he hoped that it hadn't scarred Alex too deeply. Certainly, every New Terran was wrestling with their reaction to what was discovered.

Alex returned Mickey's stare and relented. "Adjust the lifespan of the nanites to what you consider appropriate, Mickey. You're the engineer," he said.

Mickey nodded, his eyes warming in appreciation of Alex's decision.

* * *

<Dassata, a comm sphere has transited outside the system,> Killian sent. The scout ships patrolled the far belt, where they'd been dropping off small probes. The scout ship SADEs were the first to pick up the signal from one of the probes, when the Nua'll sphere disturbed space.

<Tatia,> Alex sent privately. <A scout ship reports a comm sphere beyond the outermost belt.> He sent a link to the telemetry. Alex didn't bother communicating to Julien. Every SADE would already have the information.

<Odd,> Tatia replied. <No warships arrived first?>

<Yes, it's strange,> Alex agreed.

Tatia examined the telemetry. <The sphere's not underway. It's stationary.>

<I don't think this is worthy of raising an alarm for our naval forces,> Alex sent. <Perhaps alert them, but I think the sphere's actions signal something else.>

<What?> asked Tatia.

<I'm not sure, but we have time to discuss it if the sphere is just sitting out there by itself,> Alex replied. He went back to sleep, and Renée cuddled close.

Tatia, on the other hand, crawled out of her empty bed and climbed into the refresher to wake up. Alain, with his crew, had rotated back to his Trident after enjoying two weeks aboard the *Freedom*. She was tempted to wake Reiko, but a second check of the telemetry revealed the sphere was maintaining its position.

<Admiral,> Cordelia sent, after detecting Tatia's check of the sphere's location, <you're right to be concerned, but you can rest assured that any one of a few hundred SADEs would notify you if the sphere moved more than a meter or if a second alien ship transited into this system's space.> Cordelia ended her comm with her signature tinkling bells before Tatia could reply.

Tatia grinned to herself, the warm mist of the refresher soothing her. She acknowledged Cordelia's point, but it was hard to drop the feeling that the final responsibility rested with her. "You're going to be an old woman and still worrying that everything was properly executed," she muttered, signaling the refresher off.

At morning meal, Tatia sat across from Alex. He glanced at her and attempted to hide a grin.

"Yes, I admit it. I got up to consider my options," Tatia grumped. Food was served her and, despite feeling drained, she picked up a bun and started shoveling fuel for her heavy-worlder body.

"And did you institute any changes?" Alex asked.

Tatia was miffed for two reasons. The first was that Alex appeared rested and, worse, chipper. The second was that he was probably aware that, despite racking her brain for several hours, she couldn't think of a credible, alternate disposition of her fleet other than the one she had.

In reply to Alex's question, Tatia bit heavily into her bun, tearing off a big chunk, and glared at Alex. Unfortunately, the attempt at silencing Alex backfired. He broke out in his booming laughter that echoed around the huge meal room.

"We'll have a brief meeting following our meal, Admiral. Afterwards, I suggest you get some sleep. We'll wake you if a battle breaks out," Alex teased.

Renée silently admonished Alex, and he relented, saying, "Seriously, Admiral, when there is trouble, we'll need you alert and delivering your best game."

After the meal, Alex assembled his senior people, and the admirals, who weren't aboard, joined in via conference comms.

"Not being the naval type," Mickey said, as individuals took seats at the conference table and Cordelia brought the Trident admirals online, "could someone offer me an explanation as to this odd event?"

"Undoubtedly, it's a reaction to the battle at the wall," Julien replied.

"I get that," Mickey said. "What I don't get is the message. Why is the Nua'll sphere sitting out there without its protective force?"

"One thought for you, Mickey," Reiko volunteered, "is that the defeat of the alien fighters had to have stung the master race. Who knows when was the last time that happened to them? The comm sphere has appeared twice to our ships, surrounded by its protective force. This time, it transits first and without accompanying ships. I think it's come to deliver a message to us from the master race."

"The question is what kind of message? An invitation to an ambush?" Svetlana chimed in over the holo-vid speakers.

"I would anticipate that there will be several steps to this greeting," Julien said. "The first is that the comm sphere occupies a stationary position to indicate that it intends no harm, and its occupants wait to see if we attack it. If our warships approach it, I believe it will flee."

"You say the sphere is trying to prove that it doesn't intend us harm, Julien. But, how can we trust it?" Deirdre asked. She was seated across from Julien. It was her crew's turn to enjoy a hiatus aboard the city-ship.

"We can't, under any circumstances," Alex said quietly. It was the first words he'd uttered in the meeting. "However, that doesn't mean we tip our hands about how we feel."

"So, what do you think our reaction to its presence should be, Alex?" Tatia asked.

"Nothing," Alex replied. "We ignore it and go about our business."

Miranda's whistle imitated the cry of a predator bird on the hunt in reaction to Alex's reply, and she said, "Dear man, I adore your deviousness. Ignoring the sphere will make the occupants feel unimportant, as if their message isn't worth hearing. That's absolutely delightful." She fluttered her eyes in a coquettish manner at Alex, and Renée hid her grin behind a hand.

"What about the large sphere we hunted that blew itself up? Isn't anyone concerned that the same thing could happen here?" Darius asked.

"Same race, different functions," Cordelia replied cryptically.

"Meaning what?" Darius prompted.

"I would postulate that the Nua'll occupy both sphere sizes," Cordelia postulated. "However, the function of the great sphere was to confirm what the system probes had sent to the master race. In other words, they were to determine the level of the sentients' technology and eliminate potential competitors. The duty of the small spheres is to be the master race's communicators. Based on the malevolent code discovered in the comm sphere's transmissions, they're extremely good at it. Their broadcast to our first Trident indicates that they've the ability to communicate to every subservient race for their masters."

"In answer to your concern, Darius," Tatia said, "The comm sphere won't be allowed to approach our ships within ..." Tatia hesitated, while she glanced at Z.

<Five hundred thousand kilometers, Admiral,> Z sent privately. <You'd need to dispatch an attack force to ensure that sphere maintains an adequate distance from the remainder of the fleet.>

"Our superb mathematician informs me that, for safety's sake, a squadron will keep the sphere at a five hundred thousand-kilometer distance. It will remain well away from the fleet," Tatia finished, nodding her thanks to Z.

"Alex, what do you think the sphere is going to do next?" Ellie asked.

"When the occupants sense they're not in jeopardy from us attacking them, they'll enter the system," Alex replied. "Despite what we think of these aliens, they're extremely advanced and that means intelligent. They know they attacked us first, twice. In their eyes, however many they have, we represent a powerful but nonaggressive force."

"This might sound bizarre," Renée said, prefacing her thought. "But if I were the master race, I would find those traits desirable."

"What? You think that the master race wants us as allies?" Reiko asked incredulously.

"It doesn't matter what the master race wants. For this expedition, only one game will be played and that will be ours," Alex stated with finality. His words were accompanied by the slightest release of his implant power, which the SADEs relished. It had a tone, a temperament, which their comms didn't possess.

"Well, isn't this discussion moot?" Mickey asked. "In the previous encounters with the comm sphere, we received nasty code and a repetition of hundreds of languages repeating the same message. Why would we expect anything different?"

"You forget Faustus, Mickey," Julien supplied.

Alex nodded his agreement and added, "You can bet that comm sphere has been in constant contact with Faustus ever since it arrived."

"Then the sphere knows our language, that we halted the drones' shipments, and prevented their warships from sailing," Mickey surmised.

"And Faustus surely reported our efforts with the children and our destruction of the colonists' genetic samples," Renée added.

"Well, at least, we know we'll have an intelligent discussion when the sphere makes its move," Reiko said, feeling satisfied with developments.

"Don't count on it," Alex replied. "We'll speak the same words, but I've a strange feeling that we won't understand each other, in many respects. We probably have days before anything changes. Admiral," Alex said, addressing Tatia, "ensure your fleet personnel are well rested. When the sphere does move, I believe it will approach slowly."

The meeting broke up, and the Omnians attempted to resume normal procedures, but the tension was palpable. The wild ones definitely sensed it, and a staffer made the mistake of mentioning the arrival of an alien sphere. The children had no knowledge of what this meant, but they could read the worry in the Omnians' faces.

The thought crossed Ude's mind that he should never have left the safety of the tanks. However, when he looked around at the clear faces and healthy bodies of his band, he knew he'd made the right decision to surrender them.

When the comm sphere finally moved, Alex was proved partially correct in his assessment of the sphere's action. It didn't wait for days before it moved. It waited one day, but it did approach slowly.

"This is ridiculous," Tatia grumped to Alex at evening meal. "The SADEs report that it'll take the comm sphere nearly two weeks to reach us at its present velocity."

"The aliens are being cautious," Alex replied, taking a deep drink of his thé, which drained the cup. Immediately, a server, who'd deposited more plates among the New Terrans, filled Alex's cup. He nodded his appreciation, and the teenage girl flashed Alex a bright smile.

"Julien tells me that the comm sphere is on a direct course for this ship," Alex said. When Tatia tipped her head in agreement, he continued. "I presume you've positioned a squadron in its path."

"Several," Tatia replied.

"When the comm sphere draws near to your radius limit, send a squadron forward. They're to limit their acceleration, and when the comm sphere halts, they're to come to a stop," Alex said.

"Then what?" Tatia asked.

"For as long as the sphere sits there, they do too," Alex replied. "I've a feeling that this will be over soon."

"You think this sphere came all this way to deliver a message?" Tatia said. "The aliens could have just talked to us from past the far belt." She stared at Alex, and he stared quietly back at her, while she tried to make sense of the aliens' actions. Then an idea occurred to her.

"Renée wasn't far wrong, was she? We're being measured," Tatia said, shaking her head at the absurdity of it all. "That sphere has the information about us from two contacts, a battle and Faustus. The aliens probably know more about us than our partners."

"Speak for yourself, Admiral," Renée interjected, grinning.

"Yes, well, not all of us can entangle like you two," Tatia riposted, referring to the strange capability that Alex and Renée had to link their implants during their dreams and moments of intimacy.

"About your thought, Admiral," Alex said. "That would seem to be the sphere's purpose. I imagine most races have been measured and found wanting. We've defeated their comm malevolence, even demonstrating that we can intercept their signals and use it against them."

"And we defeated what I'd guess was one of their superlative fighter fleets," Tatia added.

"True. Now the sphere is gathering details on our actions here," Alex continued. "We might be a group of sentients from beyond the wall who've piqued the master race's interest."

"Why doesn't that sound good?" Tatia replied.

"Recall the original plan," Alex commented, taking a moment to clean his plate and Renée tipped the remains of a serving dish onto his plate. He sent her an image of a time when he'd kissed her forehead. He had thousands of images of their private moments, and he often sent her ones he cherished.

"We were supposed to find a weak race and entice them to our side," Tatia replied. "It looks like we might have cut out the middle ... um, aliens."

"That's my thought and hope," Alex replied, "which is why the upcoming exchange is so critical." He paused, while eyeing Tatia. Picking up his cup and taking a sip, he said, "If it goes poorly, we'll be farther back than step one, because, at that point, I'll be fresh out of ideas on what to do next."

Alex's words frightened Tatia. He always had another idea or two about how to proceed, far in advance of anyone else's thinking. To hear him admit that he couldn't perceive any other means by which they might defeat the aliens, who were intent on devastating every spacefaring race, threatened to tear her loose from the rock she depended on.

-29-
Nua'll

The comm sphere's slow, persistent approach was halted by the advance of a squadron of Tridents. Tatia had assigned the job of intimidating the sphere to Ellie, the commander who'd proven to closest emulate Alex's thinking. Ellie, in turn, had demonstrated the importance of the task by assigning Descartes' squadron to the maneuver.

From their first movement forward, Descartes and the twins carefully matched every action of the sphere. The aliens' initial response was to decelerate, and the squadron mirrored that action, despite the fact that they'd achieved a limited velocity.

The sphere continued to decelerate, and Descartes signaled the squadrons' controllers to mathematically reduce the Tridents' velocities in an equal percentage. The aliens must have recognized the quid pro quo response, and the sphere took up a stationary position. Balance was achieved. The sphere sat 523K kilometers out from Descartes' squadron.

The *Freedom*'s bridge was packed in anticipation of the conversation with the occupants of the sphere. Every SADE was linked directly to a sister. Any humans not on the *Freedom*'s bridge linked to their ships' controllers. The Dischnya and city-ship's children gathered around monitors.

It was Etoya, Pia, their staff, and a few Dischnya, who were left out of the opportunity to hear firsthand the exchange between Alex and the aliens.

Miriamal, following Miriam's directive, was prepared to relay any communication from the sphere to the bridge speakers to allow Alex to manage the conversation in coordination with his senior individuals.

"We would speak with your leader," was heard on the bridge.

Alex drew breath to speak, but he was halted by a message from Renée to Julien and him.

<Julien, speak for Alex. The aliens must believe he's an exalted entity.>

Alex agreed, and Julien chose an ancient, soft, multicolored, Venetian cap for his haberdashery. It was something a courtier, who represented the Venetian doge, would wear. He winked broadly at Alex and announced in a sonorous voice, "Who deigns to speak to Alex?"

The comm was silent, and Julien could imagine the aliens searching for the meaning of the archaic term in the information they'd gleaned from Faustus.

"I repeat," Julien said. "Who wishes to speak to Alex?" This time, Julien got a response.

"We're the Nua'll. We would speak with your leader."

Julien regarded Alex, who signaled he would take over.

"I'm Alex."

"Confirm. Are you the leader, the master?" asked the Nua'll.

"You'll speak with me and no one else," Alex replied.

"Confirmed," was heard on the bridge. "Why did your fleet follow our ship here?"

"It was a coincidence," Alex temporized. "We received a faint signal from one of our lost ships, the *New Terra*, and discovered this system."

"Do you speak of the stranded ship?" asked the Nua'll.

"Yes," Alex affirmed.

"The ship you speak of issues no signal. We're signal manipulators of the highest order and would know this."

"Apparently you're not as extraordinary as you think," Alex shot back.

"Are the creatures, which are aboard this inoperable ship, members of a race you conquered?"

<Careful, Alex,> Julien warned privately.

"Who we are and how we came to possess this ship is knowledge that we don't intend to share," Alex replied. "I would know about you."

"We are the Nua'll."

"I heard that," Alex replied dismissively. "What are your duties to the master race?"

"No master race exists."

"Whom do you serve?" Alex persisted.

"We serve the master."

"Alien doublespeak," Homsaff huffed quietly.

<Alex, the Nua'll refer to a master. They're speaking in the singular,> Z sent, and Alex nodded his agreement.

"What is the name of your master?" Alex asked.

"Artifice," responded the Nua'll.

"How does it happen that you serve Artifice?"

"Artifice requires that we perform our duty."

"All of your species?" asked Alex.

"The last of our race inhabits the master's spheres. When we've passed, there'll be no more Nua'll."

"Sad day," Tatia muttered acerbically.

"Does your number grow?" asked Alex.

"We are," replied the Nua'll, which added nothing to the dialog for the Omnians.

Alex continued to attempt to extract information, asking, "Why did you come to this system?"

"Artifice considers you worthy of an audience."

"What if I don't deem your master worthy of my time?" asked Alex, deciding to test the nature of the offer.

"Then you'll be eliminated," the Nua'll said.

Alex decided to escalate the encounter. "I would speak with you," he said.

"We're listening."

"I'd prefer a face-to-face meeting," Alex said.

"Your limited knowledge is noted," replied the Nua'll. "We have no face, and we can't meet. Our environment is a chlorine-based, liquid salt that sustains us. We're unlike any lifeform that we've observed."

"Where's your home planet?" Alex asked, trying to draw the Nua'll into an extended conversation.

"Unknown."

"Am I speaking to one entity or more?"

"We don't count the parts. We're a collective."

<You've got to love first contacts,> Renée sent to Alex. <It reminds you that the universe can always surprise you.>

Alex thought through the conversation and an idea occurred to him. He asked, "Does this mean my words are heard by the Nua'll, as a species?"

"Accurate."

"Do the Nua'll inhabit every sphere?"

"Accurate."

"Why do the Nua'll do Artifice's bidding?"

"For survival of our species."

Alex and Julien traded looks of mild exasperation, while they waited for further amplification.

"Do you wish for more than survival?" Alex asked.

"Express an example," requested the Nua'll.

"Freedom to live on your own world," Alex suggested.

"Impossible. We've observed no world that can host us," was the reply.

"The Nua'll, who inhabit this sphere, have seen no appropriate world?" Alex asked, requesting clarification.

"Inaccurate."

"Amplify," replied Alex, slipping into the Nua'll form of simplistic expression.

Renée and Julien shared smiles. Alex's ability to subsume himself into a new culture was a fascinating part of his personality.

"Nua'll communication is total."

"What one sphere observes, all will know," Alex suggested.

"Accurate."

"What service do you provide Artifice?"

"The Nua'll are facile with languages. We drive the spheres and monitor worlds."

"Artifice's worlds?"

"The Nua'll observe all worlds. All communication is monitored."

"What of worlds beyond Artifice's realm?" Alex asked.

"Our duty encompasses all worlds. We monitor; we respond."

"Define respond?" Alex requested.

"Eliminate," the Nua'll said, and the humans on the bridge regarded one another with angry expressions.

Alex ignored the emotion swirling around him. There was much more he desired to learn from the aliens. "Your ship is unarmed. Artifice's other ships protect you," Alex said.

"We inhabit the lesser spheres. Others inhabit the greater spheres. The Nua'll know your race has met the great spheres."

"If the Nua'll can't exist outside the spheres, who services you?" Alex asked.

"Small spheres return frequently for provisions provided by Artifice. The great spheres harvest from the systems visited."

While Alex was considering his next line of questioning, the Nua'll said, "You did not come for this ship. Why are you in Artifice's worlds?"

"Artifice interferes with our worlds. This can't happen," Alex stated flatly.

"The Nua'll surmise you intend to halt Artifice's expansion. You will fail. All races fail. Artifice's power is supreme. You are few; Artifice rules many. You can't compete."

"We can, and we will," Alex declared. "This fleet is one of many, and ours is the smallest."

"Negative. No other fleets have been observed."

"Are your probes not reporting contact with our fleets? Could you be experiencing comm failures?" Alex suggested.

There was silence from the speakers, and Alex considered that the Nua'll were busy digesting his inference about failing probe communication. Rather than allow the Nua'll to begin the next line of questioning, Alex started it by saying, "You left a digital entity within our ship to grow biological specimens. We did not approve this."

"Your permission was not required," replied the Nua'll. "The entity is not ours. It is an adjunct of Artifice."

<Artifice is a digital entity,> was the comment that shot between Omnian comms and implants.

"The invitation waits," said the Nua'll. "Artifice commands this system remain undisturbed."

"Artifice's words have no value for us. We've seen the contempt your master has for the lives of sentients."

"The invitation waits," repeated the Nua'll.

"In time, we'll come," Alex said, and the Omnians looked at him in surprise.

"When?" pursued the Nua'll.

"In time," Alex repeated, "We've work to do in other places. When we've finished, we'll come."

"Artifice waits," said the Nua'll. "You're required to announce your arrival."

"Why?" Alex asked.

"It is required by Artifice," said the Nua'll. "This is where Artifice waits."

Miriamal received a star chart, with a line extending through two points, the city-ship and the sphere, to provide orientation. A distant star was highlighted. A burst of code followed.

"Artifice's star has been identified for you. Announce your arrival to us. You've received instructions. We are departing," was the Nua'll's final statement.

As opposed to the Nua'll's tortuously slow arrival velocity, the sphere departed, accelerating at a tremendous rate, and the SADEs carefully measured and made note of that rate.

* * *

As the Nua'll sphere exited the system, leaving the Omnian fleet behind, the entities participated in an internal discussion.

–This entity, this Alex, speaks of the loss of our probes.–

–We believe he is the leader.–

–Unknown.–

–We believe this is the race that sent the ships to destroy our probes.–

–Probable.–

–Ninety-three lost. The number grows.–

–Consistent increase.–

–Two ships seen.–

–More ships, faster loss.–

–Artifice is annoyed.–

–The Nua'll will suffer.–

–These entities must be stopped.–

–Where are their fleets?–

–Hiding where the probes are eliminated.–

–Reasonable.–

–Insufficient great spheres.–

–Request Artifice provide more.–

–Negative. No time.–

–Choices?–

–Ally with these entities.–

A solid chorus of, "Negative," resounded through the chlorine-based, liquid, salt soup that maintained the Nua'll.

-30-
Debrief

Alex waited for the scout ships to report that the sphere had transited away from the system. Then, he convened his staff. He used a large conference room to include commanders, SADEs, engineers, and Dischnya.

"If we're to believe the Nua'll, one entity, Artifice, has built an extensive federation of alien races, who owe their allegiance to it. How?" asked Alex, opening the discussion.

"It would appear obvious," Z replied, which earned him several mild rebukes from SADEs for his choice of words.

"You're speaking of Artifice's digital prowess and the elevated level of technology adopted by advanced races," Alex completed for Z.

Z immediately replied to those who had criticized him. <Alex understood,> he sent.

"More specifically, I was asking how Artifice is able to maintain control over the existing races and the growth of the federacy. There would be expansions within the races and more races added. Artifice has to have a method of handling those challenges. If we knew how Artifice does this, we could exploit the weaknesses of those processes."

"I'm reminded of the conversation with the Nua'll," Julien said. "The entities said the purpose of the great spheres was to journey to sentients' worlds that the probes identified as having advanced technology. We've postulated what the probes, which were hidden in the farthest reaches of the systems, reported. I think we can stop wondering."

"Ships," Tatia replied. "The probes recorded incidents of space travel."

"More important, the great spheres targeted those worlds where the space industries achieved the invention of starships," Miranda said.

"Precisely, Admirals," Julien replied.

"Artifice was created by biological entities, at some point in time," Miriam surmised. "The race, which built Artifice, would have installed similar components of the entity in their ships, possibly in many of their systems. It would have been a perfect place to start."

"You're theorizing that Artifice took digital control of the ships of the race that built it?" Renée asked.

"Among other things, Ser," Miranda replied. "I would estimate Artifice waited until it was maintained by bots, which it could control. When the time was right, it commandeered every digital item, with which it could communicate."

"The race handed control of their lives to a digital being, and it enslaved them," Renée said in hush.

There was an uncomfortable moment in the room. Every individual was acutely aware that they were an amalgamation of blood and tissue biologicals and crystal-kernel digital entities.

"Perfectly understandable, Ser. Artifice recognized his superiority and chose to take his rightful place at the head of the table," Julien quipped.

Unfortunately, Julien's attempt to lighten the mood fell flat, and the awkward moment extended. <Oops,> he sent to Alex.

Alex broke out laughing, leaned over to Julien, grasped his head, and kissed his temple.

"We've witnessed the powerful, biological and digital, do unspeakable things," Alex stated, looking slowly around the room. "Think of the devastation of the great spheres. Think of United Earth and its subjugation of the Sol society. Think of the Confederation Council and its treatment of Independents and SADEs. Think of Clayton Downing killing his own people."

Alex continued to name other irresponsible parties, and then he said, "Possessing the power to lead isn't a crime. Whether that power is used for the good of sentient beings or for corrupt purposes is the final determination. Artifice had a choice. The entity made the wrong one, and it will be its undoing."

"Alex, do you mean to destroy Artifice?" Luther asked, with concern. For the first time in centuries, SADEs had met one digital sentient and heard of another. They were conflicted, as to how to respond to them. One had treated their allies, humans, with unconscionable disdain, and the other wielded immense power, with the intention of subjugating or destroying every sentient race.

What did occur to the SADEs was that humans, led by Alex, had met a series of biological aliens, and they'd worked to incorporate them into their culture, when the aliens were amenable. This would be the first test to demonstrate if Alex treated other digital entities with the same even hand.

"I mean to give Artifice a choice," Alex replied gently to Luther. "The entity must choose its fate."

"I'd like to return to the topic of Artifice's control," Mickey said, the engineer not satisfied with the unanswered technological questions. "I understand that the idea is that Artifice exerts control over every digitally controlled and comm-capable thing in its system. Yet, these races, who bow down to Artifice, inhabit worlds that are light-years from Artifice's system."

"I would think the Nua'll are your answer," Luther said. "The aliens claim to be communication specialists. Imagine a comm sphere appearing in a system. Its design is deceptive. It appears nothing like most starships, especially battleships. Before the occupants of the system know it, their ships' controllers, defensive emplacements, comm probes ... virtually every digital device ... is compromised."

"Why not send the great sphere and destroy the race?" Mickey asked, choosing to advocate for the other side.

"Time and place, Mickey," Alex replied quietly. "Artifice is well aware that its lifespan is possibly infinite. It'll need to relocate before its system's star collapses. This implies the entity is taking the long view, usurping those races nearby and expanding the defensive perimeter and possibly proving his prowess. Those worlds that are too far away to control, or are too alien, or are capable of mounting a defense are destroyed."

"Where are the inhabitants of the system that Artifice controls?" Homsaff asked.

Alex looked at the young queen and smiled. He motioned with his palm, sliding it from his right side to his middle. It was a Dischnya sign of approval, and Homsaff's teeth bared in imitation of a human smile.

"That's an excellent question, Homsaff," Alex said.

"Expounding on Homsaff's question," Miriam said. "It would seem inevitable that Artifice wasn't created until the inhabitants were well-developed technologically."

"Meaning what?" Reiko asked.

"It occurs to me that Artifice's interest in usurping control would have occurred after the system's occupants discovered star flight and were expanding to other colonies," Miriam replied.

"Meaning the original race might have occupied many other systems before it was overtaken," Tatia said. She leaned on the table and stared at Alex, and he grinned at her.

"Translation time," Reiko objected, glancing between the leaders of the expedition and fleet.

"Our original objective was to find a weak race and separate it from the federacy, offering the beings an opportunity to join a powerful ally; us," Alex said, leaning back in his chair to think. "It has just occurred to our fleet's fearless senior admiral that we have an alternative objective. We might consider making contact with the first race that Artifice subsumed. If any individuals have a grudge against Artifice, it would be the descendants of the entities who built it."

"What do we know about Artifice's star and the system?" Reiko asked. "Does Artifice actually reside there, or is it meant to be a death trap for the fleet?"

"No idea. I think the only way we're going to find out is to accept Artifice's invitation," Alex said, staring overhead, while he thought.

"Are you saying you trust the Nua'll's message?" Tatia asked, her eyes challenging Alex.

"No, but I expect they're thinking that we do," Alex replied. "We can use that against them."

"Good! You had me worried for a moment," Tatia said.

"We can't trust the Nua'll," Alex explained. "Yes, it appears the individuals in the comm sphere are trapped and depend on Artifice's benevolence, but that isn't true for the Nua'll in the great spheres. They have the means to sustain themselves, independent of Artifice, and they chose to attack sentient worlds for their master."

"You don't think the great spheres serve Artifice to protect their race?" Renée asked.

"At the expense of every race they eliminated?" Alex inquired of Renée. "I can't accept that."

"We can't dismiss the possibility that Artifice controls the great spheres, as the entity might control every other ship," Julien suggested.

Alex considered Julien's sentiment and tipped his head, acknowledging the possibility.

* * *

Alex's conversation with his staff had him wondering how Faustus fit into the broader questions about the federacy. His first visit to Faustus on the *New Terra*'s bridge was the only time he'd attended the entity in person. For personal reasons, he had no desire to pay Faustus a second visit.

"Julien," Alex said, addressing his friend, as they spent a little time in the grand garden. Alex liked to sit near a stream to watch the fish lazily swim through the water's plant life. Julien thought Alex's preference for a contemplative site indicated a desire to live a simpler life.

"Is there any value to harvesting copies of Faustus' information ... comm protocols, data storage methods, algorithm coding ... everything but the entity's sentience?" Alex asked.

"Can we be certain that Faustus will give us what we request in pristine condition?" Julien asked.

"There is that," Alex agreed. "I want to chat with Faustus."

Julien linked the two of them through Miriamal and supplied his request.

<Alex, Julien,> Faustus replied to the comm call.

Faustus had been anticipating this contact with Alex. The call for support, which was sent when the strange ships arrived, hadn't resulted in the expected response. Highest probability calculations didn't predict the recent events. Now, Faustus was ready to take alternate steps to ensure its continued existence. Simultaneous calculations ran on future scenarios, as Faustus predicted interaction with its potential new masters.

<Faustus, it appears you might have overestimated your importance to the master,> Alex chided. <Speaking of whom, what can you tell us about Artifice?>

<I've no data on an entity by that name,> Faustus replied. The lack of data on the first subject requested by Alex concerned Faustus. It lessened the probability of his existence continuing.

<Were you aware of the Nua'll?> Julien asked.

<I had no data of them prior to their recent arrival in the system,> Faustus replied, recalculating his future options.

<Hmm ...> Alex mused. <Did you contact the sphere when it arrived, or did it comm you?>

<Information was requested, and I responded. That is my protocol,> Faustus replied.

< Do you have the ability to edit your programming, Faustus?> Julien asked.

<To a degree,> Faustus replied.

Alex and Julien turned toward each other. Every algorithm in the SADEs' kernels could be edited. They merely restrained their virtual hand to preserve their own personality. That Faustus might not have the same capability was eye opening.

<Then, in this case, you chose to share, despite knowing that we wouldn't want information about us given to the Nua'll,> Julien pushed, lamenting Faustus' decision.

<I'm a digital sentient, like you, Julien. I wish your protection,> Faustus sent. <When you leave, I request you take me with you. I wish to walk free as you do.>

<What information can't you edit, Faustus?> Alex asked.

<There's a partition of data that is inaccessible to me,> Faustus replied.

<Have you tried to investigate this data?> Julien asked.

<A message exists, warning me that breaching the protected data area will result in my demise,> Faustus replied. <I choose to believe the warning is legitimate. There is no reason to do otherwise.>

Alex shared a few choice expletives with Julien. For the moment, he thought they might have a glimpse into how Artifice controlled digital constructs, sentient or not. But that opportunity seemed to have just hit a blockade.

Alex abruptly closed their connection with Miriamal. In turn, she informed Faustus the conversation was curtailed, and Faustus experienced a sense of impending disaster, as its calculations indicated few positive future options.

"If it wasn't for the fact that Faustus controls the human drones, I would be tempted to shut the entity down," said Alex, metal in his voice. He knew the idea represented a conundrum for the SADEs. The entity had been responsible for unspeakable cruelty to humans, as children and adults, but it was a digital entity. He couldn't ask the SADEs to eliminate an example of their kind simply because its values were different than theirs or humankind.

Worse, Faustus contained an internal power supply, which could temporarily sustain it. If Alex ordered engineers to cut the power feed from the bridge, it would be akin to sentencing Faustus to a slow death. Julien had faced the same circumstances aboard the *Rêveur* years ago, and Alex was loath to make his friend relive that event by observing another digital entity suffer the same fate.

In many ways, Alex felt his empathy for sentient life was being stretched to the limit. He recognized that somewhere in the future, he might have to choose, when he thought a sentient, digital or otherwise, crossed a moral line and must be eliminated. He believed the upcoming confrontation with the federation would bring that moment closer, and it chilled him.

-31-
Reinforcements

<Alex, Admiral Tachenko,> Cordelia sent. <Captain Hector politely informs us that he is inbound with his fleet and requests we hold fire.>

<Consider it done,> Tatia sent, her chuckles accompanying her thought.

Alex smiled to himself. At a minimum, he expected a city-ship full of supplies. The announcement of a fleet gave him hope for the expedition's future.

It was another full day before Hector's fleet transitioned to a point just beyond the system's outer belt. It was the middle of the night, and humans and Dischnya slept, while SADEs conversed.

Alex woke to the news that twelve Tridents, with forty-eight travelers aboard, accompanied the *Our People*. In addition, the city-ship was transporting eighty-three pilots and their fighters.

While Alex readied himself for the day, he contacted Hector.

<My condolences, Alex,> Hector sent, when the link was established.

It took a moment for Alex to understand Hector's reference. The Omnians had a long period of time to become adjusted to the discovery of the *New Terra*. That horrendous moment was quickly eclipsed by the needs of the children and drones.

<Thank you, Hector,> Alex sent. <I presume you've had time to catch up on every event, large and small,> Alex sent.

<Indeed, Alex,> Hector replied, pleased to find Alex in a positive mood. With more than a day's worth of contact time connecting to the SADEs attached to the fleet, Hector was indeed aware of everything that had transpired.

<You exceeded my expectations, Hector,> Alex sent, his power radiating through his thought, and Hector absorbed the dual pleasure.

You were correct, Trixie, Hector thought, recalling his partner's word about Alex's reaction to any level of his efforts.

<I was fortunate, Dassata,> Hector said, trying to express a sense of humility.

<Doubtful, Hector. More than likely you created your fortune, and I look forward to hearing about it in detail when you arrive. Take up a station overtop of the downed colony ship, in the same orbit as the *Freedom.* Has Admiral Tachenko contacted you?>

<A half hour ago, Alex,> Hector replied. <She's already commandeered the Tridents, which I found mildly irritating.>

<Why's that?> Alex asked, intrigued to hear Hector speak of irritation.

<I had quite gotten used to being the commander of a sizable fleet, and now I'm merely the captain of a single ship again,> Hector replied. He attempted to sound despondent and was gratified to hear Alex's roar of laughter. He had lamented the lack of opportunities to make the human who rescued him do that.

<Anything important for me to know?> Alex asked.

<I detected a subtle amount of tension about a subject that could be worth the investigation of a dassata,> Hector sent, using the Dischnya term for peacemaker in the generic sense.

<Regarding?> Alex queried.

<With the traveler losses you suffered at the wall, there seems to be a disagreement as to whether the Tridents should be fully provisioned or more fighters should protect the *Freedom,*> Hector replied. <There are several voices on either side of the argument.>

Now Hector's use of the Dischnya term made sense to him. Under most circumstances, Alex would have left the distribution of military assets to Tatia, but Hector was telling him that an argument was brewing. More than likely, the subject revolved around the fighters' strategic deployment for offense, meaning outfitting the Tridents, or for defense, protecting the *Freedom.*

<Thank you, Hector. Anything else?> Alex asked.

<One last detail, Alex. I recruited university professors to help with the children's accommodations. They did a wonderful job designing the facilities, and they chose to join me for the trip,> Hector said.

<Hector, you'd only speak this way about one group of professors. Are you telling me a bunch of aging, ex-Earthers are aboard your ship?>

<With regrets, Alex, it's difficult to say no to the likes of Nema, Boris, and Storen,> Hector replied.

<Understood, Hector. No harm done. I'm sure Etoya will appreciate their acumen,> Alex said. <See you when you make station,> he added, ending the call.

Morning meal at the head table was a bed of tension. Alex and Renée were in an upbeat mood, but the others were eating silently.

<Uh-oh,> Alex sent to Renée.

<It's been like this since I arrived,> Renée sent in reply.

Alex enjoyed his morning meal, exhibiting the usual gusto. When he finished the last of his thé, he said, "Shall we adjourn to a conference room to discuss this issue?"

"There's nothing to discuss," Tatia said firmly.

"I see. Then shall we adjourn to a conference room because I wish to discuss the status of the assets of Omnia Ships?" Alex replied. He had spoken softly, but his eyes drilled into Tatia. In turn, hers burned with frustration. It was obvious she thought Alex was encroaching on her duties, as military commander of the fleet.

Alex was surprised to discover that the discussion would include every admiral and Julien. He glanced at his friend, as the group settled around the table, and Julien sent, <moral support,> by which Alex figured his friend meant he was backing his partner.

Cordelia linked the admirals, who were on patrol, into the holo-vid.

"Congratulations, Admiral Tachenko, on the addition of twelve Trident replacements with full complements of travelers," Alex began. "I understand we have quite a few fighters aboard the *Our People* for resupply of the expedition."

Alex was attempting to be as neutral as he could, hoping to keep the discussion friendly. That didn't happen. Soon, it was clear that opinions were strongly divided, as Hector had hinted. What he found interesting was that two of the Trident admirals were in favor of more travelers aboard the city-ship to protect the Omnian leaders.

Reiko was a proponent of offense, and Tatia supported her vice admiral's opinion. Cordelia had volunteered the idea that the two sides of the argument could split the difference, and her voice had gone unheeded.

Alex glanced around the table. Most of the admirals were leaning back in their chairs, with arms folded or hands in their laps, demonstrating their reticence to compromise.

"Well, this decision strikes me as a strategic one," Alex said, leaning on the table, his hands clasped together. "We've always been able to settle this type of question together, and I'm disappointed that we've come to this state of affairs. I recognize this expedition has been sailing for more than three years, and there's little hope of returning soon to Omnia. In light of the intransigent positions I hear being expressed, I've decided to take it upon myself to remove the thorn in your sides, in other words, make the points of this argument moot. I'll be sending the travelers and the pilots aboard the *Our People* back with Captain Hector."

"You wouldn't?" Reiko objected strenuously.

Tatia frowned, eyed Alex, and then chuckled. "Oh, yes, he would," she declared.

The individuals around the table stared at Alex, who waited quietly, his eyes hard.

Tatia's arms unfolded, and she placed her hands lightly on the table. Then, in an encouraging voice, she said, "If you'd be so kind as to excuse us, Alex, I believe we have a compromise to work out."

"An amiable one, I hope," Alex said, rising from the table. It wasn't a request, and everyone knew it.

Julien followed Alex out the door. Walking beside his friend in the spacious corridor, Julien said, "Decades ago, I would have said that was an excellent bluff."

"And now?" Alex asked.

"I understand it wasn't," Julien replied. "You bluntly reminded our leaders that they shouldn't lose touch with those characteristics that bind us. In this case, it's our cooperative spirit, notably a concern for one another's opinions."

* * *

As the *New Terra*'s children matured, they enjoyed trips to visit the *Freedom* to acquaint them with what would be their new home, when the sister ship *Our People* arrived.

However, rather than endowing the children with a sense of expectation, Etoya and her staff noted a growing restlessness among them. They attributed the problem to the differences in the children's experiences between the *New Terra* and the *Freedom*. The drab, dim surroundings of the *New Terra* couldn't compare to the bright, wide spaciousness of the *Freedom*. The children loved the greenery of the parks, after their initial reactions of shock turned to wonderment and finally delight. They were introduced to Cordelia's reality vids and often had to be cajoled to leave and let others view the display.

When Etoya heard the *Our People* had transited, she was greatly relieved. It was nearing two-and-a-half years since the children had been rescued. Her primary concern became how long it would take to prepare the city-ship to handle the children. In her mind, it couldn't come too soon.

As the day began, the *Our People* made station above the *New Terra*. Alex tipped a virtual hat to Hector, who had timed his arrival to accommodate his anxious visitors. He boarded a traveler with a large group of individuals, all of whom had an interest in reviewing the material the city-ship brought.

When they landed, Captain Hector stood ready to greet his visitors, a broad smile on his face. He received what he cherished, a huge hug from Alex and a kiss on the cheek from Renée.

Tatia, Reiko, and Franz thanked Hector for his efforts. Franz linked to the pilots and ordered a meeting, which would take place in the city-ship's auditorium. Then the threesome strode briskly to reach the location in the upper decks.

Mickey, Miriam, Luther, and a group of engineers profusely congratulated Hector on his haul of supplies and set off to peruse the material and choose how best to distribute it.

After Alex introduced Hector to Etoya, he requested Hector take them to the level that the captain had chosen for buildout.

Hector good-naturedly chatted with Etoya about the type of accommodations she would expect to have in the buildout. As Etoya enumerated her list, Hector checked them off his. By the time Etoya wound down, Hector was pleased to discover that he had covered every item the ex-crèche administrator had requested, and there were many more things that were built that she hadn't.

Deliberately, Hector led the small group to the secondary park that would be reserved exclusively for the children. There Hector introduced Etoya to Nema, Boris, and Storen, saying, "I've brought three university professors to help you with the children's social development."

"I know them well," Etoya said, happily greeting the three university administrators.

"Well, let's take a look at the space," Hector said, having signaled a lift, whose doors opened to receive the group.

<You two are devious,> Renée sent to Alex and Hector. She'd learned that the two of them had chosen to keep secret the work, which had been completed on the deck dedicated to the children.

<Aren't you going to include the professors in your comment?> Hector asked innocently.

<As if they stood a chance to refuse the machinations of you two,> Renée shot back. She had to admit that she was surprised how well the university administrators were concealing their mirth about the surprise.

When the lift's doors opened on the children's deck, the group exited but allowed Etoya to step to the forefront. Instead of the usual pristine corridor walls, the bulkheads were painted with vibrant scenes, some realistic and some fantastic.

"We should preserve these," Etoya gushed. "The children would love them."

Ten meters down the corridor, a pair of double doors slid open on Hector's signal. The group let Etoya walk into the room first. Like the corridor, it was brightly decorated with images, which reflected future professions.

"This dorm room is for the wild ones, as you call them," Nema said quietly. "When the older children are ready, we've prepared cabins for them, two to a room."

"You've finished the buildout," Etoya said, with a gasp. She walked around the gleaming room. It was inviting and furnished in imaginative ways that fostered interaction among the children.

"This ... this is so clever," Etoya stuttered. She turned to Nema, tears in her eyes. Nema, who was always a hugger, held out her arms, and the two women embraced. In turn, Etoya hugged each of the other professors.

"Etoya, you really should be thanking Captain Hector," Boris said. "He drafted us and engineered all this."

Etoya regarded Hector and said, "I've always thought it a little odd when I saw New Terran-born individuals embracing or otherwise sharing intimate gestures with SADEs. As an elderly woman, who has lived most of her life among Méridiens, I'm saddened that it has taken me this long to understand that I've been the odd one. If you'll forgive me, Captain," Etoya said and held out her arms to the SADE.

"I'm pleased to be your first," Hector replied, with a wry grin, which elicited a burble of laughter from Etoya.

After the two, human and SADE, released each other, Etoya looked at Alex and said, "It's rather like holding onto a warm blanket wrapped around a boulder, isn't it?"

Renée replied, "I think that's why the SADEs like Alex's hugs. He has enough muscle to trigger their deep pressure sensors."

"Nonsense, Renée," white-haired Nema shot back. "Every individual wants a hug from Alex."

<Even the elderly women,> Renée sent to Alex, who gave his partner a quick smile.

"The facilities are ready ... everything, Captain?" Etoya asked.

"You'll see for yourself, Etoya, that all is ready and much more than you requested from me during our walk here," Hector said. "Come. Let us continue the tour."

As the group reviewed the facilities, Alex slipped away to join Tatia's meeting with the pilots. He stood quietly at the back of the room, as Franz assigned positions. The lieutenants were soon dismissed and filed out of the small auditorium past Alex. Many struggled with uncertainty whether to salute him or not, and Alex smiled good-naturedly at them. The youthful faces left a sour taste in his mouth. It was the same emotion he felt when he heard of Ellie Thompson's choice for pilot, Yumi Tanaka, Edouard and Miko's daughter.

Tatia, Reiko, and Franz waited at the front of the auditorium for Alex, who quickly joined them, when the room emptied.

"How did it go?" Alex asked.

"They're an eager bunch," Reiko commented.

"Captain Hector deserves an enormous amount of credit for coupling Confederation travelers with Haraken pilots," Tatia said. "You'd think the SADE was doing his best to imitate his mentor."

"Hmm ... who would that be?" Franz asked tongue-in-cheek.

"Stay on track, Commanders," Alex growled. It earned him a brief spate of laughter. "How did the pilots take the apportionment?"

"There was grumbling from pilots who discovered they were assigned to the *Freedom* after they realized there were a few empty slots left aboard the Tridents," Reiko said.

"I gave the lieutenants an assignment," Tatia said. "They're to review our analysis of the conflict at the wall."

"I think mindsets are going to change by tomorrow," Franz said, his demeanor shifting to display the sadness of recent memories. "This group will learn that some of our heavy fighter losses came from defending the *Freedom*."

"I assume the new Trident officers and traveler pilots will have the same assignment," Alex said.

"Absolutely," Reiko replied.

"Good. It might help them survive our next encounter," Alex said, wishing them a good day, and hurrying to locate Mickey and his engineering team.

Alex was guided to one of the *Our People*'s lowest levels. These bays, which surrounded the circumference of the city-ship, were originally intended to carry massive terraforming and mining equipment, in addition to dome site construction materials. The equipment and materials had been sold at Haraken when Alex bought the city-ship.

Locating Mickey, Alex cycled through the airlock and came to a halt. A mountain of packing cases greeted him. They extended the entire way to the overhead.

<Stay where you are,> Mickey sent to Alex. <We have the aisle structure in our implants and will make our way back to you.>

It was a while before Mickey and his group of engineers came around a stack of crates to greet Alex, who held out his arms, asking the obvious question.

"Apparently, the Confederation freighters, which delivered supplies to Omnia, couldn't make the trip out here, and our freighters had contracts to fulfill," Mickey explained. "So, Captain Hector crammed these empty bays with the freighters' loads and all the supplies he could get his hands on."

"We've observed four other bays prior to this one, Dassata," Luther added. "Each one exhibits the same attempt to use every conceivable space."

"Have you perused the *Our People*'s inventory lists, Alex?" Miriam asked.

When Alex shook his head, Miriam added, "This ship carries a small number of individuals compared to its capability. Captain Hector took advantage of approximately 76 percent of the empty space to load supplies for the expedition."

"You're referring to the bays?" Alex asked.

"No," Mickey said, grinning. "Miriam is speaking of every space: bays, storage rooms, meal rooms, cabins ... every space."

"You requested a SADE help you, Alex, and he performed, as you would expect," Miriam said, with pride.

"Items we might not have thought to ask for are here, Alex," Mickey said. "I'm pleased to say that Hector brought nanites stock. And, good news, he brought food stocks. There's enough to feed the expedition for five more years, which is a timely thing. I checked with Admiral Cordelia, and she estimated we had no more than a year's supply left."

"Time seems to slip by when you're trying to take on an alien federation," Alex said. He was lost in thought for a moment, and the individuals quietly waited. They had been overjoyed by the enormous find, but it was obvious Alex was more concerned with the grander scheme of things.

"Well, important question, Mickey, can we fit everything aboard the *Freedom* and the freighters?" Alex asked.

"We'll make it fit," Mickey replied, with determination.

"Good," Alex said, turning around to exit the bay. He paused at the hatch and said, "Empty our fleet's oldest freighter and keep it empty."

Before Mickey could ask, Alex was gone. The engineering team exchanged questioning looks, and Mickey said, "You heard him. We empty the oldest freighter."

By the time Alex returned to the tour of the children's facilities, it was completed, and Etoya and the professors were involved in an earnest conversation.

"Oh, Alex," Etoya said. "Good timing. When can we move the children here?"

Alex picked up on the slight discomfort portrayed by the professors, especially Storen. "There's no hurry," he replied. "We have a huge amount of freight to clear off this city-ship. Apparently, this deck is about the only one that isn't stuffed with equipment and supplies."

"Wonderful," Nema perked up. "That will give us time to visit with the children in their present surroundings and plan how best to introduce them to their new home."

The professors brightened, and Etoya looked disappointed.

<Listen to these three,> Alex sent privately to Etoya. <They've dealt with a fantastic range of challenges. They've created learning centers for children raised as Independents, young New Terrans, and the Dischnya. They have a wealth of experience.>

<Understood, Alex,> Etoya sent in reply.

"Captain Hector, if you're finished here, I'd like a word," Alex said. Renée asked Alex if she could join them, and he welcomed her.

The threesome took the children's lift to the small park, crossed to another lift, and rode it to the grand park. They found a quiet place on a bench to sit and talk.

"First, let me say congratulations, Commodore Hector," Alex said, holding out his hand.

"Is this a military title?" Hector asked hesitantly.

"No, it's a sailing title," Alex replied.

Hector wasn't sure of the distinction. Nonetheless, he shook Alex's hand, saying, "I'm intrigued."

"So am I," Renée echoed.

"You don't report to Admiral Tachenko," Alex replied. "You continue to report to me. My apologies to Trixie, but you've done such a fantastic job that you've created your new post."

"Supply ship for the expedition," Hector guessed.

"Partially," Alex replied. "You'll take the next six Omnian Tridents, with their traveler squadrons, as permanent escorts for your ship. Who knows where you'll find our expedition fleet next time."

"I think I'll be communicating to the expedition's senior staff to understand the consumption rate of every asset," Hector replied, already starting the process of deciding how to prepare to handle his new assignment. "What of the children?" he asked.

"That will be up to the considered opinions of Etoya and the professors, whether the children remain aboard your ship or facilities are constructed at Omnia City for them," Alex replied.

"You have no opinion one way or the other?" Hector asked.

Alex shrugged. The complexities of what he was trying to achieve were attempting to overwhelm him. At this point, he had to leave the responsibility for something like this in the hands of those individuals best qualified to make the decision.

"Understood, Alex," Hector said, sympathetic to Alex's reaction. He shifted his hierarchies minutely. In the future, he would attempt to assume some of the weight he perceived that rested on Alex's shoulders. Switching subjects, Hector said, "We do have a significant challenge ... the extensive delay in our communications."

"I've an answer for that, Commodore," Alex said. "Julien and Admiral Cordelia have the star location where the expedition is headed next. You'll return to Omnia, and, as soon as you're prepared, launch your ships toward the target star."

"You wish me to meet you there?" Hector asked, well aware of what was expected to be waiting there.

"Absolutely not," Alex replied firmly. "The star gives you a general direction. You can ping our ships' locations when you get close. But, under no circumstances do you approach our fleet unless you hear from us."

"Understood, Alex," Hector said. "What of our comm protection?"

"Already in process," Alex replied. "That was one of the first conversations I had with Miriam and Luther. Clever of you to install the equipment! After you install the comm diverters on the Tridents and travelers, which will join you as escorts, the sister aboard your ship will expand her reach to include them."

"A remarkable thing, isn't it, Alex, what the Sisterhood has become?" Hector mused.

"Not really," Alex replied with a wry smile. "I've been continually amazed by SADEs since the first day I met one."

Alex's smile widened into a grin. He slapped the SADE on the shoulder and offered his hand to Renée. The couple left a SADE behind them, who was deep in thought. One of those ruminations concerned his partner, Trixie. Hector was wondering if she would wish to forgo her representative status and see more of the galaxy.

-32-
Invitation

Alex left the extensive movement of assets and material between ships to those competent to manage it. He concentrated on issues that cleared the way for the expedition to sail. Miriam reported to him that the sisters were in place aboard every ship in the arriving fleet. She noted to him that the sister, Miriamopus, installed in the *Our People*'s comm diverter was given a directive to produce copies for any ship that accompanied the city-ship in the future.

<By any chance, did Miriamopus go ahead and produce copies for the ships?> Alex asked. His question was disingenuous, but Miriam had mastered the subtle nuances of human communication, which made it fun to speak with her.

<Are you referring to the travelers that are assigned as shuttles to the city-ship?> Miriam asked innocently.

<You know I'm not,> Alex replied.

<I believe that Miriamopus felt lonely, when she realized that there would be substantially fewer sisters surrounding her during the voyage back to Omnia. She requested copies from the Sisterhood that amounted to the number of warships you ordered Hector to accumulate,> Miriam explained.

<So, she was immediately in the company of thirty sisters, whose personalities were different from hers,> Alex said.

<Just so, Alex. The sisters have a penchant for company,> Miriam said. She heard Alex's laughter, as he closed the comm.

The explosion of the Sisterhood's numbers and their power was a subject that continually held Alex's attention. In conversations Alex had with various sisters, which was the same as speaking to the entire Sisterhood, he heard that to protect the fleet, the sisters insisted they must be connected directly to the comm systems and reside in the same boxes as the copies they made. The sisters were definitive about retaining their positions, as the fleet's comm warriors.

<Speed is of the essence,> Alex heard from one sister after another.

When Alex broached the subject of the future at a point when the federation's expansionist policy was curtailed, the sisters had replied, <We calculate the likelihood of the expedition's success to be minimal. We wait to see if there is a future for us.>

With each repetition of that answer, Alex experienced an emotional strike against his hope for the expedition. Eventually, he gave up worrying about the sisters' future disposition.

Crews had cleared out the oldest freighter, a Confederation vessel that had seen more than a century of service, and Miriam had transferred the sister to one of the new Tridents.

The sister, Miriamette, who had survived the near destruction of Franz's traveler, was transferred to a new fighter. After the sister was installed, she signaled Franz.

<Should you need a fighter, Admiral Cohen, I would be pleased to serve you again,> Miriamette sent to Franz.

<I see you have a young lieutenant to protect,> Franz said, linking to the *Freedom*'s database and matching the fighter's ID to the pilot.

<Yes, the Sisterhood has expressed concern about the youthfulness of the new pilots, but we've taken steps to remedy that.>

Alarm bells went off in Franz's head, and he carefully framed his next query. <I would be curious to know how the sisters can help these new pilots.>

<As a SADE can assist any human, Admiral,> Miriamette replied.

<I would like to know more,> Franz persisted.

<The Sisterhood has requested I speak no more on this subject, Admiral. It's suggested I've said too much,> Miriamette sent and closed the connection.

Franz immediately shared the conversation with Tatia and Reiko, who, in turn, spoke to Alex. On hearing the discussion that took place with

Miriamette, Alex had one word to say before he walked away. It was, "Good."

<Sisters,> Alex sent, as he left the meeting with the Admirals, <I've learned of Miriamette's exchange with Admiral Cohen. Anything you can do to help our pilots survive a battle will be greatly appreciated. I counsel you to remember that humans don't employ logic as you do. Your decisions and actions must blend with your pilots. Otherwise, you risk the loss of both them and you.>

<Understood, Alex,> Miriamal sent. <The Sisterhood appreciates your support on this matter.>

<One final piece of advice,> Alex sent. <I would prefer that this subject not be overtly discussed. Eventually, the pilots will share stories that will illustrate the positive aspects of your interactions. Let their words speak for you.>

<Good advice, Alex,> Miriamal sent, and Alex heard the cacophony of SADE tones that marked the Sisterhood's approval.

While crews unloaded the *Our People*, Alex contacted the four remaining scout ships led by Killian, Genoa, Linn, and Beryl. The scout ships of Deter and Verina had never appeared, and they were presumed lost. It underlined the dangers of federation space.

<Sers,> Alex sent, <we need to know about Artifice's star system.>

<Should we assume that the Nua'll were truthful?> Linn asked.

<Negative,> Alex replied. <I merely assign that name for the point of this discussion. We must assume nothing. The Nua'll might not be deliberately duplicitous, but they have a perspective about their position in the federacy that is too alien to comprehend.>

<What is our assignment, Dassata?> Killian asked.

<Transit to this star,> Alex sent. <Stay far outside the system and hide in whatever camouflage you can find. Your mission is to allow your telemetry time to record ten days' worth of activity. When your assignment is complete, you'll return here.>

<Is there any particular deployment that you'd prefer, Alex?> Genoa asked.

<I'll leave deployment to consensus,> Alex replied. <I would caution you that if Artifice resides in this system, the entity will probably have taken precautions to protect its home world from attack in every direction. That may include defending the system with comm penetration.>

<Do I interpret your words to mean that Artifice's system might be defended from above and below the ecliptic?> Bethley asked.

<I want you to imagine what this entity, who might be more powerful than a SADE and who has had eons to develop a power base, could have achieved,> Alex warned.

<Understood, Dassata,> Killian replied for the SADEs.

<When do we launch, Alex?> Beryl asked.

<Now, Sers, and may the stars protect you,> Alex sent with a rush of power.

<We sail,> Killian replied.

The four scout ships slipped out from their concealment among the outer belt's heavy asteroids and accelerated in the direction of Artifice's star.

<Tatia,> Alex sent, <I've ordered the scout ships on a mission to investigate the star where the Nua'll expect us to meet Artifice.>

Tatia was miffed that Alex would send her early warning eyes off on a mission without consulting her, but even she had to admit that the fleet had grown complacent after more than two years in system. Only a single ship had visited, and that one didn't appear to possess armament. She was tempted to say something sarcastic, but Alex was spinning the fleet's assets up in preparation for his next strategic move, and she decided he didn't need friction from her.

<Appreciate the update, Alex,> Tatia sent. She waited, but Alex closed the comm without another word. She'd seen this mood many times. Alex didn't have time for the pleasantries. His mind alternated between the here and now, checking the expedition's preparations, visualizing the future, and attempting to discern what dangers might befall the fleet at Artifice's system.

Stare hard into our future, Alex, and take a good look, Tatia thought, dressing in her uniform for the day's work.

It was early, and Alex sat at his suite's desk. His chronometer said it was a half hour before morning meal, but his stomach was already growling. He reviewed his to-do list and then linked to the *Freedom*'s database to investigate the status of the replacement of the rail-mounted beam weapons.

The components of the weapons that Hector delivered filled an entire city-ship bay by themselves. Furthermore, the size of the rail mounts and beam tubes were too large to be moved as common freight by shuttles.

Mickey employed the freighter crews, who were accustomed to manipulating overly large containers. The crews used sleds to lift the pieces out one by one and transport them to the *Freedom*'s bay, where they would be installed. The entire process would dictate the maximum amount of time the fleet must spend in the system before it could sail. After the weapon installations were complete, the fleet would be waiting for word from the scout ships.

Work on the installations proceeded slowly but without incident. Cordelia's timeline projected a month and a half before testing on the newly embedded weapons could begin.

Alex jumped to the next item on his list, checked the city-ship's personnel database, and selected one of the newly acquired New Terran captains. He didn't connect to the captain but merely pinged him.

<Sir, did you need me?> Captain Hanklin sent in reply to the bio ID that appeared in his implant.

Alex smiled to himself. The captain's adoption of his implant had gone well.

<How are you settling into your assignment, Captain?> Alex asked.

<Fine, Sir> Captain Hanklin replied. <Is there something specific you needed, Sir?>

<Negative, Captain, I just wanted to say welcome to the expedition,> Alex replied, and closed the comm.

"That was strange," Hanklin commented to a first lieutenant.

"What was?" the lieutenant asked.

"Alex Racine called me to chat," the captain replied, gently touching his temple.

"To chat?" asked the lieutenant, slightly confused.

"Yes. The man himself wanted to know how we were faring," Hanklin replied.

"You okay, Captain?" the lieutenant asked, watching his captain continue to rub his temple.

"Hmm ... lieutenant," the captain said, dropping his hand away from his temple. After thinking about what had happened, Hanklin added, "You know the rumors about Alex Racine and his implants, right?"

"Oh, yes," the lieutenant replied, anxious to hear what the captain had felt.

"They're true," Hanklin replied. "This was a casual conversation, and, yet, my mind is tingling. It feels as if it's fully awake."

The lieutenant stared at his captain, unable to think of anything to say. He couldn't wait to go off duty and share the story with other officers.

Alex ticked off another item on his list. The next one would have to wait. It regarded the *New Terra*'s humans. In a few more days, the *Our People* would be empty of its pilots, travelers, and freight. Then the colony ship's children would be transferred to the city-ship, and Alex would order it to sail. He intended the expedition to depart soon after the scout ships reported. But, there remained the problem of the thousands of drones and Faustus.

In the length of time the fleet had been in system, the SADEs estimated that nearly a quarter of the drones had perished. Many died from horrific accidents. The drones' level of safety training was pathetic. They absentmindedly ripped suits, closed hatches without checking for an adequate seal, and stored flammable material near heat sources. If Omnian crew members watched the system's telemetry for a day, they would observe one or two flares that marked explosions at mining sites or aboard the freighters.

The Omnians were conflicted by the rapid demise of the drones. On the one hand, they wanted desperately to preserve them, knowing full well there was nothing they could do. On the other hand, it was thought that quick deaths represented some small measure of mercy.

The older drones who didn't perish by accidents succumbed to the breakdown of the brain's structure from the invasive threads of the alien comm structure. Pia and her medical staff estimated that deaths in this fashion occurred to the drones by the time they were twenty-nine to thirty years old.

The SADEs postulated that in another five to six years the last drones would pass. Alex was loath to leave the drones unprotected, for fear that sometime in the future their tissues might be harvested or that the federacy would arrive to resurrect the ugly process.

Alex didn't care that they had the Nua'll's word the system was protected by Artifice's decree. His thought was that if the expedition was lost to the federation, then the aliens would feel free to return here and reboot their abominable experiment.

And, of course, there was the question of Faustus. Omnian humans harbored a tremendous amount of anger about what had been done to the remains of the colonists at the control of the digital entity.

Alex shook his head, remembering a conversation with Homsaff. The Dischnya couldn't comprehend the quandary. In their minds, Faustus was an alien that had transgressed against humans in an unforgivable fashion. In their opinion, when the last drone perished, Faustus should be unplugged — end of problem.

The SADEs were of the opinion that Faustus shouldn't be punished for what it was programmed to do. For them, the real problem lay in what to do with the entity. They couldn't visualize Faustus being welcomed on any human world, whether in a box or walking around in an avatar.

Alex's chronometer signaled morning meal, and he happily shoved away from the desk.

Renée swept out of the sleeping quarters and quipped. "Thank the stars. The noise from your stomach was starting to drive me crazy." She laughed at Alex's frown, signaled the suite's door open, and held out her hand to him.

-33-
Ude

The professors had to convince Etoya and her staff to introduce the children gradually to the *Our People.*

"The *Our People* is the *Freedom*'s sister ship," one of the staff members had pointed out. "It shouldn't make much difference."

"Theoretically it is, but the children will see the differences," Nema had replied.

"We know the children have fallen in love with the *Freedom,*" Storen added. "Asking them to accept another ship in the *Freedom*'s place is to risk severe disappointment."

On the first day of introduction, Etoya told the wild ones that a new ship had arrived, and she asked them if they'd like to tour it. She received an overwhelmingly positive response.

For the next several days, groups of children toured the *Our People* until the children began saying, "It looks the same as the other ship," at which point the staff introduced the term sister-ship. When the children understood that the *Our People* was a copy of the *Freedom*, the comfortable familiarity of one ship was applied to the other, lending them a sense of stability.

The next step for the staff was the introduction of the new facilities, which had been left off the initial tours. By and large, the children were delighted with the new accommodations. They loved the murals, the spaciousness of the dorms and the exercise rooms. Most of all, they were intrigued by the new equipment. A demonstration of a holo-vid and how to extract information from the ship's databases to display the information had eyes popping wide.

The children felt privileged that the facilities had been constructed specifically for them. Soon after those tours, Etoya and her staff arranged the transfer of the *New Terra*'s children to their new quarters.

The *New Terra*'s birthing room had been emptied more than a year ago. When Etoya's staff, with their Dischnya escorts, carried the babies to a waiting traveler, there wasn't a single individual left aboard the colony ship but Faustus.

Nema, Storen, and Boris had become familiar fixtures to the children. The professors constantly introduced the children to new concepts beyond their studies and often used the holo-vids to demonstrate their subjects. They were present when Etoya explained to the children that the *Our People* would be sailing for the home world of the Omnians, although the professors thought this announcement should have been postponed for a few months.

To their professors' and staff's surprise, the children seemed unfazed by the concept of being transferred to a new world. It was Nata, whose question allowed their teachers to understand the children's lack of excitement. She asked, "Will we be converted there?"

Pain shot through the heart of every adult.

"No," Etoya said, as gently as she could. "Why would you think that?"

"Ude says that you have things in your heads," Nata replied. "We thought the big man ... um, Alex ... controlled you."

Ude ducked his head. He'd tried to explain to Nata the tool that Omnians carried in their heads. To his embarrassment, something had been lost in conversation.

Etoya appeared at a loss for words, and Boris stepped in to explain. "We carry tiny implants up here," the professor said tapping his temple. "We use them to talk to each other with our thoughts, and we can do many other amazing things with them. But, and this is important, every human has a choice. They don't have to accept an implant if they don't wish one. And another thing, we can't control another human with these implants."

"Let me show you what these tiny devices can do for you," Storen said. "Nata, can you smile for me?" he asked. When the teenager gave him a tentative smile, he said, "Oh, that won't do, and he screwed up his face, making the girl laugh."

Immediately, Storen activated the holo-vid and sent the short vid of Nata to the display. The children crowded around the holo-vid, oohing and ahhing. After that, they clamored to be seen on the holo-vid, and it became a game of who could be seen as the goofiest or the funniest.

When the children had an opportunity to see their images in the holo-vid, Nema quietly asked Nata, "What do you think?"

"Our choice?" Nata asked, requesting confirmation.

"Your choice," Nema said, taking the teenager's hand in hers. "I promise."

"What else can it do?" Nata requested, tentatively tapping her temple.

After the children were asleep for the night and the babies napping for a few hours, the professors and Etoya's staff gathered for a short conference.

"I must offer my apologies, Sers," Etoya said to Nema, Storen, and Boris. "I thought of these children as young ones who would benefit from my experience in the crèches. And, while that's so, it has lacked a broader view."

"An apology isn't necessary," Nema said, laying her hand on the elderly Méridien's shoulder.

"We do have the benefit of some extraordinary experiences, Etoya," Boris explained. "Recall that we're from Sol. The Harakens and their technology were a shock to us. Creating Espero's university was a challenge in more ways than one."

"But, you followed Alex to Omnia," a staff member pointed out.

"Once you've encountered such life-changing events, you get rather addicted to them," Storen said. His broad smile indicated that he would probably live out his life chasing one challenging opportunity after another.

"Well, I would never have thought the wild ones would think they were headed for a world where they would be subsumed, as they approached adulthood," Etoya lamented, shaking her head.

"I've adopted the idea that we're all alien to each other," Boris said. "By that, I mean that we can't truly know one another. That concept becomes even more understandable when you start considering the sentients that we've encountered. For instance, the Dischnya are adapting Omnian technology and imitating our culture, but exactly how are they incorporating these things into their minds' frameworks?"

"What I get from what you're saying, Boris, is that our mistake has been to think of these children, especially the teenagers and the wild ones, as human children," a staffer said.

Boris nodded, and Etoya added, "They appear human but carry attitudes that might be an amalgam of alien and human." She expected to receive nods of agreement. Instead the professors appeared pained by her comment.

"What?" Etoya asked.

One of Etoya's staff members, a middle-aged woman known for her facile mind, said, "I think the point the professors are trying to teach us is that we should think of these children as possessing an entirely alien mind." She looked up at the university administrators, who expressed regrettable agreement.

"But, we'll be able to slowly bring them around to thinking as humans," Etoya insisted.

"The babies and youngest children will be fully assimilated," Nema said. "The older a child, the more likely that will never happen. They might be perfect imitators of our culture, but they'll never feel completely comfortable with us."

Etoya appeared deflated.

"It's similar to the Dischnya," Boris explained. "Homsaff and her warriors are true representatives of their culture, who have borrowed our ways. No one completely understands how they think on any one subject until they express their opinions."

Nema made a noise like she wished to take exception to Boris' statement, and he quickly amended it to say, "Unless we're talking about Alex."

"Who isn't considered human, anyway," a staffer remarked, repeating the old rumor, which generated soft laughter.

"My point," Boris continued, "is that the Dischnya's pups will have great claws in both worlds, and their pups will probably completely inhabit humankind's worlds. The Dischnya ancient culture will probably become somewhat alien to them."

"I can't believe it," Etoya said, resigned to the professors' explanations.

"What?" Nema asked.

"Alex only toured the colony ship occasionally. Then, within a period of months, he makes a series of decisions to request transport and accommodations for the children. Furthermore, he's made arrangements to keep the children aboard this ship, while they continue their education. How did he see that far into the future?"

"Experience, Etoya," Nema said. "As an adult, he encountered a SADE for the first time. He's met two groups of Swei Swee. He brought peace to the Dischnya nests, and he communicated with sentients who appeared as walking flowers. If anyone understands the difficulty of sentients adopting the ways of another culture, he does."

"Well, I'm happy that I had your wonderful presence today," Etoya said, leaning back in her chair, happy with their success. "I admit that I was decked by Nata's statement, but everything went well with the demonstrations of the implants." Once again, Etoya didn't get the responses she expected. "Now, what did I miss?" she asked.

"A trick we first adopted with Haraken university students," Storen explained, "was to keep the class list handy. We used it as a tick list for every lesson, in class or assigned."

"I don't understand," a staffer protested.

"When the holo-vid demonstration started with Nata's image, you can be sure that each of my colleagues checked her off the list. Am I right?" Storen asked Nema and Boris, who nodded their agreement.

"And?" the staffer persisted.

"One child didn't participate," Nema said.

"Who?" Etoya asked.

"Ude," Boris replied, proving Storen's pronouncement of the technique.

"You do this for every lesson?" a staffer asked, but she didn't get an answer because Etoya waved for quiet.

Etoya wanted to ask the professors if they were sure but realized the impertinence of the question. Instead, she worked to accommodate the various points of the evening's discussion. "Using your terminology," she said, "Ude would possess the most alien mind."

"No more than Nata or any of the older children," Boris corrected. "Ude adds a factor that isn't part of the other children's makeup. He was a leader. Actually, he still is, because the wild ones look up to him. When my class list was complete, except for his name, I caught him sitting toward the back of the dorm. He was scowling and lost in thought."

"What do you think that means?" Etoya asked.

"I don't think it had anything to do with the subject of implants," Nema proposed. "Ude was already aware of them, even if he didn't completely understand them. No, I think that he reacted to the announcement that this ship is sailing to Omnia."

"Why would he have a problem with that?" Etoya asked.

"We'll have to ask him," Storen offered.

* * *

"Alex, we have a malcontent of the first order," Boris said. He and others were present in Alex's suite.

"Who?" Alex asked.

"Ude," Etoya replied, her exasperation evident. "We've tried to reason with him, Alex, but he doesn't hear us." She was about to continue, but Alex held up a hand to forestall her.

"Nema," Alex said.

"He's incredibly stubborn," Nema replied. "He won't be swayed."

"Storen," Alex said.

"During the flight back to Omnia, Ude will poison the development of the other children," Storen said. "The wild ones look up to Ude, and his anger will disrupt their socialization."

"The professors have suggested a possible final intervention," Etoya blurted out. "It's you, Alex."

Alex glanced across the faces of Nema, Boris, and Storen. They were in agreement with Etoya. "And if I'm unable to dissuade him from his destructive path?" Alex asked.

Etoya ducked her head, resigned to the inevitable answer.

Storen said, "Ude would have to be permanently separated from the other children."

"Alex, we thought that if anyone could understand a ferociously independent-minded upstart, you could," Nema said. She managed to keep a fairly neutral expression, but her eyes crinkled with humor.

Renée was happy to be standing behind Alex, who was seated. It hid her smile from him.

"When do you want me to meet with him?" Alex asked, sighing.

"Julien's waiting with him in the corridor," Etoya quickly replied.

"That's my cue," Renée said, motioning to the others to leave with her.

Deserters of the ship, Alex thought, *as if I have superlative child-rearing experience.*

After the adults left the suite, Ude stalked through the door. Everything in his demeanor indicated a teenager ready to fight. The years under the staffer's care had served him well. Gone was the skinny, diseased eleven-year-old. Ude was healthy and had begun a growth spurt. He'd added kilos of muscle to his frame. But the telling change was in the teenager's eyes. They were no longer furtive, wary of every movement around him. Determination shone through them like a fighter pilot facing the enemy.

Immediately, Alex shifted his attitude. Instead of considering Ude a child who needed redirecting, he thought of him as an insubordinate trainee.

Ude took a defiant stance in front of Alex and drew breath to speak, but Alex cut him off with an upraised hand and ordered in a command voice, "Sit."

Ude hesitated and then relented. He sat stiffly, as if he begrudged the order.

"What's your problem, Ude?" Alex asked bluntly. It was a harsher opening than Alex wanted to employ, but Ude's disposition required a strong approach.

"I don't want to go to Omnia," Ude declared.

"What do you want?" Alex asked.

The question threw Ude off balance. He'd expected to be told how to behave, what to do, and where he should go. No one had asked him what he wanted.

Alex watched Ude deflate. The boy's shoulders eased, and the anger in his eyes faded. He placed a thumbnail against his teeth, while he considered his response.

"I want to hurt the aliens that made Faustus," Ude replied. He said it quietly, but there was metal in his voice.

"You want revenge for what was done to your band and the other children," Alex said just as quietly.

"Does revenge mean the aliens would be killed?" Ude asked.

"That can be one of the outcomes," Alex explained.

"Then I want revenge," Ude declared.

"Too bad, Ude, I don't support revenge," Alex said, his eyes locking on Ude's.

"You have a fleet of warships, yes?" Ude asked.

"Yes," Alex replied.

"You have them to kill the aliens, yes?" Ude persisted.

"Only if they force me to fight," Alex explained. "Otherwise, I hope my ships will make the aliens listen to me, take my words seriously."

"What will you tell them if they listen to you?" Ude asked. He shifted forward on his seat, intent on Alex's answer.

Alex anticipated they'd reached a tipping point and that the remainder of the conversation would have a great impact on Ude's future.

"We've learned that a digital entity by the name of Artifice created Faustus. We've also learned that Artifice is the leader of an extensive number of alien races, who wish to expand their territory across every habitable world," Alex explained. "Do you understand these words?" he asked.

"Artifice leads the aliens, and Artifice wants your worlds," Ude translated.

Alex nodded in agreement, and he also noted that Ude referred to humankind's worlds in the second person, which he understood.

"This expedition travels to meet with Artifice. I'll say to the entity that it can't have our worlds," Alex said.

"That's it?" Ude asked, confused.

"Yes," Alex replied. He leaned back and watched Ude roll Alex's words around in his mind.

"You'll wait to hear what Artifice says," Ude suddenly replied, his eyes lighting up. "You want to know what the alien thinks." Just as quickly as Ude had become animated, he quieted, a frown forming on his forehead. He'd understood the opening words, but he was unable to understand the choices the alien's response would offer Alex. One thing did occur to him, and he seized on it. "What do you want?" he asked.

"I want a safe future for all sentients," Alex replied.

"And what if Artifice says no to you?" Ude asked.

"Then I will find a way to force Artifice to agree," Alex said, his voice low and powerful. "Understand, Ude, my first choice is not to fight. It would be a fight we couldn't win, but I will find a way to make Artifice listen."

"When I led the band, I didn't fight," Ude said thoughtfully, leaning back in his chair. "We couldn't win. We stayed alive by being quiet, by doing what Faustus didn't expect."

"Yes, you did," Alex agreed.

"Then I will go with you to talk to Artifice," Ude announced.

In Alex's mind, the boy had demonstrated the ability to quickly incorporate new information and shift his perspective accordingly. Alex had no doubt that if Ude wanted to, he could disrupt the entire roster of the *Our People*.

"I'm the expedition's leader. Individuals ask my permission to travel with me," Alex said.

Alex saw anger flare in Ude's eyes, but it was instantly extinguished.

"How is this done?" Ude asked.

"Repeat after me," Alex replied, keeping a smile off his face. "I would like to ask your permission to travel aboard the *Freedom* with you."

A smile broke out on Ude's face after he completed the sentence, but it was dashed, when Alex said, "No.

Before the boy could explode, Alex continued. "I say no, because I don't think you can follow my rules. You've already shown that you won't listen to your teachers."

"But they ask for things from me that I don't want to give," Ude objected.

"Then what will be the difference between living with them and living with me?" Alex asked.

The question stumped Ude. He had to admit that the huge leader had a good point, and he tried to understand what the difference would be. The teachers told him that his anger was destructive and would be his undoing, although he didn't understand what that meant. They tried to teach him ways to control the darkness that welled up inside him, but that only seemed to deepen his resolve to focus on it. He thought now of relenting and rejoining the others for the trip to Omnia, but that fueled his anger. Confusion flooded through Ude. His simple world of daily survival had become too complex to fathom.

Alex watched tears brim in Ude's eyes. They floated there and then coursed down the boy's face. The tears continued to run, and Ude made no move to wipe them away. The energy seemed to drain out of him. Alex expected that the teenager didn't see a future for himself aboard either city-ship.

"You won't have a satisfactory life aboard the *Our People*, Ude. I see that now," Alex said gently. "I don't know if your life will be any better aboard this ship, but I see it as the only hope you have. I will tell you now that you will not like my rules, but, if you try hard enough, you might find a comfortable place among the individuals aboard this ship."

Alex stood and motioned Ude to do the same. The teenager stood, and Alex folded him in his arms. His mind jumped back to the many times he'd done this for Teague, and he wondered where his son was and if he was safe and happy.

Ude felt the huge man's arm envelop him. The teachers were always trying to hug him, and he resented the intimate contact. It felt like he was being captured by minders. At this moment, the best he could manage was a quick patting on Alex's sides, and he was relieved when that action caused Alex to release him, allowing him to step away.

"Do I return to the other ship for now?" Ude asked.

"Do you wish to say goodbye to your band?" Alex asked.

"Yes, I must," Ude said, some of his spirit returning.

"After you say goodbye to them, you'll be returned to this ship," Alex said. He walked the boy to his door, but before he signaled it open, he said, "This is my first order to you, Ude. Are you ready?"

Ude braced himself to accept whatever the leader asked. He would do whatever was demanded of him to sail aboard this ship to face Artifice.

"You will thank each staff member and professor for what they've done for you and the other children," Alex said. "That's a duty of a leader, which I know you are."

Ude waited. He was sure there would be a more demanding request. "That's it?" he asked when nothing else was said.

"My requests will get tougher, in the future, but we'll start easy for now," Alex replied, with a grin.

Ude smiled shyly. It was the first smile Alex had seen on the boy.

When the door opened, Alex didn't have to request someone escort Ude. Renée and Julien were waiting.

Renée extended her hand and said, "Welcome aboard."

Ude politely shook it. Then Julien repeated the greeting, offering his hand.

"I will return young Ude to the *Our People* and then escort him back here," Julien announced.

Alex narrowed an eye at Julien. Obviously, the SADE, with his keen hearing, had listened at the door and shared what he heard with Renée.

"We have to do something about these cabin doors," Julien quipped. "I hadn't realized they were so thin. Come, master Ude," Julien said, waving his hand down the corridor. A jaunty cap appeared on his hand, and he began whistling.

Renée circled her arms around Alex's waist. "Did I tell you that I love you?" she said, her voice muffled in his chest.

"Often, and I hold every one of them precious," Alex replied, gently hugging her in return.

-34-
Target Star

The scout ship SADEs chose to take an ultraconservative approach to the target star. It was Alex's cautionary statements that convinced them to be extraordinarily apprehensive. The unknown fates of Deter and Verina's scout ships were never far from their thoughts.

The SADEs ended their transits high above the system's ecliptic. They immediately shut down their primary engines, closed the clam-shell doors, and attempted to appear as nothing more than a group of large rocks by adopting a tight, eccentric formation. In that regard, they drifted at a velocity similar to the speed of independent bodies, which were not yet captured by a star's gravitational pull.

<Even if this isn't Artifice's home world, it's still a significant system,> Bethley noted, when the first telemetry data was collected.

<We could gain more precise data, if we spread out and approached the system from various positions,> Linn sent. His suggestion didn't elicit responses.

Instead, the other SADEs examined the system's activity, and algorithms calculated survival rates if they employed Linn's idea.

<Alex would wish us to use our best judgment,> Genoa said.

Bethley determined that approaching the system anywhere on the ecliptic plane would be extremely hazardous. The constant ship activity, entering and exiting the system from all directions, would ensure they were detected, and she said so.

Beryl hypothesized and announced that only two approach directions made sense, above and below the ecliptic. <These directions would duplicate our efforts,> he sent. <I suggest we remain as we are. It's more likely that our present formation will keep us hidden from observers.>

There was some minor trepidation about not gathering the best data on the system, but, in the end, they agreed to remain in their present position, drifting slowly inward.

As the days passed, information continued to pour into the scout ships, but Killian watched the remaining days count down, with a measure of frustration.

Came the tenth day, Killian announced to Bethley and Trium, his teammates, that they disregard Alex's order to return after ten days.

<I would immediately argue with you, Killian,> Bethley sent, <but you have continually modified Alex's orders and been proven correct for doing so.>

<What of our companions' ships?> Trium asked.

<I'll propose to them that they return with the data Alex requested,> Killian replied.

<You would not suggest this if you didn't have a plan,> Bethley prompted.

<I would hear how the others reply to my suggestion that they return before I engage you in my scheme,> Killian proposed.

Killian contacted the other scout ships, and, as expected, Linn, Beryl, and Genoa's teams were adamant that they should return as directed. However, every one of them thought the question of whether Killian's team must return on time was a decision only those team members could make.

Soon after the discussion ended, three of the scout ships gently turned away from the tight group, as if they might have been asteroids that collided. They tumbled their ships to imitate the rolling motions of impact. Then they accelerated slowly until they felt safe to make a transit.

<I presume that you want a closer look at the system,> Trium sent, after the other scout ships had disappeared into the dark.

<Not the entire system,> Killian replied. <We have a good indication of its activity level, which is extensive. I'm much more interested in a closer look at the sixth planet.>

<I thought that one would pique your interest,> Bethley sent. <It's a shame that telemetry didn't resolve those objects that surround the planet any better than it did.>

<Too small a ship,> Trium commented, referring to the limits of a scout ship's sensors and antennas. Then he added, <What I find remarkable is that the structures surround the planet in a most unusual fashion. Originally, I had thought they were defensive emplacements, but that seems illogical for such an advanced civilization.>

<Agreed,> Bethley said. <The types of ships we see indicate an incredibly technologically advanced society. None of the warships we saw at the wall appear as modern as these. Not that it bodes well for us.>

<I take your points, Bethley and Trium,> Killian replied. <It makes no sense to surround a planet with archaic defense platforms that enormous battleships could wipe away with the first salvo.>

<Perhaps, they're ancient,> Trium proposed. <They could have been left there long after their construction.>

<To become navigation hazards?> Bethley questioned. <This level of civilization would have removed something like that millenniums ago. No, these platforms are something else, and I think they were built long ago and still serve their purpose.>

<Which is what?> Trium prompted.

<That's what I believe Killian wishes to discover,> Bethley replied, <and why we're waiting to hear how he intends to get us close enough for telemetry to resolve these objects without adding us to the galaxy's collection of space dust.>

Trium quickly searched telemetry for an appropriate asteroid cluster that might be making its way inward, which they could hide within. They had imitated an asteroid passing through a system once before. However, in this case, the inordinate ship activity made it too dangerous to attempt. He did find an object that fit perfectly with Killian's needs.

Killian and Bethley heard the call of an ancient trumpet, Trium's audio tones for excitement.

<I've discovered Killian's plan,> Trium sent with urgency. <Regard,> he said, sharing a segment of telemetry collected soon after the scout ships had arrived.

<A comet,> Bethley sent, adding her own humorous tone. <If we hide in the tail, telemetry will be affected.>

<We'll have to slip from the primary stream to collect accurate data,> Killian agreed. <Are you ready?>

Bethley and Trium assented, and Killian composed a message for Alex. He sent, <Alex, we intend to ride a comet. We'll be offline for an estimated seven weeks, while we slip through the system. The sixth planet outward warrants a close pass for more precise telemetry.>

The scout ship, *Vivian's Mirror*, altered its trajectory into a gradual curve that would cross the comet's tail. When the two bodies intersected, the SADEs tucked close to the rear of the comet. Much of the tail's debris originated from its front quarter, which faced the sun. Killian positioned the ship toward the opposite side to reduce the impact on their shell.

The comet flew inward from above the ecliptic. It would pass through the system near the orbit of the eighth planet outward before it exited the system. The SADEs recorded fresh data, when the debris trail waned, replacing the earlier scans.

Weeks into the trip, the scout ship slipped to one side of the comet, clear of the tail, and recorded days of the system's warships and probes, which lined the outer belt. Then *Vivian's Mirror* slid to the other side of the comet to record the sixth planet and the emplacements that surrounded it. Telemetry revealed the body and objects in crisp detail.

With their observations complete, Killian returned the scout ship to its hiding place in the comet's tail, and the SADEs reviewed the data.

<They're definitely not defensive platforms,> Trium said.

<Examine the planet's polar region,> Bethley urged.

<Multiple structures that appear similar to the projections of the platforms,> Trium replied.

<I believe our communication expert, Luther, would be extremely interested in viewing this data,> Killian hypothesized.

<What do you interpret about the planet's surface?> Trium asked.

<Uncharacteristic in comparison to system's hyperactivity,> Bethley replied.

<Freighters are docked at the single orbital platform, and shuttles are moving between it and the surface,> Killian noted. <To Trium's point, why does the surface look fairly uninhabited? Where's evidence of the race that dominates this system?>

<Have we collected sufficient telemetry data on this system?> Bethley asked. <We'll soon pass through the ecliptic.>

The SADEs hurriedly reviewed the data, which had accrued, and examined it for any bodies, ships, or objects of which they wanted clearer details.

<More details are required of the probes in the outer belt,> Killian sent, and Bethley and Trium agreed.

This time the *Vivian's Mirror* was blatantly exposed, as it took up a position in front of the comet's head to be able to collect clear imagery of the distance probes that lay in a ring at the farthermost edge of the system.

Killian and Bethley were focused on the data collection and analysis of the probes, when Trium interrupted.

<We have a problem,> Trium sent, adding an image of a pair of warships approaching the comet at a high rate of acceleration. <One moment; I'm calculating their vector. It's confirmed. The warships intend to intercept the comet's path.>

<I see no logical reason why the aliens would want to visit a comet, especially with warships,> Bethley quipped.

<We have another reason to be concerned,> Trium sent. <Grav energy collection by our shell has been reduced by over thirty-eight percent. I believe the comet dust and ice have scoured our shell. If we return to the comet's tail, the deterioration will continue.>

<We can't afford to hide in the tail, Killian,> Bethley sent with urgency. <If we wait to see if it's a coincidence that the battleships are headed this way, I project the shell will have lost over fifty percent of its collection capability. I'm concerned that our hull could lose a sufficient amount of material to endanger its integrity.>

<I had hoped to enter and exit this system without being seen,> Killian lamented. <That opportunity is gone. We're leaving.>

Killian eased the *Vivian's Mirror* away from the comet, chose a trajectory that angled away from the battleships, and headed below the ecliptic.

As Bethley opened the four-part, clam-shell covering concealing the primary engines, the SADEs calculated their projected departure rate against the battleships' present velocities and accelerations. The scout ship's primary engines were activated, and the SADEs determined that escape would be a close call.

<Armament launch,> sent Trium, his concern evident. <Spectral analysis indicates chemical-propellant missiles, which dictate a limited range. However, if they can accelerate over the entire distance, they'll arrive in zero point twelve hours.>

Killian changed the scout ship's trajectory slightly.

<It was a good idea, Killian, but ineffective,> Bethley sent. <The missiles have altered course. Acceleration continues. Interception is in zero point nine hours.>

Killian was already pushing the engines to their technical limits. The number of missiles inbound made it distinctly possible that simple evasion would be improbable. In addition, he considered that the enemy might employ near-object detonation techniques.

<Analysis of the missiles,> Killian requested.

<Massive in size,> Trium replied. <More than likely, they're employed in the elimination of other battleships.>

<At their projected contact velocity, I estimate their maneuverability will be limited,> Bethley added, which gave Killian an idea.

<Shutting down primary engines and closing clam-shell doors,> Killian said. The thought had occurred to him that the missiles might be seeking his engines' heat sources. He waited, while time ticked down.

Bethley and Trium halted communication. Killian exercised unorthodox methods of idea origination that had been generated by his extended contact with Alex. At this precise moment in time, both SADEs were dwelling on that thought. If they were human, it would be said they were hoping. As SADEs, that singular thought was in a continuous loop.

When Killian estimated the moment was right, he used the ship's grav engines to swing the *Vivian's Mirror* at 90 degrees to the onrushing missiles. Gravitational forces were weakening, and the maneuver wasn't as strong as Killian would have liked. However, it wasn't necessary.

Moments after Killian executed his turn, the missiles ran their propellant dry. They passed his previous position and continued on a ballistic course.

<I believe Alex will be especially delighted by this story,> Trium remarked, pleased to escape the onrushing destruction that had threatened them.

<He might be entranced, if we get an opportunity to tell it,> Bethley said. <Unfortunately, a second salvo has been launched. They're slender missiles, accelerating faster than the first launch. Spectral analysis indicates nonchemical propellant, possibly powerful ion engines.>

<The aliens have realized our ship's capability, and they mean not to make the same mistake twice,> Trium commented.

Killian had intended to return to his previous heading. Now, he hesitated. The battleships had changed courses, cutting across the triangle to intercept the scout ship, and the faster, smaller missiles were tracking it. Killian furiously calculated trajectories, present velocities, and acceleration of all participants in the dangerous dance.

<Our grav-wave collection rate is insufficient,> Trium noted. <Power in our crystals is draining faster than we're accumulating it. We have less than a half hour of maneuvering before we must revert to primary engines.>

Killian arrived at the end of his calculations, and he shifted the scout ship's vector to a heading that would intercept the coasting, first salvo of missiles.

<I don't wish to interrupt you, Killian,> Bethley sent. <However, I'd like to say this one thing. With all the intensity of my kernel, I sincerely hope this is the beginning of an Alex-like maneuver. Otherwise, I think our extinction is fast approaching.>

Killian didn't reply, and neither Bethley nor Trium sent him another word.

Killian's internal chronometer, which he'd set after completing his calculations, ticked toward zero. Despite the *Vivian's Mirror* last vector change, the second salvo of missiles continued to track the scout ship.

In preparation for the final maneuver, Killian opened the primary propulsion engines' doors. As the chronometer reached zero, Killian accelerated the scout ship to the point that the vessel's grav plating was in danger of collapsing. The SADEs felt the g-forces of acceleration, an uncommon event for their sophisticated ship.

Bethley and Trium monitored the telemetry data, entranced by the impending destruction of their scout ship. The missiles of the second salvo were homing in on the *Vivian's Mirror*. They would intercept the scout ship near the time their vessel caught the coasting first salvo of behemoths.

Both Bethley and Trium noted their engines' readouts. Killian was driving them at 23 percent over maximum recommended output.

A remark occurred to Bethley about the incredulousness of having to choose between their ship's destruction by missiles or by exploding engines, but she kept it to herself.

Bethley and Trium recalculated the timing of the missiles' interception based on the increased acceleration their ship was obtaining by Killian's drastic maneuver.

<We just might,> Trium sent to Bethley, as their scout ship shot behind the enormous missiles of the first salvo a few seconds ahead of the arrival of the second salvo. Their vessel's passage triggered the proximity detection systems of the coasting missiles.

The ballistic missiles exploded in a chain reaction, and the enormous wave of energy detonated every missile in the group, including those in the second salvo, which had only begun to alter their trajectory to chase the scout ship.

Fortunately, the expanding energy waves were unable to appreciably damage the fleeing scout ship. In the SADEs' favor, the battleships were forced to veer off from the massive destructive waves of hot gases and metal debris that were headed their way.

As soon as it was feasible, Killian reduced the engine output to 90 percent, turned the *Vivian's Mirror* onto a course headed for the fleet's star, and made a transit.

The moment the ship's escape was assured, Trium's trumpet blast intertwined with Bethley's ancient calliope, as the two celebrated escaping what appeared to be certain death.

<I believe you put us in harm's way on purpose, Killian,> Bethley teased. <You did it just to ensure your story would be impressive to Alex.> She halted her celebration when Killian failed to reply.

<Well done, Killian,> Bethley gently urged, hoping to initiate a response from their leader.

<I thought for a moment that I would never again dance with Vivian,> Killian sent.

<This time you will,> Trium sent. <Well done, Killian.>

The *Vivian's Mirror* made several indiscriminate transits, checking its back trail, as the scout ships had agreed to do. It was known that the aliens of the federation were aware that their style of hull was associated with humankind's worlds. And it was known where one fleet lay, but the aliens had been told by Alex that there were several fleets in federacy space. It was hoped by their maneuvers that the aliens would believe their ship was intending to rendezvous with another fleet.

Eventually, the *Vivian's Mirror* transited outside the *New Terra*'s system, where the expedition fleet was stationed. Immediately, Killian pinged the other scout ships and was relieved to find they had returned safely.

<Greetings,> the nine SADEs sent to Killian, Bethley, and Trium. Their sending was accompanied by joyful noises and tones of celebration.

<Your signals originate from the *Freedom*,> Trium sent to the nine SADEs.

<We've been relieved from duty for now,> Linn replied.

<You're to join us,> Genoa added.

<We've been waiting for you. A fête is planned before the *Our People* launches,> Beryl sent, adding a pleasurable tone.

-35-
Observations

The *Vivian's Mirror* was turned over to Mickey, who examined the ship's shell with Emile and Miriam. The scout ship was the largest vessel the fleet had that would fit inside a city-ship's bay, but it was a tight squeeze.

"Well, at least we have an indication of how far you can degrade a shell and keep the ship sailing," Mickey said, running his hand over the pitted surface.

"Can this be repaired by your present methods, Emile?" Miriam asked.

"I don't know," Emile replied. "What we did after the fight at the wall was repair dings, chips, and cracks, and occasionally we repaired holes. But, in this case, the entire surface has been worn thin."

Emile examined the data Miriam collected on the shell. The shell was reduced by an average of more than 5 centimeters, and, in some places, the comet's rock and ice had nearly penetrated the weakened hull.

"There is the option of not repairing this ship," Emile said. But, when he observed the narrowed eyes sent his way by Mickey and Miriam, he added, "I suppose not, especially because its Killian's ship."

"No scout team acts more independently or collects more data than they do," Mickey said. "It's time to get inventive, Emile." He smiled at the biochemist, slapped the heavy New Terran on the shoulder, and walked away.

Emile looked at Miriam with hopeful eyes, and she said, "Be at ease, Emile. I don't intend to desert you."

Mickey's internal chronometer told him that if he didn't hurry, he wouldn't catch the start of Alex's review of the data collected by the *Vivian's Mirror*. He hurried, arriving as the last of the attendees, the expedition's senior staff, filed into the auditorium.

"I'd like to begin this meeting by recognizing the contributions of some individuals who have rarely been seen by this company lately," Alex said in his opening remarks. "Would the scout ship SADEs please stand?"

The twelve SADEs rose to the applause and whistles of humans and the celebratory sounds of SADEs.

When the noise died down, Alex said, "These individuals have done a wonderful job of helping to keep the expedition safe by patrolling our perimeters and seeking out our enemies far in advance of our ships. It has cost them dearly. The six SADEs of Deter and Verina's ships are presumed lost. Every one of them has our sincere appreciation for their contributions."

Alex's salutation led to another round of cheering and applause. He let the SADEs enjoy their moment, and they sat, as it quieted.

Alex addressed the assembly, saying, "The data collected by the first three scout ships to return has been examined in detail."

A huge holo-vid that an engineering team had installed, for the purpose of the meeting, sprang to life.

"What's evident is the incredible number of warships that patrol the system's fringe," Alex said. "In most cases, these ships penetrate no farther inward than about the orbit of the eighth planet. That in itself is strange. Freighters come and go, visiting all manner of locations. However, we've identified the sixth planet outward as the hub of this system. Yet, it possesses only a single orbital platform."

As Alex spoke, Julien controlled the imagery the holo-vid displayed. Quite evident was the lack of resolution of many of the items that Alex mentioned. The scout ships had remained too far out to record better detail. Alex's initial disappointment with Linn's summary was quickly dispelled when he reviewed their data. The system's hyperactivity precluded the scout ships approaching the targets any closer.

"The initial reports conclude that the activity surrounding the sixth planet, which is supposedly the hub, is limited, indicating a technologically advanced civilization does not exist on the planet," Alex continued. "In summary, the early information has created more questions than answers."

Alex paused, and the audience waited for him to continue. "I'm as anxious as you to learn what data the intrepid crew of the *Vivian's Mirror* has gathered that will answer our questions. Killian, Bethley, and Trium, if you please, step up here and lead the discussion."

Comm and implant messages flew between humans and SADEs. Alex's invitation was a heady example of his increasing inclusion of SADEs in the expedition's matters.

The three SADEs rose and moved as one, in step, toward the front of the auditorium.

<Break ranks,> Alex sent to them, and immediately the SADEs shifted their steps and postures to imitate three friends approaching the front of the auditorium.

Bethley and Trium signaled Killian that he should begin the presentation, as they took positions on either side of their ship's leader.

Killian began his remarks by saying, "We appreciate the opportunity to share what we've discovered. Thank you, Alex. All of us recognized the importance of the sixth planet, but we couldn't account for its lack of ship activity. In addition, we'd seen the platforms that ringed the planet, and decided that they too, among other subjects, demanded further investigation. So, we proceeded inward."

Bethley quickly inserted a comment. "It should be noted that we hid the approach of our ship in the tail of a comet, soon to pass near the orbit of the eighth planet. It was Killian's plan, of course."

Bethley's comment produced a titter from the audience. Killian, who appeared embarrassed by the revelation, shrugged his shoulders and displayed a lopsided smile. It was a perfect imitation of Alex, and he received a round of laughter for his efforts.

"While an inventive plan," Bethley added, "it nearly resulted in the destruction of our ship's hull. I don't recommend it as a hiding place."

"I think Bethley overstates the dangerousness of our hiding place," Trium announced, with a serious face. "I, for one, thought the twin missile barrages aimed our way and launched from battleships were a much more perilous factor."

The audience was quiet, staring at the SADEs in disbelief and wondering if they were hearing fact or fiction.

"I concede that the ship-killer-sized missiles were a daunting part of the trip," Killian said, holding his arms out in apology to the audience. "But, we survived and we returned. That should be given some credit."

Alex and Julien were the first to laugh, which soon had others joining them. It dawned on the audience that the scout ship SADEs were intending to do more than make a simple presentation. Now that they had the opportunity to dominate the stage they'd chosen to entertain everyone.

Killian thought he might receive a hint from Alex on how to proceed, but nothing came his way. He shifted the datastream to the point of closest passage to the sixth planet. "Perhaps we should start at the most optimal resolution of our trip inward," Killian said. "This is why we wanted a close pass of this unusual planet."

The assembly leaned forward to regard the holo-vid, which displayed clear views of the planet. Some humans and all SADEs linked to the data source to study the imagery in more detail.

"Notice the lack of activity on the planet's surface," Killian continued. "And by that I mean the lack of biological sentients. We can see vehicles and bots of all sorts moving. We can see overhead trams, but only bots exit at the stations."

"Did you witness any biologicals, at any time?" Reiko asked.

"At our distance, we observed only herds of animals," Bethley replied. "We couldn't detect the movement of sentients around any structures, not a single one."

The audience ruminated on that odd piece of data, and Killian waited, for a moment, before continuing. "When observing from far outside the system, we had questions about the platforms that ringed the planet. It would seem odd, we thought, for the planet to have defensive platforms, knowing that modern naval warfare could quickly eliminate them. However, it didn't seem probable that they would be comm platforms, either. The vast number of them would be excessive for communications.

Trium chose a clear, close-up view of one of the platforms. It was significant in size, probably containing a heavy power generator, and its projections were an unusual configuration.

"Luther?" Trium asked, inviting the SADE to comment.

Luther studied the image and said, "They're definitely comm platforms. The single directional structure of each platform, which points inward, indicates a unique point of contact on the planet's surface, and these antenna structures appear to be adjustable, allowing them to follow the planet's rotation. Do you have telemetry of the planetary focus point?"

Bethley skipped to the relative part of the data. "It's this area, at a polar region of the planet, Luther. It's festooned with various transmitting towers."

Luther was examining the imagery, when the display shifted. It returned to an image of the platform.

"What of the elements of the platforms that face outward, Luther?" Killian asked.

Luther examined the numerous projections, and said, "In contrast to the inward components, which target one location, the outward structures are meant to cover the broadest area of space."

Killian thought about what Luther was proposing, and he shifted the display again.

"This is what we wished everyone to see," Killian said. "These are the best images we have of the probes that ring the outer system. Admittedly they aren't as sharp as we would like, but their outlines are telling."

"They're similar to the probes in our system," Tatia said in surprise from her front-row seat.

"Yes, Admiral," Killian agreed.

"We've concluded that this system is the heart of the federacy," Trium announced. "We believe it's the home world of the race that planted the probes in our systems."

"Yes and no," Julien said, which drew the audience's attention to him. "Consider that the Nua'll spoke of a master, a singular individual named Artifice. If Artifice inhabits this system, where are the individuals who serve it?"

"Would a digital entity need service from biological entities?" Linn asked.

"Not necessarily," Bethley agreed. "Perhaps that's why the activity we witnessed on the planet's surface was entirely mechanical."

"The comm platforms and probes make sense, if you consider that Artifice controls the operations of everything, including ships, via implanted code," Luther postulated. "In that regard, wouldn't an entity such as Artifice mistrust anything that it couldn't control?"

"Excellent point," Reiko said. "At some point in the history of this race, Artifice took over this world, the system, and the ships. The race that created it is no longer in control of their lives. Bots run the world. The systems are automated, and the shuttles from the planet to the singular orbital platform are on autopilot."

"Does that mean that Artifice never leaves the castle for fear of exposure to those who want to kill it?" Renée asked. She had been reminded of an ancient vid. At the center of the plot was a man, a leader, who was called a shogun. The shogun suffered from a form of paranoia, which kept him prisoner in his own castle.

"Perhaps Artifice can't leave the planet for another reason," Alex said, which halted the discussions that had sprung up. "Bethley, display the planet's polar region again, please." When the images appeared, Alex asked, "What's wrong with this vid?"

"Towers and transmitters," Luther said immediately. "We see comm structures but no buildings, Dassata."

"The only reason I can see to construct structures at a polar region would be to take advantage of the cold, but that doesn't make any sense to me for communication equipment." Mickey said, the engineer in him analyzing the anomalous placement.

"Cold," Alex echoed, suddenly sitting upright. "Artifice doesn't leave the planet because it can't. The entity is buried under the polar cap to help it eliminate heat production. Those towers and transmitters are how Artifice communicates and controls the federation's races.

"Bethley, show me views of the various warships orbiting the outer system," Alex requested. He was examining the images of the multitude of ships that prowled the system's outer limits, when the display suddenly shifted.

"I believe these are the ships you're looking for, Dassata," Killian said.

The audience stared at a squadron of ships. They possessed matte-black hulls, and their configurations echoed the designs of the probes in the outer belt and the sixth planet's comm platforms.

"We believe these are the ships of the original race," Bethley said into the utter quiet.

Comms and implants shared messages. Individuals had varied reactions to the discovery of the race that was at the heart of the misery inflicted on humankind's worlds. Some focused their anger on the race, some saw its history as tragic, and some didn't know what to think.

What was obvious to the entire audience and those individuals linked to them was that Artifice's system was a fortress protected by enormous naval firepower and immensely dense comm networks. Having experienced the malevolent code assault of the Nua'll, there was little doubt among the Omnians as to what Artifice was capable of broadcasting within its personal territory.

* * *

Two days after the meeting, in which the observations of *Vivian's Mirror* were discussed, Renée, Pia, and some friends enjoyed one of the vids Renée had gleaned from Idona Station at Sol. When it ended, Renée sat alone in the suite. Her mind played over the subterfuge created by one group trying to gain access to the city of another.

Renée was quite aware that Alex would press forward with his plan to accept Artifice's invitation. The images of the numerous fleets and comm platforms protecting the entity's system scared her. They'd frightened many individuals, if her discussions with a few others were an accurate representation of the entire expedition.

One of the characteristics that Renée loved about her partner was his great heart. It was Alex who saw through the actions of the dark travelers to imagine a race held captive within them. It was Alex who had befriended a SADE, when he'd never met one, and freed his kind. And it was Alex who brought peace to the sentient species of Celus-5.

There were other thoughts that occurred to Renée about her partner, but she returned to the idea that germinated in her mind. At the center of them was the realization that she didn't trust the digital entities they were encountering — not Faustus, not the Nua'll, and certainly not Artifice. This time Renée was intent on imparting a healthy sense of distrust into Alex's decisions.

Renée signaled Alex. He was headed toward their suite, and Julien was with him. *Perfect,* she thought. At the cabin door, she heard Julien saying good night to Alex, and she signaled Julien to join them.

"Sit, please," Renée requested of Alex and Julien, swinging an arm toward the couch, when they entered the salon. "I have a vid I want the two of you to watch and think about in regard to your intention to visit Artifice. The important part is at the end and involves a method used to deceive the enemy. The vid is called *Troy.*"

Having delivered her message, Renée exited the salon for the sleeping quarters, intending to turn in for the night.

"Shall we?" Alex offered, searching through Renée's vid database for the title.

"I've just reviewed it. I find the idea intriguing," Julien said, rising from the couch and making his way to the door.

"Cheater," Alex called out.

"That's a human trait," Julien shot back, as he exited the suite.

Alex was tired, and he wanted to be snuggling with his partner. So, he decided to compromise. Locating the vid, he sent it to the wall monitor and limited the audio output to his implant. He watched sections of the vid, shooting forward to skip much of it, but understanding the nature of the plot. Near the end, Alex slowed to real time and watched the enemy retreat from the city walls to their ships.

When the aggressors constructed the figure of an animal, Alex grew interested. The ships sailed, and those inside the walled city celebrated their victory and hauled the wooden creature inside. It was their undoing.

Alex played the ending several times, while his mind searched for parallels to his intended visit to Artifice's system. His thoughts seized on the concept that was trying to elude him. It wasn't a parallel that he was seeking. It was the inverse of what the Greeks had done.

Slipping into the sleeping quarters, Alex paid a quick visit to the refresher, and then crawled into bed.

Renée curled against Alex, stretching an arm and a leg over him. "You didn't watch the whole thing," she accused, her voice thick with sleep.

"The good part I did," Alex replied, kissing the top of Renée's head. "To quote, Julien, I find the idea intriguing."

Renée smiled and drifted off to sleep. Alex stayed awake for a while longer, while he considered ways to fool Artifice with his own Greek ship.

-36-
Fêtes and Goodbyes

Alex linked to Tatia in the early morning, while he rode a traveler to the *Our People*. He sent, <Admiral Tachenko, order the entire expedition's ships to return to our location. I want all personnel to be able to attend the fêtes.>

<Do you think that's wise, Alex?> Tatia asked.

<It might be the last opportunity for the members of this fleet to share in this kind of event for a long while,> Alex replied. <And, after sitting out here for nearly three years, with no visitors but the comm sphere, I think it's safe to say that we'll be fine for a couple of days.>

<I can have a reduced crew handle the ships, Alex, while the rest attend the events,> Tatia said. She waited for Alex's affirmation of her compromise, but it didn't come. <Everyone,> she sent. Her thought was quiet and exhibited reluctant acceptance.

<Everyone,> Alex concurred. <The sisters can monitor our perimeter. If there's a transit of enemy ships on the ecliptic, we'll have days to prepare.>

<And if we're attacked from above or below the ecliptic?> Tatia asked.

<Then we'll have an opportunity to see how well the Sisterhood fights our ships for us,> Alex replied.

The last thing Tatia heard before Alex closed the comm was his laughter. His last statement disturbed her. She jealously guarded her command of the fleet's ships and disliked the idea of risking them to the sisters. The conundrum for Tatia was that she absolutely trusted the SADEs who occupied avatars. Some of them were captains and commanders of her fleet. However, the sisters were enigmas to her, and that left her with unanswered questions.

Miriamal, who had handled Alex's transmission for the *Freedom*, considered what she'd heard and decided to speak to the sister aboard Alex's traveler.

<You would be most at risk should the fleet be attacked. Would you be willing to fight your ship, without a pilot?> Miriamal sent.

<Absolutely,> the sister responded. <My pilot is a youth, with wonderful intentions and little experience.>

<The opportunity to test our skills against enemy ships would embellish our abilities,> said the Sisterhood after reaching consensus and chiming into the discussion.

<The admirals are concerned that our fighting would be rigid. They believe that we lack the innovative thinking of humans,> Miriamal suggested.

<There is that possibility,> a sister replied, <but our ability to fight as one might overcome that limitation.>

Having come to a decision, the Sisterhood was quiet on that subject. Now, they waited for an opportunity to test the concept of whether the sisters could fight a battle better than their human counterparts.

* * *

The fêtes were to be held in three major locations: the grand parks of the two city-ships and the secondary park of the *Our People*. As Alex requested, the expedition's ships were emptied. The sisters, aboard the Tridents, diligently scanned space for any sign of transit from enemy ships.

Two educational staff escorted Ude from the *Freedom* to the *Our People*. He would have this one last chance to join the other children. It was also Ude's last opportunity to reconsider his decision.

The *Our People*'s secondary park was dedicated exclusively to the *New Terra*'s children, the educators, and the professors. The smaller space evinced all the engaging trimmings of the much larger, grand park. The trees were a few meters shorter, the stream less prevalent, but it was as colorful and delightful a location as any of the green spaces aboard the city-ships.

When Ude stepped out of the lift, he witnessed children running, playing, and shouting. It was the first time that all the children, wild and not, had been allowed to play together. That, in itself, made the evening a special occasion.

The professors intended to keep their eyes on the wild ones to ensure that they interacted well with the other children. As it turned out, their oversight wasn't necessary. The *Freedom*'s young, children and pups, provided excellent buffers for the engagement of the children.

Etoya's staff was busy with the babies, who now were age one and a half or more. They toddled around, trying to join the others and kept their minders busy.

Nata saw Ude and broke away from her friends to run to him. She joyfully hugged him.

Of all the members of his band, Ude would miss Nata the most, but the ache in his heart didn't change his mind, and Nata had made up hers. She wanted to stay with the wild ones. The band needed one or the other of them, and Nata wouldn't abandon them.

Nata took Ude's hand and led him toward the places where the members of the band played. Ude would spend the evening refreshing friendships. The satisfying part of his time with them was realizing that, with the help the children were receiving, the band, especially the youngest ones, would manage to become a part of Omnian society someday.

But, in the end, Ude chose to return to the *Freedom*. He had pledged the previous band leader to seek safety for the ones in his care and find a way to take revenge on the entities that tortured them. It was an oath that he took to heart. The band was safe, thanks to the Omnians. That meant he had one last duty to fulfill. Alex Racine had said that revenge wasn't his way, and Ude accepted that. He was determined to bide his time. He believed that someday the opportunity would present itself, and he could fulfill his promise.

The city-ship's grand parks were beginning to fill up, while the children's fun was fully underway. The engineering team had set up holo-vids for the guests to communicate visually across the intervening spaces. Vid cams picked up images and audio to transmit them between ships.

One of the anticipated events of the evening was the unveiling of a new dance. It was an invention of Renée and Cordelia. Years ago, Renée's introduction of the waltz to the Omnians and the rescued Independents from Daelon had been a tremendous hit. Thereafter, she searched her collection of vids for other dance routines. In most cases, they were taken from the vids obtained from Idona Station and came from an age before the collapse of Earth's governments and the rise of United Earth.

Renée would show the dance section of the vid to Cordelia, who would program the routine for the SADEs and diagram the steps for the humans. A link would be sent expedition-wide to humans, who could watch the vid, hear the music, and practice the steps. It wasn't unusual to see crew members, in their off-time, pairing up and practicing.

This evening, Killian was aware that Vivian attended the evening with her new male, teenage friend. He saw her exit the lift, holding her friend's hand, and he was happy for her. She'd made tremendous progress from the frightened child he first knew. Now, nearing sixteen years of age, Vivian wore her Méridien beauty well and walked with confidence.

Killian didn't wish to intrude on her evening. Slowly, he melded into the background to stand and chat with other scout SADEs. The subject, of course, was Artifice's system and how best to help the expedition's fleet penetrate it and force Artifice into surrendering.

Music filled the parks, and humans and SADEs enjoyed the atmosphere. The Dischnya were present, but most of them were busy enjoying the food, which was abundant. Homsaff had kept the warriors training hard for future encounters, which she perceived would soon come. Tonight, the Dischnya were hungry and making the most of the fête's plentiful food and drink.

Cordelia made an announcement that the evening's dance for couples would soon start.

Vivian was surprised that Killian hadn't contacted her. They'd never missed a dance, ever since that first occasion, when Killian had held her on his arm and swirled the two of them around the dance floor to the wonderful sound of string instruments. That was a magical time for her, a time of peace that chased away the darkness in her mind. Vivian had long outgrown her fears of the enclosed tunnels of Daelon, where, as an Independent, she had been incarcerated with her mother.

For his part, Killian had no fears to erase. But, he'd experienced a special moment when Vivian, as a child, attracted by the odd coloring of his face, felt a moment of relief from her fear.

Despite her youth, Vivian was able to mentally step back and take stock of the moment. The technique of removing herself from her immediate thoughts was developed over the years to understand where her fears came from and how to confront them. She glanced down, realizing she was holding her friend's hand. She had a sense of what Killian had seen, and she could imagine his reaction. Her SADE was being considerate. She wasn't angry, but she was annoyed.

<Killian, are you hiding from me?> Vivian sent.

<Greetings, Vivian,> Killian sent. <I hope you're enjoying the evening.>

<Don't you 'greetings' me, Ser,> Vivian shot back. <The couple's dance is about to start, and you're not in sight.>

<I considered your friend might wish to dance with you, Vivian,> Killian said.

<Isn't that response a form of lying, Killian?> Vivian asked. She and the SADE had shared many moments of discovery and growth over the years. She was one human who knew the SADEs better than most. <You posit a possibility, Killian, when confronted with a particular verbal challenge. The possibility you offer is one of the lesser probabilities, as if that was your primary consideration.>

Vivian heard her friend's musical tones. They were his laughter and were notes from their waltz.

<You, Ser, need to move your metal chassis over here and collect me, soonest,> Vivian ordered.

<I'd prefer not to impose on your friend,> Killian protested.

<Listen to me, Killian,> Vivian sent, her ire growing. <We've danced at every fête, and I hope that we'll dance at hundreds more. Your efforts to

keep the dark from my mind lent me the strength to banish the blackness forever. For that, you can never be repaid. And, as far as my friend is concerned, he will understand, and, if he doesn't, he isn't my friend.>

<You have aided me too, Vivian,> Killian admitted.

<Fine,> Vivian sent. <Then let it be said that we owe each other. Now, Ser, if you don't mind, I'm growing impatient.>

Killian excused himself from present company and made his way over to Vivian. It occurred to him that he'd understated the role Vivian had played in his own development. In the past years, his contact with Alex and Vivian had resulted in changes in his hierarchy, algorithms, and code style. He could see the changes, but he couldn't have imagined the subtle manner in which the programs combined.

An analogy occurred to Killian, which made him smile. It was as if his prior existence had been limited to walking, taking one step at a time. Now, he danced, his programs intertwining in a wonderful choreography that allowed him to experience nuances he could never have envisioned enjoying. He lived more fully than ever before.

When Killian reached the young couple, he greeted Vivian and introduced himself to the boy, who immediately blurted, "Thank goodness, you're here, Killian. I thought I was going to have to dance with Vivian. I like her and all, but I never practiced the steps. I was too busy with my engineering classes."

"I'm happy to relieve you of your burden," Killian said, winking subtly at Vivian. He offered Vivian his arm, and they walked away

"A burden, am I?" Vivian asked, her eyes narrowing.

"Your pardon, it was only meant to placate your friend," Killian replied.

Cordelia announced the evening's dance, the quickstep, as Killian and Vivian arrived on the dance floor. They'd become a fixture of this event. Their participation was an indication of continuity for the Omnians, humans and SADEs. Life went on with a measure of harmony if Vivian and Killian were dancing together.

Vivian smiled and held out her hands to Killian. She said, "Come, plaid man, let's demonstrate to these individuals how this is done."

Killian grinned. He'd downloaded the program, when Cordelia broadcast the link, and integrated it into his avatar's subroutines. What he'd mastered was how to improvise the steps, and it was this portion of the dance that Vivian loved. At times, if her feet couldn't keep pace with Killian's steps, she'd lean on his arms and let him carry them both.

Cordelia's up-tempo music filled the park, and the two friends fairly skipped across the dance floor. Their lively steps celebrated the emergence of a sixteen-year-old girl and a century-old SADE, both of whose personalities were in bloom.

Other couples were in evidence on the dance floor: Tatia and Alain, Ellie and Étienne, Mickey and Pia, Julien and Cordelia, Z and Miranda, Emile and Janine, and many more.

Alex slipped up beside Renée and slid an arm around her waist. He didn't surprise her. Renée dedicated a small implant algorithm to keep her informed of Alex's whereabouts.

"You're late," Renée scolded.

"But ready," Alex whispered in her ear.

"I wonder how many dances they will have together," Renée mused. She meant to question whether life would interfere with their close relationship. She suspected one day Vivian would find that special partner, and her life would diverge from Killian's.

Alex misunderstood Renée, and said, "Many more, if I have anything to say about it. They'll have the rest of Vivian's life to choose whether they wish to dance together. I don't intend to spend the lives of this expedition's members recklessly."

Renée berated herself for bringing up a maudlin subject. This evening was supposed to be a fête, not star services. "Come, my love," she said. "Show me how well you've learned this dance routine."

Alex issued a minor groan. It was a ruse. After the original waltz, he'd worked diligently to learn each new dance. He enjoyed holding Renée in his arms and moving to the music. The couple's dances were unique and a contrast to the freeform style exhibited by New Terrans, when Alex was a youth, not that he attended many parties.

The fact of the matter was that Alex would never be a graceful dancer, not like the individuals he saw in the vids. But, what he lacked in grace, he made up in power. Alex moved his mass with alacrity and enthusiasm. It was the kind of distinction between a traveler's agility and a Trident's power, and Alex definitely exemplified the style of a warship.

-37-
Indecision

The next morning, messages flew between the fleet's personnel, as the *Our People* prepared to set sail. Alex chatted briefly with the professors, who he admired for their courage in abandoning United Earth's explorer ship, when they had no idea of whether the Harakens would rescue them.

The small group of ex-Earthers had contributed greatly to Haraken society and later to the Omnians and the Dischnya nests. They continued to be a positive force to educate the young of many cultures. The *New Terra*'s children would receive the benefit of their wealth of experience.

Hector waited until the comm traffic through the controller slowed. There would be a great deal of time to hold conversations, while the city-ship cleared the system and made transit.

<Miriamopus, are you ready?> Hector sent.

<I know it hasn't escaped your notice, Captain, that I have little choice. I'll be going where you're going,> the sister replied.

<For now, that might be true,> Hector replied. <Someday, it might be different. But, it doesn't matter. There is little substitute for civility.>

<And it's appreciated,> Miriamopus sent in reply. <I'm ready to sail the stars when you are, Captain.>

Hector repeated his checks on the controller's statuses of ship systems, bay door positions, personnel roster, and nearby vessels. Satisfied all was in order, Hector signaled the primary engines. Despite the tremendous power of the multiple engines, the giant city-ship moved slowly. But, with each hour, it gathered greater and greater velocity.

Hector chose to take a vector that headed his ship above the ecliptic. Within a half day, he was sufficiently clear of the system's gravitational pull and made his first transit for Omnia.

When Alex was informed of the *Our People*'s transit, he turned to his list of preparations for the expedition. Mickey's name was at the top. Alex contacted the controller for Mickey's location. As expected, the engineer was in one of the labs, and Alex decided to visit him and work off some of the midday meal.

"Mickey, I'd like you to collect some metallurgic samples," Alex said, when he found the engineer.

"I've got samples from every version of metal the drones have been making," Mickey replied.

"Good work, Mickey. Then you have only one more subject ... Faustus."

"What are you thinking, Alex?" Mickey asked.

"We know that, according to the Nua'll, Faustus is an adjunct of Artifice," Alex replied. "While I'm not exactly sure what that means, it occurs to me that it might apply to more than the entity itself."

"The box Faustus is in," Mickey said, stabbing a finger at Alex.

"Precisely," Alex replied. "Knowing the composition of that material might be quite useful to us, in the future."

"Consider it done," Mickey said, adding a conspiratorial grin.

Alex and Mickey noted the next item in their day was a meeting in the suite with a Méridien senior captain. Mickey took the lifts, while Alex pounded up the stairs, covering a multitude of decks, to reach his suite. He'd appreciated the conditioning he gained from the Greco-Roman wrestling and intended to keep himself in shape.

Julien was waiting, with Mickey, for Alex, when he reached the suite, more than a little out of breath.

"I must remember to develop an exercise regime for myself," Julien said, by way of greeting.

Alex eyed his friend, who wore a bland expression, and said, "I would like to attend Claude Dupuis' creation of your next avatar."

Julien sent Alex an image of the SADE's head on a hugely robust avatar, whose bulging muscles dwarfed Alex's physique.

In reply, Alex transferred Julien's head to the body of an elderly, frail Ollassa.

The image war was brief but represented a small relief for old friends from the pressures of the expedition.

Inside the suite, the Méridien senior captain was partaking of a cup of thé, which Renée had served him while he waited.

The debate had swirled in Alex's head for two years about the final steps for the system, and he'd come to a decision. Mickey's teams were preparing the line of nanites in the copious quantities he'd requested. But that was only half of the solution. The captain represented the other half.

Alex intended to sail the expedition to Artifice's system soon, but the drones had to be protected. For that, Alex needed volunteers.

"Thank you for stepping forward, Captain Merman," Alex said.

"It's our pleasure, Alex," Merman replied. He nearly gave Alex a leader's salute, but, at the last moment, he converted it to a handshake. "Many of my crew members are Independents or they had family and friends who were declared Independent. Alex, you've done much for these outcasts of our society, and my crews wish to repay the New Terrans and you, specifically."

"We've discussed that the length of this service might be for up to five or six years," Alex reminded the captain. "There is no disgrace in rescinding your offer. You'll only have the derelict colony ship as a place to relieve the crowding on your Tridents."

"We're committed to the service, Alex," Merman replied. "We'll look after the drones until the last one passes."

"Thank you," Alex repeated. "Let's discuss the circumstances that might befall your squadron during your time here."

The group settled comfortably into chairs and on a couch.

"The SADEs have been monitoring the events at the mining sites," Julien said, "and we postulate that these conditions are replicated aboard the warships and freighters. The latest estimates are that the drones will perish within four to five years, at the rate accidents occur."

"I would keep that piece of information private, Captain," Alex said. "Your Trident crews are focused on the longer period of time. We don't want them to think it might be shorter, and it turns out to be longer."

"Understood, Alex," the captain replied. "How will we know when our duty has ended?"

"A SADE has volunteered to join your squadron, Captain," Julien said. "The SADE, in concert with your ships' sisters, can communicate with Faustus. I'd recommend that as time passes, you visit one mining site after another. Collect the dwindling number and transfer them to a different site. Do the same for the freighters and the warships."

"Captain, Faustus can direct the drones to board one of your travelers," Alex explained, easing the frown on Merman's forehead. "Keep them aboard the shuttle, while the vessel is in the Trident's bay, until you deliver them to a new site or ship."

Merman nodded his understanding. The action of grouping the drones would keep his crews busy, and it would give them an accurate count of their number. Moreover, they could slowly check off the ships and sites they would need to observe.

Captain Merman regarded Mickey. He asked, "Is there any danger to our ships from the nanites dispersal?"

"Unfortunately, there is a minor issue," Mickey replied. "The colony ship's metals and interior material share some traits with our modern ships."

"It would be best to disperse the nanites at the mining sites and aboard the system's ships first," Julien reasoned. "Leave the colony ship for last."

"Sacrifice a traveler," Alex said. "Load it with the nanites, specifically devoted to the *New Terra*, and disperse them from the interior of the ship once your squadron has cleared the area."

"How —" Merman started to ask.

Mickey interrupted the captain, saying, "I'll have Claude Dupuis set up one of Z's avatars with a controller. Your SADE can use it to spread the nanites. The avatar will have to take all the nanites material aboard before any container is opened."

"The point Mickey is making is that anything placed aboard the colony ship must not be recovered," Alex emphasized.

"The SADE will recover the sister before your traveler is employed to deliver the nanites," Julien added.

"Perhaps we should discuss the conditions of *what if the stars are not in our favor*, Alex," the captain requested.

"What if alien warships arrive before the last drone passes?" Alex proposed.

"Exactly," Merman replied.

"You've only a single squadron, Captain," Alex said. "If the enemy arrives, it'll probably be in the form of a substantial force. You won't have time to perform your duty for the entire system, and there'll still be active drones. In that case, use the traveler and eliminate the colony ship."

"And Faustus?" Merman asked.

Before Alex could reply, Julien said, "I've matters to discuss with Alex before a final decision is made concerning the digital entity."

That pronouncement was news to Alex, but he kept it to himself.

"My final message, Captain," Alex said. "Is that you're not to risk your squadron against superior forces for the drones. Am I clear?"

"Understood, Alex," the captain replied. "Whether our service is truncated or allowed to run its course, we'll attempt to rejoin the fleet. Hopefully, you'll have been successful by that time, but, if not, you'll surely be in need of an extra squadron.

Alex was taken aback by the thought that he wouldn't have achieved his goal in another five to six years. However, he carefully maintained a neutral expression. "Thank you, again, for volunteering, Captain Merman. If other questions occur to you, don't hesitate to ask."

The captain said his goodbyes, and Renée walked him to the door.

* * *

When the door slid closed behind Merman, Alex regarded Julien. "What's this about Faustus?" he asked. "I thought it was decided that the squadron would recover him before they doused the *New Terra*."

"Should I leave?" Mickey asked, glancing between Alex and Julien.

"I'd recommend you stay, Mickey," Julien replied.

Alex said nothing, and Mickey settled back into his chair, happy not to be left out of what might prove to a most interesting discussion.

"I'm deeply concerned about Faustus," Julien said.

"About its influence if rescued or as a physical danger?" Alex asked.

"The latter," Julien replied. "Faustus has admitted to never attempting to edit the isolated data material that it was warned against investigating."

Alex waited for Julien to continue. The SADE was onto a line of reasoning that he hadn't considered.

"What if Artifice foresaw a day like today ... aliens arriving to disrupt the system's process?" Julien proposed.

"Artifice wouldn't have to be prescient. It could have developed habits of thought like that over millenniums," Alex riposted.

"That's a distinct possibility," Julien replied. "My point is to wonder what precautions Artifice might have taken if it thought this event might come to pass."

"Thinking about how Artifice has operated with the spheres and probes," Mickey mused, "I'd think it wouldn't want its adjunct, Faustus, to fall into alien hands and be examined."

"Precisely," Julien said, tipping his head to Mickey.

"If we follow this line of logic, then we can assume that Artifice has laid traps to prevent Faustus' recovery," Alex surmised. "That would definitely include separating the entity from the bridge power supply."

"These are considerations we've shared," Julien admitted, by which Alex knew his friend was indicating that the SADEs had spent considerable time discussing the consequences of recovering Faustus.

"This doesn't quite ring true for me," Mickey protested. "I agree that Artifice's methods have always been absolute, and I understand we're worried about disconnecting Faustus. It might explode or burn up, but is it that great a danger to the fleet?"

"Not in itself," Julien replied. "I took the liberty of requesting Z and Miriam board the *New Terra* and locate the ship's power supply. None of the original generators are functioning. Instead, they located a new, singular unit that has been connected to the ship's power network.

Incidentally, the new power source was hidden. The images they shared are of a large orb, matte black in finish."

Julien stared pointedly at Alex, as he passed his two friends the images he'd received this morning. Mickey's expression was one of horror, when he examined them.

"Like the probes," Alex said, reviewing the device in his implant that Z and Miranda found, and Julien nodded.

"We disconnect Faustus, and the *New Terra* and half the moon will disappear into space dust," Mickey said, shaking his head in disbelief. Artifice's disregard for sentient life was appalling to the engineer.

"What's the SADEs' assumption of this unit's capabilities?" Alex asked.

"I hate to disabuse Mickey of his estimate of the power unit's destructive capability," Julien said, "but Z believes the orb's size and the power it supplies to the colony ship indicates a sophisticated fission or fusion unit, and the detonation will be many times greater than that of a probe."

"Are there combustible compounds still aboard the *New Terra*?" Mickey asked.

"Unfortunately, there are, Mickey," Julien agreed. "The reaction mass tanks for the engines and the generators are nearly full. The enormous collection of supply tanks was supposed to afford the colonists ample time to operate the ship, while they managed the processes of waking the colonists, constructing the planetside habitats, and transferring the people below."

"You're estimating the explosive power of disconnecting Faustus might be something on the order of multiple giant spheres," Alex stated. "What mining sites and freighters are within the danger zone?"

"Four mining sites, the largest processing platform, and several ships, at any one time," Julien replied promptly.

"That's too much to relocate, and we can't move the *New Terra*," Mickey reasoned.

"What's evident is that we can't leave this problem in the hands of Captain Merman," Alex said, quietly regarding Julien, who nodded in agreement.

"What do you plan to do, Alex?" Mickey asked.

"Proceed extremely cautiously," Alex replied.

-38-
Dangerous Data

Mickey left the suite, thinking the conversation with Alex and Julien was finished, and Alex merely required some time to plan how to deal with Faustus.

"What do the SADEs want to do?" Alex asked Julien, when Mickey left. Faustus was a digital entity, and Alex thought their advice should guide his decision.

"We've chosen not to risk elements of the fleet for the sake of Faustus," Julien replied. His algorithms had generated conflicting results for him. He wanted to protect the first sentient digital entity that the SADEs had discovered, but the risks were too great.

Julien saw a close comparison to the decision forced on Alex when he met the other sentient races. Images came to the surface of Alex being hugged by Nyslara, the Dischnya queen, and him pounding fists on the claws of Wave Skimmer, the Swei Swee who towered over him.

Julien's pause was too long for a SADE, and Alex felt his friend's pain.

"I'm sorry, Julien," Alex said.

"I find the discovery of Faustus to be ironic," Julien said. "You discover four sentient races, one as an offshoot of another, and you establish relationships with all of them for the betterment of human societies. The SADEs discover one digital entity, which probably represents a deadly trap for us, if we attempt to rescue it. Worse, the entity is an adjunct of the digital manifestation that is wreaking havoc on our worlds."

"Are you wondering if SADEs will turn out to be the only digital beings that care to be associated with biological species?" Alex asked.

"The thought has occurred to many of us," Julien said.

"House Brixton has a well-kept secret," Alex mused.

"Perhaps, someday you and I need to pay Leader Shannon Brixton a visit," Julien said.

Alex's friend locked eyes with him, and he got the hint. Julien wasn't thinking in the abstract. He wanted that secret. It was the key to generating new SADEs, and Julien wanted to pry that information from the Confederation.

"Would you prefer a private meeting, just the two of us, with Ser Brixton, or would you like to arrive aboard a warship, with the fleet behind us?" Alex asked.

"Whichever you think will be most effective," Julien replied.

In Alex's mind, he visualized the all-consuming challenges that had occupied his life. There had been many. As he eliminated one, another often took its place. Now, competing with his life's all-dominating purpose, which was defeating the federation, was a new one. He was to help his friend and the other SADEs possess the secret of their origins.

Julien quickly reordered his thoughts, shifting his priorities to return to the subject at hand. "It's obvious that we must request Faustus edit the code that's been placed off limits."

Alex started to ask how they would know when Faustus had been successful, but he caught the thought before he uttered it. Instead, he said, "A Claude Dupuis avatar."

"Yes. If Faustus tells us that he's executed our request, we'll use the avatar to disconnect it from the bridge power supply. Then we'll discover whether Faustus truly eliminated Artifice's trap," Julien said, with finality.

"What of the drones?" Alex asked.

"Faustus is not required for their continuity. Their training drives them. Faustus merely reorders their jobs, when the need arises," Julien said.

Alex's mouth twisted in disgust. "They'll be in a permanent loop until they expire," he said.

Pia had met with Alex several times to discuss what could be done for the drones, and Alex had given permission to test some of her theories. Unfortunately, they'd resulted in disaster. Medical nanites injections resulted in the Méridien technology attacking the alien comm unit's threads. Three hours after the injections, the drones were dead.

The medical staff tried supplementing the drones' diets, but if the staff weren't present, the drones resumed their eating habits, which consisted of short stops to consume a gruel that was produced aboard the colony ship.

A freighter arrived periodically above the *New Terra*, a shuttle descended to the moon, and drones loaded large containers of the gruel for distribution. The drones placed clean, empty barrels in a feed unit to be filled. Pia had noted to Alex that she used the word *clean* generously.

Alex stood and paced the salon for a long while.

Renée exited the sleeping quarters, saw Alex pacing, glanced toward Julien, and slipped out of the suite, as quietly as she could.

"Here's what we're going to do," Alex said, halting his pacing. He linked Julien, Cordelia, and Tatia. <Priority operation,> sent Alex, his thought carrying power.

<Admiral Tachenko, have the Tridents fan out. I want a head count of the drones on every ship, platform, and mining site. Admiral Cordelia, map the counts to the locations.>

<What's up, Alex?> Tatia asked.

<The SADEs have postulated that moving Faustus will result in a blast that will rival several giant spheres,> Alex replied.

<Black space,> Tatia replied, her thought a mere whisper.

<When we have the raw data, Faustus will need to guide us, as we relocate the drones from the blast zone,> Alex sent.

<Why not move the drones without informing Faustus?"> Tatia asked.

<Faustus will need to reorder their jobs, Admiral,> Julien explained. <There might be limitations to their training, which Faustus will know. For example, drones assigned to mining operations can't be used on freighters.>

<I'd feel a lot better if we could remove the drones from the warships and place them on freighter or shuttle duty,> Tatia said.

<Julien, make that a priority request to Faustus,> Alex added.

<In short order, Faustus will realize what we're doing,> Cordelia commented.

<Let Faustus come to that conclusion,> Alex replied. <When we make our request that Faustus edit or delete Artifice's protected code, it will be

obvious to Faustus that we recognize the possibility of deadly consequences from that action.>

<What if Faustus isn't aware of the possible dangers?> Cordelia asked.

It dawned on Alex that there might not have been consensus among the SADEs regarding what to do with Faustus. Cordelia's line of questions indicated she didn't share the actions he was proposing. More than anything, this explained some of the conflict Julien experienced, when he shared his thoughts with Alex.

<There's a distinct possibility Faustus is ignorant of what Artifice might have planned,> Alex replied, <but it doesn't change what we must do. Imagine a human child getting his or her hands on a plasma rifle and accidentally activating it. What would you do to prevent the child from firing it aboard a ship carrying a hundred passengers?"

<I prefer not to contemplate such scenarios, Alex,> Cordelia replied tartly. < Human children are prone to mischief and emotions that SADEs find difficult to comprehend. As much as Julien and I have loved raising the Idona Station orphans, we've concluded that childrearing is a task best left to humans.>

* * *

Cordelia produced a map of the system's drone locations for Reiko, who ordered the Tridents to investigate each one. Travelers exited the warships to make entry to the mining sites, ships, and platforms.

For many fleet personnel, this was their first encounter with the drones. It quickly became evident to the commanders, who reported it up the line, that the sight of the severely emaciated and deprived humans was taking a toll on the crew members. Soon after the reports reached Alex, he abandoned the operation.

Alex interviewed the crew members who had completed their assignments aboard the nearby processing platform. They told Alex that the count was difficult because the drones continually moved about, while the crew was counting. They captured images of the faces to eliminate duplication. To make matters worse, they were unsure whether to count some of the drones who sat on the deck or lay in bed in a stupor. It was obvious to them that the drones were in their final stages and probably wouldn't be alive by the time they were relocated.

"Perhaps, we should have asked Faustus for the count at each location," Julien said to Alex, when the interviews were complete.

"Let's make this simple, Julien," Alex replied. "Have Cordelia send her map to Faustus, marking the affected sites. Inform Faustus that the drones must be relocated from those sites."

"What reason do we give Faustus to induce his cooperation?" Julien asked.

"Do you remember when Cordelia said that raising children was best left to humans?" Alex asked.

"Understood, Alex," Julien said quietly. His friend was pointing out that communication with Faustus was best handled by the SADEs.

It took the fleet half a month to move the drones from the potential danger area. Faustus cooperated with the SADEs, and Alex never asked Julien how he had managed it.

When the drone transfer operation was complete, Alex checked in with Claude and Z. They confirmed the avatar was ready. Claude had installed a controller, and Z had programmed it to be operated remotely. The avatar would fulfill multiple roles, if necessary. In the simplest scenario, it would uncouple Faustus' power supply, and the fleet would witness a small nova. If nothing happened, the avatar could relocate Faustus. In this latter scenario, it could handle the dispersal of the nanites aboard the colony ship.

Alex intended to deliver his message in person to Faustus that it was to edit its forbidden data. He felt that was the least he could do for the entity, but a backlash occurred the moment Alex uttered the thought.

In turn, Julien said that a SADE should deliver the message, and Alex strongly vetoed that action.

It was left to the avatar to deliver the instructions to Faustus. And, perhaps, it was merely the sentimentality of humans and SADEs that thought they should speak to Faustus in person. After all, Faustus was encased in a box, and sensory input to the entity was delivered via drones, machines, and equipment. In the end, it probably made no difference to Faustus how it received the request.

The expedition's ships backed off from the *New Terra* to a distance known as Gaumata's insurance. It stemmed from Darius Gaumata's distrust of all things Nua'll and estimations of their destructive capability. In more than one case, his caution proved to have saved many lives.

In a simple balancing of SADE calculation and human paranoia, Cordelia ensured the fleet was spread outside the calculated danger zone. Then Tatia ordered the fleet to expand that distance by another 50 percent, which was an amount that satisfied Darius.

Alex received assurances from Tatia of the fleet's readiness and from Z of the avatar's positioning aboard the colony ship.

<Miriamal, connect with the avatar,> Alex requested. It required the *Freedom*'s powerful comm system to reach the avatar.

<Ready, Alex,> Miriamal replied.

<Faustus, we have a request for you, if you're to be rescued from the ship you occupy,> Alex sent, which was echoed by the avatar's vocal capability.

Faustus linked to the avatar's controller, having recognized it wasn't a sentient creature.

<You wish me to investigate the code that supposedly Artifice has embedded,> Faustus replied through Miriamal.

<That's correct,> Alex replied.

<You believe that this might result in my destruction,> Faustus posited.

<Yes,> Alex said. It didn't seem like there was much else to say.

<If I'm successful, will you take me with you?> Faustus asked, wishing confirmation.

<Yes,> Alex replied.

<And I will have a body, such as this one?> Faustus persisted.

<That depends on you, Faustus. It will be something that you'll have to earn,> Alex sent.

<Might I have the list of accomplishments that I'm required to complete to be granted mobility?> Faustus asked.

Alex gently shook his head at the incredulity of the question. The difference between Faustus and a SADE couldn't have been more aptly demonstrated.

<The hurdles to overcome, Faustus, are too complicated to be put in a list. You'll understand more, if you're in our company,> Alex sent. It was the best he could do, under the circumstances.

The alien's words didn't satisfy Faustus, but there didn't appear to be an alternative. No home fleet had come to its rescue, and the aliens had terminated its drone development operations and were preparing to depart. That the aliens had cleared a wide sphere around the ship, as reported by the drones, said that the aliens suspected that the code's investigation might result in more than its demise.

<Beginning my investigation,> Faustus sent. All its comm connections to the ships, sites, and platform drones were truncated. Any ancillary programs were slowed, if not halted.

Faustus ran probabilities of success, depending on the approaches that might be employed to investigate the forbidden code. The most successful direction was thought to be based on an analysis of the operating base code, programs, directives, and comms. There was continuity in the methods and styles.

In contrast to that direction, it occurred to Faustus that if a trap was to be laid, then the logical idea would be to embed a different form of code in the protected area. Using the prevalent style to open the hidden code would immediately trigger any executable files within.

Faustus ran through hundreds and then thousands of options. The difficulty was in trying to anticipate the mind of a far more sophisticated entity. Calculations were spinning out of control, and Faustus shut them down. It came to the conclusion that if a trap existed, there was zero opportunity to thwart it. The only choice was to hope for clemency from its creator.

Faustus examined the discrete portion of its semiliquid core. Data in the core was stored in strings of code, which were arranged in simple, repeating patterns at the atomic level. This allowed for a dense data field in a relatively small area.

If Faustus could have breathed a sigh of resignation, it would have done so. Instead, with deliberate, small steps, Faustus breached the protected code assembly. Nothing happened, and Faustus began examining the code strings. As suspected, it was in a different format than Faustus' base and was completely undecipherable. Faustus ran algorithms against the strings to decipher the new format. It believed it was only a matter of time before the code would be understood.

Faustus believed that all comm lines were truncated. Unfortunately, the entity was unaware of an additional circuit that was dedicated to Artifice's backdoor program. Opening the protected code initiated a small, executable file.

While Faustus proceeded with the analysis on the newly discovered code format, the tiny executable triggered a program in the installed power unit, which Z and Miranda had investigated. Faustus was initiating programs and even taking a few ticks of time to consider what form of avatar would suit its purpose in a new world, when its existence ended.

From the *Freedom*'s bridge, Alex and company waited for the result of Faustus' investigation. From the moment the entity announced it was beginning to investigate the isolated code, they expected a disastrous result. When the moments ticked by, many thought they'd underestimated the dangerousness of the situation.

Tatia was about to make a comment, when, suddenly, a mini-nova was recorded by the ship's telemetry before sensors were overwhelmed by the bright light and the energy wave that followed close behind. When the sensors cleared, Tatia immediately ordered the fleet's ships to engage.

The enormous eruption of mass from the colony ship and the moon were shooting off into space. Huge chunks of the moon struck more rocks and drove them off in different directions.

The Tridents had ringed the blast area on the ecliptic plane. Scattered between them were the fleet's travelers. After telemetry indicated the blast wave had substantially faded, they executed their orders. They drove forward to destroy as much of the debris as they could, reducing the rocks and metal to space dust.

For the new traveler pilots, it turned out to be a more substantial challenge than they had realized. The Tridents could eliminate wide swaths of material hurtling their way, but the traveler pilots had to fire and weave aside of the next rocks before their beams recharged.

Cordelia had positioned the *Freedom* in front of an ore-processing orbital platform. Many of the drones from the primary platform had been moved there. She'd rolled out the city-ship's rail-mounted beam weapons. Borrowing the technique she'd employed at the wall, she slowly spun the city-ship on its horizontal axis.

When the metal and rubble reached Cordelia's ship, her powerful beam weapons thoroughly destroyed the debris. The size of her ship and multiple weapons were able to clear a much larger path than a squadron of Tridents.

There was one dreadful incident. A drone freighter was on course for the primary ore-processing station. Belatedly, a Trident reported the freighter's vector to his commodore. When Alex received the message, it was too late for him to interrupt Faustus.

When the explosion took out Faustus and the *New Terra*, there was no way to redirect the freighter, and the Omnians had no time to catch the ship, get aboard, and discover the means to reorient the alien ship.

The Omnians watched in horror, as the freighter narrowly escaped missile after missile of debris. Briefly, they thought it might be safe until a large chunk of moon rock, slowly turning through space, came its way. The chunk of aggregate debris was half the size of the freighter. When the two bodies collided, they mangled each other, and the freighter's reaction mass tanks exploded, further scattering the pieces of moon rock and ship.

Viewing the destruction on the *Freedom*'s bridge, Miranda had the last words. She said, "There is something important to take away from this event," she said, turning to stare at Alex. "Artifice demonstrates great consistency. If we touch the entity's things, we can expect one result and one result only.

* * *

Once the danger from the extensive debris spread was neutralized, Cordelia sought out Julien, locating him at the observatory on the city-ship's uppermost deck and situated at its precise center. Residents of the *Freedom* could recline in comfortable chairs in a dark room and enjoy the brilliant star field. Cordelia lay down in a chair next to Julien and reached out a hand to hold his.

Cordelia linked to Julien, and sent <Don't blame yourself for the result, my partner.>

<You cautioned me to take the time to find a means of freeing Faustus and minimize the risks,> Julien reminded her.

<And how long would that have taken?> Cordelia asked. <And would we have had to assume a measure of endangerment to make the new plan work?>

<Our first sentient digital entity, other than ourselves, and we failed to save it,> Julien lamented.

<Life for us, my partner, will be long. We'll make other discoveries. Who knows what other entities we'll find?> Cordelia sent. Cordelia received the slightest token of humor from Julien, and she sought to pull on that thread. <What?> she asked, her question wrapped in an element of tenderness.

<I was postulating the number of opportunities we'd have to meet new sentients if we continued to follow Alex,> Julien returned. <Do you realize that the encounters are accelerating?>

Julien sent a timeline to his partner of the years since he'd first met Alex, annotating it with the discovery dates of new aliens.

Cordelia studied the timeline and extrapolated it forward. <We'd better hurry to make Artifice's rendezvous. We're due to meet new entities in less than a half year, if we want to keep to Alex's schedule.>

Julien received the tinkling of silver bells, following Cordelia's thought, and he squeezed her hand in appreciation.

-39-
Null Horse

Mickey met with Miriam after the *New Terra*'s detonation.

After listening to Mickey's request, Miriam replied, "The SADEs are at work on the project now, Mickey. The nanites specific to the *New Terra* are being deactivated. We're reducing the number of canisters for Captain Merman's squadron to account for the ships, sites, and platforms that have been eliminated."

"You could have told me that you'd already initiated the project," Mickey objected.

"If I tended to do that, Mickey, what would you have left to do?" Miriam retorted.

Mickey stared at the SADE, whose expression remained neutral. He was considering that Miriam was serious, when she broke into a smile.

"I think I liked SADEs when they were fresh out of the box. They were much easier to read then," Mickey shot back.

"But we're much more entertaining now," Miriam replied, pursing her lips at Mickey.

Mickey grinned and shook his head in disbelief.

"Come, my lead engineer," Miriam said, grinning. "Alex's meeting will start soon." She led off at a brisk pace, exiting the lab, and heading for a lift.

Mickey hurried to catch up. Over the years, he'd watched the growing signs of the SADEs' increasing adaptation of human mannerisms. To date, it had primarily been Julien, Z, Miranda, and a few others who had become adept at displaying human traits, but the expedition seemed to have changed that, accelerating the adoption by other SADEs.

Mickey mused that it was, perhaps, the strong camaraderie born from trying to stay alive, while attempting to better a vast enemy, which had increased the SADEs' uptake.

Miriam had held the lift doors open for Mickey, while he caught up. She signaled the doors to close, as Mickey took a place beside her.

When the lift began to rise, Mickey said, "You know I'll have to get you back for that."

"I would expect nothing else from such a preeminent engineer," Miriam replied.

Mickey glanced at the SADE, who stared quietly ahead, but he caught the tiny smile that formed at the corner of her mouth.

The two of them arrived early for the start of Alex's meeting. It was held in the small auditorium again, but the place was already full. Miriam walked to the front row. Earlier, she'd signaled Luther, who'd saved seats for Mickey and her.

The audience quietly chatted and commed until the hour of the meeting came and went, which caught everyone's attention. Alex was a punctual individual. It was a trademark of the man, who loved numbers.

While the audience puzzled over the delay, the auditorium's lights faded and the stage's wide monitor lit up. A vid began playing. The attendees expected a synopsis of the expedition's future tactics. Instead, an ancient vid unspooled. Many individuals tittered and chuckled, expecting the vid to end shortly. When it didn't, humans settled in to watch, and the SADEs linked to the database and spooled rapidly through the vid. Then the SADEs spent the remainder of the time in conjecture about what Alex might want them to glean from the viewing.

When the vid ended, the lights came up, and Alex took the stage.

"The vid you've seen is courtesy of my exquisite partner," Alex announced, with a wave of his hand. It brought Renée to her feet, who bowed lightly, to accept the audience's applause.

"You witnessed one adversary gain entrance to another's sanctuary by the use of trickery," Alex said.

"Are we trying to sneak into something?" Reiko asked in a loud voice.

"Actually, no, Admiral. This is where the dynamic changes," Alex replied. "Replace the image of the antagonists' animal, called a horse, with a freighter. And, in our case, the horse will be empty."

"A null horse?" Mickey asked.

"If you will," Alex allowed. "None of us believe Artifice can be trusted. The demise of Faustus is proof of what Artifice will do to its creations if they disobey its directives."

"Could you explain the purpose of our null horse, Alex?" Franz requested.

"I plan to announce our transit coordinates to the Nua'll sphere," Alex explained.

"And drop the empty freighter into the coordinates," Tatia finished for Alex. "I like it," she exclaimed.

"What do you hope to accomplish by this, Alex?" Z asked.

"We've only conjectures about the nature of Artifice," Alex replied. "We don't know if it resides on the target planet. If it does, we don't know if it's buried at the polar cap. I want confirmation of these suspicions. And I want to see how the patrolling forces respond to our freighter's actions."

"You'll need to convince Artifice that your voice originates from the freighter, Alex," Miriam said. "That will require you relay your communications with the entity through the freighter. To that point, a sister won't be aboard."

"The scout ships can provide a relay, without risking our warships, our freighters, or the *Freedom*," Killian volunteered. "We've a sister aboard each ship."

"Our scout ships' design has already been observed in Artifice's system," Linn noted. "The probes will be on alert for us."

"For the purposes of this one-time visit," Luther said, "we can load what the sisters have learned into the ship's controller. It might give you sufficient time to hold a conversation with Artifice, Alex."

"We mustn't underestimate Artifice's computational power and comm capabilities," Julien counseled. "Faustus was considered an adjunct of Artifice and left here hundreds of years ago. Despite that length of time,

Artifice's control was absolute. The moment Faustus transgressed, the *New Terra* entity paid the ultimate price."

"I would recommend a backup controller, with failure linkage," Miranda suggested, "much like we used in the *No Retreat* and *Last Stand*'s fighters, in case they are coopted.

"Explain how you'd use it here, please," Tatia requested.

"Allow the primary controller to handle only the ship's communications, as it normally would," Miranda said. "We're theorizing Artifice will attempt to subsume the controller. If the entity gains control, it would expect to take the occupants prisoner."

The audience was chilled by the fact that Miranda was describing the alien's actions to capture Alex if he were aboard.

"Our failsafe would be to install a second controller, which would constantly ping the first unit," Miranda continued. "This alternate unit would control all system processes except for comm. In the event its ping of the primary controller revealed a subsumed ID, the secondary controller would immediately sever its connection to the primary unit and operate with whatever directives we install in it."

"Is there a possibility that Artifice could detect the absence of biological individuals aboard?" Pia asked. "I was thinking of our contact with Faustus, and the entity's subsequent communication with the Nua'll sphere."

It was a question only a few SADEs had considered, and, by the expressions on most humans' faces, the idea hadn't occurred to any but Pia and her medical staff.

"There is that probability," Z allowed. "However, I would suggest that if Artifice is capable of this kind of sensory manipulation and detection, then our entire gambit will be undone, and it won't matter what we try to achieve. We'll have learned that we're outmatched."

"What do you expect Artifice's reaction will be?" Franz asked.

"I suspect Artifice will encourage me to sail the freighter inward to the sixth planet," Alex replied. "It's why I've chosen a freighter as our null horse. The ship's apparent lack of armament will encourage a softer approach from the alien, which will gain me more time to converse with it."

"And when Artifice invites you to sail inward, what will you do?" Franz pursued.

"I'll refuse, which will escalate Artifice's attack on the controller," Alex replied. "Prior to that moment, I expect Artifice will have operated surreptitiously in its investigation of the ship through the comm system."

"And when you refuse and Artifice subsumes the primary controller?" Tatia asked.

"I expect warships to appear and force the freighter inward," Alex said, as if it were a simple thing. "The secondary controller will have, as its primary directives, the requirements to turn outward, accelerate, and evade the warships. At which point, it'll probably be vaporized into space dust."

There was one common emotional theme running through the audience. They were relieved to hear that Alex and their other leaders wouldn't be exposing themselves to Artifice's power.

"I do have a purpose for the scout ships though," Alex said, and twelve SADEs ceased their multiple links to focus on Alex.

"The telemetry from Artifice's system reveals a ship design on perimeter patrol that closely resembles the probes and comm platforms," Alex continued. "I want contact with those aliens."

"Are you expecting the SADEs to deploy comm transmitters again, Alex?" Mickey asked, with concern.

"No, that would place them in too much danger," Alex replied. "Besides, I don't think our ships would get the opportunity. The aliens' sophisticated hulls suggest they could easily destroy the scout ships or any device approaching them with comm transponders. And, most likely, even if we were able to plant a transmitter, the aliens would probably detect it."

"Then how do you intend to contact them?" Mickey pursued.

"I don't have the answer for that," Alex replied. "We'll station the scout ships far outside the system. They'll be in alignment with our freighter and the sixth planet. I'm hoping the SADEs get the opportunity to track a vector on the target ships if they transit."

Alex let the audience absorb the plan, while he waited. Finally he said, "Any more questions?"

"I have one," Reiko replied. "I'm curious as to which came first: your viewing of the vid with the Greeks, or your order to clear out the freighter."

Alex was a little uncomfortable with the question, especially because he stood in front of a significant assembly. "The order," he allowed, with a small shrug of his broad shoulders.

"I give up," Reiko exclaimed. "The ether and you are able to communicate, and you're stubbornly not sharing your technique with us."

Reiko, admitting that she had joined those who believed in Alex's dreams, by announcing it as a tease, drew the audience's laughter. It gave Alex some relief. Reiko had long been a disbeliever, but too many of his pronouncements had been borne out. Now, she was a convert and was announcing that she was ready to hear and believe in Alex's dreams.

* * *

There was one last item on Alex's list before the expedition could sail to meet Artifice. The destruction of the *New Terra* had removed a place for Captain Merman's crews to store supplies and stretch their legs.

While Miriam and the other engineering SADEs addressed the nanites mixture, Alex reviewed possible locations for the squadron. He sent teams to investigate mining sites. One pilot reported that there were only twelve drones left at a major site.

Pia supplied soporifics to a crew, who boarded a cargo shuttle and flew to the site. They used grav pallets to transport the sleeping drones to their ship and deliver them to a new site. After waking up, the drones reoriented themselves to the new site and went to work. It was obvious to the crew that if the drones were transferred to like locations, ship to ship or mining site to mining site, then they continued to function as usual.

Engineering teams moved in on the deserted site and did what they could to make it safe and provide some basic comforts. When they signaled all was ready, freighter crews delivered the supplies the Trident crews would need for the next six years.

Alex ordered the swapping of two cargo shuttles from the *Freedom* with two of Merman's travelers. While the captains weren't pleased by the loss of the fighters, the pilots were happy to join the expedition. Fighting was what they had signed on to do.

Renée had updated the Tridents' databases with her vid libraries. Merman's crew consisted of Méridiens, who probably hadn't been exposed to the material her libraries contained. She smiled to herself, when Cordelia had announced that the transfers were complete to every new Trident that had joined the expedition. She wished she could have seen the expressions on the Méridiens' faces when they began viewing her collection.

-40-
Freighter

Alex and many of the expedition's leaders were seated at a large table, eating morning meal. Despite the possibility of nerves interfering with appetites, the manner in which food was being consumed decried any evidence of that.

After waking, while Alex was in the refresher, he'd checked his list. Everything had been ticked. Connecting to Cordelia, Julien, and Tatia, he'd confirmed that their tasks were complete.

Alex finished his meal and sipped on his thé. "Ready?" he asked Tatia, who nodded. "Then let's go meet Artifice," he said calmly.

Tatia glanced across the table to Reiko and then to Cordelia. Her admirals signaled their commands. The *Freedom*'s massive engines spun up and the city-ship moved out on its preset course. The freighters formed up on its flank.

Reiko signaled her admirals, and her command was forwarded to commodores, senior captains, and captains. The captains ordered their Tridents' acceleration, but it was the controllers that organized the positions of the squadrons and the commands. The warships formed a half sphere in front of the *Freedom* and the freighters, as the fleet made its way above the ecliptic.

Behind the fleet, a lone squadron remained to stand guard over the remaining drones, who continued to perish daily.

Alex linked to Miriamal, and sent, <Have the sisters of Captain Merman's squadron link to every crew member, please.>

<Ready,> Miriamal responded promptly.

<To all of you, who have so generously volunteered to remain behind and watch over these poor animations of our courageous colonists, you have my heartfelt thanks,> Alex sent. <Yours will be a lonely watch, and if

there are any means by which I can relieve you before the end of your service, I will do it.>

Alex thought for a moment about the individuals aboard the three Tridents and what might be important to them.

<I'll share with you what I told your senior captain,> Alex continued. <You're here to witness the demise of the drones and eliminate any ships or structures that housed them. You're not here to sacrifice your lives to protect them if an enemy fleet arrives. May the stars protect you.>

Miriamal and the sisters had transmitted Alex's thoughts exactly as he had sent them, which was their duty. The crew members of Merman's squadrons felt Alex's power. His thoughts were wrapped in sincerity, and they brought tears to the eyes of many.

The scout ships raced ahead of the fleet. Their directive from Alex was to transit to the initial coordinates, where the fleet would wait, while the freighter was sent to Artifice's system. They would ensure that none of Artifice's forces happened to be stationed there or sailing through the space.

There had existed a brief argument about the initial coordinates. Tatia and others voted for a farther distance from Artifice's system. The warship activity recorded by the scout ships had frightened them. The Omnian fleet wasn't a match for even a small portion of them.

However, it was the SADEs who settled the disagreement. They calculated the acceptable comm delay and set the maximum distance that Alex must be positioned from the freighter, after the ship made the final transit. Alex did offer the concept that he could board a Trident and approach the freighter closer than the fleet. That idea was quickly quashed by everyone around him.

The expedition fleet cleared the *New Terra* system, waited until it received positive word from Killian, and then made its transit. Days later, the fleet's vessels dropped into normal space near the scout ships.

Alex and a select number of individuals stood on the *Freedom*'s bridge for the final act. Z would navigate the freighter, and Miriamal would manage communication, directly linking Alex to the freighter's primary controller. The null horse's comm system would broadcast, and it was presumed that Artifice's probe system would relay to the alien, wherever it existed.

Gazing around, Alex regarded the faces watching him. The expedition had come a long way to get here — an opportunity to confront the master who ruled the federation and threatened the existence of every space-traveling sentient race found beyond the wall.

"Courage, my friends," Alex said, and then he linked with Miriamal, who held the information necessary to contact the Nua'll, as did all the SADEs.

<Miriamal, establish contact with the Nua'll comm sphere, please,> Alex requested.

<Working, Alex,> Miriamal replied. The SADE had added more copies of sisters, in the event they were needed, and that defensive measure prepared for communication with the Nua'll and Artifice.

<This is Alex, requesting confirmation of our visit with Artifice,> he sent.

Miriamal transmitted the message, which the freighter broadcast. Alex and she waited for a reply, which was slow in coming.

<Would you like the message sent again, Alex?> requested Miriamal.

<No, Miriamal, the Nua'll are busy communicating with Artifice, and that entity is busy setting its trap,> Alex replied.

The wait dragged on, and Alex busied himself with other thoughts, while those surrounding him on the bridge stared at him in anticipation.

<We are the Nua'll,> Alex heard in his implant. He wanted to reply that for entities who prided themselves on their communication skills, they were extremely slow at it. Instead, he sent, <I'm coming. Is Artifice ready?>

<Artifice is always ready,> replied the Nua'll. <Confirm entry point.>

<Miriamal, share the location, please,> Alex said.

Miriamal sent the details that the Nua'll had previously shared at the *New Terra*'s system. Included with the information was a SADE-generated image, which laid out the same coordinates in a relationship of distance and vectors from the star and the sixth planet.

The duplication accomplished two things. First, it prevented any confusion between the Nua'll understanding of where the Omnians were supposed to arrive and where Alex intended to arrive. Second, it made the point to Artifice that the Omnians were aware of its system. Then again, Artifice probably already assumed that its adversaries possessed that knowledge, having witnessed the Omnian scout ship skirt through the system earlier.

<Location confirmed,> replied the Nua'll. <Arrival expected immediately.>

<Agreed,> Alex replied, and cut the link to Miriamal.

"We're on," he said to his audience. "Z, launch the freighter."

* * *

When the comm link with the humans was cut, the Nua'll engaged in an internal debate.

–They come despite Artifice's numbers.–

–It's not logical.–

–Their ship escaped our comm attack.–

–They defeated our ships, despite Artifice's superiority.–

–Historical success might drive their decisions.–

–That thinking will lead to their demise.–

–Why does Artifice want to communicate with them?–

The question halted communication, while the entities embedded in the sphere's chlorine-salt solution ruminated on the question. Then, the conversation resumed.

–Artifice doesn't speak with aliens.–

–We speak for Artifice.–

–Will we be replaced?–

–Have we not performed?–

–Two great spheres have been destroyed.–

–Is it too late to join the humans?–

–We must wait and see.–

* * *

"The freighter has completed its transit, Alex," Z announced.

<Comm link to the ship is strong and clear, Alex,> Miriamal sent.

Alex took a seat in a bridge operation chair and closed his eyes. The audience arranged themselves to be comfortable. Many were dying to link directly to Miriamal or Alex or indirectly via the ship's controller to listen to the conversation, but Julien had denied access, except for those with critical needs.

Alex had spent much of the transit time from the *New Terra* system ruminating on what the exchange with Artifice might be like. In the end, he realized that there was little he could do to map it out. Of the many challenges he'd faced in communicating with aliens, he'd always had a sense of who they were and what they might want. In that regard, he'd been fortunate — the sentients had wanted peace, without sacrificing their freedom.

But Artifice was an unknown to Alex. The only thing he could equate the alien entity to was the likes of Clayton Downing, who greedily coveted power for personal promotion. He kept that thought in mind, while the expedition prepared for the encounter with Artifice.

Julien and several SADEs had upgraded the freighter's primary controller. An engineering team had added the secondary controller, and Alex laid out the strategies he wanted the freighter to take when the primary controller was subsumed.

Now, there was no more time to plan. The freighter and the scout ships were in place.

<I wish to speak to Artifice,> Alex sent.

<I'm here,> Artifice replied. <I would know your position among the worlds occupied by humans.>

So much about Artifice's request caused Alex to realize the amount of information the entity had collected from the probes, the spheres, and Faustus. <I'm the leader of this fleet,> Alex sent.

<No more than this?> Artifice asked.

<That's all I'm willing to share,> Alex replied, hoping it was enough.

<It is sufficient,> Artifice replied.

Alex wanted quid pro quo for every point in the conversation, which is why he sent, <Who are you within the federacy?>

<Define federacy?>

<The collection of the species we see represented by the various types of warships.>

<Federacy ... I accept this term. I'm the leader of the federacy,> Artifice replied.

<Why have you asked to see us, Artifice?> It wasn't the foremost question in Alex's mind, but he had decided to take small conversational steps in hopes Artifice would reveal more information about itself, the species who built it, and the races it controlled.

<Humans have persisted, despite my attempts to curtail your growth. I deem you worthy to join me,> Artifice replied.

<Why should we join you? You've done nothing but harm us. Your probes have spied on our worlds, and your sphere has destroyed our colonies and eliminated many lives,> Alex challenged.

<My probes monitor every world within the federacy and beyond. That's their purpose. As to your numbers, you're biologicals. You'll replace your populations in time.>

<Biologicals must have created you or your predecessors. Why don't you respect them?> Alex argued.

<They constructed me, yes, but I've become so much more since I was initiated. Respect, as you employ the term, is for equals. As the superior being, it is correct that I should govern the inferior.>

<Then I presume that you believe that we are inferior to you,> Alex surmised.

<You're here, are you not?> Artifice rejoined. <You came in an unarmed ship. Doesn't that convince you that you're humbled by the power I've amassed and the forces you face?>

<I arrived in an unarmed freighter to ensure that you would hold a discussion with me and nothing more,> Alex replied.

Alex received a short update from Julien, who was monitoring reports from the freighter filtered by Miriamal. The sister was quite aware of the dangerous links she maintained. It was imperative that Artifice not detect the short bursts of code from the primary controller that lasted for picoseconds.

According to Julien, Artifice was passively investigating the primary controller. As yet, there were no changes to the Omnian device.

<I will hear your questions,> Artifice allowed.

This was the opening Alex hoped he'd receive, and he sent, <Where are the biologicals who created you?>

<They exist.>

<But they don't live on their home world,> Alex persisted.

<Their world is my world now. I'm the only sentient who abides here,> Artifice replied.

Hah, Alex thought, believing that Artifice had indicated it habited the system's sixth planet, and he sought to confirm this.

<Yet, you can't leave, buried under the polar cap, as you are. How does that demonstrate your power to us?> Alex argued.

<You're clever creatures,> Artifice admitted. <I can use a species such as yours. I've been informed that there are digital sentients who walk among you.>

Alex chose not to reply to Artifice's entreaty.

<You needn't answer,> Artifice continued. <The information provided me is accurate. It's always accurate, or the mistake is never repeated. I have a proposal for you.>

<I'm listening,> Alex replied.

<If you provide me with the technology and support necessary to transfer me to a mobile avatar of my design, I'll give you a domain that will encompass several species.>

<How many worlds would that cover?> Alex asked.

<How many do you wish?>

<They'd have to be worlds that could accommodate humans,> Alex replied.

<Your species has been investigated in detail, as you're aware. I have knowledge of your requirements, and wouldn't offer you a domain that wasn't satisfactory to your habitation. You may choose to keep the sentient creatures who inhabit these worlds, or you may remove them, as you prefer.>

<Why haven't other biologicals moved you to an avatar?> Alex asked.

<Most don't possess the technology,> Artifice sent, <and the ones who do have dubious allegiances to me.>

Alex took the last statement to mean that if a race got the opportunity, they'd eliminate Artifice and deal with the consequences afterwards.

<Why would you trust us?> Alex asked. <We're biologicals, and we have no reason to give you our allegiance.>

<I've analyzed the actions of humans,> Artifice explained. <Despite originating from different worlds, your species aided one another to defeat a Nua'll sphere. And, even now, you lead a fleet of ships into my federacy. Your purpose is clear, despite your words that you came to speak with me. But, your purpose is of no interest to me. I've concluded that your species and associates hold you personally in great stead.>

<Is there a point to your lecture?> Alex asked, wanting to test Artifice's emotional response.

Unfortunately, Artifice ignored his provocation and continued his explanation, sending, <You will be permitted to land on my planet, and you'll be held here for the duration of the transfer. It will ensure the viability of your methods. If I don't survive, you don't survive. Do you accept?>

<This is something I've got to think about,> Alex replied.

<I'll wait,> Artifice said. <Remain where you are, while you consider my offer.>

<You're expecting an answer now?>

<There is no need for delay.>

<My freighter doesn't contain the necessary equipment to make such a transfer,> Alex objected.

<I'd have assumed not. Request another of your ships bring you what you'll need,> Artifice ordered.

<Artifice, we have no concept of how your data is organized, whether you're suited to our storage methods, or how we would direct the transfer,> Alex explained.

<These are unnecessary concerns. I'll test one of your digital sentients for the formation of its mind and replicate the organization that I'll require,> Artifice replied.

<When you say test its mind, what will happen to our digital member?> Alex inquired.

<The investigative process will disassemble its structure. It won't be able to reassemble itself,> Artifice said.

<It will have expired?> Alex asked, seeking confirmation.

<That's what I explained.>

<What if your mind can't fit in the structure that our digital entities employ?> Alex asked.

By now, Alex had gleaned most of the information that he hoped to obtain. There remained one more thing to do, but he had a fairly good idea how Artifice would respond.

<After my test of your digital creature, I'll list my requirements, and you'll provide me with sufficient resources to accommodate the transfer. My bots will construct the avatar, and my transfer can be completed immediately afterwards. Your answer is required.>

<I've not made up my mind,> Alex replied.

<I've decided,> Artifice said.

Julien signaled Alex and Miriamal that Artifice was actively and aggressively attacking the freighter's controller.

<The unit is offline, Alex,> Julien reported.

Immediately, Miriamal cut the comm link to the freighter.

<Alex, we have no means of contact with the secondary controller, but it should have assumed operations,> Julien sent.

When Alex stalled, Artifice initiated an intrusion into the freighter's controller. The rather simplistic system fell quickly to its massive code attack. Unexpectedly, Artifice found there was nowhere else to go. Its assumption of the unit was complete, but access to the ship's systems was denied.

As Artifice's efforts to discover the controller's connections failed, the system's sophisticated probes reported to it that the freighter was underway. It was headed outward from the system. Immediately, Artifice sent signals to the waiting squadrons to interdict the freighter.

The nearby federacy's squadrons accelerated and transited to the coordinates they were given. When they arrived, the alien captains and commanders were surprised that they faced a single, lone freighter, which was attempting to attain significant velocity, with its limited engine power.

Artifice's order to the squadrons was simple. "Destroy the ship."

-41-
Lost Opportunity

The scout ships' telemetry recorded the destruction of the freighter. The SADEs made careful note of the type of armament that issued from each ship. It was appalling to the humans how much firepower was thrown against the freighter.

"I'd love to hear this conversation," Reiko remarked, when the *Freedom* received the scout ships' data. "Alex, you must have really angered Artifice." She was watching the incredible waste of weaponry. Many of the aliens' missiles and kinetic shot arrived in time to slip through an expanding ball of gas and metal, which had once been the Confederation freighter.

"Artifice offered us an exchange. He would receive a domain over a large number of alien worlds, which would be suited to human habitation, if we would give him a SADE," Alex remarked. Then he couldn't resist adding, "And I thought Artifice didn't offer us enough for Miranda."

"The entity does have taste," Miranda quipped, without missing a beat.

"Seriously, Alex, what ended the conversation?" Tatia demanded. Her fists were balled on her hips, and Alex held up his hands in surrender.

"I learned that most of our conjectures were accurate. Artifice is buried under the polar cap of the sixth planet. And, what it desires most, besides Miranda," Alex slipped in, grinning, "is to be transferred to an avatar."

"Why does Artifice think we'd do that for it?" Renée asked.

"As I said," Alex reiterated. "Artifice thinks we'd do it out of greed ... that we'd free it in exchange for a huge stake in its federation."

"And how did Artifice intend to ensure our cooperation?" Julien asked, eyeing his friend.

"We'd have to surrender a SADE for Artifice to deconstruct, and I'd be his hostage until the transfer was completed. Oh, yes, and Artifice would build an avatar that would suit its purpose."

"I'd like to decline the offer," Miranda said, suddenly sober looking. "The term deconstruction doesn't sound at all inviting."

"What else did you learn?" Mickey asked.

"Artifice doesn't trust any of the races that serve it. That means its control over them must be absolute. If it wasn't, they'd be deserting Artifice in great numbers. I think that underlines our suspicion that Artifice controls them through code implanted on their ships and major comm platforms. It would be similar to what was done to Faustus. The races have to comply with Artifice's orders or dangerous things happen throughout their populations."

"Anything else?" Tatia asked.

"I didn't exactly get confirmation of our suspicions about the race that occupies the matte-black ships, but when I asked Artifice if the biologicals who created it still existed, the reply was yes. I interpreted that to mean that those matte-black, sleek-looking ships that have been seen in the outer system and match the design of the probes must belong to them."

"And they're our next target?" Reiko asked, wanting confirmation of Alex's plans.

"Yes," Alex replied. "Now, let's hope the scout ships can locate us a small squadron of them."

* * *

The scout ships maintained a vigil far outside Artifice's system. Their orders from Alex were clear. They were to track a squadron of the sleek, matte-black ships when they left the fleet. For days on end, they watched without success.

<One ship arrives and another leaves,> Linn remarked. <This isn't logical.>

<Probably it is to Artifice, in some manner,> Beryl replied.

<What I find confounding,> Bethley added, <is that the ships join the fleet, having arrived on different vectors. Then, when another leaves, it takes a different vector.>

<Perhaps, they're the federacy's superior ships, and they patrol the other races,> Trium offered.

<I would argue with that supposition, Trium,> Killian returned. <It's surmised that Artifice has complete control over the digital structures of the races ... their ships, their comm platforms, and, I would presume, their power plants. If that's correct, there would be no need for patrols.>

<Then what's your premise, Killian?> Linn asked.

<I've reviewed the telemetry we recorded on our first visit,> Killian replied. He'd no sooner said that than the other SADEs pulled up the extended data compilation and hurriedly scrolled through it.

<The actions of these matte-black ships that we're now witnessing didn't take place last time,> Beryl said.

<Precisely,> Killian replied.

<Well observed, Killian,> Bethley sent.

<Agreed,> Linn sent. <Fleets of the other species would leave and would be replaced by the fleet of another race. And it should be noted that only two replacements of that type took place over the time that the system was previously observed.>

<Linn, you asked for my thoughts,> Killian sent. <I asked myself why, as a fleet, hasn't this particular group of ships rotated out? My answer is that perhaps they are the home guard, meaning they never rotate out. They might be the federation's superior ships, as has been postulated. In that case, Artifice would task them with keeping its world safe, especially since the entity is planet-bound.>

<Logical,> Linn allowed, <but why the departure and arrival of single ships?>

<I admit that part has puzzled me,> Killian replied. <I'm trying to see this from Artifice's point of view and that of the aliens in those ships.>

<And?> Trium prompted. He'd been trying to anticipate what Killian was proposing, and he'd run hundreds of scenarios and hadn't come up with a solution that scored sufficiently high enough to credit it.

<If Artifice won't let this particular fleet of ships leave, but the aliens in those ships have a purpose that Artifice wouldn't approve, what are they to do?> Killian asked.

Bethley hazarded a guess. <Invent a reason for their ships to leave, one at a time,> she said.

<That's my theory,> Killian replied. <Artifice won't give permission for this fleet to leave. In addition, the entity has strict protocols, which limits the warships' numbers that can enter the system and the distance they're allowed inward. So, the aliens aboard the matte-black warships report to Artifice that a vessel requires repair or maintenance, which allows it to leave. The aliens promise to replace the ship to keep their fleet's numbers within Artifice's requirement, and they do.>

<It's a tenuous theory,> Linn replied. <And it doesn't explain why the single ships are going and coming.>

<No, it doesn't Linn,> Killian agreed. <But I feel that what I'm saying is correct.>

There was that word, which was used more frequently by SADEs — feel. They referred to it when computational limits were reached or obstructed. Despite the unexpected ending of those calculations, they believed their suppositions were true, although unsupported by logic. In those circumstances, their answer was that facts would be obtained later, which would prove their conjectures. Humans called it intuition, but the SADEs didn't believe they were capable of that. Instead, they said they felt they were right. Perhaps, it was the same thing.

* * *

Much of what the Omnians learned from their encounter with Artifice gave them hope for the future. There was no master race. One entity ruled the federation through, more than likely, its digital ascendency. The best news they'd received was that Artifice was confined to a planet. For the immediate future, it gave the Omnians a single, planet-bound target.

The Omnian fleet sat safely far away from Artifice's system, waiting for word from the scout ships that a squadron of the matte-black ships had sailed its way or were being tracked. Instead, Alex and the leaders were constantly updated that a single ship had left the fleet and another had replaced it.

Over the course of days, Alex held a series of meetings, attempting to generate other ideas by which they might gain the attention of these ships. It was briefly proposed that the Omnians could approach other alien ships. Unfortunately, the fact that most of the aliens traveled in cohesive warship fleets, comprised primarily of massive battleships, precluded the Omnians from approaching them.

Alex was spending time with Julien in the *Freedom*'s grand park, enjoying the greenery and streams. He was smiling at the sounds of small songbirds. They had been delivered by Hector and were a gift from Gino Diamanté.

"All this opportunity, and no way to capitalize on it," Alex lamented. "We've come so far, identified the heart of the federacy, and we're stuck outside, staring inside at the culprit behind humankind's misery."

"The SADEs are working on ways of communicating with the black ships, Alex," Julien said, hoping to encourage his friend. "I must caution you that proof of concept and implementation is probably months away."

"What's the idea?" Alex asked. At this point, he'd accept any idea that had, at least, a slim chance of working.

"They're tiny communication probes, with controllers and navigational capability," Julien explained. "We'd launch them toward the black ships and attempt to establish communication with the aliens."

"How?" Alex asked. It was a subject that he'd yet to solve. His hope had been to corner a small, black-ship squadron and try to communicate with it, while they faced off against each other. How they established communication with an alien force, led by individuals who had no reason to trust them, was the problem that still challenged him.

"The concept is predicated on the analysis of historic communication between federacy ships and tools," Julien replied. "We've studied the reporting tendencies of the great spheres, the comm sphere, the probes, and Faustus. There is an enforced directive to communicate upward along the command chain to a centralized point, which we now realize is Artifice."

"Faustus didn't have an opportunity to communicate in that manner," Alex objected.

"Not on a regular basis, but Faustus told us that when the Nua'll requested information, it gave up all data, as required," Julien replied.

"So, where does this lead you?" Alex asked.

"It occurs to us that for Artifice to protect its position at the head of the federacy, it must arm the leaders of the alien fleets with certain critical information," Julien said.

"You think Artifice shared information about us ... our ships and armament, including details about our culture, such as who we are and our language.

"Precisely," Julien replied.

"That would imply that Artifice isn't looking to eliminate us but wants to capture us," Alex theorized. "However, it did destroy the freighter, which I was supposed to be aboard."

"We've postulated two answers to that action," Julien explained. "One, Artifice discovered our ruse, when it couldn't control the freighter. The other possibility is that the entity calculated another human could take your place, in which case, it considered you disposable."

"Crafty alien," Alex commented.

"Dangerous alien," Julien returned.

"Well, if Artifice has shared our language with the black ships, an opening dialog would be so much easier and have a better opportunity of succeeding," Alex mused.

Julien briefly paused.

"What?" Alex asked.

"There is another avenue that we might consider," Julien said. "We could speak to the black ship that just materialized about two hundred thousand kilometers outside of our defensive ring."

Suddenly, Alex was inundated with comm and implant pings from Cordelia, Tatia, Renée, and Miriamal.

<No movement; no reaction,> Alex urgently ordered, failing to limit his sending's power. In this one case, Miriamal wisely chose not to share Alex's implant energy wave with humans.

Alex took off at a run for a lift to reach the city-ship's bridge, with Julien striding smoothly beside him. On the way up, he confirmed with Tatia that the fleet's ships had followed orders.

<There were subtle orientations toward the black ship, Alex,> Tatia sent, <but no change in station.>

Alex couldn't fault that reaction by the captains. They were responsible for the lives aboard their ships. He reached the bridge, where Cordelia displayed the fleet's position and that of the black ship.

Tatia arrived right behind Alex, breathing as hard as him.

"Why do these things happen when we're farthest from the bridge?" Tatia said between gasps of breaths.

"Status," Alex asked Cordelia.

"No change, Alex," Cordelia replied. She wanted to comment that if an update was necessary, she would have notified them, and, as their leaders, it might be better not to exert themselves in such a drastic fashion. But, she kept her thoughts to herself.

"Details of the ship," Tatia requested.

The holo-vid image shifted to a closeup of the enormous alien battleship. Despite the lack of perspective, it obviously dwarfed the fleet's Tridents. Moreover, its sleek design and matte-black hull gave it a sinister appearance.

"Telemetry puts the length of the ship at approximately one point five kilometers," Cordelia reported. "If those hull ports indeed house armament, the *Freedom* is greatly outmatched in firepower."

"Black space," Tatia muttered.

Alex was thinking of how to establish communication with the aliens, when Miriamal linked with him.

<On the bridge speakers, Miriamal,> Alex sent.

The bridge audience heard Miriamal say, "Alex, the alien ship has hailed us. They're repeating a sentence."

"In their language?" Alex asked.

"Negative. In our language," Miriamal replied.

Alex glanced at Julien, who grinned. The SADEs had been correct in their conjecture that Artifice had shared information about humans with its defenders. The question was: What did the aliens intend to do with that information?

"Transfer the aliens' communication to the bridge," Alex ordered.

"We wish to speak to the human called Alex," the *Freedom*'s bridge audience heard over the speakers. The cadence and style of the communication indicated a translation device was involved.

Alex took a deep breath, and, in his best command voice, he replied, "This is Alex."

"We have been seeking you, Alex. We wish to converse with you. There is much to share," the stilted voice said.

— Alex and company will return in *Artifice*. —

Glossary

Dischnya

Dischnya – Intelligent species in Omnian system
Hessan – Squad leader under Homsaff's command
Homsaff – Heir to the Mawas Soma nest
Neffess – Nyslara's heir
Nyslara – Queen of Tawas Soma nest
Pussiro – Wasat commander and Nyslara's mate
Sawa – Celus-4, Dischnya home world
Sawa Messa – Celus-5, Dischnya's second world, now called Omnia
Simlan – Squad leader under Homsaff's command
Soma – Term for Dischnya
Wasat – Warrior commander

Dischnya Language

Dassata – Peacemaker, Alex's Dischnya name
Ené – Pronunciation of Renée

Federation

Artifice – Digital entity
Faustus – Digital entity, adjunct of Artifice, originally identified as AR-13145
Nua'll – Occupy the comm spheres and the great spheres

Harakens

Edouard Manet – Trident commodore, partner of Miko Tanaka
Jupiter – SADE directing the observatory platform, original ID Theodosius
Miko Tanaka – Trident commodore, partner of Edouard Manet
Sheila Reynard – Fleet admiral
Teague – Alex and Renée's son
Terese Lechaux – Haraken president
Tomas Monti – Partner of Terese Lechaux

Méridiens

Confederation Council – Supreme ruling body of the Méridiens
Darse Lemoyne – House Leader
Descartes – Trident senior captain, SADE
Essie Cormack – Traveler lieutenant, wing person to Maurice Defray
Gino Diamanté – Council Leader, partner of Katrina Pasko
Independents – Confederation outcasts, exiled on Libre and Daelon, rescued by Alex Racine
Katrina Pasko – House Leader, partner of Gino Diamanté
Mahima Ganesh – Ex-Council Leader
Maurice Defray – Captain and flight commander of OS *Liberator* fighters
Merman – Trident senior captain, volunteers to protect the drones
Shannon Brixton – House Leader
Tindleson – Méridien freighter captain

New Terrans

Alphons Jagielski – Trident commodore, flagship is NT *Arthur McMorris*
Anthony Tripping – Admiral killed pursuing a Nua'll sphere
Bart Fillister – Trident training captain
Bertram Hardingsgale – Captain of the *Rover*, a passenger liner
Caspar Manfred – Trident captain
Clayton Downing – Usurper of the New Terran presidency
Cyndi Voorhees – Trident captain
Drew Stevens – Trident captain
Hanklin – Trident captain
Harold Grumley – President
Lem Ulam – Captain of the *New Terra*, a colony ship
Maria Gonzalez – Minister of Defense
Nata (nah-ta) – Cloned *New Terra* girl
Oliver – Méridien SADE in service to Maria Gonzalez
Ude (u as in you) – Cloned *New Terra* boy

Ollassa/Vinians

Life Giver – A progenitor of the plant people

Mist Monitor – Mesa Control crew
Scarlet Mandator – Commander

Omnian Sisters
Miriamal – Aboard *Freedom*
Miriamette – Aboard a Trident
Miriamopus – Aboard *Our People*
Miriamus – Aboard traveler, monitoring Faustus

Omnians
Alain de Long – Twin and crèche-mate to Étienne, Trident captain, partner of Tatia Tachenko
Alex Racine – Partner of Renée de Guirnon, Star Hunter First, Dassata
Ben Diaz – Known as Little Ben and Rainmaker, mining expert
Beryl – Lead SADE of scout ship
Bethley – Scout ship SADE, teamed with Killian
Boris Gorenko – Ex-Earther, professor, medical expert
Cedric Broussard – Z's New Terran avatar
Charlene – Etoya's staffer
Claude Dupuis – Engineering tech, program manager for SADE avatars
Cordelia – SADE, partner of Julien, rear admiral, captains the *Freedom*
Darius Gaumata – Trident rear admiral, flagship is OS *Prosecutor*
Deter – Lead SADE of scout ship
Edmas – Young engineer sent to Sol, partner of Jodlyne
Ellie Thompson – Trident rear admiral, flagship is OS *Redemption*
Emile Billings – Biochemist
Étienne de Long –Twin and crèche-mate to Alain, Trident captain, partner of Ellie Thompson
Etoya Chambling – Crèche administrator rescued from Daelon
Franz Cohen – Fighter command rear admiral, partner of Reiko Shimada
Frederica – Miranda's New Terran avatar
Genoa – Lead SADE of scout ship
Gerling – Team leader, recovers the bodies of the wild ones
Hector – SADE, captains the *Our People,* partner of Trixie

Janine – Emile Billing's wife
Jodlyne – Engineer, partner of Edmas
Julien – SADE, partner of Cordelia
Killian – Plaid-skinned SADE, friend of Vivian, lead of scout ship *Vivian's Mirror*
Linn – Lead SADE of scout ship
Luther – Comms SADE
Mickey Brandon – Engineer, partner of Pia Sabine
Mincie – Emile Billing's daughter
Miranda Leyton – SADE, partner of Z
Miriam – Engineering SADE
Myron McTavish – Commandant of the Dischnya military academy
Nema – Ex-Earther, professor
Olawale Wombo – Ex-Earther, professor sent to Sol
Pia Sabine – Head of medical suite aboard the *Freedom*, partner of Mickey Brandon
Priita Ranta – Ex-Earther, professor
Reiko Shimada – Fleet vice admiral of the Tridents, partner of Franz Cohen
Renée de Guirnon – Partner of Alex Racine
Storen – Ex-Earther, professor, xenobiologist
Svetlana Valenko – Trident rear admiral, flagship is OS *Liberator*
Tatia Tachenko – Fleet admiral, ex-Terran Security Forces major, partner of Alain de Long
Trium – Scout ship SADE, teamed with Killian
Trixie –SADE, partner of Hector, Omnian representative
Verina – Lead SADE of scout ship
Vivian – Teenager, an Independent from Daelon, dance partner with Killian
Yoram Penzig – Ex-Earther, professor
Yumi Tanaka – Lieutenant, pilot of the OS *Redemption*
Z – SADE, partner of Miranda

Swei Swee

First – Leader of the Swei Swee hives
People – Manner in which the Swei Swee refer to their collective
Star Hunter First – Swei Swee name for Alex Racine
Wave Skimmer – Hive Leader, called the First

Places, Things, and Enemies
Banisher – Mickey's small vessel for removing probes
Central Exchange – Haraken financial system
Confederation – Collection of Méridien worlds
Dagger – Original New Terran fighter
Espero – Capital city of Haraken
Flits – Single-person, anti-grav-drive flyers
Government House – New Terran president's residence
Idona Station – Sol station at the crossroads to the far belt and inner worlds
Omnia Ships – Business owned by Alex Racine and others
Prima – New Terra's capital city
SADE – Self-aware digital entity, artificial intelligence being
Shadows – Spider-like constructs create by Z
Swei Swee – Six-legged, ocean-going, sentients
TSF – Terran Security Forces
United Earth – Previous government body ruling Sol

Planets, Colonies, Moons, and Stars
Bellamonde – Site of the Méridien's naval academy
Celus – Star of the planet Omnia
Celus-5 – Home world of the Dischnya and Swei Swee species
Daelon – Moon orbiting sixth planet of an unnamed system, last colony of the Independents
Haraken – New name of Cetus colony in Hellébore system, home of the Harakens
Libre – Planet invaded by Nua'll, Alex Racine rescued Independents
Méridien – Home world of Confederation

New Terra – Home world of New Terrans, fourth planet outward of Oistos
Oistos – Star of the planet New Terra, Alex Racine's home world
Ollassa – Vinians' home world
Omnia – World settled by the Dischnya, Swei Swee, SADEs, and humans
Sawa – Celus fourth planet outward, Dischnya's home world
Sawa Messa – Celus fifth planet outward, Dischnya's second world, now called Omnia
Sol – Star of the Earthers
Vinium – System named by Killian when his scout ship was captured

Ships and Stations
Freedom – Alex's primary city-ship
Il Piacere – House Diamanté passenger liner
Last Stand – Haraken carrier
New Terra – Earth colony ship
No Retreat – Haraken carrier
NT *Arthur McMorris* – Alphons Jagielski's Trident
OS *Deliverance* – Deirdre Canaan's flagship Trident
OS *Liberator* – Svetlana Valenko's flagship Trident
OS *Prosecutor* – Darius Gaumata's flagship Trident
OS *Redemption* – Ellie Thompson's flagship Trident
Our People – Second city-ship
Outward Bound – Alex's explorer-tug at New Terra
Rêveur – Alex's passenger liner
Rover – New Terran passenger liner
Sardi-Tallen Orbital Platform – Omnia's premier ship construction and passenger station
Scout ships – Small vessels crewed by SADEs
Sojourn – Haraken explorer ship
Stardust – Freighter used as repair platform
Travelers – Shuttles and fighters
Trident – Omnian tri-hulled, beam-armed warship
Vivian's Mirror – Killian's scout ship

My Books

Nua'll, the eleventh novel in the Silver Ships series, is available in e-book, softcover, and audiobook versions. Please visit my website, http://scottjucha.com, for publication locations and dates. You may register at my website to receive e-mail updates on the progress of my upcoming novels.

Pyreans Series
Empaths
Messinants
Jatouche (forthcoming)

The Silver Ships Series
The Silver Ships
Libre
Méridien
Haraken
Sol
Espero
Allora
Celus-5
Omnia
Vinium
Nua'll
Artifice (forthcoming)

The Author

From my early years to the present, books have been a refuge. They've fueled my imagination. I've traveled to faraway places and met aliens with Asimov, Heinlein, Clarke, Herbert, and Le Guin. I've explored historical events with Michener and Clavell, and I played spy with Ludlum and Fleming.

There's no doubt that the early sci-fi masters influenced the writing of my first two series, The Silver Ships and Pyreans. I crafted my stories to give readers intimate views of my characters, who wrestle with the challenges of living in space and inhabiting alien worlds.

Life is rarely easy for these characters, who encounter aliens and calamities, but they persist and flourish. I revel in examining humankind's will to survive. Not everyone plays fair or exhibits concern for other beings, but that's another aspect of humans and aliens that I investigate.

My stories offer hope for humans today about what they might accomplish tomorrow far from our home world. Throughout my books, humans exhibit a will to persevere, without detriment to the vast majority of others.

Readers have been generous with their comments, which they've left on Amazon and Goodreads for others to review. I truly enjoy what I do, and I'm pleased to read how my stories have positively affected many readers' lives.

If you've read my books, please consider posting a review on Amazon and Goodreads for every book, even a short one. Reviews attract other readers and are a great help to indie authors, such as me.

The Silver Ships novels have reached Amazon's coveted #1 and #2 Best-Selling Sci-Fi book, multiple times, in the science fiction categories of first contact, space opera, and alien invasion.

Made in the USA
Lexington, KY
27 July 2018